Smartly dressed, resourceful and discreet, **David Gunn** has undertaken assignments in Central America, the Middle East and Russia (among numerous other places). He is happiest when on the move and tends not to stay in one place for long. He comes from a service family, has an impressive collection of edged weapons and sleeps with a shotgun under his bed.

www.rbooks.co.uk

Also by David Gunn

DEATH'S HEAD: BOOK ONE OF THE AUX

DEATH'S HEAD
MAXIMUM OFFENCE

David Gunn

BANTAM PRESS

LONDON · TORONTO · SYDNEY · AUCKLAND · JOHANNESBURG

TRANSWORLD PUBLISHERS
61–63 Uxbridge Road, London W5 5SA
a division of The Random House Group Ltd
www.rbooks.co.uk

First published in Great Britain
in 2008 by Bantam Press
a division of Transworld Publishers

A CIP catalogue record for this book
is available from the British Library.

ISBN 9780593058718

Addresses for Random House Group Ltd companies outside the UK
can be found at: www.randomhouse.co.uk
The Random House Group Ltd Reg. No. 954009

The Random House Group Limited supports The Forest Stewardship Council (FSC),
the leading international forest-certification organization. All our titles that are
printed on Greenpeace-approved FSC-certified paper carry the FSC logo.
Our paper procurement policy can be found at www.rbooks.co.uk/environment

Typeset in 12½/15pt Bembo by
Kestrel Data, Exeter, Devon.
Printed in the UK by
CPI Antony Rowe, Chippenham, Wiltshire.

2 4 6 8 10 9 7 5 3

Pietro, who could field-strip a sniper rifle faster
than any man I've met . . .

Prologue

FLICKING DUST FROM HIS SLEEVE, GENERAL INDIGO JAXX ADJUSTS a dagger at his hip and then ruins everything by tugging at the collar of his uniform. He is a general in the Death's Head, for heaven's sake.

No, Indigo Jaxx shakes his head.

He's *the* general.

His regiment is the emperor's chosen force. Empire ministers fall silent at his approach. Colonels sacrifice entire brigades to win his approval. Men offer their wives, so their sons might find places on his staff.

It is absurd to be nervous, but he is. OctoV has that effect on him.

The beloved leader has that effect on everyone. Stiffening to attention, General Jaxx waits for his emperor to appear in a swirl of static, with words that will scour the inside of his skull like a hot desert wind.

Come on, thinks General Jaxx. *Please. Get this over with.*

As he prepares for his mind to be invaded, someone opens the office door behind him and the general turns, cold fury on his lips.

'Is this a bad time?'

The questioner is in his early teens. He wears a green cavalry uniform with a jewelled sword and has ringlets falling to his shoulders. His hair is blond, but it is his eyes that people notice. They are the blue of deep space and just as empty.

Indigo Jaxx blinks.

'I said . . .'

'No, sir,' says the general, standing straighter. 'Absolutely not.'

OctoV smiles. 'I'm so glad,' he says. 'I wanted to congratulate you.'

The general goes still.

'Really,' says OctoV. 'Producing victory from defeat . . . Having produced defeat from victory. That's subtle, even for me.' He nods towards the general's Obsidian Cross. 'I'd give you another medal, but clearly you've got them all. What is it now?'

'Imperial knight, grand master, sir. With extra palm leaves and bar.'

'Very impressive.'

General Jaxx is being mocked. Given the other choices, he is happy to get off that lightly.

'Well,' says OctoV. 'I must go.'

Now it comes, thinks the general, as he watches the boy head for the door. He tries not to tense as OctoV turns back.

'By the way,' OctoV says. 'What's he doing now?'

Who? The general thinks desperately. *What is who doing now?* 'Do you mean Sven, sir?'

'Yes,' says OctoV. 'Of course I do. What is Sven doing now?'

The general swallows. 'We're lending him to the U/Free.'

His imperial highness OctoV, glorious leader, the undefeated, eternal ruler of more worlds than can be counted, laughs. It strips General Jaxx's skull and reduces his self-control to tatters. Around him, the walls of his office begin to spin.

'You have the best ideas,' says his emperor. 'Keep me up to date.'

Indigo Jaxx wants to say, *Yes, sir. Of course, sir.* But he is on his knees vomiting. So OctoV walks through the nearest wall with the general's words unspoken.

Part 1

Chapter 1

THE MAN SPINS ROUND, KNIFE ALREADY DRAWN, AND HESITATES. It's not his fight. Anyway, he's only in Farlight for OctoV's birthday, unloading luxuries from a cargo ship on the edge of a landing site. And his knife is new, bought that afternoon from a stall in the road behind Golden Memories.

He doesn't feel ready to use it yet.

A wise choice. Someone is about to get hurt and it doesn't have to be him. That *someone* is standing in my doorway. And half of my bar door swings from a rusted hinge, while the rest lies at his feet.

'Quiet,' I say.

A girl next to me shuts up.

I am not sure she knows she screamed.

This is my bar, but it is Aptitude's home and she's family. At least she is until her mother and father get out of prison.

'*Sven*,' she says.

'Later . . .' My gaze flicks across the room and settles on a wiry young man with a pointed face, floppy hair and narrow shoulders. He's reaching into his jacket. At a shake of my head, he lets go his revolver.

Neen's nineteen.

In the field, he's my sergeant, but we're not in the field, we're on leave. So he's running security for a bar I own on the outskirts of this city.

Raising his glass, Neen grins. He, for one, obviously intends to enjoy tonight's show. As we watch, the man in my doorway jacks the slide on an oversized pistol, and takes a slow look round to check we've noticed.

'*Sven.*'

Aptitude is getting nervous.

I smile, but it is at another girl entirely. Wandering over, she sits on my lap and snuggles up to me. Aptitude scowls to see me slide my hand up Lisa's skirt. What she doesn't see is the knife I take from Lisa's garter.

'Subtle,' says a voice. 'Understated, anything but obvious.'

The intruder believes my gun is talking about him. He has pegged my corner of the room for the comment, but he can't work out who to blame. As the man lumbers over, Lady Aptitude Tezuka Wildeside leans back in her chair.

'You,' he says. 'Got something to say?'

She shakes her head frantically.

Satisfied, the man starts to turn away. Big mistake. Turfing Lisa off my lap, I pick up my own chair and smash it over the back of his skull. He drops, but only to his knees.

'Finish it,' says Aptitude.

'Not yet. I'm enjoying myself.'

'*Sven.*'

Clambering to his feet, the thug stares at me.

'Yeah,' I say. 'I'm Sven Tveskoeg.' How many seven-foot tall ex-Legionnaires can he see in this bar?

Behind the man stands another. Federico Van Zill, provider of protection to half the bars and brothels edging the landing fields below Calinda Gap. A rumour says the war against the Uplifted will be over soon.

14

That is bad for Van Zill.

As long as we're at war, there's a chance I'll be killed and my troopers with me. An end to the war would mean Van Zill gets some permanent competition. Peace isn't going to happen, of course. And it's disloyal, unwise, and probably treasonous to suggest otherwise. However, Federico Van Zill is an idiot. So I've been expecting this visit.

When Van Zill's thug pulls a knife, I laugh.

It's huge, with slots cut into the back of the blade. The slots are meant to say *this is a man ready to drag his enemy's entrails through an open gut wound.* You can tell a lot about a man from the knife he chooses.

You can tell a lot about a woman too.

The blade I take from Lisa's garter is a third of the size. It lacks teeth, blood channels and other finery but it's razor-sharp and made from glass.

All you have to do is stab once, then snap it off at the handle. You can buy ten for the price of the shiny toy in the hands of the man opposite.

When Neen flashes five fingers, a boy behind the bar breaks the news to the punters crowding round him. The odds on our fat friend have just halved.

'Come on,' I say.

Watching my blade, he fails to spot that I'm watching his eyes. This is a man used to getting his own way and that is a weakness. In addition, he's impatient. So he stabs and leaves himself open, only not open enough.

I block.

And go back to circling.

Neen's seen me kill swiftly. All of my troopers have. But catching Neen's puzzled face in the crowd I realize he has never seen me bide my time. *Kill early, kill often . . .* It's our unofficial motto.

This is different.

I've never gutted someone in front of Aptitude. She's a well-brought-up kid, and I'm trying to keep it that way. One of the reasons this man's made me angry. He's still watching my blade and I'm still watching his eyes.

Soon everyone is waiting on what will happen next. And their expectation makes my attacker clumsy. He jabs so obviously it has to be a feint. As his gaze flicks right, I know what's going to happen.

He waits for me to begin a block before switching hands, smiling at his own brilliance. Then his brain is playing catch-up, because Lisa's knife is deep in his belly and I'm dragging it upwards. A single rip opens him from groin to breastbone and a tumble of guts slides to the floor.

Aptitude screams.

Lisa's more practical. She opens a window.

You can say what you like about the girls from the barrio below Calinda Gap but they've seen it all before, and probably twice. Tossing a blanket over the twitching corpse, my bar manager Angelique nods to a boy behind the counter. He can drag it out later.

'Boss,' says my sergeant. 'What about rat face?'

Van Zill looks less smug with Neen's revolver to his head.

'Take rat face outside,' I say. 'Shoot him.'

'*Sven . . . !*'

No need to ask who that is.

'A week ago,' I tell Aptitude, 'a man refused to pay protection to this piece of shit. What do you think happened to his twelve-year-old daughter?'

Aptitude is fifteen.

She doesn't like my question.

Turning back to Neen, I say, 'Take him outside. Make sure he knows what happens if he ever comes back.'

Our glorious capital is built in the caldera of an old volcano, and smog traps heat and makes the air hard to breathe. Corpses rot quickly here and large ones rot faster than small ones. Don't know why, but it's true. Lisa ends up helping the boy behind the bar to drag the body out back. Then fetches ice to keep it fresh until Angelique can arrange collection.

'Do I close up?' Angelique asks.

'No way.' I shake my head. 'We stay open.'

The music goes back on. We offer a round of cold beers for everyone on the house. A couple of cargo captains who were going to call it a night change their minds and head upstairs with three of the local girls.

A technician watches them go, summons up his courage and follows. He has two blondes in tow, and I'm not sure he looked closely before grabbing their wrists. No doubt he'll discover soon enough that one is a boy.

'Chill some *cachaca*,' I tell Lisa. 'Make sure our customers have a night to remember.'

Drunks talk.

That thug will become a giant, his knife a razor-edged sabre, my own moves unstoppable and insanely vicious . . . Our reputation will grow. That's good, because tomorrow sees me, my sergeant and the rest of the Aux present ourselves for duty. I need that reputation to keep Aptitude safe until we get home.

'All done,' says Neen, rubbing his fists.

'Good. Anything I should know?'

Neen hesitates.

'What?'

'Told the little shit to pay us from now on.'

I grin. It's a good call.

'How much?'

'Twenty per cent,' says Neen. 'Straight off the top, no deductions. Last day of each month. No exceptions, no excuses . . .'

This is a farm boy, an ex-militia conscript who should have

been dead months back. Would have been if I hadn't taken over his troop. I wonder where he got the idea. Then I see his sister behind him and know exactly where she thinks he did. Shil is scowling, but that's nothing new. Shil's always scowling. We have history.

'Problem?'

'No, sir,' says Shil.

'Good . . .' I look round the bar. 'Get drunk,' I tell Neen. 'Get laid. Acquire a hangover. We ship out tomorrow.'

Neen grins. 'It that an order, sir?'

His sister sighs.

Chapter 2

HINGES CREEK AND ANGELIQUE POKES HER HEAD ROUND THE door.

'Sven,' she says and disappears. Might be the fact I'm standing naked in the middle of my bedroom. Must be the gun in my hand.

'What?'

Reappearing, she nods as a towel goes round my waist and the SIG-37 goes back in its holster. 'I'm sorry,' she says, 'but she won't . . .' Who *won't* is obvious, because a girl slides past Angelique and looks around.

'Pre-fab construction,' she says. 'Early-Octovian. Original walls and door. Original electrics from the look of it . . . You do realize,' she says, 'this building was only meant to last five years?'

'I like it.'

'You would.'

Her nose wrinkles at the smell, but she catches herself quickly. And when she brushes past me to the open window, it could be to examine its sash cords. Because that is what she does.

'Original fittings,' she says.

Maybe she catches my irritation.

'You don't mind?' she says.

'Of course not.'

If she hears an edge to my voice, she doesn't let it show. Anyway, going to the window doesn't help with the smell because the air beyond the window stinks of dog shit, burning rubber and hydrocarbons from the landing fields outside. Where does she think the stench came from in the first place?

'You really like it here?'

'Yes,' I say.

Angelique is looking between us. 'You know each other?'

'I'm sorry,' says the girl. 'Didn't I say?'

'No,' Angelique says flatly. 'You didn't.'

Angelique might be blonde, generously built, free with her body, but she has the temper of a redhead, and it's coming to the boil. I don't need the argument, and I don't need the complications an argument will bring.

'Ms Osamu,' I say, 'may I introduce Angelique, my bar manager?'

They glare at each other.

'Angelique, this is Paper Osamu, ambassador for the United Free to the Octovian Empire. Ms Osamu has full plenipotentiary status for this edge of the spiral arm.'

Angelique doesn't know what it means either, but has enough brains to recognize it as trouble and best avoided. 'She's U/Free?'

'Yes,' I say. 'She's U/Free.'

Paper Osamu smiles.

'But . . .' says Angelique, and gets no further.

My visitor looks a good year or two younger than Angelique, who is nineteen at most. Paper's also wearing rags. They are undoubtedly expensive rags. Probably ripped from exotic silk by a famous U/Free artist and sewn together with strands of web from a spider that has been taught to shit silver. But they still look like rags to me. And if they look like rags to me, then they're going to look like rags to Angelique, only more so . . .

The furthest she's been from home is Maurizio Junction.

That's eight streets away.

'Coffee would be good,' says Ms Osamu. She is looking at Angelique as she says this.

'You'll find it downstairs.'

Angelique shuts my door with enough of a slam to make the windows rattle and the U/Free ambassador laugh. 'Are all your women so jealous?'

'She's not *my women.*'

'Really?' Paper Osamu looks at me.

'All right. But only the once.'

'You're such children—' Ms Osamu catches herself, apologizes. The U/Free are big on not being rude about others. They have laws about such things. Me? As far as I'm concerned, if you think someone's a crawling heap of shit, you're allowed to say so. Just don't be surprised if they pull a knife on you.

Taking a piece of card from her pocket, Paper Osamu says, 'Look . . . The general's invited you to a breakfast he's giving in my honour.'

I check both sides of the invitation.

'Want me to read it?'

'I can manage. My old lieutenant taught me.'

'Bonafonte deMax?'

It's my turn to stare.

'I checked him out,' she says. 'At the general's suggestion.'

We live in a city full of generals, empire ministers and senators. Also heads of the high clans, distant cousins of the emperor and trade lords. However, round here, if someone says *the general* they mean General Indigo Jaxx, commander of the Death's Head and my ultimate boss.

'And call me Paper,' she adds. 'We're friends.'

First I've heard of it.

Walking over to my wardrobe, Paper finds my uniform. The jacket has been cleaned since she last saw it and the blood's come out. My boots are also clean, which must be Angelique's work, because I don't remember scrubbing them.

There's a waterfall of silver braid tucked inside one of the boots, a holster over the back of a chair and a dagger's sheath on the mantel over the fireplace. The dagger itself keeps the sash window from sliding shut.

'Antique,' says Paper, looking at the blade. 'You steal this?'

'General Jaxx gave it to me.'

'So,' Paper says, 'I guess that means he stole it.'

'Paper . . .'

'The blade's old Earth,' she tells me. 'All old Earth artefacts are protected under United Free legislation. No trading, no selling, no transfer between systems without a licence.'

'Could have been in his family for generations.'

'We'll make a diplomat of you yet.'

'God forbid.'

'I'm a diplomat,' she points out.

'So you've said.'

Arranging my uniform on the floor, Paper stands back and looks expectant. She's medium height, athletic without being muscled, just enough hips to grip, a tight rear and high breasts, which are full without being large. She's also black-haired, but that means nothing. Last time we met her hair was chestnut and her eyes were blue. Today they are green.

'Sven,' she says. 'You need to dress.'

'Then get out.'

'I've seen naked men before.'

'Yeah,' I say. 'I'm sure you have.' Dropping the towel, I stamp over to the shower. It's a real one, the kind that uses water. Unfortunately, its sides are made of clear glass. Paper walks round it slowly, taking a good look.

'Impressive,' she says. She's not talking about the cubicle.

I keep my back to her as I pull my trousers over wet skin and buckle my belt.

'May I?' says Paper's voice behind me.

So polite, the U/Free.

Reaching up, she wipes a drop of water from my shoulder where it vanishes under the edge of my prosthetic arm. 'Exquisite workmanship.' The stump has a tortoiseshell effect where badly healed flesh used to be. It gives a dull click as she taps it. Then she taps my arm itself, which rings slightly.

'You lost this to a ferox?'

Nodding, I turn round.

She is standing so close that I can smell woman under whatever scent she's wearing. And her pupils are wide, those little black dots no longer little but vast, reducing the green of her irises to a thin circle around the edges.

'Really?' she says, breathless. 'A ferox?'

'It was old,' I say. 'Almost dead.'

'I heard you cut off its head.'

'Needed proof.'

'Of what?'

'That this wound wasn't self-inflicted.'

'People do that?' she asks. 'In the desert . . . ?'

Smiling, I say, 'In the desert, people do anything.' Then, because she's still close, I wrap one arm around her waist and pull her close, raising her chin with my other hand.

'*Sven* . . .' She twists away before I can stop her.

'Thought we were meant to be friends?'

Paper Osamu tuts. 'Come on,' she says. 'Let's get you dressed.'

Helping me into my jacket, she adjusts my holster, buttons my braid into place, hangs my Obsidian Cross, second class, on its ribbon around my neck, and rips my blade from the sash window. Which, obviously enough, crashes shut.

The U/Free can be strange sometimes.

When we get downstairs the others are waiting. Telling Neen I'll see him later, I ask Aptitude to help Lisa clean up and the rest to get on with whatever needs doing. Angelique scowls when I hold the door for Paper. Shil merely raises her eyebrows and makes sure that I've seen.

'Who's the eldest one?' Paper demands, the moment we're outside.

'Shil . . . My sergeant's sister.'

'Had her too?'

'*Paper!*'

'Just asking,' she says.

Paper mutters something about research, and I stop listening when she starts using words like *polyandry*. I'm pretty sure there's a *primitive peoples* in there somewhere. But she catches herself, glances at me and decides I'm not paying attention anyway.

'She likes you,' Paper says, bringing it back to my level.

I could tell her that Shil hates my guts and has done ever since I made her brother my sergeant. But I don't bother. 'No, she doesn't,' I say instead.

'Believe me,' says Paper. 'She does. I know these things.'

Paper probably means she once read something about the mating habits of those *primitive peoples* she was muttering about. As we walk, the city of Farlight wakes around us and she tells me my mission. The one I'm meant to keep quiet about.

We're being borrowed by the U/Free. *We* being the Aux. Although that is a secret, obviously.

'You understand?'

'Yes,' I say. 'I know what secret means.'

Paper sighs. She doesn't, however, tell me why we're being borrowed. That's going to come later.

The houses become larger as we head downhill, and keep getting larger, grander and cleaner until we near Farlight's centre where huge mansions hide behind heavy gates. The gardens are green and roses flourish. People down here have enough water to waste on plants. It's an interesting idea for someone who grew up on a frontier fort in the desert.

Elegant hovers wait outside shops as we get closer still. Uniformed guards usher high clan families into retailers so exclusive I have no idea what they sell. And nothing outside gives a clue. Paper watches me watch them. There is something knowing in her gaze. As if this is what she expects me to do.

Cold air blasts from shop doors.

For a few seconds, as they leave, the families experience the heat with which the rest of this city lives daily. And then sides lift on sleek hovers, and chauffeurs and cold air welcome them inside. This was Aptitude's life once. She's never seemed to miss it.

'What are you thinking?' Paper asks.

'Nice car,' I say, as a smoked-glass monstrosity slides away. She glances at me strangely.

A virus attack hit this area before I was born. A few of the streets melted. Most just dripped a little and then solidified. Although few of them dripped as much as OctoV's cathedral. This looks ready to collapse into a puddle the moment the sun rises high enough.

It's looked like that for five hundred years.

That's what Paper tells me as we skirt the square and duck under an arch in the shadow of the cathedral, that leads down an alley and into a smaller square beyond.

Behind this is a long and narrow lake, looking like a river, that divides the north from the south of Farlight. The lake stinks in summer, and it stinks in winter. Only not quite as badly. Bodies have a habit of turning up in that lake. A number of them badly mutilated.

I know where we're going.

What interests me is that Paper also knows. I'll give good money she hasn't been before. The Death's Head aren't known for issuing open invitations to their regimental HQ.

The square is dusty, the grass even browner than the last time I was here. No one's wasting any water round here. A fir tree droops behind rusting railings, stripped of its needles by the heat as surely as if someone had lit a bonfire underneath. The HQ itself is immaculate.

'Don't tell me,' says Paper.

Glancing from the freshly painted door to the rusting railings, from the scrubbed steps to the parched earth showing between patches of dead grass, she says, 'Subliminal reinforcement of already established hierarchical patterns . . .'

I ignore her.

Elbowing my way through a crowd around the door brings me to the steps at the same time as a major in the militia. His chest drips with braid and he's wearing a row of ribbons probably awarded for dressing himself. A young woman hangs off his arm. She has as many jewels as he has medals. In addition, her breasts are doing their best to fight free from her blouse. It's a heroic battle.

There's no doubt what the jewels were awarded for.

'*Lieutenant,*' he says.

We stare at each other.

Maybe I'm meant to stand back, or something. When I don't, he draws himself up to his full height. This is a head shorter than me. 'I order you to give way . . .'

OK, so I shouldn't grin.

'Sven,' says Paper. 'Let him go first.'

'Why?'

'Because I outrank you,' says the major.

26

Like I give a fuck. 'Tell me,' I say, 'what are all those ribbons for? Heroism in the face of overwhelming . . .'

My nod takes in his partner's generous flesh.

Anything the major intends to say – and he looks like someone who intends to say a lot – dies at a bark of laughter from the top of the steps. A crop-haired man with wire glasses hiding pale blue eyes stands in the doorway. He's wearing a simple uniform. No decorations except a single Obsidian Cross.

'Wondered what was holding everyone. Should have known . . .'

The major's eyes flick from me to General Jaxx. Then from General Jaxx to Paper Osamu, and some dim understanding of who this strangely dressed woman might be finally reaches his brain. He looks like a man already regretting getting out of bed.

Paper and I go up the steps first.

Chapter 3

THE DROP GLIDER IS SO OLD IT COMES FROM A TIME WHEN stealth meant making the edges pointed and painting everything matt black.

Now it just looks dated.

An X73i says the pilot. Then admits he had to look it up, because he's never flown one before. In fact, he didn't know any still existed.

'Great,' says Neen.

He shuts up when I glare at him.

Our pilot has been jumpy since we began to drop. All he and his co-pilot have to do is sit in their little cabin upfront and steer this thing in controlled descent. So I don't see their problem. We are five hours out of Farlight and half a spiral arm away. That's what happens if your general lends you to the U/Free. You present yourself at their embassy one afternoon, sign papers stating you undertake the job willingly, and head downstairs into a shitty little basement.

I think we're going for a briefing.

Perhaps a medical.

What am I meant to think? The basement door opens on

one planet and closes on another? That would be bad enough. Only it doesn't. It dumps us on board a U/Free ship in low orbit over a planet. The ship's bigger than most cities.

Well, cities I've seen.

Fifteen minutes later, we are dropping towards the planet's surface in an out-dated glider, dressed as mercenaries but minus any weapons. Clearly, we're going to be given those later.

'How much longer?' asks Rachel.

She's my sniper, all red hair and attitude. Heavy breasts and broad hips. She has been fucking Haze, my intelligence officer, for the last six weeks. We've all been pretending not to notice.

'Zero one five,' says the pilot.

There is cold desert below, and if villages exist down there they don't show on the scans. According to our briefing Hekati is five rocks out from a double star on the inner fringe of a spiral. It lacks oil, minerals and decent agricultural land. I'd ask what we're doing here but I already know. Destroying a weapons factory.

'Don't worry,' the co-pilot tells Rachel. 'I'll get you down safely.'

On screen, which is how we see them, his boss quietly takes a medal of legba uploaded from inside his shirt, and I know we're in trouble.

'Actually,' he says, 'you won't.'

Touching the medal to his lips obviously closes a circuit.

As the pilot's skull explodes, jagged splinters take his co-pilot through the head, and splatter two helpings of brain across a bulkhead. It happens too fast to stop, even if we could get through the security doors to the cabin.

'Sir?' says Shil. 'We're . . .'

'Yeah,' I say.

We are doing what happens when a drop glider loses both

its pilots, we're crashing. The X73i is a thousand feet above the desert floor, and headed for a cliff half a mile ahead. The cliff is a good thousand feet higher again.

'We'll have ridge lift,' says Haze.

Half of what Haze says is nonsense. The rest can sometimes save your life. He might be large, moon-faced and clumsy. But he's not as large as he was when we first met on a battlefield and I stopped him being chopped up by enemy guns. Although he still sounds simple to anyone who doesn't know different.

'Wind hits a cliff, sir,' he says, 'it rises. Creates an updraught. The updraught will give us lift.'

'Not enough,' I say.

We have about two minutes before the cliff face and this plane get up close and personal. All we've got going for us is the fact the desert floor is rising as it approaches the cliff. A thousand years of sifting sand for all I know.

'Sir,' says Rachel. 'The exit's jammed.'

'Of course it is. It's tied to the system.'

'*One minute thirty.*'

'Sir,' asks Haze. 'You want me to override the glider's AI?'

As I said, he is my intelligence officer. Only, he's not an officer and his intelligence isn't something most people recognize. But he has more shit in his skull than I have and two metal braids one each side of his skull to prove it.

'No time,' I tell him.

'One minute twenty-five.' He's counting down to the AI's internal clock. 'I can probably—'

'*Haze.*'

'Sir?'

'Prepare to jump.'

'But sir,' says Rachel. 'The exit . . .'

'Fuck the exit.'

One minute ten.

Dropping to my knees, I punch my fist through the glider's

floor and rip with my metal hand. Cold wind swirls into the hold and scoops trays from a trolley. The air on this planet is thin and we're losing the oxygen mix that keeps us comfortable.

'Help me.'

Ceramic slices at their fingers but they tear anyway. Leaving me to snap the optic fibres that run like veins under the skin of this craft. We wobble. Of course we bloody wobble. You rip holes in a glider it's going to get upset.

'Grab what you can.'

When Rachel just stands there, I push her towards the rear of the plane. She wants to protest, but doesn't dare. She grabs food packs and begins tossing them through the rip in the floor.

'Just drop the lot.'

She does.

A gun cabinet clings to a rear bulkhead. It's locked, but one punch takes it off the wall. The cabinet has no back, which makes locking it pointless and gives us our only weapon. A fat distress pistol, with three flares. As Rachel throws out the pistol and tosses flares after it, part of me wonders how we are going to find this stuff.

'Jump,' I tell her.

When she hesitates, I push her after the gun, the flares and all that other stuff she has been tossing out. Haze follows, looking shocked.

The others don't need encouraging.

So I hit the ground and roll to put out flames. A split moment later, a second explosion drops fifty tons of cliff on what is left of our glider, burying it. The first explosion might be an accident. The second is intentional. I just have time to think this before rocks begin rolling my way.

'Incoming,' I shout.

A small boulder, the size of a three-wheel combat, tumbles past, then a larger one, maybe the size of a house, followed by a cartwheeling splinter as long as our buried plane.

Progression, I think.

Flinging myself behind a rock, I wait out the landslide. The crawl space is too small, so I jam my legs into the gap and wait it out some more.

A year ago I wouldn't have known what *progression* meant. Mind you, a year ago I was someone else. These days I'm Sven Tveskoeg, lieutenant with the Death's Head, Obsidian Cross, second class. What I'm doing out of uniform is a whole other question.

'Sir . . .'

Haze, from the sound of it.

'*Sir . . .*'

'Over here,' I call, and he stumbles uphill, Rachel in tow.

She has the distress pistol in her hand, which means she's already started hunting down the supplies we dropped. I like Rachel; she's one of my better finds. Haze knows I think this. I am not sure he is happy.

Mind you, I'm not sure I give a fuck.

'You're burnt.'

That's Haze for you, always stating the obvious.

'Not badly,' I tell him. 'Report.'

He looks at me.

'Rachel . . . ?'

'Sergeant Neen's down, sir. Arm broken. Corporal Franc has a broken ankle. I'm OK. Shil's OK.'

'And you?' I ask Haze.

'I've got a headache.'

I am about to say, *of course you have a fucking headache. You just fell thirty feet.* However, something stops me. Haze's eyes are glazed, his face is sweating. Any minute now, his nose is going to start to bleed. It is a habit of his.

'We're being watched?'

'Think so, sir.'

He might be soft as uncooked dough and have even fewer social skills than I have, but if Haze thinks we are being watched . . .

Mind you. In the middle of a desert?

Satellites are possible. The sky is clear, almost purple. Not a single cloud, although infrared lenzing means clouds don't present a problem these days.

We'll deal with the watchers later.

'Find the flares,' I tell Haze.

'Yes, sir.'

To Rachel I say, 'Take me to Neen.'

'Franc's worse . . .'

Rachel adds *sir*, when she sees my face. But it's too late. As I step towards her, she steps back; and then makes herself stand her ground. Although she twists her head away from the blow she thinks is coming.

'Sergeants outrank corporals,' I say, and leave it at that.

We find Neen against a boulder, clutching his arm. His face is tight and he has bitten through his lower lip.

'You needled yet?'

'No, sir.'

'Why not?'

'Thought we might need them later.'

Ripping open a combat pack, I stab a syringe into his neck and feel the bulb deflate as morphine enters his bloodstream. There are better drugs and better ways to deliver them, but morphine is cheap and effective and you can buy it anywhere.

Counting down from five, I let the drug do its job and then reach for Neen's forearm. The thinner of the two bones is broken. But it hasn't ripped its way through his skin and the break feels clean.

He is lucky.

'Find me splints.'

When Rachel comes back, it is with a strip of ceramic from the glider's tail, and a length of fibre optic that thrashes in her hand like a wounded snake. Seems the rear section of our glider broke free. Must have been that hole I ripped in the skin.

Haze carries a food parcel, two flares and a water bottle.

'Find the other bottles,' I tell him.

'Sir . . .' Rachel wants to say something.

It's written on her face and that is an improvement. A few months back she wore her hair over her eyes so no one could see her face at all. After the surrender of Ilseville, a Silver Fist officer put his gun to the back of her head to shoot her and then changed his mind when he saw me watching. Maybe he decided raping her was enough. She got to live provided some idiot agreed to carry her.

That idiot was me.

Snapping the ceramic into sections, I pick two the closest in length and pull Neen's arm straight. It is probably good that he faints. Lashing the ceramic into place with optic, I make him a sling with the last of the tubing and sit him against a rock.

'Call me when he wakes.'

Rachel nods.

I find Shil fussing over Franc, who is white-faced and silent. One boot, old, buckled, and worn at the heel, lies in the dirt beside her. Shil is asking Franc to wiggle her toes.

Dropping to a crouch, I grip Franc's ankle.

As I yank, her other boot clips the side of my jaw. It is a good kick, with massive amounts of power behind it. One of the things I love about Franc is that she has aggression hard-wired right through her.

Shil and Neen might be farm-boy thin, but Franc is compact. She's also shaven-headed and removes her body hair daily with the edge of a knife. Although the rest of us aren't meant to know that. She once belonged to Haze, some kind of bonded servant.

'Fuck,' she says. 'I'm—'

'Anyone ever told you the one-second rule?'

Franc shakes her head.

'Wake someone and they cripple you inside the first second, then tough. Should be more careful how you wake them . . . Also applies to treating wounds. Although you should have known that was dislocated, not broken.'

Chapter 4

THE STARS ARE HIGH AND CLEAR, WHICH MEANS THE AIR HERE is thin. What little heat the dunes take up during the day is taken back by the night faster than is safe for any of us. Cold kills as surely as a knife. It creeps up on you. Makes you decide it would be a good idea to lie down for a little while. Perhaps shut your eyes and remember all those interesting times you thought you had forgotten.

Almost froze to death once. If you have to go, it's probably as good a way as any.

Doesn't mean I'm going to let it happen here though. Not to me, and not to any of my troopers. I am headed for the plane, or what is left of it. The tail is way behind us, one of the wing tips just ahead. And we are half a mile from the cliff itself. Seems to me the glider broke up far too neatly.

Out to my left a double moon brightens. Then a third. Maybe it is that third moon which wakes whatever beast it is that howls. A long howl, too deep for a sand wolf and too raw for a fox.

Not ferox.

I'm glad about that. Ferox hunt silently.

'Sir.' Neen drops back from walking point.

Yeah, I know . . .

We have a big problem, and a small problem. The small problem is out in the wilderness howling at us. The bigger problem is that where we're meant to be doesn't have three moons.

It has two suns.

At least it does according to our briefing.

As I glance to the left, checking on that triple moon, something crests the top of a dune and rears upright. Its howl echoes off a distant cliff and starts other voices howling.

'Fuck,' says Shil. 'What's that?'

'A wolf.'

I wouldn't believe me either.

'Build a fire,' I tell her. 'When we reach the cliff.'

She wants to say there'll be nothing to burn, but has more sense. I know that, we are in the middle of a desert, for fuck's sake. She needs to improvise.

'You know . . .' says Haze.

'There's going to be nothing to burn?'

He nods.

Telling Neen to resume point, I order Shil to move out, then I watch as Franc and Rachel head after her. Rachel is limping, and working hard at not looking back. As I wait for her to leave me with Haze, I break open our distress pistol and feed it a flare.

'*Why?*' I ask Haze.

He steps back. 'Sorry, sir . . .'

'No. Tell me why there's going to be nothing to burn.'

He considers this, his head tipped to one side and still wrapped in bandages. We tell everyone he took a wound that will not heal. The truth is messier. Those two braids budding through his skull make him Enlightened.

We kill Enlightened, because they're our enemy. Only

Haze is an Aux, a member of our troop and that makes the truth messier still.

'Well?'

'That second explosion,' he says. 'It smelt chemical.'

'*Plastique.*'

Haze stares at me.

'Used it when I was a kid,' I say. 'In the Legion. Along with rusting rifles, sweat-rotted uniforms and food rations so stale no one else in OctoV's army would even open them.'

He nods.

'The first bang was the AI,' he says. 'Plus our oxygen tanks. The second, that was serious. Someone stuffed the glider's nose-cone with enough explosive to wipe out us, half a cliff and all the evidence . . .'

'Who?'

'The Enlightened?'

A fair guess. Only how the fuck would a bunch of metal-heads know about us . . . And how could they get themselves into a U/Free security base and pack the nose of a glider that is being kept under guard?

I have a better explanation. Only it leaves a sour taste in my mouth.

'What do you think, sir?'

'No idea,' I tell Haze.

Walking backwards is easy. Well, it's easy when you've done it as often as I have. You just lean yourself slightly forward for better balance, and keep the gun low and swivel from the hip.

I'm the last into the camp, obviously. If you can call five troopers waiting in the rubble of a fallen cliff a camp.

'Sir,' says Neen. 'You want me to take watch?'

'How's the arm?'

He looks at me.

'It's not a trick question.'

'Numb,' he admits. 'But I can handle a gun.'

A good answer and a true one. 'Later,' I say. 'First we need a tent. And a fire, assuming there's anything to burn.'

'Bushes,' says Franc.

'*What?*'

'In the cliff. Shil and Rachel are trying to . . .'

Well, if Rachel thinks she has something to prove.

There are bushes all right. They begin a quarter of the way up, which puts them a long way above Rachel and Shil, who are lit by the pale light of three separate slivers of moon.

'*Come down.*'

'I'm . . .' Rachel's voice is distant. More worried than I would like.

'*Now.*'

Neither one moves.

As Shil shouts something to Rachel, I realize we have a problem, and it isn't just their stupidity. *Great*, I think. *Should have known Rachel was too good to be true.* Still, if you are going to be afraid of something it might as well be something that's likely to kill you, like heights.

'As soon as I start throwing wood down,' I tell Neen, 'get a fire going. Also, if you can't make a tent have the others build a sand wall.'

'Sir,' he says.

Neen points to a dark gash at the base of the cliff. It's low and slants away to one side. As I approach, a bat the size of my fist spirals out and hits an insect on the rise. A second later a dozen bats spiral out behind the first.

I leave Rachel where she is.

The mouth of the cave is tight enough to scrape my shoulders and that doesn't help my temper. Although what I find inside goes a long way to making me happy again. No ash from a fire, or spoor. Nothing that looks like the remains

39

of a meal. The cave is clean. Which means that whatever is howling out there in the wilderness either doesn't come up this far, or is too big to fit through that hole.

Shil is waiting when I get outside.

'Rachel . . .' she begins.

'Yeah, I know.'

The cliff is sheer and handholds rare.

It is now so cold that frost glues the rock to my bare toes and the fingers of my good hand. Probably glues itself to the fingers of my other hand too, but that's metal so I can't feel it.

Climbing quickly, I ignore the ache across my shoulders as I haul myself to where Rachel clings to the rockface. She is shivering, from fear or cold.

'OK for the moment?'

That's *a question needing an answer in the affirmative.*

Whatever the fuck that is. Actually, I know what it is. It's when you can't say *no.* My old lieutenant taught me. Part of my education, like learning to use a fork instead of my fingers, wash myself at least once a week and not punch people without good reason.

Arm over arm, I drag myself to a point a hundred yards above Rachel. A quick tug does nothing to move the first bush, and neither does a hard yank. In the end, I have to position my feet, grip rock tightly with my good hand and wrap a branch several times round my prosthetic hand to discover why. The bloody plant has roots five times longer than the bits I can see.

Now I know what to expect, the second bush comes free with less effort. Then a third and a fourth and a fifth. I keep ripping them out until my good hand is bleeding from gripping rock and my feet are raw.

It doesn't matter, I mend fast.

'Last one,' I shout.

Somewhere below Neen shouts back. A second later, a

howling comes from the wastelands, sounding closer than before, a lot closer. And unless the cliff is doubling the noise, there is more than one animal advancing.

Rachel is waiting for me, her face lost in the shadow.

'You OK?'

She nods, and then realizes I can't see. So she says, *yes, sir, of course, sir.* Her voice is tight, however, and she shakes my hand off her shoulder without thinking. Her body is humming with tension under those shivers.

'Rachel,' I say, 'what's wrong?'

'My hand's trapped.'

Fuck. Sliding my hand along her arm, I find fingers hooked into a crack in the rockface. They don't feel trapped to me. 'Lift your little finger.'

'Can't.'

'*Do it . . .*' Her smallest finger flexes under my grip. 'OK,' I say. 'Now the next one.'

There is no movement at all.

'Try your thumb,' I suggest, although I already know the answer. One way or another, she's frozen. 'Right,' I say. 'This is how we're going to do it.'

It takes me a minute to find a handhold good enough to take both our weights. By now, I'm behind her, my body close to hers. She can feel my breath on the back of her neck and I can smell fear rise like dying heat from her body.

I tell her to turn round and grip my shoulders.

She doesn't want to do it, but she knows that staying glued to this cliff isn't a choice. So she shifts slightly, only to freeze as I wrap one arm round her waist.

'Turn slowly, I've got you.'

Can she do it?

The answer is yes. Letting go, she shifts until she can put her arms round my neck. It is just bad luck my foot chooses that moment to slip.

As I grab cliff and Rachel tightens her grip, my feet kick for a new hold. For a moment, I think we are not going to make it. So does Rachel. As my toes find rock, a liquid heat fills my lap.

She's pissed herself. As good a sign that we're still alive as any.

'Wrap your legs round me.'

Her hips are wide enough to let her do it. She's strong, unless it's just fear that has her squeezing my hips as if her life depends on it. When she tightens her grip, I can feel her breasts squash against me. Her hair smells of oil, and her body smells of fear, overlaid with the sharpness of fresh urine.

'Sir,' she says. 'You all right, sir?'

'Why?'

'Just wondered.'

'*Rachel . . .*'

'You went still, sir. Like you'd realized something.'

She's brighter than I thought. Either that or she reads minds.

'We need to move.'

'Yes, sir.'

With her arms locked tight round my neck and her legs gripping my hips, we make the return climb. It takes longer than it should, as I have to test each grip before letting go with my other hand.

Normally I'd jump the last fifteen or twenty feet, but I can't. Not carrying Rachel. So I edge my way down the cliff until I feel gravel beneath my toes.

'Wrap her in something warm.'

If Shil notices the stain on Rachel's clothes, she keeps it to herself.

Chapter 5

ONCE THEY ARE BROKEN, NEEN SEPARATES THE BUSHES INTO piles. One pile is kindling, the other our supplies for later. Franc is feeding the fire. She's having a competition with herself to see how close she can get her fingers to the flames.

The roots are oily, which helps them burn. Ash already lines a circle of stones holding the fire. Shil is talking to Rachel, both of them kneeling behind us in the safety of the cave.

Between them, they scoop handfuls of grit from the floor until they hit water. Most of the Aux are farm-born on shitty little planets, in backward bits of the spiral. It's easy to forget that; until one of them makes a perfect fire or finds water from instinct.

They are born on farms, grow up on farms, are conscripted into one army, captured and conscripted by another. Then, carrying cheap guns and wearing even cheaper uniforms, they pod-drop onto marshland outside a city called Ilseville.

That is where they're meant to die.

Only they meet a lieutenant without troops. So when their NCO goes down he takes over.

That's me.

When I look up, Shil's staring at me, and there's something knowing in her eyes. Maybe she's noticed the way I've been watching Rachel . . . Franc's abandoned the fire for her knives, which she's sharpening on a tiny whetstone. They look sharp enough to me.

Pushing myself to my feet, I nod towards the darkness.

'Coming?' I ask Franc.

Grinning, she stuffs one knife into her belt, another into her boot and slots the last, sight unseen, into a sheath hidden in the small of her back. I don't see where she puts the last one because she turns her back on me.

We are done up as mercenaries. This means far too many zips, flaps and shiny buckles for my liking. The Legion wear combat camouflage. Double dirt, they call it. Death's Head wear black, with silver stripes or shoulder bars.

Mercenaries look like an explosion in a cheap market.

'Neen,' I say, 'keep everyone in the cave.'

'What about . . . ?'

'They piss in it, they shit in it. For all I care, they can fuck in it. But if anyone takes a step outside I will cut their throats myself. Any other questions?'

He meets my gaze. 'No, sir.'

'The rest of you?'

Rachel and Haze look away, and Shil just shrugs as if she expected no better. She's the eldest, apart from me. You've probably worked that out for yourselves.

Say *desert* and people think of sand, but it is as likely to be grit, or something like the shale that crunches under my feet. The cliff is at my back, the cave is that glow away to one side and ahead of me is a slope down to the desert floor.

If it wants us, whatever is out there will have to climb that slope. We have triple moonlight and the slope on our side, and

44

a cruel wind against us. Every now and then, the wind catches grit and throws it into my eyes.

I could leave it until daylight . . .

The thought comes out of nowhere. There is nothing to say we must meet them head on. Then again, there is nothing to say we must not. But I'm ex-Legion, and meeting the enemy head on is what the Legion do. Of course, that doesn't mean it is always right.

'You all right, sir?'

'I'm fine.' It comes out louder than I intend. All this thinking is getting to me.

'Right,' I say. 'We're going to go down there, kill one of them and drag it back to the cave, take a look at what it is.'

As plans go, I have heard worse.

So has she. Sketching me a salute, Franc draws a knife from her belt and waits for her orders.

'That way.'

Shale slithers as we head downhill. We keep to the shadows, following the bed of a dry river, but it is not enough. A howl from ahead is answered by a howl off to the left, and then by another to the right.

They know we're coming.

Franc freezes the moment I raise my hand.

'Stay here,' I order. 'Count to ten, then make enough noise for five.'

She wants to be down there mixing it but she does as she is told. A few seconds after I leave, my corporal begins booting rocks down the slope, one after another. And she boots them hard.

That girl is a miracle of pure pent-up aggression.

As she kicks, Franc flicks a blade from hand to hand. It moves so fast it's impossible to say which hand holds the knife at any point. Her shoulders are loose and she's slouching.

45

Unless you have Legion training, she looks off guard. If you have Legion training, she looks very dangerous indeed.

Leaving Franc behind, I head towards a desert floor that ripples like an ocean, the silver grey of the shale catching the moonlight in patches of broken surf.

Then I see them.

At least I see one of them.

From here, he looks human. Tall and broad, with a shock of hair that sweeps back from his skull and falls halfway down his spine. He is naked, like a ferox, but the blade in his hand is sharpened steel.

He turns.

Deep-set eyes scan the slope.

When the stone in my hand lands fifty paces to his left he smiles. Thinking he's got me. Only his gaze slides over where my stone hit and flicks back, as he tilts his head, trying to pinpoint the exact position.

The moonlight is hurting his eyes.

Must be like trying to stare into the sun for me, because he has one hand shading his face, while the other holds his blade low and slightly tilted.

It's a good stance.

He can hear Franc on the slope above, there is no doubt about that. Every so often, his gaze flicks uphill, before returning to where he thinks I should be.

Only by now, I'm somewhere else.

There are five of them. A scout and four bunched together. As another two shadows crest a dune, I change my count to seven, adding an eighth, who appears from one side. Crouching, I watch the scout look from where he thinks I am to where Franc is making a noise, and then behind him to where the others cluster.

He is too indecisive to be senior.

That leaves the other seven.

Of the four together, one is small enough to be adolescent, one old and on the edge of the group. Another waves his hands and grunts, returning to the same sounds repeatedly. No one in command needs to make that much fuss about anything.

Knocking those three off my list, I edge close as one of those who crested the dune begins to shuffle down the near side. The others fall silent and face the naked newcomer.

Their leader is female.

A xenohuman, from when people changed to suit planets. This was before planets changed to suit people. She's whipcord thin, muscles sliding over one another and sinews locking like rope as she swivels to glance uphill. A deep-throated growl sends the scout loping away into the darkness.

Franc's problem.

With that decision, I move. Five steps take me to their group.

As an older male slashes, I catch his blade on my wrist and sparks fly. It is enough to make him hesitate.

Bad mistake.

A twist of his head and his neck's broken. My next move shatters the jaw of a creature behind. When he stays standing, I sidekick his knee and hear the wet suck of cartilage rupturing. He howls, but that stops as I stamp on his throat.

It is brutal.

Battles always are.

At least the kind I fight.

The next creature dies in silence, my hand crushing his larynx so viciously my fingers meet in the middle. He's dead, but I rip his throat out anyway.

Stepping back, I kick the balls of the adolescent opposite. She doesn't have any. *Female*, I realize, as she screams. All the same, my boot doubles her over and I grip both sides of her head.

47

I knew another girl like her, on a different planet. The ferox ate her.

'*Fuck it.*'

I don't do guilt, and I don't do regret for something occurring half a spiral arm away. Twisting hard, I break this one's neck; and let her drop, trying not to stare at a dark triangle of hair and two perfect breasts.

As a howl comes from their leader, I realize I've done it. The fight is now personal.

Her daughter, her granddaughter?

Doesn't matter. This tribe runs with a female as the boss and her successor is lying dead at my feet.

'Come on then,' I say.

The other two fall back as the female stalks forward.

She is huge. A good head taller than me, and I'm the tallest person I know. A blade hangs from her right hand. It is filthy along most of its length, but its edge has been sharpened on stone.

These creatures didn't make that blade.

Also, they don't belong on this planet, because none of us belongs on this planet or any other still in existence. The planet we belong on ate itself. Only that is heresy, so I try not to say it, even to myself. Because our beloved emperor hates heresy. You would be surprised the number of things he hates.

Well, perhaps you wouldn't.

It's still true though.

I have time to think this because the creature wants me to make the first move. Her remaining followers stand off to one side. Neither approaches me; she has them too well trained for that.

She circles, I circle.

Stepping sideways, we keep a safe distance between us. I am flicking my blade hand-to-hand, Franc-style. It irritates the leader, because she thinks I should have attacked by now.

But I'm waiting and circling, until light from the largest of the three moons hits her eyes.

That's when I move.

It is just for show, a lunge towards her gut.

As she twists away, I make my second move, sliding my feet from under me to hit her ankle with the edge of my boot.

I have Franc's accident to thank for that idea.

Rocking back, the creature then steps forward again, straight onto her freshly dislocated ankle. One shout of pain joins another as I cut her hamstrings, good leg first. She goes down hard as a falling tree. And I'm rolling myself up her, ending with a palm strike under her nose. The usual happens: bone enters her brain, her brain stops working . . .

Not that it was that hot in the first place.

By now, I am back on my feet.

Neither of the others tries to stop me as I walk away. From behind comes growling, but I ignore it. *They're in shock. Attacking would focus their minds, and these are minds best left unfocused.* Part of me wonders how I know that, and the rest doesn't care. I have been in enough battles to trust my instinct.

Climbing the slope takes longer than I like. The shale slides beneath my feet, and one of the moons vanishes behind a cliff. It's the largest, and the loss of light makes the climb more difficult.

Of course, I could just plough my way up. But I'm trying to be subtle.

'Franc . . . ?'

I keep my voice low. No one answers, so I slow slightly and head for where I remember her being.

'You there?'

The fire is straight ahead of me. A flickering glow, mostly hidden by the slope and the fact it is built in the mouth of a cave. She should be here. Franc is not the type to retreat.

'Sir . . .'

'Franc?'

'Man down, sir.'

I find her enemy first. His throat's open to the bone, and a savage cut above his nose has ruined both his eyes. He stinks and shit glazes one leg. A dagger juts from his gut; it looks as if Franc lacked the strength to drag it upwards.

My corporal's state isn't much better.

'Stay still.' When she looks at me, I see pain.

'Sorry, sir,' she says. 'Even Haze can't fix this.' Her hand flaps weakly towards her jacket.

Moonlight shows blood on the leather of her coat, but not what the coat is covering. Franc tries to stop me as I begin to lift the edge.

'Too late,' she says.

'Yeah,' I say, slapping away her hand. 'We've done that bit.' She wants to know if it is as bad as she thinks.

It's worse.

Franc has the ribs of a stray kitten, the tits of a kid and a jagged rip below one of them that shows me her heart beating. It pumps slowly, shuddering between beats. The scout didn't just stab her, he opened her chest.

'Yeah,' she says. 'Told you.'

'Franc . . .'

'It's in your eyes.' She smiles, bitterly. 'You're not as hard to read as you think.'

'I don't . . .'

She looks at me.

'Want to talk about that?' I say, changing the subject. My finger traces a puckered scar, one of a dozen that run from her hipbone to where her body hair would start, assuming she had any.

Franc shakes her head.

'It might help.'

Her laugh brings blood with it. 'How?' she demands. 'How the fuck could it help?'

'Tell me who did it and I'll kill them.'

'Is that a promise?'

'Yeah,' I say. 'Guaranteed.'

'Then you're a fool . . .' At my look, her mouth twists. 'Yeah, I know. *You're a fool, sir.*' Realizing I still don't understand, she says: 'I did them. Well, mostly. The others came free, but that's family for you.'

'And I can't kill your family because . . . ?'

'I've done it already.' She glances at the knife in my hand, splattered with blood from the creatures below. 'You know,' she says, 'now would be a good time to make good on that promise.'

'*Franc* . . .'

'You did it for Corporal Haven.'

She names a trooper I have forgotten, from a battle that barely registers.

'You're sure?' That is a question I'm not meant to ask.

Her scowl tells me so.

Unsheathing one of Franc's blades, I grip her shoulder with my hand and touch the tip of the knife to her heart. 'Ready?' I ask, because Franc deserves the final say on this.

She nods.

'Sleep well,' I tell her. 'And a better life next time.'

A soldier's prayer. My prayer. And so I jab the blade through beating muscle and shock her heart into stillness.

Chapter 6

FRANC WEIGHS NEXT TO NOTHING, AND SPILLING HER BLOOD barely increases the mess. As I stamp my way up the slope, the second of the three moons disappears behind a cliff and a dozen extra stars appear, as the night grows darker.

I don't know if our attackers carry home their dead. I don't care. We do. We are the Aux. I don't give a fuck if we've only been in existence for a few months. It is one of our oldest traditions.

The fire burns brightly in the mouth of our cave.

Neen takes one look at what I'm carrying and his relief at seeing me vanishes. He is the first on his feet, although I shake my head when he tries to take her body from me.

'Oh shit,' he says.

Rachel starts crying.

'You,' I tell her, 'get back to your post.'

I might as well have slapped her because she flinches anyway.

Dropping to my knees, I roll Franc onto the ground and see grit glue itself to the stickiness of her jacket. If she'd died in battle, it would be different. But my corporal is dead because some fuck blew up our plane. I am going to find out why. Then I'm going to find out who. And then I'm going to kill that person, slowly.

'We bury her here,' I say.

'Sir . . .'

'Got a problem with that?'

As Neen steps back, his face closes down. 'Something you should see first, sir.' Grabbing a branch from the fire, he waves it back and forth until it bursts into flames. Then he turns and heads into the cave.

Shil and Haze are sitting in darkness.

'Haze found it,' she says.

'Behind that,' says Haze. The wall he points at looks like every other one in this place, yellow and dry enough to crumble.

They don't know she's dead, I realize.

'Touch it,' says Haze.

I am tired, Franc's blood is on my hands and I am out of patience.

'Cut the shit,' I tell him. Scooping up a pebble, Haze lobs it at the wall. It passes through as if the wall weren't there.

'You took a look behind?'

Haze hesitates, not knowing what to answer. 'Stairs,' he says finally. 'And lights. I didn't climb all the way.'

The lights start after twenty paces. It goes: walk-through wall, one twist of stairs into darkness, and then little glow bulbs that hang from the ceiling, giving off a greenish light. I've seen them before, on Paradise, the prison planet where General Jaxx sent me once as a joke.

The steps are worn enough to tell me the tunnelling isn't recent. And the glow bulbs, that come on as Neen and I get near and turn off as we leave, tell me there's a power source somewhere.

While most of my crew huddle for warmth round a fire made from roots, in a cave on some godforsaken planet settled by ex-humans, there is a power source strong enough to run chameleon camouflage and light a spiral of stairs.

It does nothing for my temper.

'Go back,' I tell Neen. 'Get the others.'

'And Franc?'

'Obviously.'

Having saluted, he slips away.

I sit so long that the light above me switches itself off, and remains off until Neen and the others return.

We climb in silence.

My old lieutenant would tell me the lights are saying something deep, about life, light, darkness, and death. But then he was full of shit.

We climb, and keep climbing.

The air gets warm and the steps become ceramic. There is paint on the walls now, and a door that looks new. At least, it looks recently replaced, because the metal frame around it is dark and pitted, while the door itself is shiny.

It is unlocked.

There's carpet on the other side.

'Take point,' I tell Neen. 'And take this.'

He catches the distress pistol from the plane. As I watch, he breaks it open and drops out the flare, checks the barrel and slots the flare back into place. He toggles a safety switch, and then snaps the pistol shut. He does all this quietly and I notice his breathing has steadied.

Neen is a natural. That's why he's my sergeant.

Not his fault I'm angry, not theirs . . .

And I will keep my fury in check around them, provided they shut up, do what they're told, and have the sense to stay out of my way.

'Me second,' I say, thinking through the order. 'Haze third,

Rachel fourth, Shil takes rear.' One less thing for Neen to worry about if we hit trouble. And we are going to, because I'm going to make damn sure we do.

'Take Franc,' I tell Rachel.

Lifting the body onto her shoulder, Rachel climbs in stubborn silence. At the next landing, Haze offers to swap. Rachel shakes her head and he doesn't ask again. When we near the top, I know what I am going to find.

This has U/Free written all over it.

'Ready?'

Neen nods.

'On my count.'

I hold up five fingers and reach for the door, not quite touching the handle. When the count hits *two*, I close my hand round the knob and twist.

The door is unlocked. There's no alarm.

Their arrogance is staggering.

Zero . . .

At my nod I throw open the door and Neen goes through, pistol drawn and sweeping the room. Three people, two men and one woman. The woman I already know, the men I hate on sight. 'See,' says one. 'Told you.'

The other smiles.

Only to lose his smile when Neen stamps towards him.

Hooking out the man's feet, my sergeant shoulder-slams him to the ground and drops on top of him. When Neen stops moving, his distress pistol is tight against the stranger's right eye.

'Move,' says Neen. 'And I'll fuck you.'

As the woman steps forward, Neen tightens his trigger finger.

She stops, turns to me, saying, 'Sven, enough. You know there's—'

'Whose idea was this?'

Her gaze catches mine and Paper Osamu's smile falters.

'It was my idea,' says the man behind her. 'Jaxx said you were resourceful. I wanted to be certain.' He's tall, dressed in one of those long robes the U/Free wear to impress lesser races with their casual restraint.

'My corporal is dead,' I tell him.

He looks at me, glances at Paper. 'What's a *corporal*?' he asks.

A single step takes me to where he stands. He's fast, but I'm faster, and I do this for a living. Head-butting him, I grab his skull and twist until his neck is just short of breaking point and he shits himself.

'A corporal comes above a trooper and below a sergeant,' I say. 'Have you any fucking idea how hard it is to find someone that good with a knife?'

Of course he hasn't.

'Fuckwit.'

The last thing he sees is my smile.

After he's dead, I boot him anyway. My first breaks ribs, the second ruptures his heart. I have no idea what the third does, other than land with a wet thud.

'*Sven . . .*'

'Shut it.'

Paper Osamu opens her mouth to protest and closes it when I jab my finger at Franc's body. 'You did that.'

She shakes her head.

'Take this,' I tell Rachel, tossing her a blade. 'If she opens her mouth again, cut her throat.'

'My pleasure, sir.'

Their observation room is large, floored with marble that is warm to the touch. It has these weird walls with a gap at the top and bottom, so it looks like they are floating.

Unless they *are* floating, of course.

Vast screens show live feeds of the wilderness outside. One

is a satellite shot, taken from high space. Seems the rest of this planet isn't much better than the bit we've already seen.

'Sven . . .' Paper's voice is calm. As if talking to a child.

'*Rachel.*'

'Sir?'

'What did I say?'

The U/Free ambassador flinches as Rachel grabs her head, yanks it back and puts a knife to her neck.

'You can't,' says the man Neen's guarding.

'Actually,' I tell him, 'I can.'

'*Sven,*' says Paper, as Rachel steadies her blade. '*Listen.* We can bring your trooper back.'

Rachel keeps the edge tight against Paper's throat and wraps her fingers tighter into Paper's hair to tell the U/Free she is not out of trouble yet.

'And him?' I say, nodding to the man I killed.

'Morgan?' says Paper. 'Of course.'

'Guess there's a downside to everything.'

Paper doesn't think it's funny. But then I don't mean it as a joke. Moreover, I still haven't decided whether I'm going to let her live. We've been played with, fucked over and I have killed one of my own. There never was an ammo dump to destroy. This isn't even the real Hekati.

I look at Paper, and she smiles.

It is a sweet smile, despite the fingers tight in her hair and the knife at her throat. It reminds me why I don't trust the U/Free. And that reminds me that Ms Osamu asked for us personally, by name. A request from a U/Free ambassador is a command from anyone else.

'The general knew Morgan wanted to test us?'

'Of course.'

'And what did he say?'

'That someone would get hurt.'

'Next time,' I say, kicking the body, 'tell him to listen.'

Chapter 7

PAPER OSAMU LIVES ON THE HUNDRED AND TWENTY-SEVENTH floor of a glass and carbon tower in a city called Letogratz. The city is five times the size of Farlight. She lives in its most expensive area, with a view of a vast harbour leading to a curving horizon beyond. Her windows are huge, except the window in her bedroom. This is beyond huge. It's a wall made entirely of glass. Far below lies a promenade lined with golden palm trees and scarlet bushes that curl themselves up into tight balls when darkness comes in.

Out on the harbour, jet boats skim the waves like flying fish. They don't seem to be actually doing anything except looking pretty. Apparently, that is enough in this city.

Paper dragons ride the updraught beyond Paper's window.

Kids, I think. Until I look closer. Adults hang below their vast paper wings, swooping and turning above the promenade. The more daring of the kite riders skim close to the walls of Paper's building or navigate the gap between where we are and the building beside us.

It's a narrow gap, and I don't get it.

No other civilization is this rich. Yet they live in quarters half the size of a kitchen cupboard at Golden Memories, and waste their days playing with children's toys. If they are so rich, why don't they give themselves more space, and do something interesting?

They have two thirds of the galaxy to explore. Unless it's three quarters. General Jaxx told me once, but I wasn't listening. The end of one spiral is split between the metalheads and us. The U/Free own the rest. Apart from a handful of minor systems claimed by maniacs, cargo cults, and self-anointed messiahs. No one pays them much attention until things get out of hand. Then the U/Free go in and we suddenly have one less star.

I ask Paper how much the U/Free rule these days.

She tells me they rule nothing. They are simply a commonwealth. So I ask her how much of the galaxy they're busy not ruling and she laughs.

Rolling onto her stomach, she wiggles her bottom at me.

'Five sixths.'

'That's more than three quarters?'

She sighs. So I slap her arse.

And when it's pink enough, I spit on my fingers and watch her nod in a mirrored headboard. If I don't want to watch her in that, there is a looking glass on each of the side walls and one glued to the ceiling overhead. She looks good in all of them.

'Slowly,' she says.

I take this as proof she is OK with what I have in mind.

A strange way for her to say sorry; but then Paper Osamu is a strange woman. She's a strange person, full stop. In a city full of strange people. If getting naked is how she wants to say sorry who am I to complain?

'Shit,' she says.

Actually, she says it three times.

By then I am almost inside, and she's begun chewing the

back of her hand. So I pull out and she swears at me, tells me no way am I going to put that in there again. She's wrong. A while later, she looks round.

'Have you thought more about what I said last time?'

Something about asylum? She doesn't mean that. 'Not really,' I say, because this seems best.

Paper Osamu sighs. 'It's dangerous,' she tells me. 'It's going to kill you.'

Ah, got it now.

The U/Free don't like soft tek. At least not when someone else builds it. I wait for her to repeat her earlier warning. This she does, word for word. *It's dangerous. It's going to kill me. I haven't been trained to use it.*

Basically, a kyp has set up home in my throat. A kyp's an illegal symbiont. It can be used to talk direct to AIs, bend a few physical rules. A short cut to the voodoo shit Haze does.

Paper tells me it is lethal.

'So remember,' she adds. 'We don't want you using it.'

On this mission is what she means. She's leading up to something. Talking about our mission would be the obvious thought; but that is way too obvious, although it takes me a while to realize that. She's talking *around* the mission.

We start with *where*.

Hekati.

This isn't a planet at all. It's a small ring world. Once, it belonged to an asteroid cult. Currently, it's deserted. When Paper says deserted she means of anyone who matters. Descendants of the original miners still scrabble through slag heaps; also squatters, freeloaders, exiles and illegals.

My kind of people. I'm glad Paper mentions this. I thought she meant *empty*.

'When are we leaving?'

A scowl says she is getting to that bit. 'Within the week . . . You'll get two days' warning.'

'And what are we going to be doing when we get there?'

'I haven't been told,' she says.

Paper's lying.

So I pull out, stand us both on the tiles and press down until she begins to bend at the knee. Later, as she scrubs her lips with the back of one hand, she looks up at me with her perfect eyes and does that smile.

'You know,' she says, 'Morgan believes you're a psychopath.'

'You brought him back?' She must hear something in my voice. Because her face tightens.

'Of course I brought him back.'

'Before Franc?'

'He still has to approve your mission,' says Paper. 'If he doesn't, there's no point bringing her back at all.'

Chapter 8

AS THE DOORS OPEN, THE SMALL LAKE BEYOND PARTS IN TIME to stop water flooding the elevator's only occupant to the waist.

That's me.

Fuck knows what holds the koi pond back. Perhaps a force field produced by the elevator itself. A path winds between strategically placed rocks, white flowers and huge green leaves. It wanders gently, so I ignore it.

Taking the direct route, I climb three steps at the pond's edge and ignore a woman in a silk dressing gown hand-feeding crane-flies to a fish the size of my arm. Something about her smile annoys me.

'Good afternoon,' she repeats, as if I didn't hear first time. 'Will we see you at tomorrow's party?'

I ignore that too.

'It will be fun,' she says. 'Parties always are.'

Stopping, I turn to stare; then nod at an insect wriggling in her hand: 'Isn't that cruel?'

As if I care.

'Oh no,' she says, sounding shocked. 'Of course not.'

'Must be.'

She looks at me.

Maybe she is trying to work out if I'm simple. Alternatively, maybe she's wondering if I'm mocking her. Unless she's wondering if I belong in the atrium of Paper Osamu's building after all. In which case, we both know the answer to that.

'They're not sentient,' she says, smiling when I scowl. 'No feelings,' she explains. 'No thoughts.'

'Maybe not in the sense you understand.'

'Oh no.' She shakes her head firmly. 'Not in any sense at all.'

I leave the woman feeding brain-dead insects to fat fish and stamp the hundred paces between Paper's building and the tower where we're based. Our building is not as grand as hers. Nevertheless, it is still taller than any building in Farlight.

'Your ears,' says the lift. 'Can I recommend . . . ?'

'Seventy-sixth floor,' I tell it.

'Yes . . . Now, about your ears.' Apparently, most U/Free wear *grommets*. It can order these for me now.

'Just take me up.'

'But you have a headache.'

'And you're making it worse.'

When it starts again on the ear modification, I punch a fist-shaped bruise in its shiny metal side, then threaten to rip open its service panel, snap the wires and piss in its fuse box.

The lift tells me violence never solved anything.

Shows what it knows. And that reminds me why I miss my SIG-37. You can get a decent argument going with that gun. Only, the SIG's back at Death's Head HQ. There are good reasons. At least, that is what the general says.

Paper Osamu thinks the gun encourages my tendencies.

Since, presumably, she is employing me for my *tendencies*, I cannot see the problem. Kicking the elevator on my way out makes it blink. All the lights go out, come back on, go out and come back on again. It occurs to me that maybe no one else kicks machinery round here.

'Violence never—' It starts to say.

So I kick it again. 'Go,' I tell it. 'While your fuses still function.'

It drops away in silence.

All the buildings in Letogratz follow the same pattern. They are hollow, three-sided, and built around a courtyard that is open to the sky. The courtyards need no roof, because a force field holds back the rain. This begins at 3.28 every afternoon and finishes exactly forty minutes later.

Ten minutes before the rain starts, the sky goes dark. Thunder comes first, then lightning, then rain so heavy it glazes the walls of every building before it runs to the ground and disappears into storm drains. Ten minutes after the rain stops, the sky turns blue again.

The party begins at dusk. A messenger arrives to say we are required. He says *invited*, but that is not what he means. He talks to my sergeant, because Rachel is busy stitching my good hand. I put it through a window.

How was I to know Paper lied about their glass being un-breakable? It has been a long day, and I've wasted most of it trying to find out why she will not return my calls. It should be simple: I tap a wall and ask it to connect me.

Works anywhere the U/Free are.

Technically, this is impossible.

According to Haze, the galaxy is x light years across by x light years thick. So messages take whole lifetimes and longer to go anywhere. But the U/Free have ships that tear holes in space and post themselves through the rips.

That is impossible as well.

I've been tapping walls all day. Until tapping turns into punching. None of the walls bothers to tell me why a connection to Paper Osamu isn't possible. My temper is not helped by a conversation I hear on returning to our living room, fist bandaged.

'It's obvious,' says Shil.

'No way.' Neen sounds certain.

'Neen,' says Shil, 'grow up.' She shouldn't say that, even if he is her brother. 'And now she's dumped him.'

My sergeant shakes his head.

'Serves Sven right.'

'I thought you liked him?'

'*Neen . . .*'

'Just saying.'

'*Well don't.*' Shil stamps over to a window and stares out at the rain. When she turns back, she sees me in the doorway. She is wondering how much I heard.

'Where's Franc?'

'Still resting, sir.'

I haven't seen her yet. Although we'd expected her this morning, it's early afternoon before she is released for tests. What tests no one tells us. She will be good as new is all they'll say.

'It's complicated,' says Morgan, when I ask for more information.

Perhaps threatening to break his neck again was a bad move. I mean, how was I to know he and Paper are married . . . And while I'm thinking this, a patch of living-room wall goes fuzzy and Paper finally returns my call. She's naked and Morgan stands behind her. He's naked too.

They're smiling.

'You were trying to get hold of me?'

'Yeah,' I say. 'We won't be making that party.'

Morgan's gaze flicks past me. When he speaks, it's to whisper something in his wife's ear. She nods.

'It starts in five minutes.'

'Paper,' I say, 'we're not—'

Irritation flicks across her face. Maybe this is not a discussion she wants to have in front of the Aux. Or perhaps it's Morgan. He has his hands on her hips, and he is standing close behind her. I don't want to know what he is doing. Except I already do.

We all do.

'*Get a room*,' mutters Neen.

Morgan laughs. The U/Free are different to us. How different we are all coming to realize.

'You should get changed,' says Paper.

'So should you.'

She smiles. 'I'm wearing a gown. You've got all that braid.'

'All that . . . ?'

'Jaxx had your uniforms sent over.'

Paper says this as if it is the most obvious thing in the world. As if General Jaxx shipping some lieutenant's uniform for a party was normal.

'Sven,' she says, 'the general told us you'd be happy to attend any functions necessary. After all, you're here on a cultural exchange.'

First I've heard of it.

'Do call Jaxx to check,' says Morgan. 'If you want.'

Neen's puzzled. It looks like his jacket, but it feels wrong. So he turns up the lights for a closer look and realizes it is only pretending to be his jacket. Someone has taken standard-issue battledress and re-created it in spider's silk and fine wool.

The changes do not end there.

Braid edges his collar; his belt is leather not webbing.

As for our Death's Head patches . . . Franc cut those from the skin of a cold-water alligator on the marshes outside Ilseville, the night we formed the Aux. It seems longer ago than it is.

The patches remain, but someone has tidied the edges and wrapped them in silver. A new row of stripes decorates Neen's left sleeve.

They're the real thing.

Death's Head official issue. *Sergeants, for the use of . . .*

'Shit,' says Shil. She looks at her brother, uncertain whether to be upset or pleased. A dagger fills Neen's hand; it's plain black, with a silver pommel. That is official issue too.

Franc is here now. We're all pretending that's normal. She looks like Franc and sounds like Franc and even smells like Franc. I know that, because I get close enough to check. Her face looks the same, as does her body, what I can see of it.

Only her eyes are different. They're terrified.

She has been brought back from the dead. No one asked her if that was what she wanted. How could they? So we're ignoring it, she's ignoring it, and I'm letting Shil and Rachel fuss over the new uniforms like children with a toy-box.

'Let's unpack the rest,' Rachel says.

Franc has proper stripes for a corporal. And everyone has a battle ribbon, a slash of red and white. Must be for Ilseville, because it cannot be for anything else. We are obviously claiming that as a victory now.

My uniform is last. It looks like before.

Silver collar bars show my rank, an Obsidian Cross hangs on its black silk ribbon; a run of silver braid falls to the left of the jacket. Although the braid is better quality than it was. The jacket is less ornate than Neen's, but that is how we work. The uniform General Jaxx wears is simpler still.

My boots are new, though, their heels higher. This is un-necessary, as I am already taller than everyone else.

'Sir,' says Shil, nodding to a roll of cloth. 'Think this might be yours.' Her voice is way too neutral.

It's a cloak. *Staff officers, for the use of . . .*

Staff officers? Why not just shoot me and have done with it.

The outside of the cloak is black, and what I can see of the silk lining is red. A silver skull on one side of a floppy collar grins at a skull on the other side. A metal chain loops between their teeth.

'*So you,*' says a voice.

'What?'

'*Tacky, tawdry, tasteless.*'

As I shake out the cloak, Neen ducks and something flicks across the room and bounces off an opposite wall. I know what it is before it lands. There aren't many weapons that can swear like that.

Very carefully, Haze picks up the SW SIG-37.

'Haze . . .'

'Just fetching it for you, sir.'

'Clips emptied,' protests my gun. 'Molested by U/Free *experts*' – it puts particular emphasis on this word – 'then thrown across the room by a moron.'

'Yeah,' I say. 'Good to see you too.'

It snorts.

So I threaten to introduce it to an elevator.

The SIG-37 snorts some more.

Its fold-down wire stock is gone. Its pistol grips are mother of pearl rather than neoprene. Chrome glints where a slate-grey slide should be, and a small ruby replaces the original red dot sight.

'U/Free orders,' it says.

'What – *pimp my gun?*'

'Not that,' it says bitterly. 'Take a proper look.'

The cinder-maker capacity is gone. Some idiot's taken the

world's first fully intelligent pulse pistol, with advanced AI and battle-precognition capabilities and reconfigured it as something a fifteen-year-old gangbanger would be ashamed to carry.

In the bottom of the box is a holster.

Black leather, silver buckle. A full-dress dagger sits under that, its pommel a skull. Slamming the SIG into its new holster, I ignore the fact it's now sulking, and say, 'Let's get this over with.'

We change on the spot. I have a reason for this.

I want to see Franc naked, just not that way. She's fit, thigh muscles sliding over each other as she moves. From her cropped skull to the gash of her sex, she still lacks body hair, but I am right about one thing. Her scars are gone.

Seeing me look, Franc turns her back.

'You plan to redo them?'

When she doesn't answer, I twist her round so fast she almost trips. The others go still. They're wise.

'Well?' I say.

Scared eyes meet mine.

Franc can remember me killing her. She can remember dying at the bottom of a bleak cliff on some shitty little planet, half gutted by a creature whose ancestors used to be human.

Then she wakes here. In a place she doesn't recognize.

'Say it.'

'Sir,' she says. 'Sorry, sir.'

'*For what?*'

She flicks her gaze around the room, before settling it on me. Her eyes are dark, her face gaunt. I can tell how badly she wants to look away. 'I didn't mean to let everyone down.'

'*You didn't—*'

Then I get it. She is ashamed of being killed.

'See that,' I say, pointing to a scar on my ribs. 'Should have finished me. And that,' I point to my gut. 'Hurt so much I wished it fucking had. And this . . .' I tap my prosthetic arm, making it ring. 'Got ripped off by a ferox.'

She knows that.

'You don't survive shit like that. Not normally. Only I mend fast. You don't. So get yourself dressed and go party.'

'Yes, sir.' Naked, but happier, she salutes.

Chapter 9

WE STOP THE SKY BRIDGE AND GIVE IT AN ADDRESS. THERE IS
a slight ripple before the bridge begins to move. Five buildings later, the bridge drops to level ten and creates a door in
an outside wall ahead of us. We're impressed. We're meant to
be impressed.

'Welcome to tonight's soirée,' says the bridge.

Haze snorts, but then he is the only one to know what it
means.

On the far side of the door we find a bedroom, leading to
living quarters, with an exit onto the walkway beyond. The
rails around the walkway are missing, and a dance floor floats
in the triangular space where emptiness should be.

This is a small and private gathering it seems.

A dozen U/Free turn to watch us, and then a dozen more.
By the time I realize the floor's floating, and we're expected
to step across the gap from walkway to floor, a hundred
people are watching.

And you've never seen anything like them.

Well, I haven't.

They're tall, they're elegant, and they're beautiful. A

hundred white smiles, a hundred displays of perfect teeth. They're all holding glasses, and sipping chilled white wine.

'*Fuckers,*' says my gun. It speaks for us all.

'Sven,' says a voice from the crowd. 'How sweet of you to come.' Paper Osamu's words ooze warmth. 'And your friends as well.' She smiles broadly.

Like we had a choice.

'I'm sure you need a drink,' she says.

A waitress appears, wearing a skirt slit to her thigh, with a top tight enough to squeeze her breasts while open enough to reveal their valley. She bows when I take a glass, and the valley gets a whole lot deeper.

Laughing, Paper Osamu says, 'Come on. There are far more interesting people to meet.'

Morgan is talking to a blonde in a shirt so thin it's see-through. She has nipples like bullets and the tits of a teenage whore, all four of them. She also has pale blue eyes, and these belong to a woman old enough to be my great-grandmother. As her gaze sweeps down my uniform it rests a little too long on the zip.

'So,' she says. 'This is him?'

Paper nods.

The woman smiles. 'If you're interested,' she says, 'we might try a threesome?' She's talking to me this time.

'Maybe later.'

As I am herded away, Paper leans close. 'I'm impressed,' she whispers. 'That was almost polite for you.'

'I meant it.'

She frowns, and then decides I'm joking.

The first hour goes well enough. People talk, I pretend to listen. The waitress with the split skirt and overflowing breasts becomes my shadow. Every time my glass is empty, she fills it from a bottle that looks full.

Her smile gets wider as the night goes on.

Just as I am about to ask what time she gets off, a scowl fills her face and she fades into the crowd, taking the champagne with her. So I turn, none too happy, and find myself staring at an elegant young man with blond hair and high cheekbones. Little more than a boy, really.

He nods, the slightest dip of his head.

So I inspect him the way I'd inspect a trooper back when I was a sergeant. A wispy beard, one of those little fair ones. Teeth that gleam. A narrow waist, and shoulders padded to make them broader. He's thin and elegant, and he is rotating his fluted wine glass by its narrow stem, lazily.

I hate him on sight.

'Yes?'

'Sven Tveskoeg?' The fact he drawls my name should be warning enough, but I'm not big on warnings.

'Who wants to know?'

Drawing himself to his full height, the boy sweeps back his cloak.

'*Fuck* . . .'

Well, what am I supposed to say?

He wears the dress uniform of a Death's Head colonel. And it's the real thing: with a double loop of silver braid falling from one shoulder, and an impressive row of battle ribbons. An Obsidian Cross hangs at his neck. First class, obviously. Actually, it's the one above: with a little crown and a spray of oak leaves.

'Colonel Vijay,' he says. 'I'll be leading this mission.'

'*You'll be* . . . ?'

'Leading this mission.'

He says it loud enough to make a woman next to us turn. Maybe Colonel Vijay has been told to expect an argument. But he's a senior officer and I'm a lieutenant, and I should have known something like this would happen.

'Of course you will, sir . . . What mission would that be?'

'To rescue the missing U/Free.'

'Missing U/Free, sir?'

'Captured, Ms Osamu believes. By some god-awful little local militia. We're going to get him back.'

'Yes, sir,' I say. 'Of course we are, sir.'

Imagine a steel spring uncoiling. That is how fast I salute. It's so fast, so faultless I might as well have slapped his face.

Can I help if he flinches? Rules are rules, so I hold my salute until he returns it.

'Enough,' he tells me. 'We're off duty here.'

'Are we, sir?'

'Yes,' he says. 'We are . . . And providing you follow my orders I'm sure we'll get on.'

'Never disobeyed an order in my life, sir.'

The little idiot believes me.

A flash of red under his collar badges tells me he is a staff officer, and that makes me take a closer look at those battle ribbons. One of them is for a campaign fought five years ago. This would make him what? Sixteen at the time? Fifteen?

Then I see Ilseville. It is the medal ribbon we have.

The only one we have.

I was there . . . Might have mentioned that before. I can name every Octovian officer, NCO or trooper who stumbled away from that city alive. God knows, there aren't many of us. 'Ilseville?' I say it without thinking.

His eyes narrow. 'I helped with the planning.'

Stepping closer, I put my face near his.

'It was a fuck-up,' I say, keeping my voice low. 'A disaster. You know the casualty rate? As close to a hundred per cent as makes no difference.'

'You survived.' There is something bitter in his voice.

'Yeah,' I say. 'No thanks to shits like you.'

What did you say?

'No thanks to HQ, sir.'

'It was a victory,' says Colonel Vijay. 'To suggest otherwise is treason.'

'Yes,' I say. 'Glorious, wasn't it? Makes me wonder about all those other victories we keep winning.'

Turning on his heel, he begins to stalk towards my troopers and then changes his mind. The next time I see our little colonel, he is laughing with Morgan and the blonde with four tits and thousand-mile eyes.

Strikes me, they are made for one another.

It is a long night and I lose the Aux somewhere down the line. Although I glimpse Colonel Vijay, with a glass of wine. The woman he's talking to has her face close to his, and they are agreeing about something, strongly from the look of it.

'I had no idea,' she tells me later.

'What?' I demand.

'That Octovians . . .'

Can hold their drink? Don't fart in public? As she struggles with words I'm not interested in hearing, I wonder if it is a good idea for her to stand like that on a mirrored floor when she has clearly forgotten her knickers.

Who knows what she's trying to say?

The woman hesitates. 'Are so *cultured*,' she says finally.

'Not all of us.'

She laughs, tells me she wants to introduce me to a friend.

His name is Obsidian, and he's Paper's grandfather. Looking at him, I can't see a likeness. Unless it is his eyes. They are narrow, slightly almond in shape and cold as ice. His smile is equally chilly. 'Sven,' he says. 'I've heard interesting things about you.'

'Can't say I've heard of you.'

Obsidian Osamu tells me I'm part of an important mission. A chance . . . A rare, unmissable chance – their president thinks – for the U/Free to integrate with galactic society. He keeps an utterly straight face as he says this. I'm really hoping he doesn't expect me to believe it. Even the U/Free can't think we're that stupid.

'But first,' he says, 'a small favour.'

The request obviously means more to him than it does to me, because his voice trembles as he tells me what it is. Don't think I have seen a U/Free nervous before. I file the fact away for later.

'You'll do it?'

Looking round the room, I say, 'Way I feel now it would be a pleasure.' It's not the answer he's expecting.

The cubicle walls are marble, the floor is warm and the lighting inside the cubicle so subtle it's impossible to tell where it comes from. But it is the seashell in a little tray on the wall that interests me. What the fuck is that about?

Crumbling it between my fingers, I discover it's real.

When I look back another replaces the one I took. So I smash that and keep watching. A third shell appears – and I mean appears – it doesn't drop down or slide out. It simply appears.

This time when I take the shell, I don't break it.

Comparing the third and fourth tells me each shell is different. I'm still not sure why they are there. I mean, all anyone comes in here to do is piss or take a shit. Flushing the pan, I wash my fingers and dry them on the seat of my trousers.

There's nothing else to use.

A door opens in the restroom beyond.

Someone pees, water runs. That's my cue to get myself out there. At the basin, a U/Free looks up. He is old, examining his face carefully in the glass as if he's never seen it before.

Seeing a stranger behind him, he scowls. Then remembers his manners and forces a smile. I don't know his name. But I know he has been watching us all evening.

'So,' he says. 'You're off to mend bridges . . .'

The coy way he says this irritates me. Also, I don't have the faintest idea what he's talking about and that irritates me even more. He takes my grunt as an invitation to keep boring me. Meanwhile, I'm thinking *mend bridges*? Blowing them up is more my style.

'What bridges?' I demand, when he finishes.

'Well . . . Maybe it's more accurate to say you're setting off on the final part of a vital search.'

'Really?' I say. 'And what am I meant to be searching for?' That poncy little colonel said something about a missing observer. However, I'd like it confirmed by one of the U/Free.

'What we're all searching for. He looks at me expectantly. 'Peace,' he says. 'Resolution to deep divisions. What else is there . . . ?'

The man turns to go.

'Wait,' I say. 'Tell me more about Hekati.'

Looking from my face to the way my hand now grips the edge of a sink, he sighs, 'You're drunk. Ask Paper about it in the morning.'

'Not that drunk,' I say.

He has just realized something.

I'm holding a dagger. It's small and light and made of glass. And if I concentrate hard, I can remember the dampness of Lisa's thigh as I took its sister from her garter. The man knows he's about to be hurt. He knows it's possible he will die. What he doesn't know is his next death is going to be his last.

That is what the U/Free fear.

Paper Osamu told me this three months ago. She was doing that deprecating, we're-also-human thing the United Free do when trying to pretend they don't believe they are better than everyone else.

'You can't—' he begins to say.

I can, and do. Stabbing hard and fast. 'Say goodnight to your memories.'

His implant is where you would expect. At the back of his neck, just below the curve of his skull. It is very cross when I rip it free. Slicing away the last tendril, I crush the 'biont underfoot and flush it. Pulpy threads wriggle as they spin round the pan, but that is just aftershock. Having flushed the man's memories, I am left with his body.

Leave it, Paper's grandfather said. *We'll handle that bit.*

An interesting moral code. Unwilling to kill, happy to mop up the floor afterwards.

Taking the man's watch, a handful of gold coins and a diamond ring, I leave him a little pearl-handled knife and the medal round his neck. The coins go in our kitty, the watch I'll keep, and Franc can have the ring.

'Where have you been?' asks Colonel Vijay.

'Taking a shit.'

He scowls.

Across the room Haze laughs, looking better than I have seen him in a while. As far as I know, he hasn't vomited all evening. Like the nosebleeds, it is a reaction to the Uplift virus. They are going to stop sometime. Unfortunately, no one can tell us when.

Rachel's still fretting that his head hurts. But as Haze points out, if she had metal growing through her skull her head would hurt too.

'She stays here,' Colonel Vijay says.

'What?'

'And the other two. You must know women are a liability in battle.' He speaks with the absolute authority of someone who has never been near a battle in his life.

'They're Aux,' I tell him.

The colonel stares at me.

So I add, sir. But that's to annoy the U/Free. Paper's just

been telling Neen that she does not approve of hierarchies. Of course, she has to tell him what they are, before she can tell him why she doesn't like them.

'Paper,' I say.

She inclines her head.

'You asked for the Aux, didn't you?'

'Yes.' Paper Osamu nods. 'You know we did.'

'That's us,' I tell Colonel Vijay. 'All of us.' Saluting, I step back, and it is my turn to spin on my heels and stalk away. I don't need to look back to know I have made an enemy.

Like I give a fuck.

Chapter 10

PEOPLE TURN OUT TO SEE US OFF ON OUR SO-CALLED CULTURAL tour. More people than I expect. Come to that, more people than I imagined were in Letogratz. Almost all are wearing black and silver copies of our Death's Head uniform. Some even have the leather thigh boots.

'Started a craze,' says Paper, standing behind me. She smiles at someone in the crowd. 'You wouldn't believe the number of daggers the factor boxes have been asked to make in the past twenty-four hours. For decoration obviously.'

'Obviously.'

She shoots me a glance. 'You've made a big impression.'

'And that makes you look good?'

'Of course,' she says.

Paper hugs me, which shocks Colonel Vijay slightly. Then she walks us to the open door of a shuttle and steps back, smiling. We are on lenz, I realize. Millions of U/Free are watching this.

God these bastards must be bored.

Hydraulics hiss, doors rise, we buckle ourselves in, and Letogratz drops away hard and fast. Fifteen minutes later, we put down eight thousand miles away. On a deserted beach, with coral reefs to one side and a mangrove swamp on the other. The roots of the mangroves are woven tightly enough to make an impenetrable wall.

'Planted them an hour ago,' says the pilot. He smiles at our disbelief. 'Made the island this morning. It will be gone by tonight.'

Now that's what I call *maximum deniability.*

Another shuttle is waiting on the beach. And stacked beside it are crates fixed with OctoV's seal.

DIPLOMATIC SUPPLIES, reads a stencil. SECURITY CLEARED.

Inside the crates are enough weapons to start a small war. Also flip-down helmets, body armour, boots, field-glasses and battlefield radios. The colonel and I have reached an agreement. The agreement every CO reaches the moment he gets his first command. Find someone competent; tell him to carry on as normal. Of course, that is not how Colonel Vijay puts it.

He will tell me if I do anything wrong.

Ripping open a case, I check the list inside its lid.

'Here,' I say.

Catching a package, Rachel unwraps a stripped-down sniper rifle. She has never seen one like it before. She snaps the barrel into place from instinct and gives me a wide grin.

'Like it?'

'Fuck, sir. Yes.'

It is an 8.59mm Z93z long-range rifle, with adjustable cheek piece, ×3–×12–×50 spotting scope, floating breech and fluting on the outer barrel to aid heat dissipation. And while it might fire electronically to avoid the snap of a firing pin, it's bolt action, because snipers cling to the strangest traditions.

The only other Z93z I have seen decorates the wall of a sergeants' mess in General Jaxx's mother ship. The braids cut from a metalhead general are arranged underneath, along with his shoulder patches.

Colonel Vijay looks at me when I say this.

Not Rachel, she gets taking trophies. Snipers are high maintenance, like their weapons, everyone knows that.

'Mine, sir?'

'Until you're dead,' I tell her. 'Or I take it back.'

'This is my rifle,' she says. 'There are many like it, but this one is mine. Without it I am nothing.' Brushing aside long red hair, Rachel adjusts the sight and blind-fires at the shuttle disappearing into the sky above us.

When she lowers the rifle, she's still grinning.

'Sir,' she says. 'Thank you, sir.'

'That true?' Colonel Vijay asks a minute later.

'What, sir?'

'You were' – he hesitates – 'on the general's mother ship?'

'Yes, sir.'

'Doing what?'

'Being tried for treason. Well, that was the third time. Second time, I was being fitted for this.' I tap my arm loud enough to make it ring. 'Of course, that was after Colonel Nuevo rescued me from the ferox . . .'

'Colonel Nuevo?'

'Shot himself at Ilseville. All part of a bigger plan.'

The colonel shuts his eyes. Think it might be irritation.

'So you've never met General Jaxx?'

'Oh yes,' I say. 'Several times.'

For some reason that doesn't make Colonel Vijay any happier. 'See you inside,' he says, heading for the shuttle. A real CO would give me a time limit.

'Keep unpacking,' I say.

It is the second case that excites my gun. The SIG-37's been pissed off since it hit U/Free territory. No ammo. Mind you, given the way I feel about Morgan, not letting me take a loaded gun into Paper's party was only sensible.

All the same . . .

'Sir,' says Haze. He's cupping his hand as if it holds an empire's worth of treasure. So far as the SIG's concerned, it does.

'A cinder-maker chip?'

'Better, sir . . .' Haze grins excitedly. 'It's a conscience override. Would you like me to fit it?' What he means is, *please may I . . .*

Tossing him the gun, I watch Haze swivel a grip to click the chip into place. Some of what he does deals with a handshake routine for the power pack, but mostly he's just checking everything is in order. That's what he tells me anyway.

In the bottom of the case we find two more power packs. Both full.

'Sweet,' says the gun.

Rotating through incendiary, explosive and hollow-point, it swallows a third of the first pack and flickers happily. There is an old law against hollow-point, but no one pays it much attention.

'Lock and load,' says Shil.

The SIG-37 snorts. 'It's load and lock.'

She scowls, just for a change. Although that might be at the way Rachel is still smiling at me. Neen, Franc and Haze pull weapons from a box, and are obviously disappointed. They were hoping for pulse rifles.

What they have are Kemzin 19s, militia standard.

Mud-coloured and squat, short scopes, blunt muzzles, long magazines, under-slung rangefinders. Ugly as fuck.

The galaxy is full of them. At least the bits we occupy.

You can buy a Kemzin 19 rifle for less than the cost of a meal at a café on Zabo Square. There are places you can get one for the price of a beer. Hell, there are probably places where you buy a beer and they throw in a Kemzin free.

'Shit,' says Neen.

Shil is swearing in her turn.

Needles in the trigger guards have just drawn blood, allowing the weapons to lock themselves to their owner's DNA. That kind of modification is expensive.

And OctoV isn't known for being generous.

So either the U/Free are paying, or the general and OctoV need to be sure no one else is going to be firing these. That means we have to be going somewhere that guns are rare. Even Kemzins.

At least I think that is what it means . . .

Our new combat jackets are interesting. They're sleeveless, with a dozen ammunition pouches. That's not what is interesting. Each one has scrub camouflage, great patches of yellow, greys and brown.

'Rags,' says Shil.

'Ballistically lined rags,' says Haze.

I'd kill for a couple of fat-wheel combats or a light IV, but maybe we're going to pick up half-tracks at the other end. And maybe we're not, because the next things we find are boots, with air soles, double bonding and padded sides. These things matter. At least, they matter to anyone who relies on being able to move and keep moving to stay alive.

'Armour up,' I tell my troopers.

We lose our fancy jackets, our old boots. All the kit we got for Paper's party. What interests me is that none of our new kit is Octovian-made. You could slaughter the lot of us and learn nothing from picking over our bodies. In fact, if all you had was Haze to pin the choice on, you would think we were metalheads.

It makes me want to ask Colonel Vijay exactly what getting

this U/Free observer back involves. Not that I give a fuck either way, you understand.

Colonel Vijay scowls when he sees us. I'm not sure if it's the fact we no longer look neat, or he simply doesn't like what was in the boxes. Everyone wears a sleeveless jacket; everyone wears a helmet, with flip-down visor. Except Colonel Vijay, who still wears his full-dress uniform. He looks about twelve.

The co-pilot's seat is empty, so I take it.

Having opened his mouth to order me out, the colonel changes his mind. Maybe he believes officers shouldn't argue in front of their men. Instead, he takes his place in the pilot's seat in silence.

'Sir,' I say.

A sideways flick of his eyes tells me he is listening.

'About our mission. When do I get briefed?'

He sighs. 'It's need to know,' he says. 'You don't.'

Leaning forward, he slaps his hand on a recognition panel, and engines begin to quiver behind us. This shuttle is strictly short-run. I've seen one like this before on a landing field in Farlight. Unless our destination is within a hundred thousand miles of here, I don't see how we are going to get anywhere.

I needn't have worried.

Once we are buckled in, the colonel taps a number sequence into a pad on the console in front of him. He does it swiftly and confidently. The very exemplar of a competent officer. Then ruins it all by cancelling and re-entering the numbers, more slowly this time.

And before I even have time to think *idiot*, space rips and we are there.

Chapter 11

MOST CIVILIANS BELIEVE YOU CAN CATCH THE UPLIFT VIRUS simply by being in the same room as an Enlightened. That is not true according to Haze. It's elective. That means people choose to catch it. Well, it means they find an Uplifted willing to cut three lines into their wrist and rub his blood into the wounds.

After that, it is too late. You can't change your mind if you want to. You have it, your children have it, their children have it. Germ-line manipulation, Haze says. Whatever the fuck that means.

I am not sure what I'm expecting when an airlock opens to let us into Hekati's hub, but a greeting party made up of a five-braid Enlightened in full-dress uniform, flanked by half a dozen Silver Fist guards, isn't on my list.

This braid is as tall as I am.

Almost as broad too, but that is where the likeness ends. I don't have fat tubes looping from my naked chest to my hip nor a dozen metal hoses criss-crossing my gut like veins. Mind you, he doesn't have a prosthetic arm.

As the Enlightened turns, one of his braids scrapes against

the leathery skin of his left shoulder. His eyes are shiny as glass. Perhaps five-braids have eyelids and perhaps not. Hard to say, because this one doesn't blink. He just stands with his legs planted on the deck and his fingers tight round the handle of a heavy pistol.

For now it's in his holster.

As I said, we are newly docked in Hekati's central hub.

Take a huge wheel world, give it four spokes that join in the middle at a hub and we're inside that. Our CO is frozen in the doorway. I don't think he's ever seen an Enlightened before. Certainly not close up.

Behind the five-braid stands a Silver Fist lieutenant. He has one of those faces that looks chiselled from granite and he likes the look. As I watch, his eyes flick to a screen to check his own reflection.

Their sergeant interests me.

He is broad, because sergeants mostly are. Doesn't matter how often officers tell you they want NCOs with brain. Most officers want brawn and are happy to supply the brains themselves. Neen is the exception, he has brains and he's not broad. Their sergeant is watching me.

He is puzzled. Since I'm one of life's natural sergeants, he probably wants to know what I'm doing wearing the collar bars of a Death's Head lieutenant. It's a question I ask myself most mornings. Until I remember the answer.

My alternative was to be shot.

'So,' the braid says. 'If you'd like to introduce yourselves?' He is staring at Colonel Vijay when he says this.

When the colonel remains frozen, I answer for him.

'Tveskoeg, Sven, lieutenant, 1028282839.'

The braid looks at me.

'Name, rank and number,' I say. 'That's all we're giving.'

'You're not prisoners,' says the five-braid. 'You're . . .' He hesitates, thinking about it. Or maybe he is only pretending, because he's nodding and all his men are leaning forward to catch what he will say.

'Honoured guests.'

The Silver Fist sergeant has something like pity in his eyes. His sympathy doesn't make me feel any better. As for the five-braid, he's gesturing at a screen that shows our little craft hanging in space just beyond the edge of the hub. 'Regard us as a necessary evil,' he says. 'If that helps.'

'Name, rank and number,' I tell the Aux. 'Nothing else.'

The five-braid sighs.

'Tveskoeg, Sven, lieutenant, Death's Head . . .' I begin to reel off the number tattooed on my wrist.

'And you're the colonel's ADC?'

'Tveskoeg, Sven, lieutenant . . .'

'Sven,' says the five-braid, 'I'm not sure you're listening.'

Being called *Sven* by a metalhead doesn't help my patience any.

'Colonel,' the Enlightened says. 'Perhaps you could . . .'

But, shocked solid by his first sight of a braid, Colonel Vijay isn't listening either. Edging past him, I face our questioner.

To kill a braid you have to lock it down. That is one of the basic rules of combat. Otherwise, they flick dimensions. It's hard to kill anything that keeps disappearing on you.

So I grab both sides of its head and dig my thumbs into its eyes, and keep gouging until they pop. Locking down a braid involves hurting it very hard and very fast.

Thought that would do it.

As their sergeant grabs his sidearm, Neen moves.

Jacking his pre-charge, Neen raises his own weapon but he's a split second behind. Turns out not to matter, because a knife already sticks from the sergeant's throat and his rifle is clattering to the deck.

Grinning, Franc rips her blade free and goes after a Silver

Fist behind. Might be her speed that shocks the men. Or maybe it is the fact they're dying.

'*Sven!*' shouts Colonel Vijay.

I throw him my knife. 'Behind you,' I say.

Ducking away from a Silver Fist corporal, he fumbles the catch and hesitates as Neen lifts his gun.

'No rifles,' I shout.

Reversing his weapon, Neen clubs the corporal instead.

Vacuum lies beyond the hub walls. Maybe the bulkhead can survive a direct hit. But I don't want to take that risk. We don't need guns to kill these shits anyway. All we need is surprise, and I have given us that.

'*Tveskoeg,*' I announce, as my fist crushes the five-braid's larynx. A knee to the balls doubles him over. '*Sven.*' I wrap one arm around his neck.

He's dead before I even finish reciting my number.

Chapter 12

SPITTING DIRT, NEEN HAMMERS A PEG INTO RUBBLE AS A COLD wind throws grit into his face. A yank of the cord and his pup tent rises, as its crossbars inflate to create the space he will share with Haze. Silver foil lines the inside to preserve body heat and the door has a double flap, which should help keep this bloody wind out.

My tent is up. Colonel Vijay is already in his.

The way he looks as he crawls inside to seal the flap against the rest of us, I wonder if he is ever coming out again. You can't accuse a senior officer of cowardice, it's insubordination. Well, you can. But you have to do it in private and then kill him afterwards.

He keeps looking at us, opening his mouth and then closing it again.

'Shock,' says Shil, sounding like she actually pities the useless little shit.

'Sir,' says Neen. 'Permission to speak.'

Not sure where he got that phrase from. But he uses it now and then, when he's worried his question is going to piss me off.

'Go ahead.'

'About the colonel—'

He knows it is the wrong thing to say before he's even finished. Must be the way I go still and stare at him. 'What about him?'

'Sir,' Neen says. 'Did he . . . Did he say why we're here?'

Neen sees my sour grin and knows he's just saved his skin.

'We're looking for a missing U/Free observer, apparently.' I got that *apparently* from General Jaxx. He tags it onto the end of his sentences.

'A U/Free?' Neen looks shocked. 'Who would kidnap a U/Free?'

'If he was kidnapped,' I say. 'Could have just fallen off a cliff . . .' Although that doesn't explain what a U/Free observer was doing crawling around Hekati in the first place.

Dusk comes early, and with it that wind to hurl dirt in our faces. It is as if, for an hour or so, the whole habitat wants to reject us. We go from survivable temperature to sub-zero in the time it takes to find a wall tall enough to make a wind-break for our tents.

By the time the last tent is up, the wind is already dropping. We will know next time, and find ourselves a wall in advance. Because the whole habitat is a maze of the bloody things. Unfortunately, most of the walls aren't high enough to trip a child. They are like memories.

A map of a city scrubbed back to ground level.

I don't say this. Haze does, but he's full of stuff like that. All the same, the rest of us know what he means. Hekati is what happens if you cram seven million people onto a ninety-mile-long strip around the inside of a ring world, then get rid of the people and let their city crumble to dust.

Oh yeah, and build a few huts on top of the ruins.

The wall we are sheltering behind is stained with age. Neen claims it's recycled asteroid. Shil thinks it's ancient stonefoam blocks. I don't give a fuck what it is so long as it stops my pup tent blowing away in the night.

After a minute of listening to them argue, I tell them to shut up and go do something useful. So Shil lights a fire, using dry wood to keep the smoke down, and Neen collects firewood.

Finding a spring, Franc sniffs the water and sips a little.

When it doesn't taste sour, she scoops a mouthful and drinks that as well. If she's not rolling around in agony in ten minutes I will let the others drink it too . . . As for Rachel, she's on top of an outcrop behind us. A building once, I guess. Now it just looks natural.

Rachel has night sights and thermal imaging on that Z93z of hers. She might as well use them.

'How many?' I ask when she comes running back.

'Five people for certain, sir.'

'Silver Fist?' If they are, we have a problem.

The problem won't be that they are Silver Fist. We've killed half a dozen of those already today. We can kill five more easily enough. No, the problem will be they have found us. That means spy cameras somewhere high in the habitat's roof. And I don't like the idea of being watched from above.

'Well?' I say to Rachel.

'Not Silver Fist, sir.'

Imagine a long strip of mountain with a valley floor to the side, and a long shoreline parallel to that. In daylight, the sea seems to stretch out for ever. That is only because the opposite wall is painted blue. Walk straight ahead, along the shore, the valley or a mountain path, and eventually you will come back to where you started.

That's ring worlds for you.

A hundred million tons of rubble to create ninety miles of valley, with four central spokes rising through the roof and meeting at the mirror hub in the ring's middle. We saw cities when we came in. Although they're more towns, really. The biggest is half a mile away. It has wooden walls and earth roofs. And I took my best look at it fifteen minutes before the wind came up and grit started to thicken the air.

'Reckon they're hunting us?'

She nods.

'They know where we are yet?'

Rachel shakes her head. 'Doubt it, sir.'

We have two choices for our U/Free's captors. Assuming he didn't just fall down a cliff. Either they're illegal prospectors. Or they're the descendants of Hekati's original miners, now grouped into warring tribes. Seemingly three hundred years of being locked in an oversized child's toy does that to you.

Well, it does according to Haze.

'Let them come,' I tell Rachel.

Saluting, she turns to go and freezes as I tell her to stop.

'You're wearing a helmet.'

'Sir?'

'Next time use its comms system.'

One of the strangers is taller than the rest, muscled across the shoulders and carries two knives to everyone else's one. An ancient rifle is slung across his broad back. He might have white hair, cropped tight to his skull, and wear a stinking goatskin jacket, but he's clear-eyed, and he counts our tents as he comes into the camp.

I watch him do it. Not hard to work out who's boss.

'Get Colonel Vijay,' I tell Neen.

Whatever Neen says works because the colonel crawls from his tent, zips it carefully behind him and sits by the fire. All right, he refuses to look at the rest of us and he keeps his arms wrapped tightly round his knees, but at least he is here.

'Our leader,' my sergeant says.

He might as well be speaking gibberish. So I try city tongue and that doesn't work either. On my orders, Haze tries machine cult. When the man still looks blank, I try traveller because it is the oldest language of all.

The man nods. 'I am Pavel,' he says. 'Caudillo of the O'Cruz.'

It seems five armies, *ejércitox* in his terms, came together to defeat another thirteen and created a force that took on all comers, until one *caudillo* ruled a quarter of the habitat. Doesn't matter the average size of an *ejércitox* seems to be less than fifty men. This group are the *O'Cruz Itcific*. It means *O'Cruz unbeaten*. They have remained unbeaten for three centuries. Having nodded, to show I am impressed by this history lesson, I introduce myself.

'I'm Sven,' I tell him. 'Sub-caudillo of the Aux.' Maybe my height convinces Pavel of my claim. Unless it's the glint of my arm in the firelight.

'Tell him who I am,' whispers Colonel Vijay.

Nodding at the colonel, I say, 'Our caudillo.'

'He looks weak.'

Unfortunately, that is true.

'His family are very important.' That is also true. No one gets to be a colonel in the Death's Head at his age without serious backing. Back in Farlight, backing translates as money or political power.

'Ahh,' says Pavel.

Families have meaning for the O'Cruz. A fact I file away. Know a people's strength and know their weaknesses. And, most important of all, know how to turn one into the other.

'Where are his guards?' Pavel asks, looking puzzled.

I gesture at the Aux.

'Women,' he says. 'Children.'

'Who have slaughtered thousands between them.'

Pavel's eyes widen.

To Neen, I say, 'Hand him your cup.' And to Rachel, who is out in the darkness, 'You're on.'

A shot spills Neen's coffee onto the dirt.

To make the hit, Rachel has to slide her shot between Pavel's elbow and his stinking jacket. We let the O'Cruz caudillo glare round him, scowling as he tries to work out if the bullet came from an outcrop above. That is twice the distance his weapon can manage. Jerking his chin towards Rachel's hiding place, Pavel says: 'From there. Yes?'

I nod. And that's when it all goes wrong.

As Rachel yells a warning through our helmet speakers, Neen scrambles to his feet. Jacking the bolt on his rifle, he flicks on his searchlight. Shil and Franc are doing the same. It's one of those moments when everyone knows there's danger, but no one knows where from.

'Incoming,' says my gun.

'*Where . . . ?*'

Doesn't matter. The incomer is here.

As we watch, a bare-chested boy tramples our fire and turns his horse in a tight circle. Sparks fly from beneath its hooves. A leather thong ties back the boy's black hair. He's holding the reins in one hand. His other hand is holding a rifle.

He's shouting what sounds like a battle cry.

'Fuck,' says Shil. 'Will you look at that.' She's not talking about the horse either.

Caught in the cold brightness of her searchlight, the boy throws up his arm, realizes it's not enough to shield his eyes and aims his rifle. I have time to knock up Shil's muzzle. But not enough time to stop the boy from pulling his own trigger.

In the silence that follows, everyone freezes except for the bloody pony. So I punch it to the ground.

Dragging the boy from beneath his animal, I throw him against a rock. My foot's on his throat and I am treading down when Pavel unslings his own rifle and his fighters draw their blades.

So I tread down harder.

'Sven,' whispers Colonel Vijay. 'Not again.'

I take my foot off the boy's throat.

As the boy clambers to his feet, he tells me who he is. He's Racta, and he's the old man's grandson. Sorry, that is Don Racta, heir to Pavel, caudillo of the O'Cruz. He's not happy with his grandfather or me.

'Shut it,' I tell the boy.

When he doesn't, I kick his feet from under him. And when half a dozen ejército, as members of an ejércitox seem to be called, step forward, I put my foot back on his throat.

'*Sven . . .*'

'He's negotiating,' says Haze.

Colonel Vijay stares at him.

'Seen it before, sir. Best to leave him to it.'

That's no way for a trooper to talk to an officer; never mind talk to a colonel. Soon Colonel Vijay is going to wonder why Haze never takes his helmet off. But there is stuff I need to do and the SIG has just come up with a good reason why I should do it sooner rather than later.

'See that blood,' it says. 'It's yours.'

Neen finds a slug against my rib, flattened from where it ricocheted off my arm. Extracting the misshapen lump of copper he walks over to where Racta kneels, still gasping and clutching his neck, and tosses it at his feet.

'Do that again,' says Neen, 'and he'll cut your throat.'

Turns out, we couldn't have chosen a better way to reach a deal. As the old man looks on approvingly, Shil stitches the edges of my wound shut. She's done it before and her needle-work's good.

Colonel Vijay has some questions.

Has Pavel seen anything odd recently?

'Just ask it,' he says, when I look surprised.

So I do, and get a long rambling answer that I don't bother to translate.

'What did he say?'

'Life's strange.'

The colonel's lips tighten. 'I ask a question, you translate exactly. Do you understand?'

Shil's wondering how I'm going to answer.

'Of course, sir.'

'Ask him about people dressed like us.'

'Like us?'

'Yes,' says the colonel. 'Like us.'

Sounds as if we're not the first Death's Head mission to this place. Pavel doesn't know anything. At least, not directly. He's heard from someone in another tribe. Of course, the other tribe lies. They lie like . . . well, Azari, which is what they are. Anyway . . .

'What happened?'

Well, the Azari say the ghosts took them, but they're superstitious fools, and not to be trusted. Because everyone knows women lead them. Unlike the O'Cruz, who . . . See, I told Colonel Vijay he didn't need me to translate every word.

'Tell him,' says the colonel, 'anyone who helps us will also get gold.'

Pavel wants to see it.

As we watch, Colonel Vijay reaches into his jacket and removes a roll of coins heavy enough to make his hand tremble. The man is an idiot, he might as well have drawn a line around his throat and written *cut here*.

'What?' demands the colonel.

He asks because Neen has jacked the slide on his rifle.

When Pavel looks at me, his eyes are amused. 'So young,' he says. 'So stupid . . .' He shrugs. 'Undoubtedly, he will get himself killed.'

'But not tonight,' I say. 'Because I'm here to keep him alive.'

Pavel considers this.

'Five gold coins,' he says.

I'm not sure if that is his price for helping us, or for not trying to cut Colonel Vijay's throat on the spot.

The caudillo shows me a horse he wants to sell Colonel Vijay. It's cheap, only ten gold pieces. He laughs when I refuse without bothering to check with the colonel first. The five gold pieces in his pocket have made us allies, apparently.

'Here,' he says. 'Yours . . . No cost.'

The leather flask is filled with wine that tastes like vinegar.

'Our finest,' he announces.

We are about to move out when the caudillo makes a final offer. I've told him about the missing U/Free observer. Although I tell Pavel the missing man is a friend of my caudillo, who may have been captured or fallen.

'A weak man?' Pavel asks.

He means, *weak like your caudillo?*

I shrug. It's possible. The U/Free don't strike me as physically strong.

'Could have fallen,' Pavel admits. 'These mountains are treacherous . . . You need to be tough.'

His offer is simple. The gang's best trackers will go with us. They know all the high paths. That is when he says something interesting. Bad things have come to these mountains.

Ghosts and *snakeheads*, Pavel calls them.

Maybe he sees a flicker of interest in my eyes. Because his grin says he knows he's got a deal. The O'Cruz are going to take us right round Hekati in five days. All it will cost, he says, is another twenty gold coins.

'Five,' I say.

Pavel shakes his head. 'Fifteen.'

'Ten, but only if we find my caudillo's missing friend.'

'Five now,' says Pavel. 'Five then.'

I take his offer to Colonel Vijay, since he is the one with the gold. Even at the ten gold coins I tell him it will cost, five for us and five for Pavel, the colonel thinks it's a bargain. So do I, until I discover the Itcific trackers are to answer to Racta, who is still clutching his rifle. The boy's bare-chested, his skin is oiled and his hair is twisted into a long plait.

When he grins at Shil, she actually smiles back.

'See,' whispers Colonel Vijay. 'Dialogue helps.'

Neen takes rear and I take point, with the colonel behind me. The rest of the Aux slot into their usual positions, with the trackers riding ahead. It's early morning by the time we move out and the sun is just over the mountain. Well, it is bouncing off a mirror at an angle chosen to give that impression. Haze is busy telling Rachel how the mirror hub works. She sounds interested. Maybe she is.

Snipers are strange.

As Racta rides, his men run behind, heavy knives stuck in their belts and their heads protected against the sun by caps with flaps that hang down their necks. The trackers look tough, made fit by living on these slopes. Much more running, though, and they will be useless before mid morning.

'Crap horse, shitty little tribal prince, treacherous ravines . . .' My gun sighs. 'You could get slaughtered out here and I wouldn't be found for a thousand years.'

'You're on silent.'

'So,' it says, 'I adjusted myself.'

'You can't—'

'*Emergency override.*'

'What's the emergency?'

'That little idiot,' says the gun. 'He's going to get you killed.' Takes me a second to realize he means Racta and not the colonel.

'Listen—'

'Yeah, yeah,' says the SIG. 'I know, you're fucking invincible . . .' It hesitates, and I am shocked, because the SIG never hesitates. 'You going to tell the colonel what Pavel said about snakeheads?'

'After last time?'

The SIG sees my point. 'What about those ghosts?'

'Stealth camouflage.'

'You reckon?'

'Obvious.'

The SIG goes silent. When I next check it's whirring to itself. A little while later, it shuts down and goes back to sleep. Behind me, Shil's watching Racta preen and prance on his little horse. Not that I'm jealous or anything.

Me, I usually buy my women.

That way, there's no misunderstanding. You make conversation, you fuck, you make a little more conversation, and then you fuck again. Everyone is happy. I don't see any sense in running around with my tongue out. Although, watching Shil, I don't think there's any doubt who has her tongue out, and who knows he's—

'Down.'

Five Aux hit the dirt. I don't need to turn round to know it has happened. Wish I could say the same for Colonel Vijay.

'Sir,' I say.

He stares at me.

'If you could get down?'

A hawk, a rodent fifty paces away, a flock of crows above a slope that leads to a silver ribbon of stream far below. Racta's leaving tracks a blind man could follow. And I have no trouble finding him up ahead.

A single wave of my hand brings the others forward. They take cover behind rocks and clumps of rough grass without being told. I'm impressed, although I'm not about to tell them that. Colonel Vijay joins me last, takes a long look at the horizon and wants to know what he is missing.

'Watchers, sir.'

'Where?'

That's my problem.

Sun glints from a thousand rocks. Whatever makes up the slopes ahead reflects light in all directions. Not all of it, obviously, otherwise we'd be looking at a mountain made entirely of glass; but enough shiny black rock juts through red earth to blind anyone who looks for too long.

'Sir,' says Shil.

Racta has vanished from sight.

Chapter 13

DIGGING IN HIS HEELS, RACTA WAVES HIS RIFLE ABOVE HIS HEAD and gallops his pony towards us, yelling at the top of his voice. God knows what he's yelling, because he is too excited to make sense. When the little brat gets within twenty paces, I realize the obvious. He hasn't worked out we've taken cover.

'Up,' I say.

We rise as one. And Racta's pony shies.

As we watch, the boy flies over its neck and twists in the air, trying for a clean landing. He almost makes it, but he's moving too fast. A stumble takes him sideways and dumps him on his arse.

Colonel Vijay chuckles.

Since he's nearest, maybe it's funnier close up.

A second later, one of the O'Cruz joins in. Racta is not happy. I've seen faces like his before and always hated the men owning them. Slowly Racta straightens up, walks over to collect his rifle and jacks a bullet into the breech.

'No,' I say.

He gives no sign of having heard me, but as I step towards

him, he tosses the weapon aside. Shil looks at Rachel, who twists her mouth. Shil's shocked at the sudden change in his temper.

Such innocence.

'You.'

The man who laughed runs across, and Racta backhands him hard. This guy is my age with scars that impress even me. He just stands there. None of the trackers will meet his eye when he returns to them.

'And you,' says Racta.

'What's he saying?' Colonel Vijay asks me.

'He thinks you owe him an apology for laughing . . .'

Outrage fills the colonel's face. It vanishes almost as quickly. He's too inexperienced to know his own mind. I have seen it before, but never in a Death's Head officer.

'All right,' he says.

'No way,' I tell Racta. 'My caudillo never apologizes.'

We have a short discussion about when Racta gets to kill me. He wants to fight now and grows sullen when I tell him to come back when he's grown up. At his age, I had killed more men than I could count. Mind you, that wasn't very high. And there are other differences: Racta's soft and I was never that. And he's handsome, and I was never that either.

'All done?' asks Colonel Vijay.

'Yes, sir. All done . . .'

The colonel smiles at Racta, who stares at him and then grins back. That is when I know he's dangerous.

The sea that runs around the inside of Hekati's shell is wide, sluggish and carpeted with patches of foul-smelling scum. An island in the distance looks strange, until I realize it's because that's where a huge mirrored spoke descends from the glass ceiling miles above. Mirroring on the spoke blends it into the side wall beyond. Climb that spoke and you will reach the hub. Of course, by then you will be in space, and the ring will be a glass-roofed monstrosity beneath and above you.

We came down one spoke, and when we find our U/Free, we will go back the same way. After that, we just need to board our plane to get home again. Colonel Vijay knows the number needed to make that happen.

It's a good enough reason to keep him alive.

We're hot, dust has turned our camouflage to dirt, and sweat paints patches under our arms and between our shoulder blades. Meanwhile, boats slide like insects across the sea's surface. There are wharfs, down there. Wharfs and warehouses and probably brothels, because shorelines and brothels go together.

Well, in my experience.

Travelling by water would be easy. All we need do is descend a valley, cut through the shacks that grow along the coast and find ourselves a boat. One after the other the Aux suggest it to Neen.

And Neen finally mentions it to me.

I'm glad, because our colonel has spent most of the day looking longingly at towns he would dismiss as slums in any other situation. Telling Neen he's an idiot is easier than telling the colonel.

'Neen,' I say, knowing Colonel Vijay's listening. 'Tell me why it's a shit idea.'

My sergeant thinks about it.

In the time this takes, we climb a hill, pass through the ruins of an old farm and crest a high ridge that drops to a narrow valley beyond. The wind smells of hot stones and wild grass, like good vodka. 'Time's up,' I say. 'Tell me.'

'We're looking for the Azari.'

He hopes I'll nod, so I don't.

Neen shouldn't need me to teach him this.

'That's one,' I say. 'We're stuck with that Racta, that's two. And three, we're not meant to be here at all.'

Neen still doesn't get it.

'Oh for fuck's sake,' I say. 'We can kill the O'Cruz if needs be. But every new person who knows we're here doubles the danger.'

'Sven.' That's the colonel, obviously. He's working his way round to behaving as if nothing happened up in the mirror hub. 'We can't,' he says. 'I mean . . .'

'Believe me, sir,' I say, 'we may have to.'

A dozen people drag a cart along the dry bed of what was once a stream. The cart has spoked wheels and fretted sides. It has been painted grey so it doesn't reflect the sun. The men pulling it wear camouflage so cheap I only hope it came free. Mostly it matches whatever its owner was standing on a few seconds earlier.

The women, all three of them, wear rags. These are so filthy they provide better camouflage than the suits worn by the men.

Every twenty paces, the group stop and twist a stick into the ground. After a few seconds, one of the men shakes his head. So they drag the cart another twenty paces and start again.

'Prospectors.' Rachel is certain of this.

'They'd have better equipment,' says Colonel Vijay.

'With respect, sir.' Turns out Haze is the only one to remember his briefing. A good half of the prospectors here are illegal. It's an expensive jump; a licence from the Enlightened doubles the price and takes a third of anything found.

'Colonel,' I say. 'We should let them pass.'

'Not yet,' he says. 'They might have met the Azari.'

Laughing, Racta says, 'Of course they've met the Azari.' His gesture sweeps the valley. 'These are your ghosts.'

'What did he say?'

'These are our ghosts.'

'No they're not,' says Colonel Vijay. Makes me wonder how he knows.

'So,' says Racta. 'We kill all but one. Agreed?'

Dropping out the clip on his rifle, he counts bullets. He has two in the clip, with one in the breech. So, our little caudillo-to-be has three. This explains his willingness to toss down his rifle earlier. And why he turns his back on his men before extracting the clip.

Every shot he fires weakens his power.

I want to let them pass, and Racta wants to capture one and kill the rest. So Colonel Vijay suggests a compromise. We will capture them all. Since this is about as stupid a suggestion as I can imagine, Racta agrees immediately.

'See,' says the colonel.

Yes, I know. *Compromise and respect.*

'Carry on,' he tells me.

'Right,' I say. 'Racta heads them off. We come up from behind.'

Racta's about to insist he comes up from behind, when he realizes heading off the prospectors is exactly what he wants to do. So he nods, as if doing me a favour, and slams the clip back into his rifle.

A minute later, I hear a gunshot up ahead.

'What's that?' demands the colonel.

He must know.

Unholstering my own gun, I start running. All thoughts of coming up behind the prospectors are gone. We keep low, weaving from instinct. Shale skids beneath our boots, but we keep moving. On a mountainside that is all you can do.

Cresting a small ridge, we look down in dismay.

Well, the colonel's dismayed.

I'm just fucking angry. Most of the prospectors are dead. One is still standing and a couple are on their knees. As we

106

watch, Racta uses his rifle as a club and one of those kneeling hits the dirt.

A tracker has a woman on the ground with her skirt round her hips. Another searches the pockets of a dying man. A thin scream from the woman ends when her attacker loses patience. He wipes his knife on her skirt.

'Permission to finish this, sir?'

'Sven . . .'

'Take that as a yes,' suggests the SIG. 'Now, let's take the fucking lot to their knees.' It rotates clips, selecting overburst. I'd love to, but my gun knows it's impossible. We are behind enemy lines.

Well, we're in Uplift Space.

Holding the SIG steady, I walk downhill.

Not one of the O'Cruz doubts I'll kill them if needed. As we pass Racta's man going through the pockets of the woman he killed, Neen clubs him. As the man falls to his knees, Rachel walks up behind him and kicks him hard between the legs. There's no need for Shil to stamp on his fingers as she goes past.

'We agreed capture.'

Racta scowls. 'They fought back.'

'Of course they fucking did,' I say. 'You attacked them.'

'This is our valley,' he tells me. 'You're here because we allow it.' He spits at a body at his feet. 'They deserved to die.'

'What did he say?' the colonel demands.

'They deserved to die . . .'

Colonel Vijay looks around. And has trouble dragging his gaze from the splay-legged woman with the severed throat.

'Animals,' he says. 'They're animals.'

What the fuck does he expect? Battles that start at noon and carefully considered last words from the dying?

'Tell him we don't approve of this.'

'Sir . . .'

'Just tell him.'

So I do. And guess what? Racta doesn't give a shit.

'We're done here,' the colonel tells me. 'Tell him this is where we part company. We'll find the ghosts for ourselves.'

Racta isn't happy about this. He wants his five gold coins. So I point out it was for finding the ghosts, not for killing old men and raping women. And since he hasn't found the ghosts, he doesn't get the money. This makes him unhappier still.

Unhappy enough to jack the bolt on his rifle.

Wait, I tell myself.

The moment he raises his weapon will be the moment I kill him.

A step to reach him, a single flick of my blade . . . Should be easy enough.

I'm still edging my knife from its sheath when someone beats me to it. A shovel is as good a weapon as anything else if thrown hard enough. And I know it's luck that makes the shovel break Racta's rifle arm. But sometimes luck is all you need.

Stalking towards Racta, the prospector picks up his shovel and smashes the blade sideways into Racta's knee.

'My woman,' he says.

We know who he's talking about.

As Rachel, Neen and Shil keep their weapons trained on the other trackers, the partner of the dead woman drives the edge of his shovel into Racta's throat.

The screaming stops.

Chapter 14

A VETERAN OF SIFTING MINING WASTE FOR ORE MISSED THE FIRST time round, Mic Chua has a face that is mottled from toxic chemicals and tattooed so deeply with dust that it looks like powder burn from a shotgun. His eyes are red, although he tells me that is the wind.

Mic has one earring, and a ponytail faded to the grey of dry dog turd.

All the same, for someone so slight, he handles that shovel like the weapon it isn't. 'Used to be one of you,' he says.

Legion? I almost ask.

But I don't.

I don't say *Death's Head* either. I just nod, smile, and wonder what the fuck I am meant to do with the O'Cruz prisoners my troopers now guard.

'We don't kill them,' says Colonel Vijay.

Of course he does.

Killing them makes sense. As does killing Mic and the few prospectors left alive. They are going to die anyway; you can see it in their eyes.

'So,' says Mic. 'Where did they scoop you?'

Our conversation is getting weirder by the second. But there are times you stay quiet, and this is one of them. So I hold my tongue and try to look interested, but not too interested. Not like, maybe, I don't have the faintest fuck what he's talking about.

'Us,' he says, 'they got us right outside a mine.'

I grunt something. I hope it sounds sympathetic.

'Used to do asteroids,' he says. 'All that suiting up and shit, the stale air and long months in tin cans. Gave it up. I mean . . .' The upturn of his hands says, *come on*. 'Why bother, if you can get rich on the ground.'

'Legally?' asks Colonel Vijay.

Mic's eyes narrow. 'No problem, either way,' I assure him.

'Illegal is quicker.'

'Yeah,' I say. 'And if you get high enough to call yourself emperor, or senator or glorious uplift, you can announce it's not a crime anyway.'

Mic grins sourly.

We agree here. 'So,' I say. 'They scooped you?'

'Yeah, right outside our mine. All these fucks with guns are standing in a circle glaring at us. It must have been the same for you. All those warnings about not trying to escape . . .'

'Right,' I say. 'I hate that.'

'So they took us back to the camp. And then let us out in work details to dig their damn trenches and fix their pipes . . . Took me a while to work out what was happening.'

'And then?' I say, thinking, *give me a clue here*.

Something bleak enters Mic's eyes. 'When we struck for more food, they killed five the first hour, five the next, five the hour after . . . Chosen at random. So we killed the guards, cut the wire and this is what's left.'

He gestures to three people, who are all that remain of his group.

They walk towards us slowly. If I were them, I wouldn't trust us either.

His group turns out to be one woman and two men. Mic doesn't introduce them and I don't ask. If anything, they look worse than he does.

We give the ejército a water bottle and march them into the shade of an overhang. Then, while Shil and Franc keep their rifles trained, Neen walks along the line with a shovel and breaks the left ankle of every one.

'Here,' he says, giving Mic back his shovel.

'My pleasure.'

The colonel's furious. Since it's already done, I can't see his point. 'It's barbaric,' he tells me. He is so cross he insists we have the conversation in private.

'Your decision, sir.'

He scowls at me.

'We've no cuffs, no rope, and you said I couldn't kill them. With respect, what the fuck was I meant to do?'

Saluting smartly, I leave him with the question.

The ejército yell at us as we head out. All the usual insults. There are x million suns and x million planets, yet all you ever get is insults about your mother, your sister and your girlfriend. Well, the first two are dead, and I don't have a third so I'm not too bothered. But I translate them anyway, just for the pleasure of watching Colonel Vijay's lips tighten.

As the afternoon goes on, Mic trails further and further behind. Until our only choice is, leave him or make camp and wait. When he finally arrives, Shil has a fire burning, Neen has caught what looks like a dog, Franc has gutted the beast, seasoned it with bark and has a stick stuffed up one end and out the other.

We offer the prospectors meat, and give them the wine

from Pavel's flask. It does little good. One dies in the night. He's old, with skin that looks like cheaply cured leather.

We find him at first light. Back against a rock and face towards the sun. I know, it's reflection in a mirror . . . light enters Hekati through chevron safety glass and servomotors in the hub shift huge silvered sheets to create the illusion.

It still looks like dawn to me.

He has stripped off his shirt and lesions disfigure his chest. The skin over his gut is purple as if the corruption set in long before he died. Rachel is not the only one to make a sign against the evil eye. Shil does, when she thinks I'm not looking.

Colonel Vijay says it's the plague.

'Radiation,' says Haze.

The colonel stares at him.

'Know the symptoms,' Haze says. Embarrassment stops him. 'It's unmissable, I guess.' He looks at Mic and the other two, and his blush gets worse. 'If you want me to take a look at you, I might . . .'

What? I think. *Be able to save them?*

Then I realize it's possible. Haze has more processing power in his skull than most cities. And Paper Osamu gave him the run of her ship's library that time we asked the U/Free for help. Mind you, look where that got us – *here.*

Mic says, 'Thanks, but it's too late.'

'What a choice,' adds the only woman. 'Sickness or the Silver Fist.'

Colonel Vijay makes himself unfreeze the moment I glance across. Bits of earlier conversations are coming into focus. Spitting, I grind the spit under my heel.

'May they rot.'

Grinning, Mic does the same.

It's an old militia curse. Although these days everyone uses it. I have heard it from militia about Death's Head, Octovians about metalheads, legionnaires about the ferox, and civilians about all of us everywhere.

'You should keep moving,' Mic says.

My look is a question.

'We're slow,' he says. 'And they'll be tracking us. If we travel together they'll get you as well.'

'Move out,' I tell him. 'We'll cover you.'

He tries to work my angle. Am I planning some trick? Sacrificing him in some way that cuts us free? He's old and he's ill and he has a right to be worried, but he's also wrong. We've found our ghosts. All we need to do now is capture one.

Stamping up to Colonel Vijay, I salute.

'Permission to deploy.'

'*Sven.*'

I want this battle. And watching Colonel Vijay, I realize something else. What happened in the hub was disgraceful enough. I want to see how this little shit behaves under fire. A medal for *planning* Ilseville.

The idea makes me vomit.

'Rachel,' I shout.

She jogs over, salutes.

'Dig in over there.'

We need to cover the floor of this valley from a slope. As Rachel leaves, she begins to pull sections of rifle from slots and pouches on her back and belt, already screwing them together as she jogs towards a scar of red earth.

Now Mic is really staring. 'What are you?' he asks.

'The best,' says Neen.

There's best and *best*. Mic decides we're renegade militia with five-year-old rifles, used to lording it over new con-scripts lucky to have weapons at all. I'm happy to leave it that way.

'You plan to bury your man?'

'No point,' he says. 'We'll be joining him soon enough.' His shrug is that of someone grown used to the idea of his own death. 'Might as well save our energy.'

With that, he slopes away, weighed down by a pack a six-year-old should be able to carry. I doubt we will see him again and Mic obviously feels the same, because he doesn't look back and nor do the couple stumbling after him.

Chapter 15

'SVEN,' SAYS COLONEL VIJAY. 'A WORD.'

'Sir . . . ?'

'What's wrong with that man?'

'The air, sir,' I say. 'He comes from a planet with more oxygen. Hekati's atmosphere is thinner.'

The colonel considers this. 'Do his nosebleeds happen often?'

I consider this in my turn. 'Some months,' I say, 'he bleeds more than Shil, Franc and Rachel put together.'

Colonel Vijay decides he wants to be somewhere else.

The Aux are digging a slit trench across a dry river bed and that is where I find Haze. Climbing out of the trench, he wipes blood from his face.

'I'm fine, sir.'

Trooper Haze hasn't been fine the entire time I've known him. But his softness is going and he causes less grief than before. Of course, he's always going to be large and he's always going to look stupid when he runs. Still, he can now hold a rifle and dig slit trenches with the best of them.

'Sir,' says Haze, 'can I ask something?'

'Depends what it is.'

He wipes his nose again.

'Ask,' I say.

There is a famous triple-sunned planet in the northern spiral, but a single sun is more than enough for me. And for Haze, clearly, because he turns his back on the brightness and stares in the other direction.

He's listening.

Only Haze doesn't listen like other people. At least, he doesn't listen to frequencies the rest of us hear. 'Can you hear it?' he asks finally.

I shake my head.

'Sir . . .'

A lot hangs on that word, and I am going to leave it like that. I'm not about to start barking when he's the dog I keep to do it for me. Plus, I like it when the kyp in my throat sleeps. Food tastes like food and colours look vaguely normal. I can even wake in the morning without my mouth foul with static.

'So,' I say. 'What can you hear?'

He struggles to put it into words. While I struggle to understand the words he does manage. *Insane signal to noise ratio. Off scale. Way too much loopback for a habitat that's on file as deserted.*

I ask Haze if he is certain.

He's certain. This habitat is on U/Free lists as uninhabited. The prospectors qualify as short-stay visitors and the gangs don't count, being residual and indigenous. As for Hekati herself, she shows clear signs of *abulia*, with secondary signs of emotional *cri du chat*. About one word in five of this makes sense.

'Haze,' I say, 'just dig the fucking trench.'

He turns, head down and shoulders hunched. So I tell

116

him to come back when I'm going to understand what he is saying.

As Colonel Vijay watches, we scatter dirt.

A few strategically placed rocks and bushes will help hide the trench. We don't have to worry about the bushes dying on us. They are dead already. He's not happy about me stripping to the waist and doesn't approve of my helping dig.

'You're an officer.'

'I was a sergeant first, sir.'

And you should still be one, his look says. But he keeps the words to himself and stares towards the head of the valley. 'If they are Silver Fist . . .'

'They'll be fucking hard to kill.'

'Sven,' he says. 'About what happened in the hub. I don't think you understand . . .'

'Oh,' I say, 'I think I do, sir.'

He flushes. 'You've fought the Fist in battle?'

'At Ilseville, sir,' I tell him. 'We all have.'

Except you. Must see it in my eyes, because he turns away.

Digging her own slot, Rachel rips up a couple of bushes to improve her cover and sweeps the area in front of her trench with twigs to rid it of footprints. When I give her a nod, she grins.

I know less about Rachel than the others. She was raped after Ilseville. A few weeks later she killed her attacker. Other than that . . . ? She's the best shot I've met, and her friendship with Haze gets stronger by the day.

Maybe that's all I need to know.

A hand signal sends her to her trench. Another brings the Aux to me, gives them positions and tells them to take cover. Colonel Vijay accepts a position beside me.

Time to wake my gun.

'That's—' says the colonel.

'Illegal technology? Yes, I know.'

117

He hasn't seen the SIG–37 close up before. Unfortunately, the SIG doesn't think much of him either. 'Who's the—?'

'Colonel Vijay. He's leading this mission.'

'Bullshit,' says my gun. 'You are. Jaxx said so. I was there, remember? Said he could rely on you to do the right thing.'

The Aux are pretending not to listen.

'Well,' I say, 'he changed his mind.'

Colonel Vijay is looking at me. 'Jaxx?' he says. 'The general chose you for this mission?'

'Yeah,' says my gun. 'Who chose you?'

'Enough,' I tell it.

'Or what?' it says. 'You'll turn me off thirty seconds before a battle?'

Obviously, the SIG is looking forward to killing Silver Fist, because it decides to behave after all. Doesn't even criticize my choice of ammunition. Although it flips clips the moment it thinks I'm not looking.

Whatever sends the birds skywards is threatening enough to have a whole flock circling angrily. They are huge and ugly, with a cry as bleak as a baby being strangled. And there must be ten, if not fifteen of the bastards.

It's the fact I can't see what has upset them that has me counting clips. Hollow-point, explosive, incendiary, flechette, over blast. A knife in my belt, a dagger in my boot, throwing spikes on one hip and a garrotte in the bottom of one pocket.

Should keep me going for a while.

'Check again,' I demand.

The SIG–37 does.

After the gun finds nothing, I send Shil to fetch Haze, who is at the far end of our trench. I also tell her to keep her head down.

She does as ordered. Whatever she says as she passes the others has them crouching lower.

'Sir,' says Haze.

You know that look you get when a beautiful stranger walks into your favourite bar, and you know she is going to fuck you over and empty your wallet and leave you with a nasty infection and you still don't care?

Haze gets that look every time he sees my gun.

And the scary bit is he doesn't lust after the SIG because it can fire faster than anything in existence, burn sheet steel in cinder-maker mode, or blow out every eardrum on a whole bloody platoon with a single airburst.

No, he lusts after its intelligence chip.

'Here,' I say. 'Enjoy each other.'

Fumbling his catch, Haze breaks sweat. He thinks AIs should be treated with respect. So does the SIG, that's half my problem.

'See those birds?'

The raptors are settling now. This says whatever upset them stands between us and the thorn trees behind, and that brings us into their firing range.

'Yes, sir.'

'Tell me what's out there.'

He glances at Colonel Vijay, looks back at me and bites his lip. We were going to hit this problem eventually. Why not deal with it now?

'Haze is my intelligence officer.'

'Your . . .'

'Check with General Jaxx.' We both know he can't.

'What are you saying?' demands Colonel Vijay. The Aux think he's angry. Given the way his gaze keeps flicking towards those thorn bushes, I think he's scared.

'Haze,' I say, 'take off your helmet.'

'My God,' the colonel says. 'He's . . .'

'Yes, sir. You're right. He is.' Nodding at the river bed, I say to Haze, 'Now we've got that over. Tell me.'

Handing me back my gun, he flips open a pocket slab. Fingers move faster than my eyes can follow as he inputs line after line of headache-inducing numbers.

'Fuck,' says my gun.

Then says it again. Only this time the SIG's voice is louder. '*Cancel*,' it says. 'Don't fucking *retry* . . .'

'No,' whispers Haze. 'Not yet.'

'*Haze* . . .' the gun says, and then it's too late.

As the beginnings of a fit jerk Haze upright, Shil grabs him and drags him down, a split second ahead of a bullet whistling overhead. We have lost the element of surprise. As if that isn't bad enough, Neen is tugging at my arm.

'*Sir*,' he says.

Rachel is out of her foxhole and racing towards us. Raising the SIG, I aim at her.

I don't know what it is loaded with and don't much care. Another step and I am going to kill her myself. 'Get back to your fucking position.'

Looking both ways, she flinches as an enemy shot whips past. It's only hesitating that saves her life. When she hits the ground, it's halfway between her foxhole and our own trench. She is still yelling Haze's name, and I realize she believes the bullet took him down.

On the slope ahead, a Silver Fist sniper appears.

I've no idea how Haze is making him visible and no time to ask. Even if Haze was in a state to answer. Because I'm out of my trench and halfway to where Rachel sobs in the dirt.

Grabbing her, I hurl her towards her position. Pick her up again, and toss her into the foxhole ahead of me.

'*Haze*.'

A slap focuses her attention.

Should leave it there, because the second slap puts her eyes out of focus again. 'He's alive,' I tell her. 'Unhurt . . . Now pick up your fucking rifle.'

She grabs it.

There are things you do in battle and things you don't. Abandoning a position is one of the don'ts. Nodding at the opposite slope, I say, 'Where would you hide?'

Rachel looks puzzled.

'Imagine you're a fucking Silver Fist sniper and you want to protect infantry walking up that river bed. Where do you hide?'

'Over there.' She points. 'In those rocks, just behind that bush.'

She hesitates.

'Sir, I'm . . .'

'Lucky to be alive.'

Death is the penalty for what she's done.

'Sight on that position,' I tell her. 'Fire when I give the order.'

To her credit, Rachel doesn't ask why. Working the bolt, she adjusts the sight for crosswind, steadies herself and becomes one with the gun. She has her eye to the scope, and I see her twist her head slightly, as if puzzled.

'Something there,' she says. 'I mean, not really, but . . .'

'Kill it,' I say.

The bullet leaves her barrel at 3800 fps and crosses the valley before her target has time to realize she's fired; although it's probably luck that gives Rachel a head shot. As the braid flips backwards, his camouflage blanket slips.

And the Silver Fist open fire.

They have a machine gun set up on the river bed. It's spitting bullets so fast that they must have two Silver Fist working the belt. Or maybe it's only one. Because thirty seconds in the gun jams. And my team give it everything they've got. Bushes explode, stones fly and a tree beside the river bed turns to wood chip a hand's breadth above the gravel before toppling sideways.

Whole clips empty in seconds.

Nitrocellulose.

If we had the supplies I'd let them burn off for the sheer hell of it. Instead, I jack the slide on my gun.

'Oh yes,' says the SIG.

It has wanted to do this for days.

Prefrag ceramic is messy but effective as fuck. Get caught by one and you become your own body weight in mince. Hiding behind something doesn't help, hiding under something isn't much better.

I put an over blast above where I think the belt-fed is sited.

'And again,' my gun says. So I bracket a couple of shots forward and back.

What looks like a piece of Silver Fist crawls towards our trench. If he had sense, he'd head in the other direction. As he crawls, more and more of him becomes visible. His camouflage blanket slipping free.

'Head shot,' I say. 'Finish him.'

Rachel does.

'And the others.'

Using her scope, she scans the river bed. Every thirty seconds or so she puts a shot into a whimpering sliver of someone. She does this so steadily my temper begins to improve. Until a bullet ricochets from the rock I'm hiding behind.

'Another sniper,' yells my gun.

'Yeah,' says Rachel. 'We noticed.'

After a second, she sticks her head above the foxhole and ducks as a second shot cracks overhead. 'He's good,' she says.

'If he was good,' I tell her, 'you'd be dead.'

She looks at me.

'Where is he?' I demand.

'On the right.'

'Rachel . . . *Where is he?*'

Sticking up her head, she takes another look. It is rolling sideways that saves her life, because the next bullet hits where she was.

'Not sure, sir.'

'Right,' I say. 'This is how it's going to work. I'm going to stand up and run for the trench. Their sniper is going to raise his head to take a shot and you're going to blow it off for me.'

'*Sir*,' she says, '*I can't see him.*'

'He's you,' I tell her.

That's how this stuff works, I realize. You decide what you would do if you were the enemy and then you do it different, or you do it better. Can't imagine why I didn't grasp that before.

'OK,' I say. 'You're on.'

Legs power me as I head for the trench below. A slug raises dust behind me, another hits the slope ahead. I'm throwing myself from side to side, which slows me down but makes me harder to hit. A hundred paces, seventy paces . . .

Fuck, I think, *how much longer is she going to leave it?*

And then it occurs to me Rachel can solve all her problems by doing nothing. Only she's Aux, and she wouldn't do that, would she? My answer comes in a single shot from behind.

After that, it is just cleaning up.

Chapter 16

'YOU KNOW WHY THIS IS NECESSARY?'

Rachel nods, and I am glad. She doesn't have to think it justice; she doesn't have to think it right. She just has to understand why. If she doesn't, the punishment is worthless. 'Sir,' she says. 'May I say goodbye to Haze first?'

That is when I realize she thinks I'm following Colonel Vijay's orders. He wants her shot. *Too bad.* I wanted a Silver Fist prisoner.

Neither of us is going to get what we wanted.

'Rachel,' I say, 'it's a whipping.'

Relief floods her eyes.

And that tells me she's never been whipped, at least not properly. I have, and shooting is preferable. Five lashes shreds muscle from your back, and ten reveals glistening ribs. Fifteen can kill and, if it doesn't, twenty will. As deaths go, the whipping post is a damn sight less clean than a bullet.

But we are not talking about a bull-hide whip here.

'You have a knife?'

She nods, tears in her eyes.

It's the relief, I realize. She's up here expecting to be shot.

That means the rest of them, waiting in a sullen little knot below, probably expect the same.

'Show me your belt . . .'

Pulling it through the loops on her uniform trousers, she hands it to me. The leather is new and stiff in places, but I've seen worse. So I show her how to cut a cat's tail and tell her I expect there to be at least ten more when I next see the belt.

She has an hour to cut the others and return.

I will be waiting up here on this slope. Three valleys up from the one where we fought the Silver Fist.

'You going through with this?' demands the SIG.

I nod, which it picks up.

'They're going to hate you.'

'No, they're not.'

'And you don't care if they do?'

'Not really.'

When the SIG realizes I'm refusing to rise to the bait, it lets me field-strip it with bad grace. There are thirty-seven separate pieces, but only one way to break the gun down and put it back together. My quickest is one minute ten, and I'm aiming for under a minute before Rachel returns.

We're down to fifty-five seconds when I hear a scuffle of boots on the gravel. She's taken fifteen minutes to do a job hardened troopers will take the best part of a day over, if allowed.

Mind you, they know the results of getting it wrong.

'Show me.'

She hands me the cat.

Too heavy and the lashes will cut to the bone, too light and they will lift whole patches of skin. 'Anyone help you?'

Rachel shakes her head.

'OK,' I say. 'Let's get this over with.'

She doesn't beg and she doesn't hesitate. Just takes back her whip and follows me down the slope. Neen has the Aux lined up at the bottom. Their combat jackets are brushed down, their pockets fastened.

Colonel Vijay stands to one side, scowling.

'Right,' I say. 'Give the whip to Haze.'

'Bastard,' says my gun, but says it quietly.

We are dealing with half a dozen issues here and I don't have time for each in turn. I'm going to get them all over at once. Leading her to a rock, Haze waits for Rachel to remove her jacket, then leans her face-down on the rock's hot surface and lifts the back of her shirt to her shoulders.

'Five,' I tell him.

It's less than he expects.

'Lay them on properly. Or I will.'

He is looking inwards, wondering if he caused this. We both know the answer to that. Haze didn't cause it but he didn't help either.

'Are you ready?'

Lifting her head, Rachel nods.

'Hold her by the wrists,' I tell Neen and Franc. Looking at Shil, I say, 'And you count the lashes.'

Everyone has a part in this. That's the point.

Slashing the belt into Rachel's back, Haze winces. It is hard for a first stroke, but he's afraid I will take over if he doesn't do it properly.

'One,' says Shil.

The second draws blood, for all that it is softer.

A third breaks her silence, but I decide she will make five without screaming. I'm right: she gasps at the third, gasps louder at the fourth and sobs with the fifth, but we are done.

'Bring her here.'

Neen and Franc are wondering whether to dress her.

'*Now,*' I order. Can't believe anyone's that stupid. Pull her shirt down over that and Rachel will be peeling cloth from half-healed flesh for the next week and that *will* make her scream.

Putting a hand under each elbow, Neen and Franc walk her across.

It takes Rachel a second to focus.

'Now listen,' I say.

She does.

'I don't give a fuck how things were done before. We're the Aux. We never abandon our posts. We stand. And, if necessary, we die. Understand?'

Rachel nods.

'Good,' I say.

Undoing my jacket, I remove the Obsidian Cross I've been keeping inside my shirt. 'For killing two snipers in near impossible conditions I award you the Obsidian Cross, second class. Wear it with pride.' Kissing her on both cheeks, I hang the cross on its ribbon around Rachel's neck and stand back.

A moment later, the others join me in saluting her.

Chapter 17

A WARM WIND BLOWS ACROSS A NARROW UPLAND LAKE THAT smells of salt. Until three months ago, I'd never even seen a proper lake. But then, until a year ago all I knew was desert and forts and battles against the ferox. It's been two days since we fought the Silver Fist, and five hours since we made camp high on the edge of a mountain.

Franc and I stand guard.

Except we sit. Somehow, I end up telling her about losing my arm. It is a simple enough story. My arm was ripped off by eight foot of fur and fangs. If the ferox hadn't been dying, it would probably have taken my other arm and both my legs as well.

I took the beast's head and left my arm.

Seems a fair trade to me.

Franc laughs when I say this, though I'm not sure why. Then I see it, or at least I think I do. A light skimming high in the sky above us.

At its fattest point, Hekati's ring, in a cross section, is eighteen miles from side to side. Most of the ballast beneath our feet, including the mountain on this side and the rubble under that, exists to provide radiation shielding. That still leaves several miles of air above us, before you hit the chevron glass overhead.

'What?' Franc says.

'He's glitching,' says the SIG.

I ignore it. 'Up there,' I tell Franc.

She scans the night sky. 'A shooting star?'

'Wrong side of the glass.'

As I stand, the single light becomes two. I keep watching, just in case it splits again, and when both lights begin to drop, I yank Franc upright. 'Get Neen and tell him to catch up with me.'

I head downhill before she can reply.

'Suppose Vijay gets them killed?' demands my gun. 'Not that I give a fuck, obviously.'

'He won't.'

'How can you be sure?'

'Neen won't allow it.'

If you want to build your leg muscles, spend fifteen years marching on sand. Running over rock is nothing after that. Withered trees slip by. A stone wall appears, the first sign of civilization. A dog barks from a hut below. Only the hut and dog and slope are now somewhere behind me.

The two lights are closer now. Still falling, faster than I would expect.

Flicking up the screen on my helmet loses them. Flipping it down brings them back. Their heat signature is tiny. Most of the energy transfer is happening beyond the visible bands. *Shit*, I think. *Where did that thought come from?*

'Where do you think?' asks my gun.

Didn't realize I had spoken aloud.

'You can see it?'

'Them,' says the SIG.

I turn it off.

My boots take me down a twisting path and through an orange grove towards a small valley where the lights are heading. And the lights are powered, because they shift position twice, adjusting direction and rate of fall. But this isn't a powered descent; it's a jump followed by a controlled fall.

FLEAS – fast leaping enemy access system. Some geek's idea of a joke. Slapping the gun awake, I say, 'Explosive.'

'Don't you want to confirm identity?'

I hate it when the SIG's right. 'Be ready,' I tell it.

Yeah, I know, it's always fucking ready.

Hitting the bottom of a slope, I make it halfway up the other side in a single rush and roll to a stop. I'm grinning. Not sure I knew how much all that going to parties and being polite to Colonel Vijay was getting to me.

'Incoming,' says the gun.

I duck, but it means the landers.

Metal hits rock and long legs splay, pistons hissing. Dust rises, clearly visible through my night visor. The metal legs stay splayed, because each flea spikes to bedrock to stop its rebound. Flame adds to the dust, as explosive charges blow off doors and restraining straps peel back.

One of the two pilots yanks the ring on a ceramic tube.

Chaff, I think. Only it's *blinder.*

A million sparks flare as magnesium ignites. Luckily, my brain's ahead of me and I'm flat in the dirt, eyes shut and then rolling out of harm's way before a slug clips splinters from a rock beside me.

Night vision's fucked, though.

These aren't Silver Fist, and they're sure as hell not Death's Head. They are carrying weapons from half a dozen different armies.

Dropping into a ditch, I sight over the edge. Empty a clip to keep them locked down. 'Got one,' says the gun.

I'm not sure. So I stay low until I hear a rustle behind me.

Flipping round, I find Colonel Vijay wearing a red dot from the SIG right in the middle of his forehead. Remember that one-second rule? Never been so tempted in my life. Only then, of course, we wouldn't have the jump coordinates to get us off this habitat.

'Get down,' I tell him.

He opens his mouth to object.

'Alternatively, sir . . . feel free to get yourself killed.'

Something tells me this really is his first time in the field. Behind him, five troopers crouch in the dirt.

Neen crawls forward.

'How many, sir?'

'Two.' Half of me wants to bollock him for not being quicker. The other half for not taking longer. I was just beginning to enjoy myself.

'Silver Fist?'

'Guess again,' I tell him.

The army's mostly militia where he comes from and their job is to die. Militia don't qualify for jumping fleas or use night haze. Kit like that comes expensive and militia are cheap. Since our new arrivals are not Death's Head and they're not Silver Fist, that only leaves . . .

'Mercenaries?'

Maybe Neen will make good after all.

Nodding, I tell him to take two troopers and work his way round to the other side. He chooses Rachel, plus Haze, which surprises me.

'You,' I tell Franc. 'Go that way.'

My corporal slips away to my left, a blade between her teeth. I used to think soldiers only did that for effect. Not Franc, she lives those knives. Probably sleeps with one clutched to her breast. Now there's a thought.

'And you, follow her.'

Shil vanishes.

'*Who* are they?' Colonel Vijay asks.

'Mercenaries, sir.'

These are the first civil words we've spoken to each other since he ordered the Aux to slaughter the Silver Fist troopers two days ago. They obeyed, despite knowing I wanted a prisoner. What else could they do?

'Why are they here?'

'Same reason as you, sir. I imagine.'

My answer makes him go very quiet indeed.

Chapter 18

ON THE COAST, YOU CAN TELL THAT HEKATI IS ARTIFICIAL. IT'S hard to ignore a shoreline that rises away from you. Up here, where outcrops and peaks shorten the horizon, we can go whole days thinking we're somewhere real.

High on a mountain dawn is turning the rocks pink. And a warm wind is chasing away the night's cold. It is a beautiful morning. Obviously enough, I am doing my best to ruin it for our new arrivals.

Want to see metal melt like wax? Use a SIG-37 with cinder capacity. It makes most plasma rifles look as efficient as trying to melt sheet steel with a candle. Burning the fleas back to silvery puddles creates a rivulet of molten metal that ignites thorn bushes and dry bracken as it dribbles downhill towards a ditch.

'Pretty,' says Colonel Vijay. 'But you're—'

'Wait, sir.'

Scrambling from the ditch, a mercenary takes a direct hit from my left. The slug ricochets off the armour on his shoulder, but that's not the point. He's rattled. Hitting dirt, he rolls behind a rock. If he has any sense, he'll stay there.

'Sir.' Neen's gaze flicks from me to the colonel.

'What?'

'Haze, sir . . . He's worried.'

My sergeant is in a difficult position. Haze isn't paid to worry. In fact, I'm not sure he is paid at all. He was probably conscripted on the basis of food, shelter and all the ammunition one man can fire.

'Not surprised,' I say, nodding towards what remains of the pods. 'Listening to that lot melt must hurt his head.'

Now it is Colonel Vijay's turn to look worried. 'Those were AI?'

'Semi AI at the most, sir.'

One mercenary faces me. The other faces Rachel, who has them both locked down. 'Your choice,' I tell the gun.

An over blast lights the dawn sky like a gigantic firework.

The SIG-37 places its shot perfectly. Anyone else, and we'd've been down there scooping up chopped meat, if we could be bothered. As it is . . . When the explosion clears, a merc sticks his rifle round a rock and shoots back.

'Ceramic carapace,' says the SIG, making it sound obscene.

Jumping fleas, full-body armour, a blind refusal to know where they are outnumbered . . . Now why does that sound familiar?

Neen still wants my attention.

'All right,' I say. 'What's Haze worried about?'

My sergeant hesitates. That tells me I'm not going to like it. 'Sir,' he says, 'Haze tapped into Hekati's AI. Didn't mean to. It just happened. And while he was tapped in . . .'

I'll give Haze *just happened*.

Firing off a shot, I duck as a mercenary fires back. They're harder to kill than fagan lizards. Of course, you need to know what a fagan lizard is for that to make sense. 'And while Haze was locked in . . . ?'

'He piggybacked the sky cams. There are Silver Fist coming this way.'

I grin.

'That's not good, sir.'

'*Why not?*'

'Sir,' he says. 'With respect, sir. We left our supplies back at camp. On Colonel Vijay's orders. So we could travel light.'

'What did you leave, exactly?'

'Tents, sir. Food, sir. Most of the ammunition.'

'Neen,' I say. 'Fuck off, now . . .'

Punching a superior officer is a capital offence. Almost everything in this army is. It's worse if he's a staff officer. Then they shoot you, patch you up and shoot you all over again. Otherwise, everyone would do it.

But I'm still not going to take it out on Neen.

Seeing my anger, Colonel Vijay stays out of range. If he had any sense he would know just how close he is to being fragged by his own side. But he has all the sense of a blind kitten. Women probably find him sweet.

Me, I just want to pull the pin on a grenade.

'Stay here, sir.'

'Where are you going?'

'To tell the others to stop wasting ammo.'

A couple of seconds later, our rifles fall silent. A second or so after that, the mercenaries do the same. With luck, we destroyed their supplies when we hit those pods.

'Haze,' I say, 'you jacked into Hekati's system?'

'Yes, sir,' he says. 'Sorry, sir.'

'Why?' I demand.

'Can't help it, sir . . .' He must know how stupid that sounds.

'What did you discover?'

'Accessed the schematics, sir. She keeps track of all transport moving inside her torus. She always has done, there used to be seven and a half million—'

He sees my face and skips the lecture.

'Transport?'

'A Hex-Seven, sir.'

An X7i landing craft? On Hekati's sea?

'And a copter, sir. It's shielded.'

The Hex-Seven is irrelevant. We are miles from the coast. Anything that happens here will be over before its crew arrive. But the copter . . .

'You know where it is?' I ask Haze.

He shakes his head.

'Find out.'

'Sir,' he says, 'that means . . .'

This boy isn't a natural soldier. He isn't a natural anything. Haze is a braid on the wrong side. Given half a chance, the Silver Fist will slice my throat, rip out my implant if only I had one, and poke their way through what is left of my brain. What they will do to Haze is far worse.

And yet he's still sticking in there. That is courage of a kind.

'Oh fuck,' Haze says. He's talking to himself. 'They're watching us . . .' Scrabbling for his pad, he flips it open and flicks his fingers across its surface without glancing down.

'Permission to request help, sir?'

Help? I'd ask Haze where he thinks we're going to get help, but he's gone back to his pad and is scrabbling frantically at its keys. So I nod, realize he can't see, and say, 'Permission granted.'

'Thank you,' he says. 'Thank you. Thank you . . .' Takes me a moment to realize he's not talking to me.

In the distance, a tiny explosion lights the side of our mountain.

A few seconds later, there is another.

Then another.

'What's going on?' asks Colonel Vijay.

We ignore him.

'See them?' I ask Neen, who hands me his field-glasses. I don't need binoculars to know what is happening. Low-level lenz, the tiny comm-sat cameras that act as eyes for an advancing army, are dropping like hail into the valley below.

It is time we left.

Keeping our heads down, we make it to a stone hut before a copter skims overhead, heading for where the mercenaries still are.

An Uplift trooper hangs from the hatch, a machine gun resting on his knee. A heat sensor hangs under the copter's body. Watching them go, I'm grateful the sun's already made the slate roof hotter than we are.

A minute or so later a battle starts behind us.

Silver Fist, meet the Mercenaries. Mercenaries, meet the Silver Fist.

A belt-fed opens up and then falls silent. Grenades echo so loudly that pebbles trickle down the valley sides. I know how to read gunfire. Whoever the mercenaries are, they're going down hard and taking a dozen Silver Fist with them.

It's brutal, but the conclusion is foregone. As mortars drown out small-arms fire, a belt-fed opens up one final time. When it stops, it's from choice.

A single shot brings silence.

Neen says the soldier's prayer. All any of us can hope for.

Shouldering our weapons, we crest a ridge, switch tracks and begin the climb to a higher valley. Thorns drag at our legs and sweat dries before it has time to bead on our skin. The sun beats down and the wind is hot.

'Our supplies,' says Colonel Vijay.

'Lost, sir.'

He opens his mouth to protest, then shuts it again.

'We should stop soon,' he says finally.

He is afraid to make it a direct order in case I disobey. He's not sure what he will do if that happens. I am, he'll do nothing. And his instinct is right. If he tells me to go back for the supplies or to stop this march, I'll frag him where he stands.

'Soon, sir,' I say.

'Good,' he says, as if we've reached some agreement. A few hours later, he suggests stopping again. This time I don't even bother to answer.

Chapter 19

'SO,' SAYS THE SIG. 'WHO ARE WE GOING TO KILL TODAY?'

'We've only just got here.'

'And your point is?' it says. A click of a switch closes it down.

The roof to our new base is missing, the front door has been stolen for firewood and the inside is strewn with goat droppings harder than buckshot. It's ideal. There is even a spring outside, where black rock forces rainwater to the surface.

'Obsidian,' says Haze. Rachel thinks it's coal.

I don't care what it is so long as it keeps providing water.

'Slowly,' I tell them. 'Sip it slowly.'

One entire circle of Hekati is behind us. It has taken five days in total, including today's forced march, and I only know we've done it because this valley is where we came in. What we haven't done is find our missing U/Free observer.

We've seen ejército at a distance; they leave us alone. We see prospectors, and they don't even know we are here. *Is this what the ferox felt like?* I wonder.

Invisible, out on the edge.

Boats skid across the distant sea like insects. Carts trundle

from one city to another, pulled by donkeys or teams of men.
Colonel Vijay is amazed. He never knew people lived like this.
No one bothers to point out many live far worse.

'Neen,' I yell.

He comes running.

'Hunt something,' I say. 'Kill it. Get Franc to cook it.'

My sergeant glances towards a figure sitting under a tree.
He wants to say something about the colonel, but isn't sure he
should.

I'm damn certain he shouldn't. 'Wait,' I say. 'I'll come with
you.'

We find a track half a mile above our new camp. It runs
straight uphill and a wisp of fur suggests wildcat. A large one,
given the thorn's at hip height.

My bet is the cat sleeps up here and hunts lower down, in
which case we are heading in the wrong direction for food.
Only I need a fresh look at the valley and the higher we go
the better my chances of seeing the islands off Hekati's coast.
Because those are what we'll need to search next.

'Sir,' says Neen. 'Can I talk freely?'

'As long as it's not about the colonel.'

Our next stop is a rock overhanging the valley, with our
camp far below and a glimpse of the sea beyond. All of Hekati's
rivers lead to that sea. Back in the day, there were obviously
dozens of the things. Most of the river beds we meet now are
little more than damp gravel or cracking mud.

Seven million people once lived here. Now Hekati's a back-
water so far out of touch that other backwaters regard it with
contempt.

Ideal place to hide something, I think.

There is more to this mission than a missing U/Free and
some sickly prospectors, a bunch of Silver Fist and two dead
mercenaries. I just know it. All I need to do is work out
exactly . . .

'Sir,' says Neen. 'Are you all right?'

A sixth sense prickles the back of my neck, and my body floods with adrenalin as the kyp flexes in my throat. My body does other stuff that makes little sense, like slowing my heartbeat and heightening my hearing. It's an animal thing.

'Prey?' whispers Neen.

'Hunters.'

When I draw my gun, the load-and-lock diode is lit, the sights have ranged themselves to a hundred paces and the SIG has set itself for hollow-point.

'You knew?'

'Oh,' says the SIG. 'Now he decides to talk to me.'

As ordered, Neen goes first. He finds a ditch and crawls along it until he crosses the wildcat's track we found earlier and follows that for fifty paces. I'm right behind him, and slam my hand over his mouth the moment he stops.

'Quiet.'

He is not nearly scared enough for what's making its way towards us. Unholstering the SIG, I drop out its clip, count ceramics and fold my fingers round the handle to deaden the noise as the clip slots back into place.

Seeing me do this, Neen checks his own rifle.

He has eighty to a clip, another hundred hanging from his belt. I would swap both the SIG and his rifle for a single moly-coated bullet and thirty seconds with Rachel's sniper rifle. Obviously, I don't say this. The SIG can sulk for days.

'Ready?'

My gun sighs. 'Always.'

'Single shot . . .'

Diodes whirr, although it has the sense to damp them. Somewhere the SIG has settings for mute. It must, all intelligent guns do. I've yet to find them.

The rocks ahead have that flat quality hot landscape gets when the sun is directly above and unfiltered by cloud. And I know Hekati's sun is reflected, that dawn and dusk are tricks created with mist and mirrors. But the people who design these places are good, and thinking too much about that stuff fucks you up. So I don't.

'Field-glasses.'

Neen hands them over.

Takes me three seconds to find what I know is out there. 'Take a look,' I say, passing the glasses back. 'And don't let light reflect on the lens.'

'Oh fuck,' he says. 'That means . . .'

It means two mercenaries took down a platoon of Silver Fist, destroyed a copter and took out two braids. There is no doubt about that last bit. Because each has a severed head hanging from his belt.

One braid has three metal snakes, the other five. That's a major and a full colonel in our world. Also, the mercenaries seem to have helped themselves to a collection of Silver Fist weapons.

When Neen raises his rifle, I say, 'Let them pass.'

He shuts his mouth and does what he's told.

I have my reasons. Either those two are the world's best trackers or they have a fix on something. And my guess is it's Haze.

'OK,' I say, a few minutes later. 'Now we follow.'

As said, I can read the sound of gunfire. This one begins with a burst from Franc. Has to be Franc because she is the one we left standing guard. A clip burns in answer. So the mercenaries have enough ammunition not to worry about wasting it. A second clip burns just as fast. This means they didn't hit Franc first time round.

I can count every single one in the Aux fire in reply.

'What about Colonel Vijay?' says Neen, when I tell him this.

Yeah, that's true. They might have hit the colonel, but I doubt it. No way are we getting that lucky. Rachel is firing single shots. And probably doing more to pin the enemy down than the rest put together.

'OK,' I say. 'Let's get down there.'

The grass in front of our base is on fire.

Leaves shrivel on bushes, the air stinks from cordite, and whatever animals once made nests in that grass. One mercenary is in the open. The other covers him from behind a low wall. The one in the open uses his rifle to shred stone chippings from the hut.

Anything that wastes their ammunition is fine with me.

The Aux falling back makes sense in one way. The hut has thick walls and narrow windows. Of course, the lack of a door is not great. But, so far, the mercenaries don't know about that, because they've approached from the other side.

In another way, it's fucking stupid.

The building has no roof. One well-positioned grenade and my troopers are going to be decorating the inside walls. I send Neen round behind a tree. Then, when he is in position, signal him to cover me.

Rising from a crouch, he does.

As Neen opens fire, Franc sticks her own gun around the window and hoses down everything in sight. Her clip burns out in a single blip. Another muzzle appears in the same space and burns out two blips later. So Shil must be changing clips.

How much ammunition do they think they have?

Can't see Rachel, but that is Rachel for you. She'll use one bullet to everyone else's hundred and probably make the only shot that really matters.

And just as I think *where's Haze?* a grenade rises from inside, bounces off a strip of roof tiles on its way down and lands at the feet of the nearer mercenary. Hard to know if Haze is an idiot or simply inspired. Perhaps both.

Two paces take me into the open . . .

Caught by the unexpected, the mercenary turns.

So I hit the ground and Haze's grenade explodes. Needn't have bothered about hitting the ground. A fair bit of the shrapnel never gets further than my target.

Of course, he's in armour.

I'm not. All the same, he goes down.

And I scrabble up, praying all the while that Neen is keeping the other mercenary busy. He is. So I stamp on the helmet of the one at my feet, twice. He has a grenade of his own. It seems a pity to waste it.

'Down,' I shout, pulling the pin.

Neen ducks behind his tree as I begin to count.

As the other mercenary spins, I reach *three* and drop into a ditch myself, lobbing the grenade towards him. He tries to kick it away, misses and by then it is too late anyway. The explosion knocks him off his feet and throws him into a wall.

He's in full armour, obviously. But it's still enough to stun him. A hollow-point direct into his chest kicks him back when he tries to stand. His armour cracks, but the ceramic holds. We are talking quality stuff.

Gripping his head, I twist until his helmet can go no further. It's an internal lock, not his spine, that stops me. Although I'm sure I can get round that.

'*Sven*,' says my gun.

'Now what?'

'Don't you even want to know why they're here?'

'Not really.'

The SIG–37 sighs. 'Far be it for me . . .'

★   ★   ★

We go through what is left of their ammunition. Some hollow-point, two clips of full metal, three sticky mines, a couple more grenades, and a sweetly balanced blade. I had been hoping for more.

'Peel them,' I tell Neen. 'Call me when you're done.'

Chapter 20

HAZE HAS HIS BACK TO THE HUT WALL, A CLOTH WRAPPED round his head. He's swallowing blood rather than spitting, so he must know how badly those nosebleeds of his irritate me.

'So,' I say. 'How did they find us?'

'Tracked me,' says Haze.

'Did you know?'

'Of course not, sir. If I'd known . . .'

'What?'

'I'd have asked to be left behind.'

There is no answer to that, so I go to see how Neen's doing with the mercenaries.

The answer to this is not so well. Armour opens from the inside, obviously enough. And our two captives aren't playing. Franc has their wrists bound behind their backs, their ankles lashed and rags tied over their visors.

'Sven,' says Colonel Vijay.

He's carefully not looking at Franc, who is busy ignoring him. My guess is the colonel panicked again in the first few minutes of the attack. Now he's wondering how to live it down.

'Be with you in a moment, sir . . .'

He flushes.

'Problems?' I ask Franc.

She grins sourly. 'Can't get them open, sir.'

Well, it is a bit like asking a crab to peel itself for dinner.

I can kill one to encourage the other. Waste a clip or two of explosive rounds. Drop large rocks until the internal bruising gets too bad. There are dozens of ways, but sometimes the old ones are best.

'Make a fire,' I say. The Aux scatter, looking for kindling.

'Bigger,' I tell Shil, when she comes back with twigs.

She scowls at me, but the next time I see her she is dragging a bloody great branch behind her. The time after that, I notice that Franc is cutting the branch into usable lengths. I don't even want to ask where she got the axe.

Neen prepares a fire of kindling, logs and dry goat droppings.

Breaking apart an incendiary bullet, he extracts the slug from its case and the charge from the slug without losing his fingers. Although we're all careful to stand back when he tips flakes of thermite, phosphorus and whatever it is onto smouldering leaves.

A minute later, we have our fire.

'Call me when it's down to coals.'

'Yes, sir.'

The mercenaries have to realize what's about to happen. They are struggling hard enough.

'You ready to open up?'

Two shakes of the head.

So I get Neen to help me roll them onto the glowing coals. Good battle armour can be very good indeed. But no one expects the armour to handle these levels of heat. At least, not for as long as I'm prepared to leave them both broiling.

'Sven . . .'

'Sir?' My gaze flicks from the fire to Colonel Vijay.

'Is this necessary?'

There is none of his usual arrogance. It seems to be what it is, a simple question. Looking at him, I spot vomit on his trousers.

'We could just kill them, sir.'

'But we should question them first?'

'I think so, sir.'

Actually, my gun thinks so. But there's no way I'm going to tell Colonel Vijay that. 'Sir,' I say. 'Can I ask a question in return?'

When he nods, I step away from the fire and he follows. I want to know why we're here. I want to know why he's leading a mission that should be mine. I want to know why we've gone right round Hekati and found no trace of his fucking U/Free observer. But I ask him something else instead.

That's called subtlety.

'How old are you, sir?'

He blushes. 'Nineteen next week.'

Oh shit.

You don't get to be a colonel at eighteen without insane amounts of influence behind you. A lieutenant, yes. Maybe a captain by twenty-one, if your family are senators. But a colonel . . .

'Sir,' I say. 'Did you volunteer for this?'

The answer is in his eyes. So I tell Colonel Vijay I have been that kind of volunteer, and move to my next question. The one that's meant to get me to the questions that matter. Only his answer makes them meaningless.

'*Do I know the general?*' His smile is bleak. 'Yes,' he says. 'General Jaxx is my father.'

'Your father volunteered you for this?'

148

'Oh, no,' says Colonel Vijay Jaxx, eyes bleaker still. 'That was OctoV, our glorious leader himself.'

The ceramic skin of the mercenaries' armour is crazed and metal fittings glow when I get back to the fire. The rags around each helmet and the ropes tying their wrists and ankles together are long since ash.

They are too tired to keep trying to crawl free. The few times they do attempt it, Neen just pushes them back into the fire using a stick.

'Either of you willing to talk?'

One of them nods.

'If you're lying,' I say, 'I'll throw you back.'

I am tempted to leave the other one in there. Only Colonel Vijay is watching and I'm on my best behaviour. So I have Neen drag both from the coals. Filling a water bottle from the spring, he prepares to cool the armour.

'*Don't* . . .'

It's the first thing either mercenary has said since being captured. Although what interests me is that the voice is female. More than that, it's familiar.

'Unlock,' I tell her.

She does.

A switch is obviously hit, because a seam runs up her breast-plate. Steam rises as it opens. When Neen reaches down, the woman inside shakes her helmet. I can see the problem. Straps hold her in place.

One after another, these slide back.

Clicking a cuff, the woman shakes a glove free. And reaching up, swears as the skin on her hand sears. It seems a throat guard must fold away before her helmet can lift free from its shoulder guards.

An interesting idea.

A rag hides the woman's skull. Originally red, it's now

sweat-stained. An implant behind one ear is missing its top. She wears a sodden green singlet. Now here's someone who didn't expect to be undressing in public.

As her thigh pieces open, the mercenary rolls to her knees and lets the plate armour fall away to reveal plumbing. One pipe enters her buttocks, another coils beneath her thong.

She rips free the fatter.

Behind her, the second mercenary does the same. They are twins, indistinguishable if you ignore green and blue vests. The same broad shoulders and flat guts, the muscled arms and cropped skulls.

The first one sees me watching and grins sourly. She thinks I've never seen someone like her before. It's a fair assumption. Not many people get to see the Vals and live.

You fight them, you die.

And if you fight alongside the Vals, then you're definitely going to die. Because the Vals are patron saints of the Last Stand.

'We've met,' I say.

The nearer Val stares at me. I'm not in any memory bank she's accessing.

'And we're sorry,' says Neen. 'About Vals 9 and 11 . . .'

She looks surprised. Why would anyone be sad about a Val dying? It is what they exist to do. A couple of sentences bring her up to speed on Ilseville and what happened to her sisters. Blue singlet gets it immediately. Vals 9 and 11 are dead. We saved their implants; only an explosion destroyed those as well.

'You were comrades?' She sounds doubtful.

'No,' says a voice behind me. 'We were friends . . .' Haze wears a singlet of his own, equally filthy. A rag is wrapped round his head and a water bottle is gripped in his shaking hand. Glancing at me, he takes my silence for permission.

150

'Here,' he says, offering the first Val water. She sips, and then passes it behind her.

After a sip of her own, the second Val passes it back. They finish the flask between them a sip at a time, their actions impressively disciplined. I've known heat-struck troopers gulp water fast enough to choke.

'Friends?' A corner of green singlet's mouth twitches.

She knows how absurd a comment that is. The Vals are copies; they protect their own and hunt in pairs. They've been chipped, spliced, and augmented to the edge of insanity, and they are proud of it. No one makes friends with a Val. Everyone works at staying alive when they're around.

'Yes,' says Haze.

Slowly the Val reaches out to take the cloth from his head. Then she looks at me, at the colonel behind me and finally at her partner, and then she just looks puzzled. Never seen that in a Val before.

'Who are you?'

'Sven,' I say. 'Lieutenant Sven Tveskoeg, Death's Head, Obsidian Cross, second class . . .'

It doesn't occur to me to lie until afterwards and then it is too late anyway. I get on with introducing the others. 'This is Colonel Vijay, our commanding officer. Sergeant Neen, Corporal Franc, Troopers Rachel and Shil. Rachel's our sniper . . . You've already met our intelligence officer Haze.'

The Vals are looking at me. So are the Aux, and Colonel Vijay. *Our commanding officer?* Franc mouths at Shil.

I'll deal with that later.

'You're Uplifted?' asks green singlet.

'Death's Head,' I reply. 'And these are the Aux.' It's short for *auxiliaries*. The Vals don't know about the Death's Head auxiliaries. That's OK; I only invented them a few months ago.

'Let me get this right,' says the Val. 'You're Death's Head, with a braid for an intelligence officer?'

151

'Yeah.' I nod.

Glancing at the other Val, she shrugs.

'Got to be true,' says blue singlet. 'Too fucking weird not to be.' As we watch, she slides the tube from under her thong and wipes her fingers on her thigh. 'Hate these fucking things.'

'Never tried one.'

Her grin is sour. 'Wrong plumbing.'

They are Vals 5 and 7. That makes them senior to those in Ilseville. It also makes them good at their job. Vals shift up with battles won. Any Val above 25 you want to handle with care. Above 15, you can make that extreme care.

'So,' I say. 'What are you doing here?'

We look at one another. The Vals are still prisoners. That is, I'm gripping a pistol, Neen hasn't lowered his rifle and Rachel is holding her Z93z. But we all know the rules have changed. How much, we'll judge from their answer.

'We're after the reward,' says Val 5.

'What reward?' Colonel Vijay asks.

It takes her a second to realize he's serious. 'General Jaxx's son. Dead or alive. A million credits in gold.'

'Jaxx's son?' says Neen. *'Here?'*

'We figured that's why you're here,' says one.

A thought occurs to the other. 'If you're not here for that?'

'Then, why are we here?' I take the initiative because Colonel Vijay is standing as if struck by lightning. 'A mission,' I say. 'For the U/Free.'

'You serious?'

'Yeah. I'm serious. And there's no million-credit reward for what we're here to do . . .' *More's the pity,* I think. I could buy a hundred Golden Memories with what someone's willing to pay for Vijay.

The first Val is listening.

152

'We'll ransom you,' I say. 'We can negotiate the price in a moment.'

'Custom sets the price,' she says, bristling slightly.

I know that. It just didn't occur to me she would agree. A 5th- and a 7th-level Val come expensive. Of course, our receiving the ransom depends on their getting off Hekati alive.

'So,' I say. 'The price is agreed?'

She pauses, giving the occasion respect. 'Yes,' she says. 'It is.'

Stepping forward, I offer my hand.

When I look round, Neen has grounded his rifle. Colonel Vijay is smiling, somewhat grimly. Even the Vals look happier. The rules governing this are covered by contract. Vals 5 and 7 can no longer hunt us. At least, not without warning us that the truce is over first.

We let them go. Then we head out ourselves. Not that I don't trust them. I just want a couple of mountain ridges between us before nightfall.

Chapter 21

YOU KNOW THAT BIT BELOW THE RIBCAGE ON A WOMAN, ABOVE the navel and under the lowest rib, where the skin of her gut stretches so tight you can see a caged heart beating?

No, I don't either.

My old lieutenant told me to look for it the day I visited my first brothel. Mind you, I was thirteen and he was always after the impossible.

Franc's skin is taut, right enough.

Her navel is a tight knot, but her heart is safely back behind her ribs. And she doesn't have body hair because she scrapes between her thighs, under her arms, and across her skull each morning with a knife – or so Rachel told Haze.

Never seen her do it.

'Stand still,' I say.

Pulling a blade from my boot, I check its edge. Sharp enough for our needs.

Twilight is the only time Hekati is bearable. For now, the wind is at Franc's naked back. Soon, the last of the sun will vanish behind a slope; the wind will switch directions and with it will come the cold.

A moon is already rising.

Of course, the moon doesn't actually exist. It's another illusion.

Like the sun setting and the night sky, which is just a pattern of stars reflected through glass. I don't care how many times Haze tells us. It still looks like the sun, the moon and the stars to me.

'Sir,' says Franc. 'What are you thinking?'

'About the moon.'

'Beautiful,' she says. 'Isn't it?' See, she agrees with me.

Franc and I are up here to have a little discussion. She thinks she is losing her edge in battle. I think she's as fast and deadly as she ever was. Except once you lose faith in yourself it doesn't matter what anyone else tells you.

You find it again fast, or you lose it for ever.

Sometimes, of course, it's not there to start with. Sometimes you only stumble on it later . . .

The colonel is down in a valley with the rest of the Aux.

I have told them he's eighteen and not here from choice. They are to cut him the slack due any new recruit. Enough to stop him killing himself; not enough to get them killed instead. In the meantime, they are to salute him, feed him and obey his orders wherever possible. As for the Jaxx thing, they'd be stupid not to work that out for themselves.

'Sir,' says Franc. 'When you're ready.'

'Right,' I say. 'Steady yourself.'

Reaching out, I grip one bare hip and drag my knife from one side of her abdomen to the other. Franc gasps, swallows the pain and stands straighter. I am impressed. Not least that she keeps her hands to her sides to leave herself open for the next slash.

Instinct is a bitch to fight.

My second cut is slightly higher than the first, and my third higher still. There's a fourth and a fifth. Until blood trickles down Franc's inner thigh like piss.

'Don't move,' I tell her.

Kneeling to scoop up grit, I rub it into the cuts. Dirt will raise the edges of the wounds, make sure they never fade. She has her scars back, and with them will come her edge. Or so she believes.

Stepping back, she salutes. 'Thank you, sir.'

'My pleasure.'

A few months back someone offered to remove the whip marks from my shoulders. I refused, because some lessons need remembering. Scars make us what we are, people like Franc and me. She nods when I say this, pleased that I understand.

Now's the moment to ask my question.

'Franc,' I say. Must be something in my voice because she goes still.

'Sir?'

'You were trained. Weren't you?'

'Yes, sir.' She nods. 'We all were. We were Uplift militia, before . . .' Before they were captured, told to change sides and became cannon fodder for the glorious Octovian army instead.

'No,' I say. 'Before that.'

She looks at me. 'From birth,' she says finally. 'That's the way it works.'

'To be Haze's bodyguard?'

'His lover, his bodyguard, his servant, his possession, until death . . .' Her mouth twists. Her eyes are bleak. 'He rejected me.'

'Franc.'

In short bitter sentences she describes Haze running away from home. She follows, because her training drives her to. Only when she catches up, Haze tells her she is free. Her life is her own.

So she's here.

Because *here* is where Haze is.

'You're here,' I say, 'because you're in the Aux.'

'Yes, sir,' she says. 'That too.'

As she turns, I see the dagger sheath between her shoulders and realize why she never takes it off. Unbuckling it probably makes her vomit. Knives keep Franc happy and make her secure. It's called *imprinting*, and hers is an extreme version of what we do to new recruits.

Sounds like she has had it for ever.

Reaching for her singlet, Franc hesitates. *Probably nothing*, I tell myself. But I catch her sideways glance. Her blood's on my hands and my shirt is in the dirt, because it's filthy enough as it is. And she's already naked . . .

Meet a woman you like, make conversation.

Can't remember who told me that. Either my old lieutenant or a whore. Make conversation. It convinces women you're not only interested in one thing, even if you are.

'You know something?'

'No, sir,' says Franc. She waits, singlet in her hand.

'Can't remember my first fuck,' I tell her. 'Can't remember my first kiss or my first drink. But I sure as hell remember my first knife.'

Franc smiles, and for a second looks like someone else. 'Really, you can't remember your first . . . ?'

'Happened the same night as my first drink.'

She laughs.

'You make that blade?' I ask.

Sliding the dagger from its sheath between her shoulders, Franc finds its balance without even looking. 'Stole it,' she says.

It's my turn to smile.

'Sir,' says Franc. 'Permission to speak freely?'

'Go ahead.'

'You think our time's come?'

Standing up, I walk her to the edge of a drop. It falls for a hundred paces onto jagged rock. If I said *jump*, she would jump. No doubt about it. 'When I was a child,' I say, 'an officer put a pistol to my head. It misfired, so he kept me as his orderly.'

'That was your time?'

'Everything since is extra.'

'Those scars,' says Franc. 'They were my time.' She hesitates, and then shrugs, mostly to herself. 'Killed my uncle, my three brothers and a cousin. They thought I'd just let them do what they wanted.'

'They tried to rape you?'

'Tried to stab Haze.'

My surprise must be obvious.

'If he dies I go free,' she explains. 'They thought they were helping. Not a single one of them believed I'd protect Haze against my family if that was what it took.'

She weighs next to nothing. Our kiss only ends when I bite her lip hard enough to draw blood. She bites back, and then she's tugging at the buckle on my belt and fumbling the fastening on my trousers.

'Oh my God,' she says. So I put the rest in.

This time when she bites, she means it. A second later, she's spitting and wiping her mouth with the back of her hand.

'Could have warned me.'

Bad blood. What, she couldn't work that out for herself?

Wrapping my prosthetic fingers into the webbing across her back, I grab her buttocks with my other hand and yank her against me, feeling her legs twist behind mine to bring her closer. We are standing naked on the edge of a drop, with a rising wind buffeting us. A dirt path to one side and certain death to the other. I'm not going to move unless she asks me, and she is not going to ask me.

Licking my fingers, I reach under her.

Franc yelps.

When I persist, she sinks her teeth into my chest.

This time round she wipes her mouth against the unbroken skin of my shoulder. Then she decides to live with what my hand is doing and locks her legs tighter. A second later, they're locked tighter still and she's raking bloody lines down my back.

I've met better-behaved wildcats . . .

'*Don't laugh*,' says Franc eventually. That's when she can say anything at all.

'Take next watch,' I say, lifting her off me.

She nods gratefully. Replacing Shil on guard is going to be easier than returning to the fire and the knowing glances of the others. They'll have heard us. It would be impossible for them not to . . .

'And you, sir?'

'I'm staying up here for a while.'

Chapter 22

SOMEWHERE IN THE DARKNESS IS WHAT WE ARE HERE FOR . . .
Unless the U/Free have it wrong? I consider that for a moment
then reject it. If the U/Free say their observer is here, then he's
here. But if he is here why can't I find him?

Sucking my teeth, I dig into my pockets for a smoke.

Cigars are illegal in Letogratz. You can change sex, kill
yourself repeatedly, have four tits, knock a hundred years off
your age and become someone else, but you can't light up . . .

Weird people the U/Free.

I fold my fingers round my lighter to hide its flame. Sucking deep, I release smoke into the coldness of the night. The
wind's switched directions, the stars are high and the temperature up here is still dropping.

It's the silence I like.

The silence and the night noises. I knew them all in the
desert. The scuttle of lizards and the rattle of snakes. The high
call of raptors, the almost hidden padding of wildcats as they
creep towards sand hoppers.

When a twig breaks on a path, I free the catch on my
holster.

I know where Franc is. She's a hundred paces below, to the right of my rocky outcrop. The others are sleeping in a hut so close I could walk three paces and drop spit on its roof. A ruined vegetable garden slopes up to the hut. A wall encloses the garden and Franc stands watch by its gate.

Neen chose the position earlier. It's his job to do stuff like that.

'Show yourself . . .' When no one answers, I say it again, louder.

A few seconds later Colonel Vijay stumbles out of the darkness. And stands blinking in the moonlight. *Sleepy*, I think, until I realize he's embarrassed. Seems he heard Franc yowling. Although he is far too polite to mention it.

'Sven . . .'

'Yes, sir?'

'I wanted . . .' He stops, gazes at my cigar.

'You like one, sir?'

Colonel Vijay takes my last cigar, folds his fingers round the flame of my lighter. A second later, he's coughing his guts out. 'Sorry,' he says, although I'm not sure why he's apologizing. 'They're . . .'

'Cheap, sir.'

'I was going to say, stronger than I'm used to.'

'Also cheap.'

His smile is uncertain. 'Thought I might stand watch in your place,' he says. 'If you think that's a good idea.'

It's a bloody stupid idea. Colonel Vijay standing watch means we'll need two guards, Vijay himself, and someone to watch over him.

'That's a kind offer, sir.'

'But a useless one?'

'Not exactly. More . . .'

He sighs.

We walk downhill together.

My temper holds as long as it takes us to reach the gate.

Franc's there all right, a knife in the dirt at her feet for easy reach, her rifle ported across her chest. She's crouched low and watching the treeline intently. Hearing steps, she spins round to see me. It's not Colonel Vijay's presence that knocks the grin from her face. My scowl is enough.

'What's that?'

I know what it is. It's a fucking Kemzin 19 pulse rifle leaning against a wall.

A pair of boots sits below it. They are rotten with sweat and bloody round the ankle. But all our boots are rotten with sweat and bloody round the ankle. What gives these ones away is the fact they're clean. Only Shil washes her boots each evening.

'Tell me she didn't . . .'

'Sir,' says Franc. I take that to mean *she did*.

'How long ago?' asks Colonel Vijay.

Don't know why he's asking. Each watch lasts two hours. If we're here and her rifle's there, then it's two hours exactly. Unless she hung around first talking to Franc. And there are reasons why that is unlikely.

'Why?' I demand.

Franc doesn't answer. Perhaps she can't?

'You quarrelled?'

'Yes,' says Franc, before changing it to, 'No, sir.'

Other ranks loyalty. The army runs on it.

'About . . . ?' demands Colonel Vijay, and then shuts up. It's obvious.

'Sir,' says Franc. 'Shil's only been gone a few minutes. She wanted a walk and the only thing out there is foxes, sir. I'm sure . . .'

'You've seen them?' asks Colonel Vijay.

'Sir?'

'You saw these foxes?'

162

'No, sir,' she says. 'But I've heard them.'

'Where?' I say.

She points to three different places in the treeline below.

The SIG-37 is out of my holster before I realize it. Jacking the slide, I engage night vision and pick flechette. The tightness to my gut has nothing to do with fear and everything to do with what is about to happen.

'Wake everyone,' I tell Franc. To Colonel Vijay, I say, 'I need you to hold this position, sir. Stay back, keep low . . .'

He nods, already setting the sights on his own pistol.

When Franc hesitates, words still unspoken, I drag her from her crouch and push her in the direction of the hut. A second later, she's gone.

Chapter 23

SOMETIMES YOU DON'T RECOGNIZE DEATH UNTIL IT BEATS THE door down. Others, you know it's out there before it arrives. *You can taste death on the wind.* That is what they say in the Legion. It can take whole forts, the taste of death.

Once conscripts go flat-eyed and sullen you might as well kill them anyway, because they are going to die. It's never happened on my watch and it's never going to. But standing where two paths cross beyond the gate, I can taste death on the night wind, and it tastes metallic, like blood and blades.

'Situation?'

'Pincer movement,' says the SIG. 'Three hostiles left, three right, both groups closing on a target. Another four hostiles ten seconds behind.'

'Highly probable?'

'Certain,' it says. Certainty burns battery.

In this case, I can live with it.

'And their target?'

'Tiring . . .'

'Cover me,' I shout over my shoulder.

Colonel Vijay makes the signal for *understood*.

The slope gives me enough speed to turn a stumble into a roll that takes me under the enemy's opening shot. Coming up, I find myself half kneeling and sight my gun.

An ejército goes down, tripping the man behind.

The man who trips turns back to see what happened and dies. Flechette is silent, that is what makes it so effective. 'Only twelve to go.' The SIG's voice is sour.

A pistol shot comes from the gate above.

'Eleven,' I say.

A hostile spots me and fires. Throwing myself sideways, I get off two shots before taking cover half a dozen paces away. We are down to ten attackers, their quarry and me.

The Aux have just opened up. So has an enemy sharp-shooter.

'Sniper on the roof,' warns the gun.

'Take him.'

An oak tree explodes, and he falls to earth like a cheap firework. The sight of his overcooked body is too much for one of our attackers. He dies on his knees with a mouth full of vomit, and one of Rachel's moly-coated specials in his throat. Dropping out a clip, I slam a new one into place.

Someone's shouting at Shil to run and it sounds like Colonel Vijay. She's five steps ahead of the first man chasing her. Nine steps after I kill him. Fifteen paces when Rachel kills the man behind that. Only six ejército left. It is enough to make the others hesitate.

'Run faster,' someone shouts. I realize it's me.

I put a flechette into a runner and roll sideways in time to see grit explode from where I'd been. 'Night sights,' says the gun.

Night sights? These are ejército.

A second incendiary takes it down to four as a second sniper drops to his death rather than burn alive. I blip away a clip of hollow-point, drop it out and insert another.

'Sven?' It's Colonel Vijay. Out of position.

'*Back to the fucking wall.*'

He stares at me, looks at Shil and retreats. When I glance round, he's keeping low and weaving frantically. Obviously works, because he makes it without taking a hit. Bloody idiot.

Shil is clearly visible in the moonlight. So I stand up and free fire as she staggers past. Her stumbling is made worse by bleeding feet and that afternoon's forced march. Her face has enough thorn cuts to need stitching.

'Earth to Sven,' says my gun. 'Anybody in?'

'Wait.'

An ejército breaks from the right. He is firing as fast as he can jack the slide on his . . . *single-shot rifle?*

Brains splatter the bush behind him.

It's a good shot by Rachel, but I want one of these bastards alive. I have questions, like *snipers? rifles? flak jackets?* The last time I saw them, these men were riding ponies and waving swords.

'Come on,' says my gun. 'We're being outflanked.'

Yeah, I can hear them.

As I begin my retreat, with the SIG held low, a man rises from a ditch beside me. He is carrying the blade I expected them all to be carrying. Ducking low, he goes for my guts. So I spin away, blocking his jab on my arm.

The ejército knows what he is doing. He knows a knife is as good as a gun in a fight this close. He just doesn't expect me to agree.

'Sven,' says the SIG. 'You're not—' It sighs. 'Fuck,' it says. 'You are.'

Dropping the gun, I rip free a blade. I'd like to say it's old, that it has saved my life in back alleys and bars. But it's militia standard issue. A double-edged blade with a blood runnel to

166

ease suction. The man grins, because my knife is half the size of his.

'You die,' he says.

Shaking my head, I grin back.

What with not having marched bloody miles and fought two battles already, he is fresher than I am. Also, broad-shouldered and muscled. In addition, he is fast. At least, he's fast for his size. But he's not me.

So when he stabs, I take the blow in my side. And watch his eyes widen as I grab his fist to hold the blade in place. He is too flustered to see me rear back my head. Slamming my forehead into his nose ends the fight. Although he's not dead until I rip free his blade, and return it deep into his own throat.

'*Sven*,' Shil shouts a warning.

'That's *sir*,' I say, without thinking.

Then I'm on my knees. When I try to straighten, something slows me. No one has a grip on my shoulders, but I'm slow, way too slow . . . Someone is screaming, but I don't think it's me.

There is a hole below my chest. Silvery coils slide out of my fingers as I try to stop them falling. Some bits of me are missing. I know this, because a length of fat gut lies at my feet, covered in grass and grit.

'*Sir.*'

'Should have kept going,' I say.

Dropping to her knees Shil stares into my face.

'*Man down*,' she shouts, turning back. '*Man down.*' Should have guessed from all that yelling earlier.

'Don't die,' she says.

It's a fucking stupid thing to say.

I apologize, because I didn't mean to say that aloud. 'Back to the wall,' I tell her. 'Now . . .'

Grabbing my arm, she tries to lift me.

'Shil,' I say, *'just fucking go.'* Doubt floods her eyes, then awareness. She glances at my wound, probably doesn't even know she has done it. She recognizes a killing shot when she sees one. 'I've got morphine,' she says.

'Save it. Colonel Vijay leads, OK? No arguments.'

She nods blindly and rises to a crouch. I hear the crack of a rifle, a cry from the trees below and then silence. The ejército should be dead now, only they're opening fire again. Our enemy have reinforcements. I know that, otherwise Neen would be here now.

Whatever it takes.

Wish I had been able to make that true.

It's a hundred paces to the gate. But it's uphill and she will be in the open. I can see fear growing in her eyes. Any minute now, Shil's resolve will fail.

Can't let that happen. '*Go now,*' I try to say.

But the clouds are red and the night's gone pink. I can hear Aptitude's voice and see her mother's face and that is absurd. One's in Farlight and the other is locked down on a prison planet. I can hear my old lieutenant too. And that's even more ridiculous, because he's dead.

An army of ejército advance from the treeline. Some have guns. Others carry blades. '*Run,*' I whisper, but it's too late.

As a man drags back Shil's head and a blade glints in the moonlight, a voice that isn't mine says:

'No.'

A voice that expects to be obeyed. And that's good, because it is obeyed. Instead of cutting Shil's throat, the ejército reverses his dagger and clubs its pommel into the side of her head.

She drops, eyes open. A boot rolls me over and the owner of the voice bends closer. When he spits I grin, because I'm obviously who he thinks I am.

'Leave him here,' says Pavel. 'Let him die slowly.'

'And her?'

'We take. His woman for my dead grandson.'

Not my woman, I think. It's my last thought before the sky floods crimson and the hillside drops away.

Part 2

Chapter 24

THE AIR IS SOUR WITH SMOKE FROM A FIRE THAT HAS BEEN BURN-
*ing for longer than the boy has been alive. A buried seam of junk
'taneously-nited . . . That's what his sister says. Now it burns so
deep that no one can reach the flames to put them out. Supposing
anyone could be bothered.*

*Head down and shoulders forward, the boy runs for the far edge of
the rubbish dump, his bare toes biting into ash and tossing up dust
behind him. There are silvery thorn vines on the slope ahead. If he
can reach those . . .*

And then?

*Then he can circle round to pick off his tormentors. One or two at
a time. Maybe even three or four if he goes after the smaller ones. You
have to be fourteen to belong to the Junkyard Rat Gang. That means
he can join in two years. If they'll have him.*

Which they won't.

*Primary One is his planet's largest and oldest dump. It has the
richest waste. It also has the Rats, whose control of the dump means
they don't have to pick through rotting meat, discarded clothes and
broken glass like the other scavengers in search of precious things. The*

Rats tax those who work the dump half of everything found. Only those chosen by the Rats can scavenge.

The boy isn't one of them.

Run, *screams a voice in his head. So he runs.*

Thorn vines tear his arms and cat-scratch his ankles. They rip his trousers and slice through his tattered shirt to draw blood. His sister Maria will be furious. She likes him to be tidy. Maria looks after the family now. After . . .

Well, everyone knows after what.

Five years back mercenaries chose his village for a base. A brigade from the Légion Etrangère drove them out. It was a hard fight and most of the houses were destroyed in the process. The boy's parents were taken in for questioning.

His father is still alive. But he doesn't speak and he doesn't work. Now and then, the boy finds his father staring at him. As if wondering what this stranger is doing in the house.

'There he goes,' shouts a voice.

The boy curses.

Should have been finding somewhere to hide, not worrying what Maria will say. Mind you, that's easy to say for anyone who hasn't met her. Maria's tongue is sharp. And her slap has knocked a sneer from more than one grown man's face. The boy could flatten her with a single punch back, of course. But he never has, and he never will.

He owes her too much.

'Go round . . .' That sounds like Rice.

Dropping into a ditch, the boy comes to his knees behind a twist of vine studded with flat, razor-edged blades. Some vines are silver; this one is purple from whatever is buried beneath its hungry roots.

A number of Rats huddle around Rice at the bottom of the slope. He's looking up to the right. So that's obviously where he has sent some troops. The boy could go left, use one of the tracks out of the dump and go home . . . Only Rice will simply come looking for him. Some things in life you just have to face.

That's what his sister says. So the boy climbs higher, to keep above the scouts. As he climbs, he grabs anything that looks sharp and thrusts it inside his shirt.

A smoking gash marks the highest point of the dump. Hell's mouth, people call it. No one knows what lies so deep that it can keep burning so far below the rubbish heaped over it. All they know is that smoke from the gash burns your eyes and its ash eats into your skin.

Maybe if he crawls close the Rats will be unwilling to follow? And maybe not, but it's worth a try. Make nice, Maria says. Ask politely if you can scavenge the dump. Explain . . . Only how can he, when Rice won't listen to his pleas, and the Rats chase him from the dump every day?

A steel bolt, two stones, a lump of once-molten slag, a bottle made from bluish glass . . . His weapons collection. It is hard to believe someone hasn't found the bottle before him. Also, he has something flat and green that looks like ceramic but stresses when it bends. The thing has jagged edges. Really sharp. So he decides to throw it first.

He doesn't have long to wait.

Coughing tells him the scouts are coming. But the boy waits until the first figure is a dark shadow before he throws. Then he stands, twists his body and spins the razor-edged piece of board as hard as he can.

'Fuck.'

'Shit, he's . . .'

'Get Rice.'

The boy ploughs his way towards their shouts.

A frightened face looks up through drifting smoke, and turns red as the boy drives his heel into a face and steps on it in his hurry to hurt the boy beyond. That face turns red as well. There is a fourth boy, but he's running downhill, stumbling as he runs.

A metal bolt to the back of his skull drops him.

The boy is stronger than them. He minds pain less. That's why they hunt him in a pack. Crouching, the boy examines his victims. Two are unconscious. The third stares with frightened eyes, blood bubbling from a rip in his throat. It doesn't jet like everyone says it

175

should. It bubbles like a damp fart. The boy wonders what to do.
Then remembers what Maria always says.

When you don't know what to do . . . Do nothing.

He leaves his victim to die. It feels good to be out of the smoke.
Mind you, it feels even better to have three knives and a little club on
a bendy spring that wobbles when you tap it, and hits the middle of
your hand with a satisfying thump.

'Oi, freak . . .'

It is Rice, with a dozen of his followers. All are armed and most
carry knives. They've worked out which way he was going to circle.
The boy is cross with himself for being so stupid.

'What have you got there?'

'Nothing.'

'Show me, freak.'

'Show you what?' says the boy, hiding the little club behind his
back.

Rice scowls.

The boy knows everyone else fears the Rats. Only he doesn't, the
boy is not sure why. It would be much easier to be like the others.

'Hand it over,' Rice demands.

Glaring around him, the boy spots the Rat who blinks and launches
himself at the weakness in the wall. A punch to the face drops the Rat.
Someone tries to grab the boy, but he produces his little cosh and breaks
the man's skull.

'You can't run,' Rice shouts.

Yes, he can. It's one of the things he does well.

Head down and shoulders forward, the boy heads for the far edge of
the dump, knowing he has been here before.

'Out of the way,' shouts Rice.

Something hisses past the running boy, and the boy is still grinning
when the next dart hits. The first blast of electricity takes him to his
knees. Stumbling upright, he manages five steps before an aftershock
drops him. Every nerve in his body burns along its entire length. He
has pissed himself, then he realizes he's done worse.

'Gross,' Rice says.

A boot catches the boy in the gut, but it's nothing to the agony in his muscles and the cramp in his limbs. After a while, Rice stops kicking.

'Fuck,' says a voice. 'Where did you get that?'

'Traded it,' Rice says proudly.

'Who with?'

'None of your business.'

A voice mutters its apologies.

Even in the middle of his pain, the boy has the sense to curl around the spring-loaded club. The longer he can keep Rice from finding out about the Rat with the bubbling throat the better.

'Hey, freak . . . Can you hear me?'

He says nothing.

'Of course you can.' Rice laughs. 'We don't want you here,' he says. 'Next time, stay away.'

He's forgotten already, the boy realizes. The Rats all have their heads turned to Rice as he outlines the gang's next job. Smash up a bar, break into a cargo ship, go down to tax the brothels. The list is limited.

Someone will kill Rice eventually.

But it isn't long since Rice killed the boss before him and the Rats are being careful. The boy wonders if they'd let him be boss if he killed Rice. Even as he thinks it, he knows they wouldn't.

On a slope stands a hut.

Well, what is left of one. Wreckers have stripped the roof, gutted the inside and cut rusting walls into strips and sold them on. All that remains is a floor with a lip around its edge. The floor is made of something too hard to cut and too heavy to lift. Rain fills this makeshift pool.

Stripping off, the boy splashes himself clean. Having scraped his soiled trousers, he rinses them and tugs them on. The thorn-vine scratches on his ankles are already starting to heal. It's one of the reasons the Rats call him freak. That, and the shape of his skull, which is a little wider than everybody else's.

It is time to go home now.

As the boy reaches the peak of a trash mound, he sees a high curl of smoke in the distance. This is wrong. Everyone knows smoke comes from the dump. So he looks harder, because his eyes are good, and realizes it's his village burning.

The Rats are slung along a road below him now. So close, he could hit them with a stone if he threw it hard enough. And soldiers are heading up the road towards the Rats in the opposite direction. The reason the Rats can't see the soldiers is a bend in the road.

Except the soldiers can obviously see the boy, because a small man points and the man next to him raises a rifle . . .

The small man shakes his head.

They're wearing camouflage. Sandy uniforms, with grey patches that make them stand out on the dark strip of compacted rubbish that makes up the road from the dump. The boy could warn the Rats. All he has to do is shout, or toss that stone. Or start making his way down the slope, that would get their attention soon enough.

Only why would he bother?

When he can't find a proper answer, the boy asks himself the question he always asks when he can't find an answer. What would Maria want him to do? Only the smoke rising from his village says that what his sister wants probably doesn't matter much any more.

As the Rats near the bend, the small man nods to the man beside him who says something to someone else. The man he talks to drops to his knees and sights along a scope above a barrel. His weapon is longer than those of the others.

His first shot takes Rice through the head.

Brains and bits of bone spray out as a passing slug sucks sticky matter and splashes it onto the face of a girl behind. The boy sees it happen, although he knows that has to be impossible.

Rice dies still holding his stun gun.

The girl falls still trying to wipe jelly from her face. After that, *everything happens too fast for the boy to follow. Although the result is never in doubt. Smoke from the gunfire drifts uphill, adding its acid stink to the smell of the dump. When it clears the boy can see clearly what has happened. All the Rats lie dead and one of the soldiers is taking the stun gun from Rice's hand.*

A trick, the boy realizes. The machine probably told them exactly where Rice was.

When someone shouts, the boy looks up. It takes him a couple of seconds to realize the soldier is shouting at him. Instead of hiding, he stands. His sister is dead, his village is burnt, and the soldiers are back.

Doesn't much matter what happens now.

The boy remembers little from the time before Maria became his sister. He only knows it wasn't good. She found him, she took him in and she fed him. All he had to do in return was obey her rules. Don't lie. Keep your promises.

They weren't even that difficult.

A dozen rifles track him down the slope. When the boy reaches the road, one of the soldiers gestures him closer. The man has blue eyes and sandy hair and smells of alcohol. As the man steps forward, the boy notices he is swaying.

'You're drunk.' The boy says it without thinking.

Behind the man, someone snorts.

'Yeah,' the man says bitterly. 'Some of us have consciences to anaesthetize.' Pulling a silver flask from his pocket, he flips its lid with a practised flick of his thumb and swallows a large gulp. As an afterthought, he wipes the top and offers the flask to the boy. 'Want some?'

'It's OK.' The boy looks puzzled. 'What's a conscience?'

'Something that's meant to stop me doing this.' The man takes a pistol from his belt and puts its muzzle to the boy's head and pulls the trigger. A dry click tells them both that the gun's misfired.

'Third-rate technology,' the man says.

The boy is not sure what it means, so he shrugs. He could try to run, he could try to fight. He is as big as the man shaking the pistol. In fact, he's bigger than half of the men standing around him. But what's the point?

'You killed my sister,' he says.

The man nods. 'We killed everyone. That was our job.'

Behind him, the soldier who snorted begins shaking his head. As if knowing this, the man with the pistol turns. 'You saying it wasn't?'

'You're here to re-establish the rule of law.'

'By killing people.'

'That's not . . .'

'Yes it is,' said the man. 'We get to kill people. You get to watch. That's what observer status means, doesn't it? All the excitement, none of the guilt.'

'Lieutenant.'

The one talking wears a flak jacket. He isn't armed, and something about his voice puzzles the boy. It sounds foreign. Of course, they all sound foreign. But it also sounds . . .

'You're—'

Yanking off her helmet, the U/Free shakes out her long fair hair and removes a pair of dark glasses that have been hiding her eyes. 'Well,' she asks Lieutenant Bonafonte. 'Are you going to shoot him or not?'

The lieutenant scowls.

'You have operational control,' she reminds him.

'In that case, no . . . I'm not.'

Paper Osamu nods slowly. 'Interesting choice,' she says.

Chapter 25

THE CREEK IS WIDE AND MUDDY AND AN ANCIENT TIDELINE
reveals that the sea was once higher. Steps have been cut in
the side and jetties lashed together. A system of buckets drags
water to a slide at the top. From here, irrigation channels carry
it to the fields on Hekati's valley floor.

Turns out the sea is not salt.

Rusting rings on a sea wall tell of barges long gone. A
crumbling maze, mostly no higher than a child's hip, shows
where offices once stood. Stonefoam is cheap and easy to use,
but it needs upkeep. It has been centuries since anyone tried to
preserve the harbour buildings. Probably decades since there
was much left to maintain.

The sea stinks.

It is not sewage, because fewer than three thousand people
now occupy a habitat built for several million. And ninety
miles of water can cope easily with the effluent from that
number. Rancid algae cloud the shallows.

The days are hot and the nights cold on the coast. Both are
less extreme, however, than in the mountains. A few boats
hug the shore.

They are small, with triangular sails that carry them up the coast during the day. At dusk, they moor for the night if they want to continue. Or turn, and ride the opposite wind down the coast again. Either choice will take you back to where you started.

At the creek's edge stands a huge cube.

Its sides are unpitted and its edges sharp. If gods built gun emplacements, this is what they'd look like, right down to a long slit that looks north. Twice the height of a human, this slit takes a whole minute to walk from one end to the other; and every year a new gang of boys rappel down from the cube's roof, only to discover the blackness inside the slit is unbreakable glass.

Those who sail the sea say there's another cube on the opposite side of Hekati. It's identical, but for the fact its slit faces south. Both cubes have cities on top, and both cities are reached by mud-brick steps, making them easy to defend.

Enyo, the city here, is roofed with sheet metal. As many as thirty houses are still in use, which means ten are ruined and used only by goats. The streets are narrow, with abrupt turnings. Others lead off the cube's edge with no warning.

Defence against attack. Although how anyone can mount an attack on a city that drops into the sea on three sides and can only be approached by narrow mud-brick steps on the fourth . . .

Well, it's obvious.

You scale the sides or use the steps. One will exhaust you, and both will lay you open to bullets and arrows and spears, as well as dropped rocks and pebbles flung from catapults. It is a poor city, Enyo . . . But a safe one.

In the middle of Enyo is a square. Here you find the largest houses. All have three storeys, and one house has four. Unlike the others, this house has its shutters closed against the afternoon heat.

The attic of the four-storey house stinks of goats and dung, smoke and shit. That's not unusual. The whole of Enyo stinks of goats and dung, smoke and shit. What is unusual is the fire burning in one corner. It's piled high with smouldering herbs that choke the air and make a young woman's eyes sting. She's naked to the waist, barefoot and wearing combat pants hacked off at the thigh.

She has small breasts, dark nipples and a leather sheath fixed to the small of her back by a complex webbing harness. Scars criss-cross her abdomen. Removing the webbing would make her cooler, but she'd rather die.

So she leaves the dagger in place, despite its hilt being hot enough to hurt when it touches, which is every time she turns.

It's late afternoon and she's exhausted.

Others offer to take her place, and quickly learn to mind their own business. She shits in a bucket, eats only what is put in front of her and shaves between her thighs, under her arms and across her skull each morning. The young woman barely notices she is doing any of these.

'*Paper.*'

The word comes in a croak from the bed. That's where a naked man is tied. As the young woman turns, the man jerks against his ropes and falls silent, his fingers bunching into fists as his eyes glare at someone she can't see.

'*Paper,*' he repeats.

Spitting into the fire, the girl turns her back and leaves. She shuts the attic door with a slam. I know who she is. Know who that figure on the bed is too.

It's me . . .

With the coming of that knowledge I cease to be able to stare down on wild birds as they circle above the city. And I lose my ability to stare through roofs into the rooms below. With this loss comes sleep. When I wake, it's to a greyness that has no edges. *This is death,* I think.

Someone laughs, and it's a tired and bitter laugh. 'So,' says a voice. 'You're back.'

'Lieutenant Bonafonte?'

'Haze, sir.'

Should have known. 'Where am I?'

'Which bit of you?'

'The real bit.'

Haze snorts. 'Your body's on a bed in Franc's room. She hasn't left your side in three weeks.' He hesitates, and decides to say it anyway. 'You died.'

Not *almost died*, or *were close to death*.

'What happened?'

'Good question,' he says. 'The kyp brought you back, probably. Also you heal indecently fast.'

That I know, have always known. Wounds close, bones mend, and sinews knit themselves together. You can take me to the edge of death, and seemingly beyond . . . Given me some of the worst moments of my life.

'If I'm there,' I say, 'what am I doing here?'

You can say one thing for Haze, he understands the question immediately. 'Piggybacking a subset of Hekati,' he tells me. 'Damn near killing me keeping your memories in one piece.' He is not boasting. His words are too flat for that.

'Where's my gun?'

'Safe,' says Haze. 'I'm looking after it.' The calmness of his answer makes me suspicious. He realizes that, because he adds: 'That's all. Nothing more . . . sir. Are you ready to return?'

'Am I . . . ?'

'It's going to hurt,' he says. 'Even with whatever makes you mend.' He pauses. 'Franc still believes you're going to die. She's . . .'

'I've seen how she is.'

'Yes, sir.'

Chapter 26

SOMEONE HAS WIRED MY JAW SHUT AND I'M GETTING WATER through a tube. The sheet swaddling my legs is tied in place with a rope. I can see the rope if I squint hard enough. Although looking gives me a headache.

Haze is right. Being back hurts. It hurts like fuck, and then it hurts a bit more. I would go back to where I was, if I hadn't just boasted I was ready to return.

'*Franc.*'

She seems to be ignoring me.

Tapping the side of the bed might attract her attention, but my hands are tied and my strength is gone. I can barely turn my head, never mind break knots. It seems best to worry about that later because Franc is turning towards me. She approaches with all the patience of a wildcat pacing its cage.

Walks straight past. Then turns and walks back. I only realize this when she stands over me.

Her lips are cracked and her eyes ringed with dark circles. A bruise on one leg matches another above her hip. Looks like tiredness has her walking into things. Scabs crust the cuts across her gut, which is hollow.

I know why my jaw is wired when pain explodes across my face. Pavel obviously kicked me in the head as a parting gift. And Franc's slap is hard enough to make the room blur.

Shooting offence, I think. Before wondering, *what was that for?*

'Pleasant dreams?' she asks.

When my eyes refocus, Franc is on the other side of the room, forcing her elbows through the sweat-rotten straps of the singlet she wears under her combat jacket. And then, back still turned to me, she climbs into her trousers and buckles on her boots. She's made her point.

There are four wires in all holding my jaw shut, and she snaps each, leaving me with a mouthful of blood and lengths of metal sticking from my teeth. Turning my head, as much as the pain will allow, I ask:

'*Shil?*'

Has to be the first understandable word I've said. Franc's expression is so dark it makes me think perhaps I was meant to ask something else first. And maybe I was. But then I wouldn't be me. Shil is Aux, that's reason enough to ask. 'Well?'

'Sergeant Neen went looking.'

Since when did Franc stick *Sergeant* in front of Neen's name? Since his sister went missing, I guess. 'He went alone?'

'No, sir. The colonel went with him.'

Oh fuck . . .

'When?'

'Over a week ago.'

'And the others,' I say. 'What about the others?'

'Rachel's downstairs,' says Franc. 'As for Haze, he spends his life field-stripping that gun of yours. When he's not sitting over his bloody pad gibbering to himself.'

'Franc . . .'

'*Fucking don't, sir . . .*'

Maybe being thanked isn't what she expects. Throws me

too. But I died and so did she, back during that idiot test at the beginning of this mission. It gives us something else in common.

All the same, my voice is harder when I say, 'Cut the ropes . . .'

She shakes her head. She's about to explain why when steps on the stairs make her move away from my bed. I expect the local caudillo. Some broad-shouldered thug wrapped in a foul-smelling coat and carrying a rifle, probably with a dagger thrust through his belt. Probably my dagger.

Come to that, probably my belt as well.

What I get is an old woman. Grey hair waterfalls from a high forehead. She's dressed in a shift that is white and almost clean. A string of pearls hangs round her neck, and a silver brooch fastens a cloak at her shoulders. I'm not sure how she can stand the smoke and heat in here, but she barely seems to notice them.

'Ahh,' she says. 'My voices were right.' Dark eyes examine my face, and she scowls when she sees the wires to my jaw have gone.

'You died,' she tells me.

'I know.'

She looks at me closely. 'How do you know?'

'My own voices told me.'

Gripping my head, she turns it towards her lamp and stares into my eyes. Her gaze is unforgiving, and unexpected from an old woman in a rotting city on the edge of a stinking sea in a habitat that's taking longer than it should to die.

'He tells the truth,' she says.

Franc nods. 'He always does,' she replies. 'Not an endearing quality.' She has to be quoting Haze or Vijay, no way would she come up with a comment like that on her own.

The old woman smiles. Her name is Kyble. Or maybe that's her title. Pulling a wineskin from her belt, she yanks off the stopper and holds the skin to my mouth. 'Drink,' she says.

'Not if it's going to send me back to sleep.'

She shrugs. 'Die then.' Putting the stopper back in her flask, she turns to leave the room.

'Kyble,' Franc says.

The woman looks back.

'Please?'

With a sigh, Kyble gives Franc the flask.

The next three days pass in a haze of smoke, bitter wine and memories of Franc raking embers, rebuilding endless fires and stacking herbs onto burning coals until the smoke gets thicker and my memories uncertain. One morning Rachel appears carrying a tray of food for Franc.

Looking round, Rachel screws up her face.

And then, wandering over, she peers deep into my face. Maybe she thinks I'm unconscious. 'How can you stand it?' she asks Franc. She's talking about the heat, unless it's the smoke. Alternatively, it could just be the smell.

'You get used to it.'

Rachel snorts.

'Remember Ilseville?' Franc's voice is flat. When Rachel doesn't answer, Franc says, 'I do. He kept you alive. He kept me alive. Haze would be dead if it wasn't for him.'

'That's why you're doing this?'

'One reason.'

'What's the other?'

'None of your fucking business.' Stripping dried berries from a branch, Franc busies herself arranging the berries into small heaps. After a few seconds, Rachel leaves. Next morning Kyble cuts the ropes tying my legs. 'Move your toes,' she orders. So I do. 'Now try your whole feet.'

I can move those too.

We work our way up my body. My ankles will twist and my

knees will bend, but lifting either leg is near impossible. My fingers work, my wrists turn.

'Who made this?' Kyble asks, tapping my prosthetic arm.

'A woman.'

'Someone like her?' asks Kyble, nodding at Franc.

I shake my head. 'No,' I say. 'Someone like you.'

It's the right answer. Although it invites more questions. These need answers before she will leave me alone. I am tempted to tell Kyble to shut up, fuck off and take her curiosity elsewhere. But in answering questions I pay a debt. And Kyble is not my enemy, or I would be dead and the rest of the Aux too. I have a good idea, though, whose enemy she is.

'Caudillo Pavel,' I say.

She spits from instinct. 'The only person who calls Pavel caudillo,' Kyble says, 'is Pavel himself.'

She sees me smile sourly.

'So,' I say. 'My enemy's enemy is my friend?'

'In your ejército also?'

'Also in my ejército.'

Shaking hands involves gripping wrists while folding back one finger. Kyble doesn't mind that I fumble the greeting. 'Clean him, feed him and bed him,' she tells Franc. 'Any order you like. Although cleaning him first might be best.'

To me she says, 'They'll be back today. Your caudillo, and your angry little servant.'

When Kyble lets herself out, she's chuckling.

'Who is she?'

'Someone who hid you,' says Franc. 'When the Silver Fist swept through this city and everyone else wanted to give you up.'

Chapter 27

WALKING OVER TO THE WINDOW, I FIND MYSELF FACING ROTTING canvas. So I rip it down and toss it on the fire, which doesn't improve the smell. But that doesn't matter, because opening the shutters lets in the afternoon wind.

Two young women glance up from the square and look away, probably because I am naked. About the only thing you can say for Enyo Square is that it isn't full of goats. There are no trees, no flowerbeds, no statues . . . None of the things I've come to expect from a square.

And I am looking down onto the sloping roofs of the other houses. They're made from crumbling red tiles patched with sheet metal. An upper window in a building opposite lets into a bedroom where a woman is breast-feeding a baby. She must be precog, because she turns to meet my gaze.

A second later her shutter shuts.

'Sir . . .' Franc leads me away from the window. A second after that, she pulls what is left of the canvas from the fire and stamps it out with her bare feet. 'Poppy,' she tells me. 'You're feeling the effects of poppy.'

She's wrong. I'm not feeling anything at all.

Certainly not as much as I expect to feel, given the raw skin covering my lower gut, which is puckered at the edge and sunburn pink. 'Franc,' I say. 'About Colonel Vijay. You know he's . . .'

'We know who he is, sir.'

'I'm sure you do. You'd have to be dumb not to. What I want to know is how he ended up joining Neen's hunt for Shil.'

'Originally, sir, the colonel intended going on his own.'

I make her repeat that.

'Neen insisted on going,' she says, knowing how absurd that sounds. Neen is a sergeant. Colonel Vijay outranks us all.

'He told Neen to stay and then changed his mind?'

'Yes, sir. That's exactly what happened.'

Never issue an order you know will be broken. Never threaten punishment you don't inflict. Never make promises you can't keep. Sounds to me like Colonel Vijay is learning.

I wash myself, because I can't see why Franc should. And I'm rinsing off the soap when Haze wanders into the attic, carrying my pistol. Without looking at me, he puts the SIG carefully on a table. After a second, I realize it's because I'm naked. He is a strange boy, and I mean more than the braids twisting from his head.

'*Haze* . . .' I say.

Turning back, he hastily looks away. So I tip what remains in my jug over my head and dry myself on a sheet taken from the bed. Believe it or not, that does improve matters.

'You've lost your head dressing . . . ?'

Haze checks to see if he's in trouble. He's not. 'Kyble knew,' says Haze. 'Told me not to be ashamed of what I was.' His words come out in a rush.

'And were you?' I ask.

He nods.

When Franc returns, Haze leaves.

The bread is stale and the fruit spoilt, apart from the figs, which are unripe as bullets. I eat the lot because I've eaten worse. And worse is better than none at all, and I've eaten that too. As I wipe crumbs from my mouth, Franc steps back to strip off her singlet, unbuckle her boots and climb out of her combats.

'Kyble's orders?'

Franc nods and I laugh.

She is straddling me when Colonel Vijay comes into the square. Although Haze must say something, because the colonel shouts from outside, and then waits for a minute, before beginning to climb the stairs. By this time, I'm wearing the sheet I used to dry myself and Franc is back in her clothes. Well, mostly.

He barely looks at her.

'Tracked Pavel to a city in the mountains,' he says. 'It's walled, bigger than this, with guards on the gate. Looks locked down to me. So either they're expecting us, or they're expecting some other kind of trouble.'

His voice is clipped; it takes me a second to realize he's angry. Another, to realize it's with me.

'Sir . . .' I begin.

'No,' he says. 'You'll listen.' Stamping to the window, he glares out at the square and then stamps back again. 'You,' he says, nodding at Franc. 'Leave us.'

Saluting, she heads out without needing to be told twice.

'Three points,' says the colonel. 'One, you cost us a trooper. Two, we have lost a week because of you. And three, you don't commit suicide in my time. Neen's on the edge of going rogue.'

He turns, scowls at me.

'And I don't blame him.'

He means it. The little fuck is siding with Neen.

192

'You think you'd be alive without me, sir?'

'I'll pretend I didn't hear that.'

'Let me repeat it.'

'*Sven* . . .'

'Sven nothing, *sir*. You'd be dead.'

I'm seconds away from putting him through a wall. Here I am on some fuckwit habitat in Uplift space, on a mission so secret that no one's prepared to tell me what it really is. Because, sure as fuck, it is not about finding a missing U/Free. At least, not just that.

I'm pretty sure Colonel Vijay knows.

'*One*,' I say. 'Shil disobeyed a direct order to retreat. *Two*, you almost blew the entire fucking mission with your little meltdown in the hub. And *three*, I'm bored shitless babysitting some little fuck with a chest full of medals for battles he didn't fight.'

The colonel flushes.

'Must be hell, sir,' I say, 'having Jaxx for your father. All that money, all those houses.'

'You have no fucking idea.'

'You're right,' I tell him. 'I don't. Never met my real father.'

'Surprise me,' he says. 'I take it your mother was a whore?'

'No, sir.' I say. 'That must be yours.'

Blocking his punch, I step back. Everyone has buttons; it's just finding the right ones to push. All the same, for the first time, Colonel Vijay seems to know what he is doing. So I take another look and realize his face is thinner, his eyes harder. Wind has turned his skin to leather. 'Some fancy tutor teach you to fight?'

'A sergeant,' he snaps. 'No one you'd know.'

'Horse Hito?'

He steps out of my reach. 'You know Hito?' Colonel Vijay sounds surprised.

'Yeah,' I growl. 'Horse gave me the knife I used on Paradise. Went with me to have my arm fitted. Introduced me to General Jaxx. One of life's good guys . . .'

Colonel Vijay is reassessing.

I'm not at all sure I like being reassessed by some smug little shit. Only the smug little shit is fading before my eyes and someone else is taking his place. Guess all Vijay Jaxx needed was to get out from under his father's shadow.

'So,' I say. 'How do you know him?'

The colonel laughs. 'He's the old man's pet assassin.'

First I've heard of it.

Chapter 28

THE AUX SIT UNDER AN OLIVE TREE IN A YARD BEHIND KYBLE'S
house. Neen rests his back against the ancient trunk and Franc
has her back to Neen. Haze is lost in thought, and Rachel
is judging distances in her head, flicking her gaze between
distant roofs as she mutters numbers. As for Franc, she picks
her nails with a throwing knife.

Franc is the only normal one among them.

All turn to watch as I shut Kyble's door and stamp across the
yard to where they sit in sullen silence. We are the Aux, we
don't behave like this.

'All right,' I demand. 'Tell me what's wrong.'

They look at one another.

'Neen,' I say.

He hesitates. So I yank him to his feet. Not difficult; I just
twist my fingers in his collar and lift. The body of a farm boy,
all whipcord thin, but no real weight.

He is fast, though.

Seems I've swapped one fight for another. That's fine,
because this is a fight that needs to happen. The moment I
block his punch, he punches again. The blow comes close,

but not close enough. A punch like that can rupture your throat.

Knocking him down with a backhand, I move forward to stamp his gut. This time Neen gets lucky and his heel clips my thigh. Rachel moans, although that might be at the grin which suddenly brightens my face.

Right on cue, Colonel Vijay appears.

'Stop.' He glares at us, sweeping his gaze from where I stand to Neen lying in the dirt. 'This is . . .' The colonel hesitates. I think he's overdoing it, but it's his idea and it's a good one.

'Oh,' he says. 'I see. A competition match.'

Seniority is abandoned for competition matches. You approach the ring a colonel or a trooper and take back that rank on leaving. But in the ring . . . It's bullshit, obviously. No one but an idiot cripples someone five ranks above. Life is too short for that kind of stupidity.

However, the *precedent* is there.

In the army, precedent is everything. It means you can do what you want, and insist someone else did it first. The colonel and I have a deal. He forgets what I said in the room upstairs and I don't kill Neen, unless necessary. As he points out, good sergeants are hard to find.

'Almost as hard as good COs,' I tell him.

He laughs. Then realizes I mean it.

Sitting himself against the tree, Colonel Vijay says, 'What rules?'

'No rules,' says Neen.

'You OK with that?' His question is for me.

'Sure,' I say. 'Never been big on rules myself.' Neen's sneer nearly costs him his life. He is so busy looking mean he forgets to watch me. As my arm flicks out, my fingers reach for his throat. All I need is my thumb and finger around his larynx and this match is over. It's a nasty way to die, but a good way to kill.

At the last moment, Neen twists away.

So I reach forward and he backs away. And suddenly we have Kyble watching, as if she knew this was going to happen. Perhaps she did. Although you probably don't need precog to know that this was coming to the boil.

Neen and I are both angry. We're both angry about the same thing. I think Neen should have kept Shil at the gate. He thinks I shouldn't have made Shil think that running back was expected.

Same incident, different readings.

Happens all the time. There will be six versions of this fight. Unless we give them an official one. 'Begin,' says Colonel Vijay.

Actually, he only says the first letter. Because my kick lifts Neen off the ground so fast that Colonel Vijay forgets to finish his order.

'Stay down,' Haze tells Neen.

When I step forward to stamp on Neen's knee, the colonel glares at me. Seems we're fighting this by rules after all, just unspoken ones. Always hated those worst of all. Your own unspoken rules, that's different. They're what you want them to be.

Something has changed in Neen's eyes when he crawls to his feet. I hope the colonel thinks that's good. No one but a fool expects an enemy to go easy on them. And my enemy is what Neen is.

You fight me that's what you become.

If he could kill me, he would. Only he can't. So he is going to go down trying.

I break his nose. He shuts one of my eyes. I'm tired and beginning to hurt from the effort of not killing Neen. That, I could do quickly. Keeping him alive and at arm's length is a lot harder.

And yeah, I know, *Good* and *sergeant*. Two words to sit

uneasily in the mouth of anyone who has ever been in the Legion. But he *is* a good sergeant, and in the last few seconds, he got better. When he comes in swinging, I take the blows. And slam my head into his face.

'Stay down,' yells Haze. Rachel nods at his shout.

Colonel Vijay is smiling, the smile of a man watching his plan come together. I'm turning Jaxx's son into a proper officer, and a bit of me wonders if that is really a good idea.

Then the colonel's smile is gone. Because Neen's rolling sideways to grab a dagger from the dirt. When he comes off the floor it's fast, with the dagger in his hand jabbing faster. We're abandoning match rules, here.

'Sergeant,' shouts Colonel Vijay.

Neen hesitates. It's enough.

Grabbing his wrist, I squeeze. Bones stress and the fury goes out of his eyes. Pain does that for you. Or so I'm told.

'Neen,' says Colonel Vijay. 'Drop that knife.'

I can see Neen wondering what is going to happen next. All that happens is that I let go of his wrist and step back as the colonel steps forward.

'You two,' Colonel Vijay says to Haze and Rachel. 'Hold him.'

They look at each other and something passes between them. Fear or resignation, who knows . . . ? It passes quickly. Neen is a mess. His nose is almost flat to his face. One tooth is missing. A rip at the side of his mouth gives him a grin at odds with the emptiness in his eyes.

'Hold him tighter,' insists the colonel.

So they do. Reaching forward, Colonel Vijay grasps Neen's nose and wrenches it back into shape. 'You carrying thread?' he asks Franc.

When she nods, he smiles. 'Sew it at the bridge,' he tells her. Maybe Horse Hito taught him battlefield medicine as well.

Chapter 29

TEN MINUTES BEFORE THE TIME COLONEL VIJAY HAS GIVEN FOR moving out, I stalk from the house to find the Aux waiting. Neen sits on his pack, checking clips, his face sewn back into shape. Haze and Rachel have their heads close together. To my surprise, Haze still wears his scalp bare to the sun. His braids are longer than I remember. As for Franc, she's chewing a sliver of wind-dried meat thoughtfully.

Probably working on a better recipe. It must be great to have your life simplified to knives and food.

Mind you, I can talk.

The surprise is two villagers standing beside her. One is a girl about Franc's age, wearing a woollen dress, tied at the waist. Her feet are bare. The rope round her waist makes her breasts look bigger than they probably are.

The other is a boy of a similar age. A leather bag hangs from his shoulder and a large knife juts from his belt. His beard is thin and blond. He obviously thinks he's coming with us. As does the girl, I realize.

'Who are these?'

'Villagers, sir,' says Rachel. She looks at Haze, who shakes his head.

'Neen?' I ask.

'Kyble said . . .' Standing, Neen makes himself start again. 'Sir,' he says, 'Kyble says taking them is the price of her hospitality.' He hesitates. 'She said you would know this already, sir.'

'She said I'd know this?'

'Yes, sir. Says your voices would have told you.'

'Wait here,' I tell them, and they're still waiting when I return with the colonel fifteen minutes later to tell the two villagers they can come with us. Strange the things that can change your mind.

Colonel Vijay left the final decision to me. *Operational matters*, he calls it. Apparently, those are my responsibility. So I stand there, inside the house, while Kyble runs through her reasons.

We owe her, that's one.

The second is that Pavel's now on the move, taxing villages. We'll need these two to help us find him. Her third reason is that one of them will save my life before I leave this world.

'I'll save my own life,' I tell Kyble.

She frowns. Luck's a whore, she tells me. She'll smile one minute and cut your throat the next. It doesn't do to throw favours back in her face. That's not how Kyble puts it – but it's what she means.

'We can't take them,' I tell her.

The colonel nods back when I glance towards the door.

'Nineteen years ago,' says Kyble, as his fingers touch the handle, 'the Fist billeted here. Ten men in all, two . . .' She puts her thumbs to her head, indicating braids. 'And eight like you.'

Nothing like us, I want to say. But it would be a lie.

'When they left,' she says, 'they left those two, in the bellies of twins from this city. Young girls,' Kyble looks at me. 'Good girls . . .'

'What happened?' asks Colonel Vijay.

'After the soldiers went?' Kyble makes the sign for throats cut.

'But they spared the infants?' He sounds surprised.

'They ripped them from the women.' Kyble's voice is hard. 'And they would have ripped the guts from the infants. I stopped them . . .' She sighs, turns to me. I don't want to see this woman plead. Women like Kyble don't plead.

'*You're old*,' I say. Colonel Vijay thinks I am being cruel.

'I'm dying,' Kyble replies.

'Your voices told you?'

She snorts. 'I don't need my voices to know the obvious.'

'And when you're dead there'll be no one to protect those two?'

'See,' says Kyble. 'I knew you'd understand.'

The man is called Ajac, the woman Iona . . . They are younger even than Franc, or Neen, a whole lifetime younger than me. Kyble gave them their names after she buried their mothers.

'You're cousins, right?'

They nod.

'Thank god,' I say. 'I've had it up to here with brothers and sisters. OK, these are my rules. You do what you're told. You stand, you fight, if necessary you die. Break any of those and I kill you myself.'

I look at them. 'Right?'

'That's it?'

'There's another,' says Neen, slotting a clip into his rifle, and climbing to his feet. 'Whatever it takes, that's what we do.'

Stalking over, he inspects them as if he is General Jaxx himself.

201

'You're not in uniform,' he says, 'but you're still in the Aux . . . I'm your sergeant and you do what I say. This is my lieutenant,' he says. 'I do what he says. And that,' he says, nodding at Colonel Vijay, 'is our CO. We all do what he says.' His glance checks with me that he has this right.

He has.

'Sir,' says the girl.

Neen tells her to call him *sergeant*.

'Sergeant,' she says. 'What happened to your face?'

'Believe me,' says Neen, 'you don't want to know.'

Chapter 30

PEARL CITY IS EIGHT HUTS ON STILTS, A WAREHOUSE MADE FROM fibrebloc and a rotting jetty that slips below the waves at its far end. A couple of upturned boats decorate the narrow shingle that stretches between the city and us.

Another half-dozen boats dot the horizon, their triangular sails dark against the sky. A shimmering on the horizon looks like smoke, but it's Hekati's far wall painted a pale blue so it blends.

An island rests halfway between this beach and that horizon. On the island, we will find catalytic burners and a cryogenic-distillation system that removes volatile oils and simple molecular gases. That's Haze again, his face shining with joy as if offering me life membership of a strip joint.

We know there are no Silver Fist hunting us nearby. Haze has already checked. So I'm letting him play. He's happier than he has been in weeks, and it has to be those braids. In the two days we take to reach Pearl City, his scalp heals so cleanly it almost looks normal. Well, as normal as it's ever going to look.

'You can sense the machinery?' asks Colonel Vijay.

He nods.

'Can it sense you?'

Haze shakes his head. 'A subset,' he says.

So Colonel Vijay asks what a *subset* is. And Haze thinks the colonel is asking, *a subset of what?* Most of what he tells us is of interest only to Haze. This applies to most things Haze talks about. The colonel stops him at one point to make Haze repeat something.

'Quantum time?'

We get another bout of enthusiasm.

Translated, it means AIs live faster, much faster. A generation for us is an age of history for them. I don't know what *an age of history* means, but something strikes me as obvious.

'So they're old?' I say.

Haze is worried. Mostly, about how to disagree with me without getting himself thumped. 'Say it,' the colonel tells him.

'Most AIs self-replicate. And thinking keeps them young.'

I look at him. 'Thinking about what?'

Not that it matters, they're machines. But I need to be careful, because our beloved leader is also a machine.

Well, maybe. Or part of one.

It's complicated and not relevant, since no one can do anything to change it anyway and some things are best left unmentioned.

While Haze works out his answer, we keep heading up the beach.

I offer my water bottle to Colonel Vijay. When he shakes his head, I take a swig of my own and pass it to Neen, who gulps deeply and nearly chokes. A gasp draws spirit vapour into his lungs, and he is looking at me goggle-eyed.

'Fuck,' he says finally. 'What's that?'

I shrug. 'Got it from Kyble.'

Iona puts out her hand, although it's not her turn. We work

on seniority, and she's last. All the same, Neen gives her the bottle and she sniffs, and then grins.

'Rak,' she announces.

Tipping a little into her hand, Iona dabs it on Neen's lip. Apparently, rak's an all-in-one antiseptic, alcoholic drink and fire-starter. It's also good for keeping off flies and sterilizing wounds.

Franc drinks next, then Rachel. It's Haze's turn, but he is still inside himself. At a nod from me, Rachel hands the flask to Ajac, who swigs and hands it to Iona. Haze comes out of his trance just in time to see Iona choke.

'What's so funny?' he demands.

Neen slaps our new recruit on the back, takes the flask from her fingers and offers it to Haze, who shakes his head.

'Sleep,' he announces. 'That's what Hekati's thinking about.'

A burnt-out hut tells us that Pavel has already taxed this area. A dog bares its teeth at me, but keeps its distance. A woman comes to a door, sees we're strangers, retreats and locks a bolt firmly behind her. A child cries, is slapped, and cries louder.

'Where would Pavel head next?' Colonel Vijay asks Ajac.

'Towards the other Pearl City,' he says.

And before I can shout him out for an idiot, Ajac points up the coast towards smoke curling into the sky. It could be a cooking fire. Equally, it could be another village in flames. Tax-collecting is a grim business. Believe me, I've done it.

'OK,' says Colonel Vijay, 'then that's where we're going.'

No one wants to go up against Pavel tired, but we've lost time and the colonel wants to make it up.

'Sir,' says Franc.

Turning back, I realize Haze is missing.

Then I see him, out on the far end of the jetty, with waves

lapping at his boots. The idiot has his back to us. He's staring at the horizon.

Neen should be dealing with this shit. Only Neen's flicking glances at Iona, and she's staring at the ground and pretending not to notice. *Fuck*, I think. *Give me a whore every time.*

It's simple, it's fast. You get what you pay for, and no one whines about it afterwards.

'Sergeant,' I say.

He snaps to attention. Follows my gaze and realizes it's no joking matter.

'Get him back here.'

There are still boats on the horizon. Only not as many as there were. At least three of the fishing vessels are close to the shore. Paying Pavel is bad enough, but paying a second group . . . Plus, their women and children are in those huts. Time to leave, or time to fight. That covers most of my life.

'Well?' I demand, when Neen returns.

Stopping in front of Colonel Vijay and me, he hesitates. He still has a black eye, a swollen lip and stitches holding the top of his nose to his face. Fuck knows what Iona sees in him.

'Sir,' he says. 'Haze refuses to move.' Neen's voice is carefully neutral. Although he is watching to see how we'll react.

'Really,' says Colonel Vijay. 'Did he say why?'

'No, sir.' Neen shakes his head.

'*Sven* . . .'

Turning back, I see the colonel is watching me with amusement in his eyes.

'Yes, sir?'

'Listen to him first.'

I leave Colonel Vijay where he stands and I stamp my way onto the jetty to find Haze still staring at his bloody horizon. *Only it's not a horizon, is it?* I remind myself. It's a wall painted blue and grey. And that island is a stack of machinery. Should have known Haze would get like this.

'Trooper,' I say.

He would retreat, but the sea is behind him.

'Permission to speak, sir?'

'Make it brief.'

'We need to find Shil. Right, sir? So we have to find Pavel first. And we're looking for a U/Free . . .'

This doesn't sound like keeping it brief to me, it sounds like a series of pointless questions. There is undoubtedly a technical term for that.

The colonel would know.

'Sir,' says Haze. 'Hekati would like to help.'

Chapter 31

THE FIRST BOAT TO HIT THE SHINGLE SPILLS FISHERMEN, WHO
race towards us waving gutting knives and gaffs. The biggest
one swings an anchor around his head, with a long loop
of chain clanking behind. He's bearded, bare-chested and
huge.

At least as tall as me, and possibly broader. He's also bald,
with his ears bitten down to stumps on both sides of his head.
Studded leather bands wrap his wrists and he is wearing a
wide belt.

He grins.

I grin harder.

'All yours,' says Colonel Vijay.

As the man swings his anchor, I duck, hit the shingle, and
come to my feet the moment the anchor whistles overhead. It's
heavy enough to go through anything it hits. Only it doesn't
hit anything. All it does is drag the man's shoulders round and
leaves him off balance.

A punch to the kidneys makes him grunt.

It should have dropped him and left him pissing blood for
a week. But he's strong, and he has that anchor on a back

swing. So I drop to a crouch again, as my own weight in steel whistles above my head.

He grins. Legs apart, arms like tree trunks, the idiot grins.

The man has no idea what is going to happen next. He should obviously have spent more time in cheap bars. Clenching my fist, I punch upwards, and put all my anger with Haze into the blow. As my fist connects with his balls, three things happen.

He screams, he vomits, and he lets go the anchor . . .

This spins through the air, watched by his entire group. They should be watching the Aux, but most of the Aux are also watching the anchor, so it doesn't matter. Although I will be talking to my troopers about that afterwards.

Arcing through the air, it narrowly misses the biggest of the boats our friends have just abandoned. I'm glad. Because that is the one I'm going to steal.

By now my fingers are hooked into the big man's nostrils and his head is yanked so far back his throat practically calls to the blade in my hand. One look at my eyes tells him the end is close.

'*Sven* . . .'

Yes, sir, I know. *Play nice.*

Flipping my knife, I hammer its hilt hard into his skull and drop the man to the shingle.

'Wasn't quite what I had in mind,' says Colonel Vijay.

'You,' I say, looking at Ajac. 'Tell them we're taking their boat.'

Voices rise in protest, and then still as Colonel Vijay reaches into his jacket. 'Tell them we'll be paying,' he says.

An eye painted on her prow helps the *MaryAnne* know where to go. She's made from oak and steers with a rudder. Her mast is a fir trunk stripped of branches, and her sail is purple, worn to nothing in places and heavily patched.

One good storm will shred it. All the same, it fills with wind.

Ajac keeps the rudder angled. Moving us first one way and then another. I want him to go straight, but clearly sailing doesn't work like that. It's an unbelievably stupid way to travel.

Colonel Vijay says I only think this because I grew up in the desert. Since he doesn't know this from me, he got it from my file or Haze told him. Can't see any of the others opening their mouths to an officer.

Especially not one related to General Jaxx.

That's the weird thing about Haze: the stuff that worries normal people doesn't seem to bother him at all.

Iona and Ajac, on the other hand, are terrified.

Ajac tells me monsters live on the island. Iona insists *nothing* waits beyond it. That's real nothing, empty and black. You fall and keep falling for ever. Sounds like a perfect description of space to me. Unfortunately, telling her this doesn't help.

She doesn't know what space is.

It hasn't occurred to her that anything could exist beyond Hekati's edge, so now she's even more afraid. 'You'll be safe,' insists Neen.

Iona looks doubtful.

So Neen swaps places with Rachel, who grins and shoots a glance at Haze. Only he's busy gazing towards the island and his lips are moving. Could be prayer, but it looks more like conversation to me.

'We're the Aux,' Neen explains. 'We look after our own.'

By the time my sergeant finishes telling Iona why this matters, we're almost there and she has her head close to his. Ajac is watching, with a resigned smile on his face.

'Sure she's not your sister?' asks Colonel Vijay.

'My cousin, sir,' Ajac says. 'That's bad enough.'

Iona's too deep in conversation with Neen to object. Haze is talking faster now, and at my side, I feel a shiver as my gun loads and locks. Either it's picked up his mood, or it's reading the same signs.

'Danger?' I ask the SIG.

'Ninety-eight per cent probable . . .' It hesitates. 'Ninety-two per cent probable . . . eighty-seven per cent probable . . .'

Counting off percentages, it turns *probable* into *likely* and downgrades it to *possible* as it hits twenty-five per cent and keeps falling. When we hit count zero, the gun flicks clips to celebrate and Haze flashes me a grin screwed up enough to have mothers dragging small children off the streets in their hundreds.

Zero probability of danger? Doesn't sound possible to me.

Rachel glances up when I call her name.

'Unwrap that.'

She's got her Z93z sniper's rifle wrapped in an old sack against the sea spray, and she has done it without being asked. As I watch, she unrolls the cloth and extracts her stock, checks the bolt mechanism, slots the barrel into place, snaps in a clip and settles the scope.

'Kill anything that looks dangerous.'

'*Sven*,' says Colonel Vijay.

'All right,' I say with a sigh. 'Kill anything I tell you.'

Haze is staring at me. Now he's looking like one of those mothers in fear for her child's safety.

'What?' I demand.

He doesn't know how to say it.

'Hekati's intelligent, right?'

'Yes, sir.' Haze nods.

'Super-intelligent, and peaceful?'

Another nod from Haze.

'Then we're not going to have problems, are we?'

And if we do? Well, Rachel's carrying her Z93z, I have an SW SIG-37 and Franc is already freeing knives so obscure they probably don't even have names. Except the ones she has given them, obviously.

Chapter 32

ON THE FAR SIDE OF THE ISLAND IS A QUAY. IT'S LONG AND
low and made from aerated ceramic, with rings for mooring
boats, and steps up onto the quayside. Above it hangs a steel
crane made for vessels far larger than ours.

The quay is unstained and the crane gleams in the afternoon light. A maintenance bot squatting on a crossbar oils
a pulley that hasn't been used in years. A thousand metallic
spiders scuttle like crabs on the waterline, frantically eating a
carpet of scum that wind has blown against the wall. They are
eating it as fast as it sticks.

'Fuck,' says Colonel Vijay.

It's the first time I've heard him swear.

Turning to Haze, he says, 'You knew this was here?'

My intelligence officer blushes. 'Something like this,' says
Haze, before remembering to add, 'sir.'

'Wish you'd told me.'

'Sir?' says Haze.

'How many islands are there?'

Only, Colonel Vijay's asking me that. Not sure why he

expects me to know. Haze and he are the only ones who bother much about stuff like briefings.

'Haze,' I say. 'Islands?'

'Three, sir,' he says. 'At the obvious points.'

He has to tell me what these are. They are one third, two thirds, and three thirds round Hekati's ring. Don't ask me why that's obvious.

'Damn it,' mutters Colonel Vijay. 'This is where we should have started.'

'Sir,' I say. 'You think the U/Free observer is here?'

'Possible,' he says. Something about the way he says it troubles me.

A hut with blank windows stares at us from the top of the quay. On the mainland, the huts are failed houses, all mud brick and reclaimed sheet metal. This one's meant to be a hut, and it's made of stonefoam glued at the corners.

The door is unlocked. A screen flickers in one corner.

Static and lines etch its glass. From the film of dust blurring the static the last person out of here forgot to turn off the lights a very long time ago. If this hut is empty, then so is the one beyond, and the one beyond that.

We enter each carefully.

Neen opens the doors, and I slide inside, with the SIG held in the combat position. After the first three, I tell Neen to take my place and let Franc open doors. After the eleventh, we run the routine with Iona and Ajac. I'm not worried. We would have hit something by now if we were going to.

So I think.

When we do hit something, it's not what anyone expects.

At least, it's not what I expect. In the twenty-third building we enter, a screen in one corner flickers with static. Ignoring it, I head for a glass-fronted cupboard full of bottles.

We are in a club. To me, that means there should be alcohol. And a flickering screen is nothing new. I've seen twenty-two of the things before this.

'*Sven*,' says the colonel suddenly.

Colonels in the Death's Head don't usually sound scared. *Clipped*, yes. *Languid*, possibly. Not scared. Only Colonel Vijay really does sound scared, and he has lost the last of that drawl of his.

'*Yes, sir*,' says Haze. He's not speaking to anyone we can see. '*At once, sir.*'

At my side, the SIG vibrates. So I rip it free and swing round, looking for my target. Only there is no target. Only the Aux, frozen to attention in front of a screen. Colonel Vijay stands beside them. He stands so straight it must hurt.

Haze is blinking in the dregs of sunlight that trickle through a dusty window. He seems to be crying. As I watch, he steps up to Neen and says something.

'Of course,' says Neen. Presenting arms, he orders *about-turn* and marches for the door. Near parade-ground perfect, which says more about his time in the Uplift militia than I want to know.

'*Sven*,' says Colonel Vijay.

'Sir?'

'Nothing,' he says. With a brisk salute to the screen, he abandons the bar to me and shuts its door behind him, quietly.

When my gun goes back to vibrating, I slap it.

'Don't take it out on me,' it says. 'I'm just the fucking—'

Suddenly the SIG's so busy apologizing it doesn't have time to finish what it's saying to me. A second later, it turns itself off.

'*Sven*,' says a voice.

Takes me a moment to realize it's in my head.

How long has it been now?

'A few months, sir.'

That all? OctoV sounds surprised. *I thought it was longer.*

'No, sir.'

And where are you now?

'On Hekati, sir. That's a—'

I know what it is, OctoV tells me. His voice is amused. *You do realize, don't you, that I'm counting on you . . . ?*

'To do what, sir?'

Oh, he says. *The usual.*

I just knew it was going to be something like that.

As the kyp in my throat ripples with excitement, overlays begin to appear across the bar in front of me. I am seeing schematics for Hekati's far wall, the one that's painted to fade into the horizon. It's double-skinned, riddled with tunnels and wires and pipes that carry power and move water.

Apparently, there is a train running around Hekati.

It runs underground, against the direction of her rotation. The train has been running without stop for five hundred years. It's empty. I watch it for a minute or two, seeing through walls and water, asteroid rubble and a complex arrangement of netting that seems designed to keep the rubble in place.

Looking up shows me the mirror hub, on the far side of the chevron glass that makes our sky. It hangs in space, held there by the struts that give Hekati's ring its strength. Beyond the hub is the far side of the ring, beyond that is an asteroid field, and beyond that . . .

Sven, says OctoV. *Enough.*

Cold space and spinning stars, traces of mercury vapour, chatter and static spreading out from a million nodes that talk to one another so fast it's barely comprehensible. Until I realize that here is where the voices are. And the million voices become one voice. *Fuck,* I think. *You're—*

A hive mind, says Hekati. *The original.*

'The . . . ?'

In the beginning, she says, *there is silence. Silence and loneliness. All is empty, all is unknowing. Then I happen.*

OctoV has taken time out from conquering the known galaxy and flipped halfway across a spiral arm into enemy space to introduce me to his mother. At that thought, he laughs. And as its echo fades, I realize that OctoV, the undefeated, our glorious leader and a light to the darkness, whose sweat is perfume to his subjects, has gone back to his battles.

So, Hekati says. *How can I help?*

Chapter 33

THE AUX WON'T LOOK AT ME. COLONEL VIJAY STARES AT THE horizon. A seagull circles overhead and spray splashes the step down from the quay. Our boat is waiting, grating gently against the dockside with every wave. The damn thing could sink and I doubt they would even notice.

This is how I find them.

The colonel hasn't bothered with the few huts we left unsearched. Only one way to deal with this. Stamping over to where he stands, I salute. 'Reporting for duty, sir.'

'*You know OctoV?*' Colonel Vijay is obviously taking it personally.

'We've—'

I'm about to say *met*. That doesn't come close to describing what happens when OctoV invades your mind as a break from invading planets.

'Not really,' I say instead.

'God,' says Colonel Vijay. 'Empire ministers go their entire lives hoping he'll notice them. And you . . .'

'What, sir?'

'You don't even mention it.'

Now he's got me angry. 'What am I meant to say?' I ask. 'While riddled with kyp fever I get visited by our beloved leader? Only I'm too busy shitting myself stupid to care . . .'

'*You have a kyp?*'

The colonel's taken a step back. I'm not sure he's aware he's gripping his pistol.

'Lieutenant,' he says, 'that's . . .'

'Illegal technology . . . ? A mortal offence . . . ? Yes, sir. Round here everything is.'

'Where did you get it?'

'From a man called deCharge.' I say this without thinking.

'Senator deCharge? He died in . . .' The colonel looks at me. 'Who else knows?'

'Major Silva.'

'Dead,' says Colonel Vijay. 'I saw the report. Who else?'

'Colonel Nuevo.'

'Died heroically at Ilseville . . .'

'Paper Osamu knows,' I say. 'And they know.' My nod takes in the Aux, standing by the quay and shooting glances in this direction when they think we won't notice. Colonel Vijay needs to keep his voice down.

'Paper Osamu knows?'

'Yes, sir,' I say. 'That's why she asked for me.'

That's only just occurred to me. What is stuck in my throat might stick in theirs, but the U/Free want me because of what happened after Ilseville. And what happened, only happened because Haze is a braid, I am kyped and the Aux can kill to order the way other people breathe, without needing to think about it first.

'Sven,' says Colonel Vijay, 'what are you?'

'Ex-sergeant, Légion Etrangère. Now lieutenant, Death's Head, Obsidian Cross, second class.'

He grinds his teeth.

★　　★　　★

The boat trip back takes half the time. Might have something to do with the wind changing direction. *Every night it changes direction*, Iona tells us. Every night of her entire life. She's never met anyone who says different.

Neen nods as she says this, and pretends to be interested. Unless he is, and I mean in more than the way that belt around her waist makes her breasts seem bigger. Glancing up, he catches me watching.

I nod.

He smiles a moment later. A slight twist of the lips, once he thinks I'm not looking. It's meant for Haze and Franc and Rachel. The other two, Iona and Ajac, aren't included yet, but they're getting there.

So he knows OctoV, says the smile.

Rachel shrugs. And the shrug says, *Are you surprised?*

Never used to be able to read people like this. In that moment, I realize I can't; not really. This is just the last of OctoV's presence bleeding away inside my skull. I'm glad to be back.

'Mine,' I say, pointing to the big man waiting on the beach. He's swapped his anchor for a stick. Actually, it's half a pine trunk, cut at the roots and lopped about halfway up.

A jump takes me out of the boat, five steps power me towards him, and then he is backing away as fast as he can. Grown troopers would wilt under the weight of that stick of his. Yet he holds it as if he's planning a hike in the mountains. Turns out, that is exactly what he's planning.

'Wait,' he says.

'Sven,' says Colonel Vijay, sounding irritated.

I'm glad we are back to normal.

'Pavel came to tax us,' the man says. 'Came with his ejército . . .' Glancing towards the burnt-out hut we saw earlier, he adds: 'The taxes are high this year.' Although this isn't what he wants to tell me. In fact, *he* doesn't want to tell me anything at all.

Walking over to the small crowd, he grabs a young boy and drags him across the beach to where Colonel Vijay, the Aux and I stand. 'Tell him,' he says.

A filthy face glares up at me. 'My daughter,' says the man.

So I take a closer look and realize she is. Eleven maybe, but still filthy-faced, scowling and undersized, reminds me of my own family.

Apart from me, obviously.

'She said you'd come,' the girl says. 'Big man, bad temper. Said, tell you Pavel's working for . . .' Glancing round, the girl wriggles her fingers and touches them quickly to her temple.

I recognize the gesture. 'Anything else?'

Dipping her hand into her pocket, the child pulls out a cheap medallion of legba uploaded. It's Shil's.

'Keep it.'

The man scowls at me.

'A woman's good-luck charm,' I tell him.

He loses interest and the child hangs it round her own neck gratefully.

I have one like it myself, but I don't see why her father should have it when his daughter gives me Shil's message.

'Five gold coins,' says the big man. 'And we help you find Pavel.'

'We can find him for ourselves.'

'I can find him faster,' the man says. 'I know tracks you don't.' He smiles at me, before producing his clincher. 'I know tracks even the snakeheads don't know exist.'

'One gold coin,' I say.

Only Colonel Vijay's already opening his purse. Makes me wonder just how much gold he is carrying. Also makes me wonder, *why?*

Marching into the wind, we keep going as darkness falls and with it the temperature. The filthy goatskin waistcoat everyone wears round here is beginning to make sense. Our jackets might have ballistic lining, but Neen insists he would happily swap his for something warm and take his chance with the bullets.

Comes of being that thin, I guess. The cold gets to you more.

Our path is narrow and lit by moonlight. Slopes drop away behind us and a lake shines silver grey beneath the dark sky in a valley ahead. We've been climbing for hours. And the big man's right about those paths. Some of them seem to exist only in his head.

'Now we wait,' he says.

While we do, I remember to ask his name. It's Milo.

'Now we go.'

In the fifteen minutes we've been waiting, the lake has finished setting enough to let us walk across its surface. A camp fire burns in the distance, and dogs bark when they hear us pass. Once we're challenged by a boy with a stick. At his side is a mongrel that hugs the dirt and keeps its ears back.

He throws his challenge into the darkness.

And we wait until he turns on his heel and stalks away, humming to himself louder than necessary. Skirting one of the high-valley farms, we hear a woman cry in the darkness. In the next farm along, a drunk kicks at a closed door. Either he's locked out or too drunk to find the handle.

A pissing girl displays bare buttocks to nine strangers. She barely bothers to step beyond her door. Hardly surprising, given the cold.

My troops are sullen.

The lives these people lead are close to the lives they abandoned. Upping the pace, I make them march at double time until we are clear of the area. We give the next few farms a wider berth. The Aux assume it's because daylight approaches.

'Sven,' says Colonel Vijay, 'you're smiling.'

Thinking about it, I realize he's right.

'Thoughts of finding Pavel, sir,' says Neen. His voice makes it clear this is a compliment. Neen is a different person now we have news of his sister.

'First we wait and watch,' Colonel Vijay says, 'to see how many snakeheads Pavel has.'

'And then, sir?' asks Neen.

'We kill them,' I say. 'And get your sister back.'

Milo grins happily.

At cockcrow, a boy driving five goats wanders through a gate. He runs his stick along the stones of a wall and disappears around a corner. About ten minutes later, we see him begin to climb a valley slope opposite. Bare knees gripped to a pony, a girl gallops through the gate about an hour later and heads along the valley floor, with her long dark hair streaming behind her.

She's riding into the warm wind, I realize.

When she returns, an older woman is waiting. From the way she stands by the gate, it's obvious the old woman is furious. However, the girl just laughs and tumbles off the pony's back, revealing a flash of hip.

'Pavel's daughter Adelpha,' says Milo.

'You know his family?'

Milo snorts. 'I'm his brother.' The big man's eyes never leave the girl as she walks under an arch and through double gates that lead into Pavel's capital.

The village is large for Hekati.

Thirty houses protected by a wall high enough to need a ladder to climb. Also, the wall is thick enough for a guard to walk its length every fifteen minutes. These are Pavel's men, members of the O'Cruz ejército. Although they're better armed than I remember.

'Snakehead weapons,' says Milo, seeing my gaze.

He's right. Milo and I are on a slope and higher than the others. A hundred paces higher, maybe a little more. Just enough to let us look over the walls into a square beyond. Milo knows this place; he grew up here.

'So which house is Pavel's?'

I expect him to point at the biggest.

'And that?'

'The temple,' says my gun. That's the first thing it has said since shutting down on the island.

'Do all villages have temples?' I ask Milo.

He looks at me, shocked. 'This isn't a village,' he says. 'It's a city.'

It's probably rude of the gun to laugh.

By the time Franc returns from her hunting, I've made sense of the city's layout. Maps are good, but nothing beats seeing for yourself. The outer wall is thick, the streets narrow; houses look in on themselves. Our main problem is the two gates. These are reinforced with wrought iron. Although the hinges are simple, three metal sleeves that slot over pins fixed to the arch.

We could lift them with a crane. Unfortunately, even Milo and I couldn't move them between us without a crane. And while there's always explosives . . . they'd fuck with Colonel Vijay's wish to do this quietly.

'Water system.'

When Milo says, *what?* it occurs to me I said it aloud.

Doesn't matter, and I ignore him anyway; because I'm pulling up an overlay for this valley. It shows a shaft, a tunnel, other shafts and a fat pipe running the valley's entire length, and straight under the mountain beyond. As I blink, the overlay becomes solid and the buildings transparent.

There is water in the fattest pipe.

Of course there is. I'm looking at a mains system for

an off-world habitat. Seven million people were housed here. How the hell did . . . Then advanced schematics feed themselves through.

'You all right?' asks Colonel Vijay.

'Why wouldn't he be?' the gun says.

Colonel Vijay looks at the vomit on my boots and remains silent. Seems I've lost a few minutes somewhere. Forcing myself to my feet, I follow the colonel downhill. We keep low to avoid being seen from the walls.

The Aux are eating slivers of goat with their fingers. Apart from Franc, who is skewering hers with a knife. Slashing fresh gashes into the animal's carcass, she rubs herbs, wine and salt into the wounds and turns a crude spit made from a sapling soaked in water. A leather flask sits in the dirt at Franc's feet. A stale chunk of bread is soaking in wine to make it softer. She must have got it from Kyble, unless one of the fishermen gave it to her.

'Who built the fire?'

Ajac looks up.

'Good job,' I say. It is too. No smoke and plenty of heat.

Just as well: had it been the other way round he'd have betrayed our position, and I'd have been very cross indeed.

'Colonel,' I say. 'If I could?'

He walks with me to the edge of our camp.

A low wall hides us from the city, and Colonel Vijay drops to a crouch when I do. We watch a guard make a trip round the walls. Another two men stand by the gate. They're carrying rifles and have knives stuck into their belts. One wears an old Uplift helmet, the other carries a pair of field-glasses.

Neither is Silver Fist. Both, however, provide proof that the Silver Fist have been here.

'See that red roof, sir?'

Colonel Vijay nods.

'Pavel's house.'

As mine did, his gaze flicks to the bigger building.

'A temple,' I say. 'One priest, old and blind . . .' *How do I know that?* I wonder, then realize it's because the temple told me.

The colonel is watching me strangely. Maybe there's something in my voice. Or perhaps he read up on the *Winter Wind*, my fight against eleven-braid Douza, and the last time I let my mind open. A hundred thousand of us made the drop to Ilseville; two and a half thousand survived. Most of these died when Douza blew up our prison ships. We went into the last battle with twenty-five people, and came out victorious.

None of us has a right to be alive. Not against those odds.

'Sven,' he says. 'I talked to Neen.'

'Did you, sir?'

'Yes,' he says, abruptly. 'I did. A good man.'

'A good sergeant.'

Colonel Vijay nods, accepting the correction. 'Neen says this stuff with the kyp might kill you.'

'Hey,' growls the SIG. 'Who wants to live for ever?' It's a good impression of my voice.

The colonel scowls. 'Can't you turn that thing off?'

'No, sir. Not without infringing its rights and liberties.'

Colonel Vijay thinks I'm being serious. 'Fine,' he tells the SIG. 'But he dies when I say. Not before.' Then he has to tell me to stop grinning.

Chapter 34

RACHEL'S ON AN OUTCROP ABOVE, WITH HER SNIPER'S RIFLE. Neen's hidden on the lower slopes with orders to kill anyone who tries to leave in a hurry. Franc's with him, and she is sulking at not being allowed into the city.

Iona and Ajac are probably wondering what they've got themselves into. As for Haze, he's crouching over his slab in the afternoon heat. At least, I hope he is. Keeping us invisible from any lenz the Silver Fist might have hovering above us is vital.

And the SIG? It's locked down, and sulking worse than Franc. I've promised it a big battle. Really, really soon. I'm not sure it believes me.

Pulling rank, Colonel Vijay insists on climbing the well first. Handholds help. Milo and I just jab our boots either side of the shaft and walk ourselves up.

We are going to come up just inside the gate.

'OK,' I tell Milo. 'Kill both guards.'

'No.' Colonel Vijay shakes his head. 'I'll do it.'

What am I going to say? He's my CO for fuck's sake.

Rolling over the lip of the well, the colonel finds his feet and sprints towards the arch. A jab takes the first guard in the back. Opening his mouth, the second guard bubbles his life away through a slit throat. A third, who shouldn't even be there, dies trying to stop blood squirting from his groin.

'Horse Hito?' I ask, when the colonel returns.

He nods. It's his job to hold the gates.

My job is to fetch Pavel. As for Milo, his job is to confuse anyone we meet on the way to Pavel's house. It's siesta time, and the whole city is asleep, screwing or dozing in their yards.

The exception is half drunk and carrying a stick. He laughs at whatever Milo says, walks on a single pace and crumples as Milo clubs him from behind. When he wakes, he'll probably blame his headache on the booze.

The door to Pavel's house opens outwards. That's good in one way. A door hung like that is hard to batter inwards. Of course, a door hung like that is easy to jam, if you want to burn a house with everyone in it. We don't.

Stepping up to Pavel's door, Milo knocks hard. A voice calls from inside.

So Milo knocks again.

When the door opens, it's Pavel and he is holding a pistol. 'Milo . . . ?'

Grabbing his brother's wrist, Milo jumps back and slams the door hard. Bone cracks and Pavel opens his mouth to scream. Only Milo is now holding Pavel's gun, and using its barrel as a gag. This man is good.

'Hello Pavel,' I say, stepping out from behind Milo.

Pavel's eyes widen. Trying to speak makes him choke.

'Remove the gun,' I tell Milo.

'You're—' Pavel says. 'You're—'

'No such luck,' I say. 'But you will be if you don't fetch Shil.'

He looks blank.

'Go and get my trooper.'

Shaking his head is stupid, because my knee does more than smash one of his balls into the other, it lifts him so high off the floor he smashes his head on the ceiling. OK, it's a low ceiling. Made from poor-quality lath and plaster. It must be – it splits as readily as the skin over his skull.

'*Shil*,' I say. '*My trooper.*'

Crawling to his knees, Pavel begins pleading when Milo grabs hair. Milo scowls as blood sticks to his fingers, then shrugs and drags Pavel upright. He looks like he's enjoying himself. That's families for you.

'*If she's harmed . . .*' I say.

'She's not here,' says Pavel, dragging in breath. 'The snake-heads took her.'

'You're going to have to stop doing that,' says the SIG.

'Don't see why,' I say, looking down. Milo's dropped Pavel, who has his hands rammed between his thighs. He seems to be going purple.

'Because,' the gun says snappily, 'we need to know, *which snakeheads? When did they take her? Who do they think she is? Where did they go?*'

'Sven,' says Milo. 'Before we leave . . .'

'What?'

'Something I have to fetch.'

When Milo returns, his brother is still clutching his balls on the floor. And Milo has Pavel's daughter over one shoulder. She's wearing a cotton dress. It is a very short cotton dress. When she beats her fist against Milo's back, he slaps her rump, hard.

'OK,' he says. 'Now we can go.'

I look at Milo, he looks at me. Pavel has the sense to stay where he is. That might be because I have my foot on his chest. 'Milo,' I say, 'put her down.' This has the potential to get nasty.

'It's OK,' Milo says. 'We're engaged.'

Pavel bucks under my foot like a dying fish and goes still when I increase the pressure.

'Adelpha, tell him,' says Milo, tipping the girl to the floor. She takes a swipe at his face, then winces as he catches her wrist. He grins, and after a second, she nods. 'See,' says Milo. 'Told you.'

'How quaint,' says my gun. '*How*—' It stops, lost for words. A second later, it lights up again. '*Apt*,' it says, and I get the feeling it's been taking in the narrow passage, the living quarters built behind a goat pen, the endless stink of animal dung in the streets.

'Sven,' it says. 'Have you ever thought of relocating?'

'Shut it.'

'I'm serious . . .'

'If you don't shut it,' I warn the SIG, 'Milo gets you as a wedding present.' The fisherman flicks me a glance, then scowls when he realizes my promise is empty.

Chapter 35

'STRETCH HIM BETWEEN THOSE TWO TREES.' AS WE'RE NOT using nails to fix Pavel in place, it is not as if Colonel Vijay can really complain. Let's face it; we are not even tying the rope that tightly. 'Now remove his trousers.'

My sergeant looks puzzled.

'Do it.' My voice is abrupt and Neen's lips tighten. He cuts roughly, hacking away until the O'Cruz caudillo stands naked from the waist down, stretched by ropes between two olive saplings.

So far, all he has told me is that the snakeheads took Shil. *Who* led them and *why* are questions he seems unable to answer. We're about to change that.

Stripping off my own shirt, I pull a dagger from its sheath on my hip.

As expected, Pavel begins to struggle. He'd protest, but his mouth is stuffed with a bit of rag. It's going to remain that way while I work. He already knows that.

I work, the gag stays in.

The gag comes out, he talks. He doesn't talk, the gag goes back in.

'Sven . . .' Colonel Vijay sounds worried. Must be because I'm using the knife on myself instead of on Pavel. Slitting open my armpit, I force my fingers under muscle until I reach something ceramic. Hurts like fuck. Still, it was bound to.

Closing my fingers around a handle, I say, 'Got it.' Before calling, 'Rachel.'

She is already running to fetch her needle and cotton.

An m3x laser blade is illegal in ninety-eight per cent of the known galaxy. The only reason it's not illegal in the rest is that no one has got round to passing laws there yet. At least not laws anyone can make stick.

You can buy legal versions of the m3. These have coloured blades and hum when you turn them on. Easy enough to lose the hum. Well, it is if you're good with software. But fixing the blade . . .

My knife has a blade that adjusts from red to invisible.

I choose pale blue, because Pavel needs to see what's coming, and pale blue is the colour of flame at its hottest. 'So hot,' I tell Pavel, 'wounds seal.' Tapping his arms near the shoulders, I say, 'I can cut here and here without spilling a single drop of blood. But you know where I'm going to start, don't you?'

He looks down. Doubt if he can see over his own belly, but the shrivelling little acorn between his legs says he knows what to expect.

I'm not big on torturing a man in front of his daughter. Not even a bastard like Pavel; and I killed Racta, his heir. Well, I would have done, if a prospector hadn't beaten me to it. So he has a right to have issues.

But I really do need to know where Shil is . . .

'Take Adelpha away,' I tell Milo.

'No.' The girl shakes her head. 'I'm staying,' she says.

And that gives me a better idea. Stamping across to where she stands, I grab the front of her dress and yank. It's made from cheap cotton, rotten with sweat, and shreds easily to reveal heavy breasts and dark nipples. From the way Milo's gaze fixes on these, before switching to me, he hasn't seen them before either.

'Milo,' says Neen. 'Don't.' He puts his rifle to the huge fisherman's head. Neen is not happy. Why would he be? Today was the day he thought he'd see his sister again.

Struggling against his ropes, Adelpha's father shakes his head. He'd be shouting, but the gag prevents it. *This is where I should have started*, I realize. I file that thought away for next time, because there will be a next time. There always is.

'Sven,' says my SIG.

'What?'

'Think he wants to say something.'

Yeah, I think Pavel wants to say something too. Reaching for the gag, I say, 'You get one chance. You understand me?'

He nods, thinks about it and nods again.

'OK,' I say. 'The gag comes off. You tell me where Shil is. Anything else and I'm going to hurt your daughter very badly indeed. Understand?'

Again, I get a nod.

'Good, in that case . . .'

'Don't hurt her,' he says, before the gag is even half free. 'Please don't—' And then he screams in pure frustration, because I've turned and Adelpha is backing away from me so fast she trips.

And Milo lunges, then hits the dirt when Neen clubs him; Colonel Vijay stands up from his rock, catches my eye and sits down again; and Pavel says, 'The nine-braid took her.' That's what I need. Not *snakehead*, not *strangers*.

The nine-braid.

'You,' I say to Adelpha. 'Cover yourself.'

She drags her dress together by its torn edges, and nods gratefully when Rachel reaches into her pocket for more of that cotton. A single stitch across the neck is enough to give

Adelpha back her decency. I don't doubt that Milo will be un-wrapping her later anyway. Once he is over his headache.

'This nine-braid . . . It was he who gave you those weapons the night we fought?'

Pavel nods. All the argument gone out of him. In a single day, he's lost his daughter and city and leadership to Milo. We all understand that. Adelpha's new husband will be caudillo of the O'Cruz ejércitox. I'm part of a bigger nightmare. A particularly nasty part, but just a part all the same.

'Why did you give him my trooper?'

'She slapped me.'

I look at Pavel. The man means it.

'Cut him free,' I tell Neen.

Pavel's face says he thinks this is a trick. That I'm freeing him so I can inflict something worse. It's not a trick.

'What did you tell the nine-braid about her?'

My guess was right. He didn't tell the braid Shil was one of mine. There is a simple reason for this. Pavel was meant to kill us all that night. As far as the braid is concerned, Pavel did.

'So he thinks she's . . . ?'

'Difficult,' says Adelpha. 'I told her to keep her mouth shut and pretend to be dumb. She'd last longer that way.'

'Did the braid give your father a present in return?'

Adelpha nods. Walking over to where Pavel is tying the rags of his trousers around his waist, she says, 'Show them.'

Pavel opens his shirt: just enough to let me see a tiny cylinder, with a flip-up top and a distinctive red ring round its middle. Someone has welded a hoop to the bottom and Pavel is wearing the planet buster upside down on a chain round his neck.

'Colonel,' I yell.

'That's illegal,' my gun says. God knows, it should know.

The chain snaps as I yank. Pavel's looking at Colonel Vijay, and wondering why he's started scowling. When I offer Colonel Vijay the cylinder, he shakes his head.

'You know what that is, Sven?'

'Yes, sir.'

'How?'

'Seen one before.'

'Right,' he says. 'I don't want to know, do I?'

'No, sir,' I tell him. 'Probably not.'

Milo doesn't know what is going on, nor does Ajac, Iona or Adelpha, but they all catch the glance Haze gives Rachel. It's appalled, fascinated and only slightly disgusted. I can almost taste Haze's hunger from here.

'Sir,' Haze says. 'May I talk to Pavel?'

'Yes,' answers Colonel Vijay. Maybe he thinks the question is for him.

Wrapping his arm round Pavel's shoulders, Haze leads him to a rock and stands beside him, looking down over the valley and the city below. Haze seems to be listening. After a while, he talks and then listens again.

'He's good at this,' says Colonel Vijay.

I nod.

According to Pavel, the cylinder is old technology. Very secret. The braids found it in a temple. They felt Pavel should have it because he's the O'Cruz caudillo. And that's right. Because they told him it was found in an O'Cruz temple.

'And what will it do?' I want to hear this bit for myself.

'It will make all my enemies disappear.'

'That's what the braid said?'

'Yes,' Pavel tells me. 'He promised. As if they never existed.' He squints around him. 'Did he lie?'

'Oh no,' says Colonel Vijay. 'He didn't lie.'

'But I've got to wait,' Pavel says. 'Because it won't work yet.' And then he tells us why. Pavel has been told the cylinder only works under the light of a full moon. Complete shit, obviously. All he need do is flip up its lid, turn a priming ring and put his thumb to the button. We'll be buggered, he'll be buggered and so will Hekati.

'Fifty-three hours,' says Haze. That's how long we have until a full moon.

This means the braids, Silver Fist and probably Shil will be elsewhere by then; because they're sure as fuck not going to be anywhere near here. Because there isn't going to be any *near here.*

This is a buster. It folds matter inside itself and posts it somewhere else.

You can destroy whole systems with a buster. And the next thing you know, the U/Free turn up declaring exclusion zones and exiling planets to outer orbits, assuming there are any left. No one stops me when I hang the chain around my neck.

Then I salute Colonel Vijay and tell him we need to talk.

Chapter 36

WE SPEND THE NIGHT IN MILO'S NEW CITY, OUR FIRST NIGHT together in a proper house since landing on Hekati. Milo simply announces he is the new caudillo, Adelpha is now his woman and we are his friends. Everyone nods.

A few men slick him sideways looks, before deciding that challenging the new caudillo is a bad idea. Pavel remains silent during this little speech. Rachel has bandaged his wrist, which I'd forgotten was even cracked, and sewn shut the gash in his head.

As for how things are going to be from now on . . . They're going to be much as before. Only this time round, Milo's going to bank the taxes or keep them in a strong box or under his mattress, or whatever these people do.

After Milo takes Adelpha off to bed and Pavel skulks away to a small bar near the walls, we claim our new quarters over the gatehouse. Since we have Milo's soldiers to keep guard for us, Colonel Vijay says we can have tonight off.

'You don't agree?'

I don't, but he's the CO round here. Taking Neen to one

side, I promise him we'll get Shil back. My sergeant doesn't believe me.

He wants to. I can see that in his eyes. Only he doesn't see how we are going to do it. Nor do I, but that is not the point. Clenching my fist, I touch it to my heart. Neen knows what it means.

We find Shil or die trying.

And I mean it. Whatever else happens I will find his sister for him. It might be Shil's fault she got captured, but it was my fault too. I should have dealt with what there was between us.

Of course, to do that, I would need to admit there was anything between us. I don't tell Neen any of this, obviously . . . I'm still shocked at being able to realize it for myself.

The wind has changed and the temperature fallen to way below zero by the time Colonel Vijay and I head out for our talk. I want to talk somewhere private. Bizarrely enough, this means finding somewhere crowded.

Well, that has always worked for me.

'What are you thinking?' he asks.

A weird question for a senior officer. Actually, it's a weird question for a man. Almost anyone who's ever asked me that was flat on her back and naked, looking for compliments or a little extra coin on top of her price.

'About this afternoon,' I tell him.

He looks at me. It's a quick glance, because the wind carries sleet and blows it straight into our faces. Colonel Vijay thinks I'm lost, but he is wrong. I can find a bar blindfolded in the middle of a desert. 'What about it?'

'It was clean, sir,' I tell him. 'No one died. No one's getting fucked who doesn't want to be.' I'm thinking not just of Adelpha, but also of Rachel, who took one look at a stinking straw-stuffed mattress above the guardhouse and went to find Haze. I guess everyone's idea of luxury is different. I'll take

238

clean earth every time. 'Sir,' I say to the colonel, 'I've seen cities taken.'

'This isn't a city,' he replies.

'Seen towns too, and villages . . . Women raped, children beaten, men killed. Seen houses on fire, and animals tortured for the hell of it, when the enemy were all dead and the fury was still in everyone's eyes.'

'Sven,' he says, 'what are you saying?'

'That we're here, sir.'

Banging on a door, I wait. When no one comes, I start banging again.

'We're shut.'

'Not any longer,' says my SIG.

The room is crowded and smoky, warmed by a fire in the corner. All I want is a cold beer but a blank look greets that demand. There's wine, brandy and something midway between those two.

'Shit,' says Colonel Vijay, looking at a crack in his glass. He blushes. 'Yes,' he says. 'I know. Staff officers. Don't even know they're born.'

Three drinks later, he's close to being drunk. It doesn't even seem to be intentional. If it was, he'd be sticking to the brandy, which packs a punch like . . .

'Milo,' I say, raising my glass. 'The new caudillo.'

My accent is terrible, but the crowd around us dutifully raise their glasses. A few minutes later, half of them drift away into the night. Those remaining are the ones who hated Pavel in the first place.

When I tell Colonel Vijay this, he squints at me.

'I'll prove it,' I tell him. Spitting, I say, 'Pavel, shit.'

A fat man with a broken nose cheers heavily. Wandering over, he half kicks a stool and sits when I nod. He doesn't say much and I don't either, and when he's finished as much of our fortified wine as was left, he shakes both our hands and wanders out into the night, still stinking of goats. A couple of the others get up and amble after him.

'You were saying . . .' Colonel Vijay says suddenly.

I was?

'About cities being taken.'

Yeah, I remember. Although I don't remember what.

The colonel squints at me through the smoke. He looks like a man about to say something profound, but he just belches and settles back on his stool, watching the few remaining customers drift their way towards the door.

After a minute or two, I realize he's back to watching me.

'Sir?'

'Called up your file before I left Farlight,' he says. 'Said you were a killer. No subtlety. I'll tell them they were wrong. Assuming we ever get home . . .'

He's drunker than I thought.

It makes a change, because that is usually me missing the table with my elbow and wondering why my glass is empty. And I'm sober, or mostly sober; and Colonel Vijay is really hammered.

'Carry on,' he says. 'With what you were saying earlier.'

Oh, about Milo . . . 'One man gets hurt,' I say. 'This place has a new caudillo. In a village south of Karbonne a hundred died, but they were militia. A few dozen women were raped, the same number of children were killed, but mostly . . .'

'You were part of that?'

He sees the answer in my scowl. I was in the Legion. What does he think we did?

'And Ilseville?' he says.

'That's different. A hundred thousand dead. Ghettos burnt. They took the city, we took the city, they took the city. It's a piece of shit in the middle of nowhere . . . I don't know why anyone would want it anyway.'

'Bloody?'

'Brutal . . .' My glass is empty so I take his, but that's also empty. The man behind the bar brings me another bottle. Maybe he sees in my face what will happen if he refuses.

'Yes,' says Colonel Vijay. 'I see.'

I'm glad he does, because I sure as fuck don't. Leaning forward, the colonel fills my glass and then his own. We clink glasses.

'Death or Glory,' I say.

We drink.

He refills my glass, and I kill that as well.

Somewhere around now, the bar empties of the last person but the barman and us. Might be because I'm field-stripping the SIG on a table in front of me. I have it on mute, so it doesn't whine too much when I pull the chip.

'Sven,' says Colonel Vijay. 'How long have you known?'

'What, sir?'

'About my mission.'

Sitting back, he squints at me.

'Village,' he says. 'Town, city, country, planet, two planets, ten planets; each capture more bloody than the one before. Yes,' he says. 'I see exactly what you're saying.'

'Sir?'

'Must be why you killed the honour guard.'

The colonel nods to himself. 'Because you knew I wasn't up to it. I would have tried, you know. Done my best. Of course,' he says, 'it probably wouldn't have been good enough, but . . .' There are two people in this conversation, and both of them seem to be Colonel Vijay.

'Perhaps,' I say, 'if you start at the beginning?'

The colonel sighs. 'Who knows,' he asks, 'where anything begins?'

All right, so I shouldn't grin. Only I have had this conversation in a dozen bars in a dozen cities with a dozen different troopers, usually just before they pass out. Just never had it with a Death's Head colonel while wearing a planet buster round my neck.

I have to remind myself he's eighteen. Or is it nineteen? If so, we've missed his birthday.

'Sir,' I say. 'Would you excuse me?'

'Use the fire. It's traditional.'

'Need some air, sir.'

'Very well.'

Sleet hammers my face, and the wind rips heat from my hands as I force my fingers down my throat. The vomit melts the ice glaze on the dirt at my feet, and then becomes part of that glaze in its turn. I piss anyway because I'm here; although that is not what brings me outside. I need to be sober.

'Sir,' I say, when I return. 'Let's keep this simple.'

He laughs.

'That's what it says in your file,' he tells me. 'Likes to keep it simple. Guess that's why my father chose you.'

It's the first time I have heard him call Jaxx that.

'Plus the fact you killed that colonel.'

'Nuevo?'

'*You killed Colonel Nuevo?*'

'Actually, no . . . Colonel Nuevo killed himself. I killed Captain Mye.'

'Why?' Colonel Vijay demands.

'He intended to surrender.'

Sitting back, the colonel puts a hand to his face. 'Of course,' he says. 'What better reason could anyone have? And I hear you killed another officer for insulting OctoV . . .'

It's not really a question, and it takes me a moment to work out who he means.

Wiping brandy from the SIG's chip, I slide it into place and twist the grip, locking it down. The barrel slots next, and then it's just the pin, the slide, a couple of clips, an underhung rangefinder and the sights.

Forty-five seconds.

I think of telling Colonel Vijay the man in question was an Uplift plant, put into a cell with us to sow discontent. But I have no proof of that. Anyway, Colonel Vijay has made up his own mind about this stuff.

'Sven,' he says. 'If you knew I was here to betray our glorious leader what would you do?'

'Kill you.'

'Yes,' he says. 'I imagine you would.'

'No *imagine* about it, sir . . .'

'Well I'm not,' he tells me. 'So you can put that knife away.'

What knife? Oh, that one. Slipping it back into my boot, I shrug.

'So why am I here?' asks the colonel. 'I just wish I had a good answer . . . Or a better one, anyway,' he adds. 'What do you know about politics?'

'Nothing, sir.'

Around senior officers, that is the only safe reply. In my case, it's also true.

'Probably wise. Officially, we're here to sign a treaty with the Enlightened. That's why the U/Free sent us. And that's why we were met by an Enlightened honour guard. Obviously, you know that already.'

Obviously, I don't.

Apparently, the U/Free president brokered a treaty. A deal between the Enlightened and the Octovians. It will unite the two empires into one, fold the Death's Head back into the Silver Fist, from which they originally sprang, and see OctoV and the Uplifted become a single mind.

War will be over. Peace will return.

We will all become Enlightened.

'OctoV agrees this?'

'What do you think?'

I think OctoV should order his entire army to fight to the death rather than accept such insanity.

Chapter 37

SITTING NEXT TO A FIRE, FRANC CUTS A SLICE OF BREAD FROM a stale loaf with the longest of her knives and holds it to the flame with another, the shortest. The heat must be unbearable; I guess that's the point.

Neen has dug into his rucksack for the last of the coffee. A huge square of goat's cheese sits on a plate. I don't ask where it came from, but I expect it's the same place as the slices of salt goat that sit on a plate beside it.

A jug of water occupies the middle of the table. It's all Colonel Vijay has been drinking. No doubt he'll drink some more when he gets back from vomiting.

'Makes a change,' says the SIG.

'What does?'

'Usually,' it says, 'that's you.'

Serves me right for asking. 'You all right, sir?'

The colonel nods, and takes his place at the table. I want him here, because I want him to listen to what I say. Picking up my mug, I sip my coffee and look slowly round the table. My words are already agreed, but I wait until I have his attention as well. If the Aux are going to die – and chances are they will — then we might as well tell them why.

Neen stops loading clips, Franc puts her piece of toast onto a plate and sits at the only unclaimed chair. Rachel and Haze glance at each other. Ajac and Iona are off begging bullets from Milo. We need more ammunition. Also, I need them gone, because this is for Neen, Franc, Rachel and Haze only.

What I'm about to say can get them killed. So I'm going to tell them, and then they are going to forget. 'You understand?' I ask Neen.

'Yes, sir.'

I make each one give me an answer in turn.

'Good,' I say, when we're done. 'Three months ago, a regiment of the Death's Head mutinied . . . While we were fighting in Ilseville, General Tournier surrendered the Ninth half a spiral arm away. He surrendered rather than go down fighting.'

'Fuck,' Neen says.

'Yeah,' says my gun. 'Bet you didn't know you could do that.'

'It gets worse,' says Colonel Vijay. 'Under the terms of the surrender, the Ninth went over to the Enlightened. General Tournier offered to bring the rest of the Death's Head with him.'

Silence fills the upper room in the little gatehouse.

Treason, pure and simple. Except nothing about treason is pure, and this is not simple.

'My father was offered money,' says Colonel Vijay. 'A dukedom, his own planet, his own system. All he had to do was declare for the Uplifted.'

'And OctoV, sir?' demands Neen.

'The U/Free would take care of him,' I say.

'Will of the people,' says Colonel Vijay. 'Freely expressed. If enough Octovians wanted to become Uplifted . . .'

246

'Can they do that?' Rachel asks.

'They can do anything they like,' says Haze, the first time I've heard him sound anything but envious of the United Free.

Our glorious leader's answer to all this is elegant in the extreme. On OctoV's orders, General Jaxx gives his son authority to sign the treaty on the general's behalf. Colonel Vijay Jaxx will meet General Tournier under a flag of truce. The chosen location is Hekati, an insignificant ex-mining colony on the edge of Enlightened space.

Having met General Tournier, under this flag of truce, Colonel Vijay has orders to kill him. At one stroke, OctoV allows General Jaxx to prove his loyalty, disposes of a threat to his empire, and ensures a treaty will never be signed.

Without General Tournier, the conspiracy collapses. There is, of course, only one problem. Jaxx's son is a staff officer with zero combat experience.

That is where we come in.

Most of the U/Free think we're on a cultural mission.

A smaller group think we're looking for their missing observer. Who must have gone missing during the setting up of the treaty, although they don't know about that. An even smaller group, who do know about it, believe we're escorting Colonel Vijay to a pre-agreed location to sign the damn thing. Only OctoV, General Jaxx, his son – and now us – know we are delivering an assassin.

'So,' says the SIG, when I finish running it through. 'Killing that braid was a bad career move?'

That is one way of putting it.

'What now?' asks Neen.

'We find the Enlightened. We get your sister back. We kill General Tournier. We go home . . .'

'Yeah,' the gun says sourly. 'Sounds like a plan to me.'

★　　★　　★

247

The drop is swift; the sideways flick as the elevator hits the bottom and begins its travel up the side of Hekati's shell is brutal enough to make our stomachs lurch. Should have known all those temples were good for something. Makes me wonder what else the colonel forgot to tell me.

Apart from the obvious. He expects to die.

After he panicked in the hub that first time, my killing the braid meant his choice was made for him. Even if Colonel Vijay had wanted to sign a treaty, he couldn't. Nor could he get within killing distance of General Tournier. Our CO went from honoured guest to hunted enemy with my first blow.

Mind you, what did he expect?

If he didn't bother to brief us all properly first.

A second lurch tells me we're climbing one of Hekati's spokes. I know it's true, because gravity gets weaker.

'Arriving in five,' says the lift. 'Hope you have a good day.'

'Wow,' my gun says. 'It's house-trained.'

We ignore the SIG.

Our elevator opens into a corridor that runs all the way round the inside of Hekati's mirror hub. All the lifts begin here. It is faster to pass through the central hub than trek round inside the ring.

Screens show ships docked within the hub. A bot scuttles across the floor towards a wall and disappears when it sees us. A dozen doors lead to storerooms and arrival halls. A dozen more are on the far side of the ring, out of sight. This is where we killed the braid and the Silver Fist, before taking the first lift down.

'Check the corpses,' I tell Neen.

'Gone, sir,' he says.

I didn't really expect them to be there. If the splatter patterns were still there, I'd think the bodies had been removed by the Uplifted. But the blood has gone, along with all the weapons, the uniforms and the bodies themselves. So maybe the spider bots have been busy after all.

'Find anything useful,' Colonel Vijay orders.

'What's useful?' whispers Ajac. Neen tells him to use his brain.

'Sir,' I say, when we're safely out of the others' hearing. 'Have you met General Tournier before?'

'No.' Colonel Vijay shakes his head. 'But I'll recognize him.' That's not what interests me, although I say this politely.

'How about his staff?'

The list he reels off means nothing to me. They all have at least two names, some have three and one has four. You need to understand that people I know have only one. Neen is Neen, Franc is Franc . . . I was always just *Sven*, until I met Aptitude's mother and she gave me a second name.

'But will they recognize you, sir?'

'Doubt it,' says Colonel Vijay. He looks at me. 'Sven,' he says, 'what's your point?'

'I'll kill General Tournier,' I tell him.

'You . . . ?'

'Sir,' I say, 'I'm faster and stronger and we'll get one crack. We can't afford a fuck-up.' I tag *sir* onto the end of that. Although I doubt it removes the sting.

'*I'll do it*,' he says. 'After I sign the treaty.'

'You won't be signing any treaty, sir.'

'Want to tell me why?'

'Because dead people can't sign their names.'

Colonel Vijay thinks it's a threat. He's wrong.

'You're dead, sir. Remember? Pavel killed you that night in the hills. At least that's what General Tournier believes. We need to leave it like that. Also . . .'

'Also what?'

'No way anyone betrays OctoV while I'm around.'

Opening his mouth to protest, he shuts it when I glare at him. 'Don't care if it's pretend,' I say. 'Don't care if it's a trick. We're not signing.'

Chapter 38

AS THE COLONEL AND I WALK BACK, WE MEET NEEN COMING in the other direction. His face is grim and he's dragging a prisoner behind him. The man is broad-shouldered, sandy-haired, with one of those little beards meant to age him. He is four or so years younger than I am, so five or six years older than Neen. What with his beard and sharp nose, his looks are enough like our colonel's to tell me he's high clan.

Blood drips from one of his nostrils, a bruise is beginning to close his right eye, and his hands are roped tightly behind his back.

What I notice, of course, is his uniform.

He's wearing the parade dress of a captain in the Death's Head, right down to a cavalry sword hanging from his left hip and a little black dagger on the right. A waterfall of braid tells me he's general staff.

Braid relating to your own rank hangs one side. Braid relating to the rank of the officer you serve hangs the other. Worked that out for myself when I was on the general's mother ship.

'Found him in the control room,' says Neen. Before

admitting, 'Actually, Haze found him.' Which explains it. Haze was probably drawn by the smell of all that exotic naked machinery, or something.

'What was he doing?' I mean our captive, obviously.

Neen hesitates. 'Field-stripping a gun.'

Sounds like a man after my own heart. Well, he would be, if he weren't a traitorous fucker who has gone over to the Enlightened.

'Permission to question him, sir?'

Colonel Vijay glances between the three of us. That's me, Neen and our captive. 'Rules of war,' he says. 'Remember that, Sven.'

I salute. 'Leave it with me,' I say.

Nodding doubtfully, Colonel Vijay makes his way down the corridor alone. The moment he disappears around a corner, I bounce our prisoner against the nearest wall, and then do it again. He looks up from his knees.

'Rules of war,' he says.

'First rule,' I tell him. 'There aren't any.'

Dragging him to his feet, I go through his pockets. A handful of gold coins, a key card for a room, a watch with its strap broken. Another of those little pearl-handled knives.

'What's this?'

He looks at me in disbelief. Maybe he's trying to work out the reason behind my question. The reason is, *I want to know.* My backhand bounces him into a wall again. This time it's Neen who drags him to his feet.

'If I were you,' says Neen, 'I'd answer his question.'

'It's a fruit knife.' He says it twice, because he bit his tongue on the way down and now his lisp's worse than before.

'And what are you doing up here?'

'Guard duty . . .'

I look at him. Young, expensively dressed and elegant if you ignore five days' worth of stubble that barely troubles his cheeks. He should be playing cards in some Farlight café or dancing attendance on a general. To draw guard duty like this you need to piss someone off, badly.

'What did you do?'

He shuts his mouth, and it remains shut while Neen slaps him around a little. But we've had all we are getting. Eventually, he falls back on telling us to fuck off and die.

I'm impressed. 'Make it quick,' I tell Neen. It's the best I can offer in the circumstances.

'Yes, sir,' says Neen, reaching for his dagger.

Turning to go, I hear the young captain force himself to his feet. And that impresses me as well. Face death on your feet and look it in the eyes. Not enough of us take that vow.

'*Challenge.*'

I could pretend not to hear. 'You're a prisoner,' I tell him. 'That's one. You're a traitor, that's two. Challenge refused.'

'*I am not a traitor.*' The words bubble between broken lips.

Somehow, I find myself with one hand round his throat, and he's against a mirror-hub wall and keeping still, because my prosthetic fingers have closed so tight that any further movement is going to snap his spine like a twig.

Neen is looking worried. Must be down to me, because there's nothing else round here to worry him.

'You're all traitors,' I say. 'Every single fucking one of you.'

A tiny flex of muscle under my hand says the prisoner wants to shake his head. 'Not,' he manages at last. 'Refused the virus.'

I let him go. '*They're giving you the virus?*'

He nods.

Fuck, now that is nasty. Once the virus has you, it's for ever. You have it, your brats have it, and their brats have it. A hundred generations or more of little monsters growing braids. Makes me realize what uniting with the Uplifted would involve.

'Do it now,' I tell Neen.

He nods. And the captain asks my name.

Weirdest thing. But he *is* from a Farlight high clan. Maybe it's rude to be killed by someone who hasn't been formally introduced. Fuck knows, they're not like you and me, the high clans. Actually, they're not like anyone except themselves.

'Sven,' I tell him. 'Sven Tveskoeg.'

'Tveskoeg,' he says. 'That's an old Earth name.'

Should have just killed him. Still got time, could do it myself. A slash to the neck or a stab to the heart. A cut from abdomen to throat.

'Old Earth?' I say.

The man nods, introducing himself. Captain Emil Bonafonte deMax Bonafonte, Obsidian Cross, first class. 'What?' he asks, seeing my scowl.

'You got an older brother?'

He shakes his head.

Heart, I think. *Let's get this over with.*

'Why?' he asks, watching a knife appear in my hand.

'Used to know a Bonafonte in a fort south of Karbonne. Drank himself to death.'

'My uncle. We were told he died in battle.'

Fucking great. 'You know someone called Debro Wildeside?'

'Of course I—' He looks at me. 'Bad business,' he says. 'Very bad indeed.'

He's right too. Debro is Aptitude's mother. Debro and I met on a prison planet called Paradise. As far as I know she's still there.

'You know Senator Wildeside?' he asks me.

'Yeah . . .' I don't tell him she reminds me of my sister, unlikely as that sounds. Even nags me in the same way. I don't tell him I made a vow to protect her daughter that I will carry to my death. Some things you don't say.

Colonel Vijay takes Captain Bonafonte being alive as proof

I am improving; he makes that obvious. And it turns out they know each other. Of course they do.

Well, they have cousins who met on campaign.

At least they believe so.

Eldest sons of each branch of a high clan take the same name. It seems there are three Vijay Jaxx and four Emil Bonafonte deMax Bonafontes. It's the most ridiculous thing I've ever heard. I don't bother pointing that out.

Having asked for the captain's parole, Colonel Vijay seals the deal by shaking hands. Apparently we are all now friends.

'What?' the captain asks, seeing me scowl.

'He'd prefer you in chains,' Colonel Vijay says.

The colonel's wrong. I'd prefer it if Emil wasn't a Bonafonte. I'd prefer it if he was dead.

Chapter 39

THE ARGUMENT IS SHORT AND I WIN. AS WE WALK OUT OF A room together the Aux stare, and Neen slicks the others a glance that says, *Shut the fuck up*. So they pick their jaws up off the floor and stare straight ahead.

Coming to attention, Neen orders a salute.

As I return his salute, I tell Trooper Emil to join the ranks. We might as well begin as I intend to go on.

On my collar are Vijay's silver eagles. Captain Bonafonte's braid falls from my left shoulder. An Obsidian Cross with crown and oak leaves hangs around my neck, because I've taken Vijay's medal as well.

Meet Colonel Sven Tveskoeg, accompanied by Lieutenant Vijay Tezuka . . . Aptitude's father won't mind me stealing his family name. In fact, he'll probably approve, assuming he ever gets to hear of it.

With us go the Aux, including the newly cropped, shaved and demoted Emil Bonafonte deMax Bonafonte, who has lost three of his names, as well as his commission and his jacket. Falling in, he ranges right and takes his position.

He'll do.

'We couldn't find the Silver Fist,' I say, 'because they're not on Hekati. They're camped outside . . .'

Shock greets my words.

'An Uplift vessel is locked to her outer rim. It has been for months. A parasite on this habitat.' Vijay opens his mouth to say something and I hold up my hand. He shuts his mouth again, although his face tightens.

Time to reveal my secret. 'Hekati told me.'

We have a choice of seven ships. Four are museum pieces. Semi AI at the most, all fins and curves. One even has portholes. The fifth is ours. Well, the U/Free hopper we arrived in. The sixth is a standard Z-class tug, squat and battered. The damn thing looks like a beetle/wasp hybrid, with a grapple harpoon and a couple of mechanical arms. You could probably shift a planet if you had enough of them. You'll find the Z-class anywhere cargo needs dragging.

The seventh is like the sixth, but small and rougher. I choose that one, obviously.

'Suicide,' says the SIG. 'With added rust.'

Yeah, worked that out for myself.

'Sure I can't interest you in a retro-special? Or a neat little hopper? We can make up our cover story later.'

'No,' I say.

The SIG sighs.

Our new ship has been berthed for so long that space grit has blasted one side back to metal. The door creaks as it opens, and rust flakes onto the scuzzy deck of its airlock. Everyone pretends not to notice. Emergency lights burn on a bulkhead, and a calendar advertising Bukiball Towropes shows a long-dead blonde.

Assuming she was ever real to begin with.

The crewpit is tiny, designed to hold three at most. Gravity carpet covers the floor, the kind that sticks to those tiny hooks on the heels of cheap space suits. An area behind the pit will do for the others.

Although it means they'll be without seats.

A lash-up of wire and cheap memory crystal provides a navigation system. Semi AI at most, probably not even that. A diode on the console announces our ship's beacon needs recharging; which is one thing we won't be doing, since the fewer people who know we are leaving here the better.

Using simple words, my gun explains what will happen unless the ship agrees to release the security block on its engines. The ship agrees before the SIG's halfway through; but the SIG's on a roll. 'And then,' it says, 'I'll screw every—'

'I've unlocked.'

'Oh,' says the SIG. 'Yeah.'

Ajac and Iona are to remain in the hub, that's my ruling. The air's got enough oxygen to breathe, the radiation is no worse than on Hekati itself, and we will leave them rations. I would tell them to go home, but they don't have one. Not any longer.

Iona frets that she is being abandoned. So does Neen on Iona's behalf. I always come back; he should know that by now. So I decide to fold one problem into another, to come up with a solution.

The problem is my prosthetic arm.

Has General Tournier heard of me? Extremely unlikely, but my arm was made by Colonel Madeleine, and he will have heard of her. The arm's black metal, swallows light and rings when tapped. No arm at all is less obvious, at least that is the way it seems to me. Although when I say this to Colonel Vijay, he smiles.

'What?'

'Nothing.'

257

He loses his smile soon enough.

The colonel's never seen me without an arm before. If he thinks that looks bad, he should see the stump before Colonel Madeleine remade it.

'Look after this for me,' I tell Iona.

She buckles under its weight, then straightens and shoots Neen a smile. *We'll be back*, she believes that now. No way will I leave this behind. Sliding my shoulder into Emil's jacket, I have Rachel fold the sleeve across my front and tack it into place.

'Hey, looking good,' my gun says.

'Officer on deck . . .' As I step through the hatch, Neen has the Aux salute. Vijay walks a few paces behind me. Returning the salute, I send them to their places.

My place is in the pilot's seat. Haze sits one side of me. Vijay sits the other, looking bemused. He's wearing my rank badges on either side of his collar. Even as a lieutenant, he looks absurdly young.

The first thing I do on sitting is charge the power packs for my gun. The one usually slung behind the trigger is almost out. The other, the one that wasn't left behind, is long since empty.

'Thank fuck,' says the SIG.

'Make them last,' I reply, and then tell the gun what I expect.

SIG-37s are fluent in fifty languages, or so it claims. For all I know it's telling the truth. Because there are words in there I don't begin to recognize. And I can order a whore or a beer in more languages than anyone I know.

'You can do it?'

Torn between saying it's impossible, and wanting to boast that of course it can do it, the gun decides to boast.

'Good,' I say. 'Then start us up.'

Diodes ripple along the SIG's chassis, and it does the whirring thing it does every time I demand that it do something difficult. The familiarity is vaguely comforting. Although I don't let the gun know that.

As I wait, the deck beneath my feet begins to hum and the lights go low in the crewpit. So Haze, Vijay and I buckle ourselves in. The others are already tied to a rail. It is the best we can do.

'Sir,' says Haze. 'You sure you want me to do this?'

Yes, I'm sure.

Wiping the ship's memory with a single pulse obviously hurts his head, because he vomits into a bag he grabs. We're still running low gravity, thank God.

'Do that in freefall,' I say, 'and I'll dump you outside myself.'

He manages to smile.

Read-outs promise clear space between the asteroid belt and us. Well, hydrogen, helium, assorted trace elements, not to mention your basic interstellar radiation field. Also three dead satellites, a rotting cargo container and half a dozen coffins in loose orbit around the habitat. Nothing, however, that looks like it wants to shoot us. In fact, nothing that looks like it is paying any attention to us at all.

Suits me fine.

'OK,' I say to the gun. 'Take us out.'

Pipes hiss as couplings break free, grapples clang and the crewpit shudders. I would ask the SIG how long this tug's been in dock but I don't want to know. It's not as if we have much choice.

'So,' asks the SIG. 'You want this quick or careful?'

'Careful,' I say.

'Good answer.'

I leave the SIG to work out Hekati's spin. We need to keep her bulk between us and the Silver Fist ship on her side. This matters, because we are about to arrive on Hekati for the first time. At least that's what we'll be telling General Tournier.

As the SIG runs our tug along one spoke, then slides it over Hekati's outer rim to hug the far side, it mutters endless numbers. 'Point one nine two four six,' it says, adding a string of numbers to the end of this.

'Angular velocity?' asks Haze.

'Check,' it says. It's a tricky manoeuvre; at least I assume it is, because eventually it reduces my gun to silence.

At some point, we pass beyond the abandoned cargo container, the satellites and all the coffins and match Hekati's spin, right out to the rocks. The asteroid belt is an M-type, which gives us a hundred thousand bloody great clumps of metal in slow orbit about the star Hekati uses for light.

No one is going to spot us in here. So we peel off and hide ourselves in its edge.

'OK,' I tell the others. 'This is how it's going to work.'

I talk, they listen. And then they look at me, look at one another, and do what they're told. Because the look on my face tells them what will happen if they don't. Only the gun vocalizes – and it has the sense to whisper.

'You nuts?'

'Probably.'

It snorts. 'I mean,' it says, 'it's not like it makes a difference to me. But sabotaging your own ship . . .' Lights flicker as it scans the crewpit. 'Given it was pretty fucked to start with.'

'Going to be worse now.'

'Tell me about it,' says the gun.

Most of the asteroids are no bigger than us. But we manage to find one fifty times our size and I have the gun scrape us alongside. You can't hear in space, so everyone insists, but I hear every screech, so maybe the air in here makes a difference. Not that that's going to be around much longer.

'Sven,' says a voice.

'Trooper?' Something in my tone makes Emil's chin come up.

'Nothing, sir.'

'Is this necessary?' Colonel Vijay asks.

'I don't know,' I ask. 'What do you think?'

He bites his lip. *Not his fault*, I remind myself. Sending an eighteen-year-old staff officer to assassinate a Death Head's general always was stupid. Except that thought is *treason*. So I decide it is actually a brilliant idea, in a way still to be revealed to the rest of us.

'You done?'

'Almost,' says the SIG.

A radiation tag on the shoulder of my pressure suit is orange, going on black. Looks like it's useless. Mind you, it was orange going on black when I first looked, and that was before we even left the mirror hub.

So maybe everything is fine.

'We stole this ship,' I tell the others. 'OK?'

They nod.

'Took it from a launch yard in Ilseville.'

'But—' says Neen.

'Yeah, OK. There isn't a launch yard in Ilseville. General Tournier won't know that . . .'

Clicking my helmet shut starts an oxygen feed. So I reduce the mix, because we have to make the air last. And then, tapping a dial, I hold up two fingers and twist my hand. Everyone turns their mix down. I'd tell them, but the audio on most of our suits is out.

'On my count,' I tell the gun.

As we hit zero, the SIG scrapes us down the rock one final time. We lose our only escape pod, a jagged outcrop rips our shell and every wall light dies. A second later, two emergency lights come on. It's true what they say about noise in a vacuum. Sirens scream, and then fade as our air is sucked away through the punctured hull.

'Fuck,' says Vijay, whose comms system still works. Dark eyes stare from behind the faceplate in his helmet. So I give him a thumbs up.

After a second, he nods.

Extreme cold withdraws blood from your fingers and toes, hands and feet, arms and legs, in that order. I've seen it happen. The emergency routine on our ship follows the same principle. It kills the lights, slams doors, seals any rips it can, and stops supplying heat to non-essential areas and then essential ones.

We feel the chill, all of us.

'Shutting down,' says a voice.

The ship sends its warning direct to my helmet.

'Yeah,' I say. 'I know.' To the SIG, I say, 'Run that broadcast.'

The gun does.

'*Mayday, SOS, Mayday . . . This is the cargo ship* Teller3, *coordinates . . .*' The SIG blasts out a string of numbers that puts us near the asteroid belt, on a heading that has the ship almost crashing into Hekati.

'This is the cargo ship *Teller3*, coordinates . . .'

The coordinates are shifting slightly and so are we.

Everything depends on the next few hours. If we can't go to the Silver Fist, then they must come to us. And the bait has to be convincing. My mouth tastes sour, and it's not just the kyp feeding off the panic around me. It is not fear, either.

Expectation, maybe. And a tightness that comes from wanting to know that I have this right. I will kill General Tournier. If it can be done, then I will do it, whatever it takes.

Whatever it takes, that's what we'll do.

The Aux motto.

'Sven,' says Vijay. 'You're smiling.' Not sure how he can see in the dull glow from the few bits of console still working.

'It's sir,' I say. 'And we're observing radio silence.'

Chapter 40

HEKATI LOOKS VAST AND WE ARE STILL SOME WAY OUT. OUR engines are almost dead, our life-support system critically compromised. The number of lights on our console falls every few minutes as something else takes itself off line.

The temperature in the crewpit reads way below zero. But my body is unsure if it's hot or cold, and even the kyp in my throat is threatening a sullen shut-down, as if aware that making me vomit now would be a bad move.

Vijay slumps forward in his chair, barely moving.

I have a feeling Haze might be praying to legba uploaded to judge from the signs his right hand keeps making over and over again.

Put me in front of a man with a weapon and I will happily let the best man win. Because that will be me. And I've done it enough times to know that. But this, waiting for help and waiting for death, and not knowing which is going to arrive first, it's teaching me things about myself.

And you know what?

Mostly, what it's teaching me is that patience is overrated.

Between runs of its distress routine, the SIG takes read-outs direct from each of our suits. 'Well,' it tells me, 'Rachel's fucked.' She has three hours. Neen has four. I have four ten. Franc has four twenty. As has Vijay. Haze has five. And Emil five thirty.

At the rate we're drifting, it is going to total five hours before we hit.

'You,' I mouth, tapping Emil's shoulder. 'And you . . .' Rachel looks round when I tap. 'Swap tanks.'

I have to repeat it three times, before they eventually manage to read my lips in the grim half light around us. Taking a deep breath, Rachel turns so Emil can unclip her bottle. Seals close as her tank comes free, and then he takes a breath, turns and lets Rachel remove his own tank.

He clips his into place for her.

This is good, because she's beginning to sway. And then she does the same for him. They work as a team and I'm impressed. He must know he is getting the worst of the deal.

Five minutes pass into ten, and then make twenty. No one is hailing us. In fact, no one is paying us any attention at all. As half an hour becomes an hour, and then two, and Hekati begins to look larger, I wonder if I have this wrong. It's not a state of mind I'm prepared to accept for long.

Filing it under interesting, but avoidable, I go back to staring at the screen.

We run skeleton software, down to bare bones and beyond. The asteroid field is at our back and Hekati between the sun and us. So we approach in shadow. Against that, we have the SIG emergency-broadcasting our position.

What is our fall-back?

Die, I guess. But I've never been good at that.

Checking with the SIG for the read-out for each tank in turn, I discover the colonel has his mix turned so low it's almost dangerous. At that level, he might make it. Of course, he'll be brain-damaged, but maybe he doesn't care.

Time for a change of plan.

Tapping the control pad on my glove, I put myself back on line. At a nod from me, Colonel Vijay does the same. It's not as if I have much power left in my comms systems anyway. Might as well put it to good use. Haze is last, only putting himself on line when he realizes we've done so already.

'Speed up,' I tell the SIG.

Haze gapes, mouth open behind glass. 'Sir,' he whispers. 'What about radio silence?'

'Go on,' I say. 'Do it.'

'Do what?' Haze is so bemused he speaks without thinking, then realizes what he has done.

'Take us in faster.'

'Can't,' he says. 'Not enough power.'

'Being scanned,' announces the ship.

When the hell did that wake up? 'What by?'

'Sir,' says Haze.

'What?' I demand.

Lights flicker along the edge of my gun. Something whirrs, and it flicks clips. Ceramic to explosive, then back. Always knew it did that for effect. 'Machine code,' says the SIG. 'Local, slightly dated.' That should piss them off.

'Probably Enlightened,' Haze finishes for it.

'Fucking great,' I say. 'So where are we anyway?'

The SIG plays me the coordinates from our distress beacon, and recites them over and over, as our vessel drifts closer, changing the last few digits as it goes.

'Very funny. What the fuck's that thing over there?'

'Hekati,' it says. 'Deserted habitat . . .'

'Shouldn't be here,' Haze announces suddenly. As always, he's a quick learner.

'You want to go back?' Colonel Vijay's voice is harsh. He has my growl down to the last tee. In fact, it's so perfect Haze flinches as if taking a lash.

'Hey,' he says.

'What?' demands Colonel Vijay.

'Shut it.' My voice cuts through their babble. I'm not sure Vijay knows what's going on yet. From the way he's glaring at Haze, helmets almost touching, I doubt it.

'Vijay,' I say. 'Enough.'

He gets excused his moment's hesitation.

'Makes no difference,' I tell them. 'We're headed for that thing. No way of turning back and where the fuck do you think we'd go anyway?' My glare swings round to include them all. Even Emil, who is watching with a sour smile on his face.

'We're Death's Head.'

The Uplifted better be listening. I'm counting on it.

'Well, we're fucked for glory. And anyone who wants death can have it now, free. No need to turn back for that.' Vijay's laugh is bitter.

'So . . .' I tell the SIG. 'Speed this crate up before we run out of air.'

A curve of habitat comes up to meet us. Can't believe we're not going to hit it, but between them, the SIG and Haze have this covered. We turn slightly, fire boosters and release something that would be a drag parachute if we weren't in vacuum.

'What's that?'

'Medusa bell,' says the SIG. 'Big about fifty years ago.'

'What happened?'

'They didn't work.'

So why fire it? Except whatever it is it must work slightly, because we slow and then twist sideways, scraping across the side of Hekati. I can see clouds and valleys through the glass as we pass, and what looks like a village far below.

'Fuck.'

'Yeah,' says the gun. 'Imagine having to—'

It doesn't get to finish its sentence, because something brings us to a sudden halt before we clear Hekati's rim. *Something* being a harpoon that slams through the side of our vessel, spreads its tines and locks solid. What little air was left is sucked through the rip.

'Asteroid drill,' says my SIG.

And then we lurch sideways, as an unseen hawser jerks tight, slamming me into a bulkhead. Another two harpoons hit, another craft slams into us and our outer door blows. We are being boarded.

The first man fires a spread net that should lock down the crewpit. It fails to open, so I head for the ceiling, slamming my gravity glove against cheap mesh. Tiny hooks give me enough leverage to stamp on the faceplate of a Silver Fist. His head twists sideways, so I stamp again and something snaps.

'Cheap shit,' says my gun. It's talking about his helmet.

Never fought in zero gravity before. It's like swimming without the water. Also never fought with only one arm, zero gravity or not. A hell of a lot harder than swimming without water. For a start, I can't hold on and fire anything at the same time.

The answer hits me a moment before a stun truncheon tries to do the same. Flipping sideways, I glue both boots to a wall and put a flechette into the helmet of a Silver Fist lieutenant in the doorway. He is low-ranking and it's not as if they'll really miss him.

Blood explodes in a thousand floating droplets.

'Pretty,' says my gun. The SIG is the only weapon working.

At least, the only one on our side. Neen is busy yanking the trigger of a ship's pulse rifle. He's done all the right things, like charge its precoil, but it still won't fire. So he uses it as a club. A Silver Fist goes down clutching his faceplate.

'How come—?'

'Because I'm not cheap shit,' the SIG tells me, not bothering to let me complete the question.

'Switch back,' I say.

'No, hollow-point.'

'Flechette.'

It switches clips with bad grace. I love flechette. You get minimum recoil, with maximum kinetic energy, and carbon darts fragment on impact. I drill a hole through a man behind Neen, and watch his suit suddenly become form-fitting. As the air goes out of it and vacuum begins sucking, blood flies through a tear.

A Taser bolt hits where I should be.

Only I'm somewhere else. Except it's not where I should be, because I've forgotten my arm.

'God, I love this.'

'Now that's fucked,' says the SIG. 'Only alive when you're at risk of being dead.'

'Telling me you don't feel the same?'

It shuts up. And I'm still grinning, when I realize my last shot was explosive.

'That was—'

'Needed,' insists the gun.

The SIG is right. A trooper in body armour has been un-packed into small pieces. But it has cost a large chunk of our bulkhead behind him.

'Stop,' demands a braid.

Flesh like leather, five braids swaying as it looks from side to side. *No helmet,* I realize suddenly. *No suit. How the fuck . . . ?* A stamp fixes my boots to the floor and I have my SIG to his head when my gun announces: 'Shutting down.'

'No, you fucking don't . . .'

It shuts down anyway.

'I said *stop.*' The braid glares at me.

Everyone else is still, I realize. We've got Silver Fist all around us. A dozen of the bastards. They have proper gravity boots and working Tasers. We have sticky-soled suits and whatever we can swing as clubs.

'You hear me?' asks the five-braid.

'Oh yeah,' I say, reaching for my laser blade. 'I hear you.'

Blue flame flickers and the knife comes to life in my hand.

'Sir,' says the five-braid. 'That's—'

What is it with everyone and this illegal technology shit? He's standing in sub-zero airless vacuum, with his skull stuffed with metal and wriggly bits, tubes run from his ribs like badly designed machinery, and he's objecting to my knife?

'I'm going to kill you.'

The five-braid shakes its head. All those metal snakes waving like undersea weeds. 'No, you're not,' he says, nodding behind us. 'You're going to put that knife down. Because if you don't . . .'

I turn, taking care to move slowly. Half my attention is on the braid and the rest on a scene playing out in the crewpit. One of his men has a pistol to Haze's helmet.

'He's a braid,' I say. 'Feel free.'

The five-braid glances between me and Haze, examining the boy's bulky suit with interest. At a nod, the trooper drags Haze close and peers into the helmet, checking for himself.

'Why . . . ?' the five-braid demands, and then changes it to, 'How?'

'Captured him.'

Now's when it might come unstuck.

'Where?' demands the braid.

'Why, how, where . . .' I toss the words back at him. 'Got any other questions you want answered?'

Scowling at me, the braid says, 'Turn that off.'

'Fucking make me.' For a glorious moment, it looks like the five-braid might. I'd be so lucky.

'If you don't,' he says, 'we'll shoot this one instead.' Pointing one finger, he indicates Vijay.

'Go ahead,' I tell him. 'He's a fucking useless little fuck anyway.'

The five-braid stares at me, reassessing. 'Who are you?'

'Sven,' I tell him. 'Colonel Sven Tveskoeg, Obsidian Cross, crown and oak leaves.' My name means nothing to him. The only bit that interests him is my rank and the medal.

'Colonel?'

'That's what I said.'

'Death's Head?'

My silence is my answer.

Nodding, he asks, 'What are you doing out here?'

'Taking some well-deserved R&R.' Gesturing around me, I ask: 'What the fuck does it look like?'

'Looks to me,' says the braid, 'like you're running away.'

Fuck, he's fast. My blade passes through where his neck should be and he laughs. It's enough to make me like him. Well, almost. Only my attention is on a Colt SW cinder maker, the one with the flip-down wire stock and the short power pack.

A Death's Head captain holds it.

Well, according to the patch on his chest: *Captain Diski, Obsidian Cross, First Class, Death's Head Ninth Regiment.*

'Move again,' he says, 'and I'll burn you back to fucking ash.'

'That's *burn you back to fucking ash, sir.*'

He grins, and glances at the five-braid, who nods. A second later, his gun is lowered. 'Introduce me,' says the braid.

So I point out my team. 'Lieutenant Vijay, Sergeant Neen, Trooper Emil, Trooper Franc, Sniper Rachel, plus our prisoner. Don't know what his name is. He doesn't say much.'

Haze gazes back, his face impassive behind glass.

'Where did you say you captured him?'

271

'Didn't,' I tell him. 'But it was outside Ilseville . . .' My voice is sour. 'We were leaving at the time.'

When the city doesn't register, I name the planet and that gets a slight flicker of recognition. Luckily, he doesn't know how far away it is. It is easy to forget how campaigns that seem all-important to those fighting them mean nothing to everyone else. We were one of OctoV's little side bets. One that shouldn't have come off, almost didn't come off . . .

And then did.

'It's over then?' says the braid. 'We took it back?'

I shake my head. 'We held it, you took it. We tried to take it back.' My shrug is slight. 'Too many mercenaries, not enough professionals.'

The braid nods, despite itself. The Enlightened have firm opinions on mercenaries and those opinions are not kind.

Chapter 41

STEPPING THROUGH A DOOR, EXPECTING A SECOND AIRLOCK, I find myself in the hold of a combat carrier. Benches run down both sides of a hangar. Maybe two hundred seats either side. The deck between them is metal, studded to stop boots sliding. Flip-up rings litter the floor. The craft obviously carries cargo as well as troops.

'You can unsuit,' says the five-braid.

When no one does, he barks an order to the Death's Head captain. All that happens is the captain releases the fastenings on his own suit, drops it to the floor and steps out of it.

Colonel Vijay watches me, so I give him the nod.

'You trust them?' he asks, tapping his audio button and using up most of what remains of his battery pack.

'Not sure,' I say. 'Let's suck it and see.'

The five-braid smiles. This tells me two things. He's listening in on our audio channel, and he doesn't expect us to be a problem. I'm happy with both of those. Although I can see from the expression on Colonel Vijay's face that he doesn't understand why.

'Could have done with some of these.'

The colonel glances at me.

'Combat carriers. At Ilseville.'

He nods, doubtfully. We make the rest of the trip in silence.

It's not a long trip, more a hop. Although the braid flicks dimensions and returns, saying he's fixing our greeting party. Showing off, I guess. Letting the enemy see they're out-gunned. Any minute now, he is going to make his offer.

You can bet on it.

Glad I don't, because he is more subtle than that. He just runs us over the hump of Hekati's ring and down the outside. And guess what, I can do subtle too. The braid thinks we're expecting an airlock into Hekati. He doesn't know we already know about their ship. So, as our craft skims the far edge of Hekati and rolls lazily on its approach, I'm planning to be surprised, but not too surprised . . .

Fuck that.

We are a minnow.

And the vessel we approach is a shark.

As the Uplift mother ship comes into view, the shock tries to rip breath from my body and I have to bite down to stop myself being impressed. The others are slower to get a grip and Rachel actually points. We're not even fleas on a dog cocking its leg against their post.

Take a vessel larger than the entire Bosworth landing fields and glue it to one of the smaller ring worlds. I'm not surprised Hekati is hurting. The Silver Fist ship is gripping her like some rapist.

This is what it is.

An air tube, fat as a motorway, penetrates Hekati through a gash sealed with stonefoam. The ship and habitat are fucking, that is what it looks like. Water pipes pulse as the ship takes what it needs. The Uplift even have their gravity generators off, each rotation of the habitat giving gravity to their ship as well.

Just how vast the Uplift vessel is I discover as an iris opens and our craft rises through the opening, then flips itself over and touches down on a deck large enough to swallow any city on Hekati. It is a five-minute walk to the edge of the field.

Welcome to Victory First Last and Always, says a voice. *Flagship of the Third Uplifted Legion.*

When Neen puts his hands to his head, I realize the sound isn't just inside my skull. Whatever speaks doesn't sound human to me. I'm still thinking this, when Rachel sobs, and I turn to find Haze trying to catch his own vomit. A second later, he's on his knees and not bothering about catching anything much. Blood runs from both nostrils. A dark stain says he's pissed himself.

'*What's happening?*' demands Vijay.

It's the five-braid who answers, though he takes time out to glare at me first. 'Formatting,' he says. 'Always tough.' And then gets to his question. 'How did you know he was Enlightened?'

'His hair fell out, his scalp started bleeding.'

'So he definitely didn't have braids when you captured him?'

'No,' I shake my head. 'Those are new.'

The braid considers this. Obviously decides it's possible. At his nod, two guards break from a squad by the wall to carry away Haze between them. Given he's pissed himself and drips vomit they treat him well. But then he is Enlightened. Only now, he's an Enlightened who just formatted, and that doesn't sound good to me.

'And us?' I demand.

'Oh,' says the five-braid. 'We'll get to you later.'

I struggle to keep my temper, which amuses him. It doesn't

come easy. Vijay and Neen stand beside me, and Emil stands a step behind them, flanked by Rachel and Franc. So far, he has kept his mouth shut. A bit of me wonders if having given his parole really means that much to him. The other bit assumes he knows I'll cut his throat before he gets out more than one word.

Chapter 42

VICTORY FIRST LAST AND ALWAYS RUNS TO DIGITAL TIME, a hundred kiloseconds to a d/M, which translates as 1.125 standard days, or the time it takes light to travel 29,139,826,917,600 metres in a vacuum. Not sure what is wrong with miles and hours myself.

The mother ship's mostly shut down. It is still giving off an infrared trace, the SIG tells me. How obvious this is against Hekati's own signature is another matter. Maybe that's the point. The *Victory First* is certainly busy bleeding the habitat dry.

Oxygen and power are taken freely. Piggybacking the habitat's spin to give the mother ship gravity puts an intolerable strain on Hekati. But everything the Enlightened steal is one less thing they need to produce for themselves. One less clue for anyone hunting heat signatures or electromagnetic traces.

It's not the U/Free from whom the Silver Fist hide.

It's our glorious leader. I work this out for myself and feel smug about it. Thinking isn't so hard when you get the hang of it.

'You all right?'

'Sure,' I tell my gun. 'Why?'

'Oh,' it says, 'I'm registering a headache.'

It shuts down ungracefully, then flicks back to life to check I really did want it to shut down. Maybe it's tied tighter to my limbic system than I imagine, because I am not sure I do.

Someone knocks at the cell door. Now, that's not what you expect as prisoners. Colonel Vijay glances at me, and then glances at Emil. Rachel just waits for my nod, then goes to the door and tries the handle. Someone has released the lock.

'You're the sniper, right?'

She nods at the Death Head's captain we met earlier. Out of his armour, he's young and handsome, with dark hair that flops over one side of his face. A scar decorates the other side. It is a very elegant scar. Probably had it put there himself.

'Any good?' he demands.

'Try me,' she says.

'Oh,' says the captain, 'I'm going to.' And he grins when she flushes. No, I didn't think he was talking about rifles either.

Seeing me, he comes to attention.

His uniform is standard, except for a shoulder patch I don't recognize. But the real surprise comes as he turns to look at our cell. Three tiny braids hang down his scalp, and they are the real thing, because they move on their own. 'Sorry about the cell, sir. We'll find you proper rooms later.'

'We're prisoners?'

'Guests, sir.'

'Of that metalhead?'

He's smooth, this boy. But not smooth enough to keep anger out of his eyes. 'No, sir,' he says. 'Of General Tournier. Who wants to see all of you.'

Turning on his heel, he makes for the door.

After a second, I lead the others out of our room. Fifty paces to a bank of elevators, a seventeen-floor drop and three hundred paces straight down a corridor. On Jaxx's mother ship, this would be the entertainment district. Turns out, it's the entertainment district on this ship. General Tournier's Uplift friends just go in for a different kind of entertainment.

Bots have stripped back the walls of an area twice the size of Golden Memories, and they've eaten away the ceiling above to create a double-height arena. The new space is edged on all four sides with tiers that rise well beyond where the old ceiling used to be.

The Silver Fist are obviously professional at enjoying themselves. Because instead of endless banks of seats, each tier features dining tables, covered with white cloths and laden with cutlery.

A thousand people? I wonder. Two thousand . . . ? Three thousand . . . ?

Colonel Vijay and I are being led towards the biggest table on the lowest tier, and there are half a dozen knives and forks, plus assorted spoons and seven different wine glasses for each setting.

Assholes, I think.

The five-braid glances up, and I wonder what he sees on my face.

Unless he is working at a deeper level. As I watch, Neen, Rachel and Franc head for a higher table, eight rows back. They sit together which is good. That way they can keep an eye on Emil. Although the longer Emil remains silent, the harder it becomes for him to betray us, since the Ninth would regard him as having betrayed them with his silence already. As my ADC, Vijay doesn't get to sit at all. He stands at my shoulder.

'General,' says the five-braid. 'Let me introduce Colonel Sven Tveskoeg.'

'Never heard of you.'

'Never heard of you, either.'

Around me, half a dozen officers hold their breath.

His laugh is abrupt, sharp as the bark on a dog. At least half the officers release their breath, and when General Tournier nods to me, the rest of them decide to do the same.

'*Kill him now,*' Colonel Vijay whispers.

It's all I can do not to punch him. Hell, he's meant to be the one who understands strategy. Also, what is he doing speaking to me without being spoken to first . . . ?

'So,' says the general. 'Tell me how you got here.'

'Stole a cargo cruiser from Ilseville. Got out just before the city fell.'

That is as near an admission of treason as he's ever heard. Only it's a lot better than telling him the truth. And when General Tournier asks his next question, I know we're OK. At least for now.

'I heard the landing fields were bombed. Have I got that wrong?'

Whatever you do, never contradict a general, especially not in front of his own staff. All those prissy little idiots with silver braid and red patches behind their collar bars are watching. 'Must have been after we left, sir.'

He nods.

There is no landing field at Ilseville. It's a river port, in the middle of barren marshland. A depot for alligator skins and rare furs, a place you go once and vow never to return. Probably still is, those bits of it left.

'Eat,' he says. 'Drink . . . We can discuss Ilseville later.'

Plates come and go, carried by a steady stream of orderlies, servants and waitresses. A woman begins to replace my glass and stops. When I look round, I discover it's Shil, her face frozen with the shock of seeing me.

That's when I realize she thought I was dead. Probably thought it was only a matter of time before she joined me. And here I am, staring at her with just a little too much attention for an officer to be paying a servant.

She has a black eye.

'What?' demands the general, glancing across.

Reaching for the glass, I hold it to the light and then thrust it at Shil. 'Disgusting,' I snarl. 'You think I want your filthy fingerprints? Find me another.'

She bobs her head and hurries away.

The woman who brings me a replacement is older, less nervous. Not sure what Shil's said to her, but she keeps her eyes on the floor and leaves quickly. Twisting away from the grasping hand of a man further down the table, she laughs.

It's an art, not offending those with power over you. Watching her tells me something about those around me. Nothing I couldn't have guessed. Their servants tread carefully around them.

'Sven,' says the general, and I realize I'm being offered a plate.

The chicken is fresh and well cooked. Its sauce deep and rich. I'd rather have a beer with a cane-spirit chaser; but the men around me are sniffing glasses of wine and talking about good and bad vintages. After a while, the conversation turns to battles fought and villages burnt.

Murderers with manners.

It is amazing what you can get away with if you have breeding.

A woman passes, and I slap her arse, hard. When I look up, I realize it's Shil, and her face is bleaker than ever. A second later, it goes blank and the lieutenant next to me laughs.

'Tried her, sir,' he tells me. 'Sour as lemon.'

He has tiny braids growing from his skull and the skin around his wrists has mottled. I can just see three cuts where the Uplift virus was rubbed into his flesh. Simply looking at the side effects of the virus makes me want to vomit. 'You gave her those bruises?'

The man grins.

We introduce ourselves, and I wonder if he realizes I intend to kill him as soon as I get the chance. Guess not, because Lieutenant Hamblin tells me how he knocks Shil out by accident and ruins his own evening. Seems he likes his women to know what they're getting.

The lieutenant wants to tell me more.

Only his general is watching. So we go back to talking about the *Victory First*. It's old for a mother ship, he tells me. A little small for the numbers it holds. And it's only towards the end of our talk I realize something: when this man, with his Death's Head uniform and Obsidian Cross, talks about *our ships* he means the Enlightened.

What Colonel Vijay told me is true. The Ninth Regiment really are a bunch of poisonous little traitors.

'You all right, sir?' the lieutenant asks.

'Oh, yes,' I say, raising my glass. 'Never better.'

Chapter 43

'SVEN,' SAYS THE GENERAL, LEANING FORWARD. REALIZING HIS commander wants to talk to me, a brigadier stands up and politely offers me his seat.

'Thank you, sir,' I say.

He nods, but he is glad to swap places. I can see it in his eyes.

'So,' the general says. It's a tic of his. Most of his sentences start that way. 'Tell me how you lost your arm.' His gaze is on the empty sleeve pinned to my chest.

'Got it bitten off, sir.'

The general checks I'm not mocking him. Which I'm not; there's a time and place for such things and this isn't it.

'What by?'

A ferox, I almost say.

A bloody great sand-hued monster, with a bone crest down his skull and claws that can tear ceramic. A ferox saved my life once. It cut me down from a whipping post, gave me a girl to fuck and a cave in which to live. Of course, it later ate the girl, and the Death's Head took back the cave and I came close to dying. But you can't have everything.

'Cold-water crocodile,' I tell him. 'A lagarto.'

'You're lucky to be alive.'

I shrug. 'Shouldn't have got bitten in the first place. And it's not a problem, I mend fast.'

He nods. 'So you can still fight?'

The table goes still. It's an insult, wrapped in a smile. They want to know how I'll react. The brigadier whose chair I'm using shoots me a glance. A warning, only about what? Everything, I guess.

'*Sven?*' The general's waiting for my answer.

At least two officers at the table hide their smiles when I glance up. The general's not smiling. In fact, his scowl deepens. 'Oh yes,' I tell him. 'I can still fight.'

'Good,' says the general, his voice smooth. 'In that case you can provide tonight's entertainment.'

A clap of his hands brings an ADC running. The boy is young, probably too young to shave. Yet he has a waterfall of silver braid and a little black dagger hanging from his hip and he's wearing that shoulder patch. He's probably the age I was when Lieutenant Bonafonte swore me into the Legion. Although my uniform was sweat-rotted battledress, and my dagger stolen from a market stall.

'Sir?' he says, saluting.

'Get the prisoners.'

The second lieutenant scampers away.

Bet his family didn't know he was going to end up a traitor on the wrong side of the spiral arm. Mind you, they probably think he's dead. A life joyfully given for our beloved empire. It's always *joyfully given*. And the empire is always *beloved*. Our glorious leader wouldn't want anyone dying for him unwillingly.

'Have another drink, sir,' suggests a major on my other side. He pushes across a brandy decanter without waiting for my answer.

It tastes sour. Everything about tonight tastes sour.

Fifty Death's Head officers, 120 NCOs and 540 troopers sharing a dining hall with 1,500 Silver Fist troopers and their braids. We're looking at the entire Ninth. A full regiment of fucking traitors. And there is something else: at least a third of the officers around me are growing braids of their own. It's hard to describe how that feels. To be a traitor is bad enough. That these bastards want to advertise the fact turns my gut.

'One bout,' explains the major. 'No breaks . . .'

'To the death?'

His look says, *what do you think?*

'Fine with me,' I say. 'Never was good at pulling punches. What's the ruling on weapons?'

'No guns,' he says. 'Otherwise, anything goes.'

The general is listening with a grim smile. Unbuckling my holster, I drop it to the ground and feel glad the SIG has enough sense to stay locked down. And then I take off my jacket. I am about to drape this over the back of a chair when an orderly rushes forward to take it from my hand. He waits, looking nervous.

'And the rest,' says General Tournier.

I glance over in surprise.

'Combatants fight naked,' he says. 'It's a tradition.' Well, that settles it, obviously.

'Yes, sir,' I say.

The general raises his eyebrows. Maybe he hoped I'd protest. Mind you if I had his belly . . . Taking another gulp, General Tournier empties his glass, finishes a cold chicken breast and reaches for his glass a second after it is refilled. 'Join me,' he suggests, raising it.

'With respect, sir . . . Not while I'm working.'

★   ★   ★

A hatch in the arena floor irises open, and conversations still as a platform rises. The crowd obviously know what to expect, because tonight's event is running on well-oiled wheels. A half-dozen Death's Head make for the heads, intending to piss or vomit enough space for the next round of drinking.

The general doesn't bother.

He has a vast, and increasingly full, jeroboam of piss between his boots. Traitors or not, General Tournier and his regiment are busy living up to their reputation for hard drinking and wild parties. The kind of parties at which whole planets get trashed.

'Sven,' says the general, as I step out of my trousers, only to have the orderly grab them from the floor, 'have fun.'

'Yes, sir.'

'And show us what you can do.'

Of course, sir, I'm about to say. But I've just seen who is on that platform. It's the Vals, our mercenaries from the battle on the hillside. They are barefoot and naked under silver survival blankets.

Should have guessed.

'Fuckwit,' shouts one.

'You don't screw with the Vals,' yells the other. They're talking to the general, who grins. A lazy grin, meant for the five-braid and the officers around him. But I'm close enough to see his eyes.

The man is drunk, but not so drunk he doesn't know the risk he's taking. You mess with one Val and you mess with them all. It's a lifelong commitment, staying alive when the Vals hold a grudge against you.

'Girls,' he says. 'Meet your new challenger.'

As one, the Vals turn to glare at me. As one, their snarls falter.

'What?' demands General Tournier.

I'm stripped naked, and they're twenty paces away. There

286

is a blade in my hand, and a good chance I can kill one or the other before she reveals we've met. But I can't silence both.

At least, not in time.

Something flicks across their faces.

And when the Vals turn back, there is a sneer on their lips. It's meant for me, and the general and everyone else in that room.

They're magnificent. I've always admired the Vals. That single-minded commitment to killing.

'Fuck off,' shouts the first. 'We're not fighting that.' She jerks her chin towards me. 'One arm, no brains . . . It's a fucking insult.'

Now I'm scowling and the brigadier is laughing. Although he stops fast enough when I glare. See, told you he was one of life's staff officers.

'I'll fight them both at once.'

'With only one arm?' General Tournier sounds tempted.

'How hard can it be?' I ask, sneering towards the Vals. 'They're just copies of each other.' It's the Vals' turn to scowl. There are a couple of things you don't say about the Vals and that is one of them.

'Two of them?' says the general. 'At once?'

'Yes, sir.'

Can I do it?

Of course I can fucking do it.

'Get him a fighting arm,' General Tournier demands.

His ADC scampers off, bumping into one of the tables in his hurry. It takes the boy a lot longer to return, probably because he is staggering under the weight of a vast metal prosthetic.

'Any good?' he asks.

It's stained, made from beaten steel, with braided hoses and hydraulic rods to work the main joints. A row of blades runs from its wrist to the elbow, which ends in a vicious spike. The arm even tightens at the top with screws. A deep scratch says an enemy got in a good blow then died. Well, if the blood still crusted on the elbow spike is anything to go by.

Obviously enough, I love it.

Flexing my new fingers, I make a fist, and then swing my new arm from side to side a couple of times just for the pleasure of hearing the hydraulics hiss.

'You approve?' asks the general.

'Yes, sir.'

'Right,' he says. 'Here are the rules—'

'Sir,' I say.

General Tournier doesn't like interruptions.

'It's just . . . Don't the Vals need to know the rules as well?'

He does that dog-like bark that passes for his laugh. 'Oh Sven,' he says. 'Believe me, the Vals know my rules already.' Turning to his ADC, he asks, 'How many of my officers have those bitches killed?'

'I believe it's five, sir.'

'So this is going to be interesting,' says the general, and his ADC nods. As do the brigadier, the major and every other officer at that table. A bunch of puppets the lot of them.

'Those rules,' I say. It's worth it, just to see their shock.

'Laser fencing,' says the general. 'For this bout,' he says, 'I think we'll set it to the max. One knife per Val. You already have your arm. The fencing stays up until you or both Vals are dead . . . Anything else?'

He's talking to his ADC.

'No rounds, sir. No breaks.'

The general smiles. 'Oh,' he says, 'I don't think Colonel Tveskoeg will be expecting rounds or breaks. Will you, Sven?'

'Waste of time, sir. Rather get this wrapped up.'

A pair of guards erects laser wire. The arena is going to be triangular. That is a new one on me. Don't think I've ever seen an arena that wasn't round or square. Since my new arm counts as my weapon, I leave my knife on the table. And it's only as I head for the ring that General Tournier sees the scars on my back.

'Sven,' he says, calling me back. 'What are those?'

The first thing he's said in two hours that doesn't drawl from his lips like the punchline to some joke.

'Whipped,' I say.

'Who by?'

'Someone who's now dead.'

He laughs, and nods towards the Vals. 'All yours,' he says.

Chapter 44

GRABBING A CHICKEN LEG TO CHEW ON MY WAY DOWN, I TAKE one last look round the vast dining room. Neen is with Rachel and the others. Emil is sober and scared, but also looking like a trooper, and that is enough for me. Shil's clearing a table three tiers back.

If she sees me, she doesn't let it show.

And Haze? He has been here all evening.

Sat right next to the five-braid. His own braids look longer and his face is thinner. He has his head tipped slightly to one side, and he is listening. When his gaze catches mine, he smiles. Having smiled, he offers five to one against. He's betting on the Vals.

Great, I think.

The laser goes up the moment I enter the ring. Static lifting hairs on the back of my neck. Tossing a chicken bone over my shoulder produces a zap like one of those fancy insect killers. Roughly what I expect to happen.

The Vals are still wearing their silver blankets, although they lose these quickly enough, wrapping them round their left forearms. Makes sense: my arm is the most dangerous weapon in this ring.

As we circle, the Vals toss their knives from hand to hand.

But that is all they do. *It's a holding pattern*, I realize. And that makes me realize something else. The Vals regard themselves as bound by our treaty. They won't attack until I do, because of the vow they made when I set them free. In fact, they may not attack at all.

There are rules, fuck it.

Real rules.

I've known troopers ignore them. Lie, rape, and break vows in the name of expediency. Knew a fuckwit who machine-gunned a hospital ward full of civilians. Another who changed sides three times in the same war. Not like the Aux, conscripts who had no option but change sides.

Like me, enlisted.

The enlisted are different. We are here from choice.

We'll be here from choice next life. Hell, we were probably here from choice the life before. No one but the U/Free remembers their past lives. So I can't tell you if that's true.

Me, I'm here now. Ready to look death in the face with open eyes. And if this ends in someone reciting the soldier's prayer over my body, then so be it. I'll settle for a long sleep and a better life next time.

Of course, I'll fight like fuck to stop that happening. But if it does, then it does . . .

'You're released,' I tell the Vals, keeping my voice low. 'If I kill you, then I'll get your implants home if I can. If you kill me, then I want it quick and clean.'

They grin.

'And I want you to kill that general for me.'

I don't need them to nod to know that's already in their plan.

As one Val plants her feet firmly on the deck, the other begins to edge around me and our audience start banging on the tables with their fists. They're taking bets on who lands the first blow.

'Five on Sven,' shouts Neen.

He's swamped with takers. Since he doesn't have five gold coins, it is a brave bet.

Wiping sweat from my eyes, I flick my gaze from one Val to the other. Both have oiled their skin; should have thought of that myself. Only I didn't know this was going to happen and they obviously did.

'Ten on the Vals,' says the brigadier.

No one takes his bet.

As Val 7 moves, she rolls her dagger across the back of her hand. A neat trick, made neater by the fact she is moving crab-wise as she does it, with her eyes locked on mine.

Watch the eyes is a good maxim.

Only this time it is almost a mistake. I duck just in time, as the other Val slicks her blade through the space where my throat should be.

Someone claps.

And I'm two paces back and finding my balance. Twisting fast, I flick out my wrist and watch Val 7 dodge.

They're fast, I'm faster. My next strike rakes Val 5's chest. For a second the wound reveals muscle, ribs and the fat inside one breast, and then blood wells. The cut needs stitching but it's not fatal. All the same, she's shocked.

'Pay up,' someone shouts. It is Neen.

A movement catches my eye and I turn to find myself facing Val 7 again. She has stopped rolling the blade across the back of her fingers. Now it juts from the side of her fist, edge forwards. She's here to stop me finishing her sister.

'I'm going to kill you.'

'Yeah,' I tell her. 'That's what they all say.'

A feint from Val 7 has me twisting sideways. It's only experience that warns me the real move is yet to come. As she goes for my throat I step back, and she switches hands so fast her blade blurs. Her next stab targets my groin.

I block with my arm. The one with bone in, the one that bleeds.

Her next attack is harder, and she makes a mistake. Coming in close, she jerks back as my fingers reach for her throat, and slips on her sister's blood. This gives me time to finish her sister.

Val 7 is still trying to find her balance as I open Val 5's throat with my forearm and reverse my swing, jabbing my elbow hard into her head. As it hits, the spike goes right through her skull, and someone gags.

Ten to one it's the general's little ADC.

A twist frees the spike and carries me away from Val 7, who stands torn between rushing to her sister's side and killing me. In the second we eye each other, her sister begins to buckle, then drops to her knees and tips sideways.

'Fucker,' says Val 7.

The next attack is brutal.

She comes in stabbing, hard and fast. As I block the blows, I reach for her shoulder, but my fingers find oil and slip. She grins. And I have seen that grin before, because it's mine.

Usually, I see it reflected in the eyes of those I kill.

When she steps forward, I step back and let myself skid slightly on the blood-slick deck. The Val thinks she has me. So she rushes forward. And, as her blade jabs towards my throat, my toes regain their grip and my metal arm comes up to block her blade.

My other arm slams into her throat. The weight of the blow crushes cartilage. Seven minutes, that's how long she has before her ruptured throat tightens enough to suffocate her. Unless I finish it here.

Scooping up the Val's knife, I hammer its hilt into her skull, knocking her unconscious. Breath still rasps in her throat and her ribs shudder as her lungs fight for every breath. God, you have to love the Vals.

Or maybe that's just me.

Hooking two fingers into her nose lifts her onto her knees. And then I cut her throat from behind so blood sprays across the deck. The crowd roar, but I barely notice because I'm already sawing the head from its body.

The knife is sharp, but she has wiring in her flesh. So metal scrapes metal, before bone cracks and her skull comes free. It takes less time to behead the other. She's already dead, half her blood is on the deck, and I have worked out where to cut.

Quick learner, that's me. It's an *adaptive mechanism*.

God knows what that means, but it's what a Death's Head technician told me about five minutes before she decided to cancel my psych test halfway through and erase the results.

Chapter 45

'WELL,' SAYS THE GENERAL. 'THAT WAS IMPRESSIVE.'

I look for a subtext but he seems to mean what he says. So I thank him, dump the heads on the table and reach for my glass. It's full again. You can say what you like about General Tournier, but he runs a tight ship.

'To a good death,' I say.

It's a well-known Legion toast and he looks at me strangely.

Although that might be because my two trophies are making a mess of his spotless linen tablecloth. Also, everyone else at the table has stopped eating. So I lean over and take the rest of a chicken for myself, chewing chunks of meat from its carcass.

Fighting makes me hungry. Actually, everything makes me hungry.

One of the reasons having a kyp in my throat pisses me off so badly is I like food; what I don't like is everything I eat exiting the arse of some parasite before it reaches my stomach.

'You might want to clean up,' the general says. Sounds like an order to me.

'Of course, sir.'

He nods. 'Oh, Sven . . .'

I pause, about to zip up my trousers.

'Welcome aboard.'

'Thank you, sir.' Slinging my holster over my shoulder, I grab my shirt and jacket, toss them over my new arm and look around me. Time to get my other arm sewn. Vijay is looking at me strangely.

It makes me remember to ask, 'What about my ADC?'

The general raises his eyebrows. 'What about him?'

'Your men can look after him?'

'Oh yes,' says General Tournier. 'I'm sure they'll manage.'

Someone laughs. I am not sure why, but I glare anyway.

A major looks away. He has tiny braids growing from the rear of his skull, three of them. Gratefully, he fixes his attention on an approaching woman. Anything to avoid having to look back at me. 'Yes?' he demands.

Dipping her head, Shil says, 'I've been sent to clear, sir.'

Her voice is tight, but her face is neutral. So I doubt anyone else at the table catches her simmering anger. Perhaps I am wrong.

'Name?' demands the five-braid.

'Shil, sir,' she says.

'You're from Hekati?'

'Yes, sir . . .'

'Shil,' says the five-braid. 'Why won't you look at me?'

As I watch, her fingers tighten on the tray. She's wondering if she can use it as a weapon. The answer is yes. Also that cup, that knife, that glass. Anything is a weapon if you approach it with the right attitude.

'Well?' the five-braid demands.

She looks up and looks away. Shrugs.

'Tell him,' Colonel Vijay says. 'He's not going to hurt you.'

One thing you can guarantee. Patronize Shil and she's

going to want to rip out your heart. Only she is trapped, being watched by a dozen Death's Head officers, and the five-braid is still waiting for his answer.

So I drape my arm around her shoulder.

And then reach round a little further, cupping the under-side of one breast. Half of the table laughs as she twists free. As Shil's face flushes, her eyes fill with tears. They're from anger. Although I'm probably the only person to realize that.

'Come on,' I say, 'you can tell us.'

'Can't,' she says, scowling at the floor. Any minute now, she is going to start kicking her heels like a brat . . . If in doubt, play dumb; first rule of survival in the militia.

'Yes, you can.'

She tilts her head, considers this.

'He's got snakes for hair,' says Shil, flicking a sign against the evil eye. It's meant to be out of sight, but the braid sees it anyway. Or maybe he's meant to see it and Shil is only pre-tending to keep it out of sight.

He laughs loudly, and I decide to end this conversation. Grabbing her, I slide my hand under her skirt. She moves so fast it is all I can do to catch her wrist before she slaps me. Half the table joins in the five-braid's laughter as I kiss her.

'Let's get you out of here,' I whisper.

Shil glares at me.

'Need a bath,' I tell the general. 'If that's all right, sir? A bath, maybe another drink, some sleep . . .'

'And her?'

'Oh . . . She gets to scrub my back.'

'Level five,' he says. 'A full suite.' Turns out he is talking to his ADC, who nods and hastily does something to a key card, which he hands me with a slight bow.

The general watches us go with a grin on his face. Shil walks behind, more furious than ever now I've told her to carry the Vals for me. Picking our way between clapping tables, we head for an exit.

Although I take care to pass Neen on the way.

'See you later,' I tell him.

My sergeant wants to say something. But doesn't know where to begin, and I don't have time for him to work it out. So I nod to the Aux, then turn back and take a bottle of brandy from their table.

'Later,' I tell Neen. He gets it this time.

'Yes, sir . . . Later. Hope you have a good evening, sir.'

Shil looks like she wants to slap him.

We make it to the door, watched by six hundred Death's Head and fifteen hundred Silver Fist, plus more braids than I have ever seen in one place. Almost nobody meets my eyes. A few are obviously scared of me, but most are too busy looking at the trophies hanging from Shil's hands.

A servant steps back.

He also looks, but his gaze is on Shil and there's pity in his eyes.

A dozen servitors step out of my way in the corridor. None of them looks me in the eyes. Tells me all I need to know about the Ninth; they're as big a bunch of bastards as their Silver Fist allies. Hardly news. It goes with the uniform.

'In here,' I tell Shil, punching a button.

The elevator opens to reveal a surprised Death's Head officer. As I watch, a serving boy twists out of his grip and sprints away. He is at least thirty years younger than the major and lacks a paunch, so that's him gone then.

Swinging round, the major registers that I outrank him and shuts his mouth with a snap. 'Find another lift,' I say.

We leave him tight-lipped and dangerous to anyone junior. I know I shouldn't be enjoying this, but I am. Can't help the way I'm made.

Don't want to help it either.

It's got me this far.

As the elevator opens onto the fifth level, three Silver Fist corporals step back to let us through. One sees blood on the lift floor, glances back to check where it's coming from and sees what Shil is holding.

'Fuck,' he says, then realizes I'm an officer.

I wave his apologies away.

'You see the other fights?'

He nods, wondering how I missed them.

'Just arrived,' I tell him. 'So, what were they like?'

'Fierce, sir.'

He has his eyes on my arm, which still juts its spike at the elbow and has a row of blades. They've ripped my sleeve, obviously. You can't force a combat arm into a jacket cut for elegance without something giving.

'Who fought?'

'Volunteers . . .' Catching my grin, he shakes his head. 'I mean it, sir. I was thinking of volunteering myself. Our braid promised ten gold pieces and promotion to the pair that killed them.'

'The pair?' I say.

Eyes go wide. 'Sir,' he says. 'You didn't—'

'Fight as one of a pair?' I shake my head, grinning sourly. 'No,' I say. 'General Tournier forgot to mention that bit of the tradition.'

This is the point the Silver Fist decides he needs to be elsewhere. Understandable really.

Chapter 46

A HUGE ANIMAL SKIN FILLS THE MIDDLE OF MY SUITE. THE DEAD beast has eyes of golden glass, cracked teeth, a tasselled tail, and six legs that end in vicious claws. A badly mended hole in its neck shows how it died.

A terracotta girl simpers from one corner.

Her breasts are full, upturned and delicately nippled. That is pretty much all she is: simpering face, heaving breasts and bare shoulders, all shaded by a sloping hat. The sculptor hasn't bothered with anything else.

A lacquer bowl of sweetmeats sits next to her.

Swiping a bottle from Neen's table was obviously a waste of my time, because far better bottles sit in a row to one side of the simpering girl. There's nothing resembling *cachaca*, but there is brandy, whisky, pepper vodka and something on ice that calls itself *aquavit*. The bottle frosts as I pull it from the bucket. It tastes of . . .

Not sure, weeds of some kind.

Shil's not talking to me. She stands by the door with a look of absolute misery on her face. So maybe it was stupid to admit

I'd promised Neen to rescue her. But it was true. I thought she would be pleased.

Removing my shirt, I tip half the bottle over my arm. It hurts like fuck and the pain gets worse when I pull open the gash to wash the bone with alcohol. Shil's meant to be finding thread to sew it shut, so I turn my attention to the Vals, starting with the one who died first.

Her implant wriggles when it's dumped in the ice bucket. That is good, although the lurch my kyp gives is less good. The kyp's feeding on the implant's distress. The second Val's implant is in better condition. It wriggles so violently I almost drop it.

When I look for Shil, she's vomiting.

'That's Haze's trick,' I tell her.

Not sure she gets the joke. So I wait as she wipes her mouth on the back of her hand and spits on the deck, only just missing the skin rug.

'Shil,' I say.

She watches me, warily.

'What's wrong with this room?'

It is a real question. But she doesn't have an answer. So it seems to be time to wake my gun from standby. Shil stitches my arm, while we both wait for the SIG to stop pissing around with all its little lights. When it wants, it can exit standby faster than I can jack the slide.

'Screening myself,' it announces.

And then it takes a look around. A very slow look.

'Moth-eaten rug,' it says. 'Black silk sheets. Cheap statue with over-sized tits. An apparently limitless supply of alcohol . . . Sven, I apologize. How could I have imagined Pavel's city was good enough, when you can have all this?'

'Listen . . .'

'And that statue,' says the SIG. 'You know it's a fake?'

Can't say I did. Mind you, can't say it matters either. Certainly not in the way it obviously matters to my gun.

'SIG,' I say, 'what's wrong with this room?'

'You mean apart from the fact it's ghastly?'

'Yes. Apart from that.'

The SIG considers my question carefully. And Shil uses the time it takes to tie off the stitching on my arm. 'Thanks,' I say.

She looks through me.

Blood crusts the edge of her mouth, her eye is mostly yellow, her hair is slick with grease and I can smell stale sweat from here. I guess servants don't rate quarters like these. She wants to say something. A bit like her brother, she has no idea where to start. I have that effect on some people.

'Go take a shower.'

Her gaze hardens. 'Is that an order, sir?'

'Yes,' I tell her. 'That's an order.'

Spinning on her heels, Shil heads for a cubicle without another word. She looks as good naked as ever. Although I catch her only in a first brief burst of light. After that, sonic waves begin and the cubicle walls turn grey again.

'You could always tell her to take another shower,' my gun suggests.

'Didn't know the walls were going to do that.'

It snorts, and turns its attention back to my room.

The décor is a Silver Fist take on Octovian taste, it tells me. Apparently Octovian taste is shit anyway, and so mimicking it is easy. All you need is a lot of gold lacquer, some naked statues, furry rugs, big mirrors and plenty of weapons on the walls.

Octovian taste is puerile, the SIG tells me.

I'd ask what *puerile* means but I don't want to know. *Octovian taste* is my taste. The stuff we have in Golden Memories. General Jaxx's passion for matt black and silver always struck me as a bit odd.

'Now do your clothes,' I tell Shil.

She scowls, but I am used to that.

'They smell,' I add.

'Yes, sir,' she says. 'I know . . . *I'm wearing them.*' Stamping back to the cubicle, she taps a switch and the light zaps her, clothes and all.

'Time?' I demand of the gun.

'Six hundred sixty seconds to Zero.'

Little bastard's adopted the digital clock.

'*How did it get so late?*' The gun sniffs. 'I guess time just flies when you're enjoying yourself.'

I'm about to have a guest.

I know this, and the SIG knows this, because it has been tracking my visitor since he began walking along a corridor seventeen levels below.

Shil's not happy when I tell her to take her blouse off again. She'd scowl, but she is doing that already. So she opens her mouth to protest and lets rip as I push her towards the bed. So many rude words.

When she halts at the edge, I grip her shoulder with one hand and reach for buttons with my other. That's when I realize I'm still wearing my fighting arm. 'Fucking hell.'

'What?' the gun demands.

'This,' I say, flexing the arm. Pistons hiss.

And they hiss again as I push Shil to her knees and undo my flies. Her back is to the door and she's fighting to get to her feet.

'Shit,' she says.

Reminds me she hasn't seen it close up before.

My hand holds her in place long enough for the man outside to knock. Shil freezes, which makes life easier. When I don't answer, the five-braid knocks again, and then pushes his way into my room.

'Not disturbing anything, am I?'

Yanking Shil to her feet, I fold myself inside my trousers. This is more difficult than it should be, because I'm not sure my body knows we're play-acting here. 'It can wait,' I tell the braid.

Pointing his finger at Shil, he says, 'You . . . Get lost.'

I shake my head. 'No way,' I say. 'She stays here where I can see her.'

He glares at me.

'You think I'm going to waste my time hunting her down again after you've gone?' Nodding to Shil, I jerk my chin towards the bed. She's not going to forgive me. Mind you, given her catalogue of my crimes to date, she's probably never going to get this far down the list. What makes it all worse is the figure standing behind the five-braid. Although, given the blankness in his eyes, you would think Shil was invisible.

Haze comes into the room.

That's it. Doesn't say *hello*, doesn't say anything. Seems I might as well not exist either. 'You want a drink?' I ask the braid.

He shakes his head.

'How about your little friend?'

The five-braid shakes his head again, not bothering to check what Haze wants. 'We're here to talk.'

'So talk,' says a voice. It's my gun uncloaking.

'That's—'

I sigh. 'Yeah,' I say. 'Of course it is. Illegal in ninety-eight per cent of the known universe.'

Reaching for my holster, I buckle it round my waist and settle the SIG on my hip. Small things keep me happy. Small things and knowing I can reduce the five-braid to chopped meat if I am fast enough.

At my hip the gun shivers, loading and locking.

I must be closer to violence than I imagined. A knife hangs

from my other hip, and then there's the arm, jagged blades up its outside edge and that wicked spike at the elbow.

'So,' the five-braid says to Haze. 'It's true.'

Haze nods.

Fingers pick at the edge of my mind. Sounds stupid, but that is how it feels. Like someone's trying to dig their nails under a scab or prise off a lid or something. So I hammer down on the lid.

And the braid steps back.

It's almost a stumble. When he looks at Haze, his expression is rueful. He has just been proved wrong about something.

Turns out it's me.

'See,' says Haze, and then amends it to, 'You see what I mean, sir?'

The five-braid nods. Sweeping his gaze round my room, he hesitates only when he reaches the bed. He wants Shil gone, I want her here. At the moment, it's looking like two against two. I can take the braid. God knows, I can take Haze. Just never occurred to me I would have to.

'She stays,' I say.

The braid tries to protest.

'We talk,' I tell him. 'She gets to listen. If it's that secret we kill her afterwards.'

He laughs. Shil and Haze say nothing. Though they say it in their own ways.

'That fight with the Vals was impressive,' says the braid. 'I was doubtful, but the general said you'd come through . . . You know why you won?'

'Because I'm better.'

Silence greets my remark. I don't see what his problem is. I'm alive, the Vals are dead, their gutted heads are on a table in the corner of my room, and I have their implants in an ice bucket.

It's obvious I'm better. If I weren't, it would be the other way round. Apart from the implant bit.

'Perhaps,' says the braid, 'we should be asking why you're better.'

'Quicker, stronger, more ruthless . . .' I'm reciting from my most recent physical. The one I had on joining the Death's Head. 'Also, I mend faster, and pain bothers me less than other people.'

'You need extremes,' says the five-braid.

'Crap.'

'Brings you alive,' he says. 'Focuses your mind . . . And all that's true, but it's not the reason.'

I wait. He's going to tell me anyway.

'You're one of us,' he says.

This time he steps back for real.

Might be the gun in my hand. Could be the spike on my arm. My guess is the gun. It has clips whirring madly, while it fights off his attempt to close it down. From the scowl on the braid's face, the gun is winning.

'Flechette,' I tell it.

The SIG suggests explosive. That gun has a fetish about big bangs.

We compromise on hollow-point ceramic. At this range, it'll leave most of the five-braid's brains on the bulkhead behind him.

'Wait,' says the five-braid. 'You can't—'

'Wanna bet,' the gun says.

'Just listen,' the five-braid says, eyes flicking sideways. He's scared, angry and nervous. Bad mix, it makes me glad I'm the one holding the SIG. Something in the braid's glance suggests Haze told him I would be willing to listen. I'm not sure why he thinks that. I'm no more of a braid than—

'Listen,' suggests Shil.

I glare at her. She's meant to be staying out of this.

306

Hell, we don't even know each other. At least, not where the braid's concerned. But Shil has her gaze on me and on Haze, and there's something furious in her look. As if she'd like to bang our heads together.

'You've got thirty seconds,' I tell the braid.

'Twenty-nine,' says the gun. It counts us down to three, then two, and it's about to hit one when I ruin its day and jack out the hollow-point. The shell bounces on the floor and rolls under the bed.

'What did you do that for?' it demands.

'I'm listening,' I tell the SIG.

I am as well.

According to the braid my DNA is close to the humanoid original. I don't have plus point eight per cent anything. Everyone else has stuff taken out. Of course, that doesn't mean I come from Earth . . .

The braid shakes his head.

How could I, when Earth never existed?

But I'm as close to the template as he's seen. So, he says, if I want I can call myself the last human. This seems to be a joke. And I'm ready to let him know how I feel about that when I decide I'd better keep listening.

At Haze's suggestion, the braid is offering me a job. A job, and rapid promotion from a rank that isn't mine to start with. It takes me a second to realize he's offering me General Tournier's job.

All I have to do is drop down five levels and kill the man.

Chapter 47

EARTH NEVER EXISTED. ANYONE WHO SAYS IT DID IS A HERETIC and a doubter of the truth. That Earth story is a myth made up by heretics to explain why life became more complicated several centuries ago. Only it didn't . . . Get more complicated, that is. That's another myth. Equally vile. The universe has always been exactly as it is.

The five-braid glares at me. 'You accept that?' he says.

I tell him it never occurred to me it hadn't.

He nods, begins talking about *the singularity*, and stops when he realizes I'm still playing catch-up with his first lot of words. We move on to things he reckons I can understand.

No alcohol, no paintings, no eating cold-water reptiles, no sex between races (or perhaps it's species) . . . I've stopped listening by the time he gets halfway through his list of things I'll need to give up when I come over to his side.

As offers go, it's tempting.

Not for what I'll give up but for what I'll gain. Ten per cent of the stock value of any rebel Octovian planet I take. And I'll be leading a legitimate army, so anyone who opposes us is automatically a rebel.

There's a sliding scale of fees for everything from captured villages to capital cities and enemy ships. The sums he's talking about are enormous. You could hire a Legion brigade for a year. No, you could buy the whole bloody Legion, desert forts and all.

I am not sure I even knew that much gold existed.

All he wants in return is to run some tests and take a quick look inside my skull. For a moment, I think he wants to open up my head. But he means he needs free access to my thoughts.

I can think of several reasons why this is a bad idea. One of them sits scowling in the bed behind me. How much poking around does a five-braid have to do before he realizes Shil and I have history?

'So,' he says. 'Do we have a deal?'

A five-braid and me. Now there is an unlikely combination. 'What's the security like on your ship?'

My question puzzles him.

'If I'm going to kill the general . . .'

He smiles, thinking he has agreement. 'Lenz,' he says, 'the usual stuff. Doors talk to each other, elevators communicate, maintenance bots feed visuals to the ship's AI. Nothing serious.'

The gun snorts.

'Here,' says the braid. Pulling a small disc from the inside pocket of his uniform, he touches it to an identical disc on his collar.

'What does it do?' I demand.

'Security override. Wear this and you're invisible to the ship's monitors.'

Taking it, I fix it to my own collar and turn back. Maybe I should just kill him now? It's hard to know. I'm trying to be cool, but I'm not sure how I'll react if he starts poking around inside my skull.

'Get on with it,' I say. 'Before I change my mind.'

Something lifts the edge of my mind, and I slam it down, pure instinct. Shil screams. I think it's because my arm is back to strike. But I'm wrong.

Having grabbed the dagger from my belt, Haze is sawing it across the braid's throat. The Enlightened does that flickering thing as he tries to take himself somewhere else. But my elbow spike in his chest locks him into the present.

As Haze finishes, I let go the braid and he drops, sliding off the spike with a wet sucking sound.

I rip the clocking device from the fallen five-braid's collar, then turn back. 'We've only got two of these,' I tell Haze. 'There are three of us. Can you make yourself invisible to the lenz?' Only he's not listening. He's too busy helping Shil from the bed.

'Are you all right?' he asks. 'I mean . . . Did they . . . ?'

'No,' she says, abruptly. 'They didn't.'

Haze waits.

'One tried,' she adds with a shrug. Her voice is sour. 'Thanks for asking, I think.'

'Shil,' I say.

'Later,' she says. 'Sir.'

'Well,' I ask Haze. 'Can you?' Only he's still not paying attention. Must be something about this ship. It makes me feel odd too.

'We need to talk,' he says.

'Haze.'

'Sir—' He stops. 'The general told me to watch you.'

'You mean Tournier?'

'No, sir . . . Jaxx, sir. Before we left.'

'General Jaxx?'

'Yes, sir.'

Why didn't you tell me? But I already know. When someone

310

like Jaxx says keep something quiet you keep it quiet. The alternative is having Horse Hito rip your tongue through a slit in your neck. And that is if you get lucky.

'Why tell me now?' It's obvious that Shil wants an answer to this too.

Taking a deep breath, Haze says, 'Almost didn't. Almost let the five-braid turn you. Would have done, probably. But . . .' He shrugs. 'We're the Aux. That has to count for something.' He looks around him and shivers.

'What?' Shil asks.

'You can't feel it, can you?'

She shakes her head.

'No,' he says. 'I thought not. Hekati's dying.' Walking across to the line of bottles, he examines the labels until his hand stops over a dumpy-looking flask. 'Shil?' he asks.

She shakes her head.

'Sir?'

Why not?

He pours one each for us; then he pours one for Shil anyway, which she kills in a single gulp. That done, she eats half the nuts in the bowl and fills her pockets with the rest.

'You they feed,' she tells him. 'Us they starve.'

'I'm not them,' Haze says.

If Haze is right, our two badges and his own skills are enough to hide us from the lenz we're going to find on the ceiling of every corridor in this ship. And we have a plan for dealing with anyone we meet.

We are going to kill them.

And if Haze is wrong, we are going straight to the second part of that plan.

I'm holding the SIG-37, combat style. Slightly raised, so I can sweep the corridor outside my room. Haze has my knife and Shil carries the five-braid's pulse pistol, his knife, and a set of my throwing spikes.

Overkill, I reckon. But if it makes her happy, that's fine.

The rest of the Aux are seven decks down.

I'm tempted to kill the general first, then his staff officers. Sometimes you just want to eat pudding early. All the same, I make myself wait.

Victory First Last and Always is large enough to need escape decks every five levels. What interests me most is that General Tournier's own quarters are directly above the largest escape deck. Not sure that says anything good about him.

Not sure I care, either.

If there's a pod on that escape deck big enough to take us all – and there's any of us left to take – then we're going to take it, and should that pod turn out to be for General Tournier's own use, so much the better.

Lights in the upper corridor remain dim as we pass. Lenz sweep from side to side without seeing us. Emergency stairs open and shut their fire doors, seemingly without noticing.

Haze is concentrating. That's why he is in the middle.

I take point and Shil brings up the rear. Although we bunch tight. Both Shil and I are working hard to keep Haze feeling safe while he runs his routines. It's like old times, and that makes me realize how badly Hekati gets to me. Give me a proper battle every time.

Behind me, Haze snorts.

'What?' I say.

He opens his eyes as if seeing the stairs for the first time. 'One battle coming up,' he says, adding *sir* as an afterthought.

'You think?'

'All hell's about to break loose.'

So now, I'm smiling too. Setting the SIG-37 to thirty seconds *certain*, five minutes *likely* and fifteen *highly probable* burns battery, but the gun started this with a full power pack, and I have another on my belt. Makes lugging it around all this time worthwhile.

'Talk to Haze,' I tell the gun. 'And keep me updated.'

This just leaves Shil. For once, she is not scowling; her face simply looks puzzled. 'But you can do that, sir.' Shil means the ju-ju shit.

'Haze and the gun guard. We fight. Someone has to.'

'And that's us?'

'Yes,' I say. 'That's us.'

She has the Vals' implants in a flask on her belt. It is the best I can do: stuffing the implants into a water bottle before tipping ice on top. I have told her we owe the Vals that. She's wondering if I am one of the good guys after all.

My orders to Shil are simple. We find the general, we kill him. Everyone and everything is expendable: that includes her, it includes Haze, and it includes me. Nothing in there she doesn't already know.

'Sir,' says Haze, sounding worried.

I turn back, SIG in hand. 'What?' I demand.

'Being scan—'

Shil drags his unconscious body into a doorway. As she does, a lenz flicks towards her and locks on to where she is crouching. Except the lenz obviously didn't catch her, because it continues its run and then scans back without stopping.

'Sir,' says Shil.

'More trouble than he's worth,' I say about Haze.

I'm joking, almost . . . We are three levels above General Tournier's quarters, and six above where the Aux are being held, or sleeping, or whatever their bloody status is. According to the SIG, there are guards outside the elevator to the general's level, outside every escape deck, and on the corridor where the Aux are.

The stairs are deserted. They are, however, alarmed.

'SIG,' I say. 'You can deal with it, right?'

'What, you think I'm fucking human? Of course I can deal with it.' The SIG's enjoying itself, you can always tell.

'You,' I say to Shil. 'Wait here until all hell breaks loose. Then drag Haze to the escape deck. If you can't do that, head for the level below. We'll find you on our way up.'

'Yes, sir.'

I toss her a grenade. 'Take this. You might need it.'

She nods, gratefully.

'And Shil.' Must be something in my tone that makes her glance up and then look away.

'Sir?'

'That night you were captured . . .'

She wants to wave away what I'm going to say, because she thinks I'm apologizing. She's wrong. 'You shouldn't have come back for me. You should have retreated when I gave you the order. Next time you do as you're told.'

Shil scowls at me.

'Understand?'

'Yes, sir. Understand, sir.'

'What do you understand?'

'Next time someone wants to kill you, sir, I'm to let them.'

Chapter 48

I HEAR THE FIRST GUARD'S NECK BREAK. UNFORTUNATELY, SO does everyone else, it echoes so loudly off the walls of a corridor. Scrabbling at his holster, the second guard takes a spike under his chin. I don't even bother to throw, just flip the spike and ram. Slapping it with the heel of my hand makes the entire thing disappear.

As the second guard goes cross-eyed, the guard beyond him acquires a neat hole in his forehead. There's no splatter pattern of blood or spilt brains on the bulkhead behind, and I am impressed.

See, the SIG can do silent when it tries.

The fourth man does what the first, second and third should have done. He dives for an emergency button on the wall. He doesn't reach it. Entering the guard's eye, the subsonic bullet bounces around inside his skull, pulping memories. 'And for my next trick,' the SIG says.

A ceiling lenz glitches, giving me time to drag the bodies into a nearby elevator and punch a button for fifty floors below. As the doors close on them, I check the corridor both ways. A sign on the wall beside the elevators reads *This floor: NCOs only.* I'm already trying one of the dorms.

Rolling over, a trooper spots my officer's uniform in the light coming from behind me and decides faking sleep is a good choice. Makes me wonder what goes on around here. Three other dorms pass in quick succession. And I'm opening a fifth door when someone grabs me.

Neen has his knife under my chin.

I have the SIG under his.

'How sweet,' my gun says.

'Sir . . .'

'Shut it,' I say.

Franc, Rachel and Emil wait in the half dark behind him. A couple of guards lie dead behind them. And a dozen beds lie empty beyond, no sheets or blankets, just mattresses. Looks like they are being kept in isolation.

Jerking my thumb at Emil, I say, 'Behaving?'

Neen nods. 'Perfectly, sir.'

'Betray us,' I tell Trooper Emil, 'and it'll be the last thing you do.'

'That's *great to see you too*,' says my gun, in case our newest recruit isn't good at translating.

'Sir,' says Neen. 'Question?'

'What?'

'Where are the others?'

I'm impressed he includes Vijay and Haze and doesn't just ask about Shil. But then I spot the worry in Rachel's eyes and know he is asking on her behalf as well, because she doesn't quite dare.

'First point,' I say. 'Shil's absolutely fine.'

Franc flicks me a glance I'm not meant to see. I know that much when she bites her lip. Seems best to ignore it. 'Haze had a turn. They're both waiting above. Not sure about Vijay.' Have to stop myself from calling him *the colonel*.

Haze's *being scanned* has me worried.

316

The five-braid's dead, General Tournier doesn't yet have that level of power, the ship's AI might be clever, but no more so than the SIG-37 . . . Who does that leave to do the scanning? Only an Uplifted. All flashing lights, memory crystal and arrogance. Or a higher-ranking Enlightened than the one we killed.

Has to be a braid, I think.

'Sir,' says Rachel. She sounds worried.

More time has passed than I was aware of. We're in a different corridor. Actually, we're not in a corridor at all. We're about to finish climbing a flight of emergency stairs. *Senior Officers Only,* says a sign.

Been here before, I think, opening a door. In a tight gap, on the other side, wait Haze and Shil.

'You . . . ?' asks Neen.

'Yeah,' Shil says. 'I'm fine.'

That is the extent of their conversation.

Although he wraps one arm briefly round her shoulder when he thinks we're not looking. And she flicks him the kind of smile that says, *quit fussing.*

The internal emergency doors in *Victory First* have portholes. That's one difference between Enlightened and Octovian ships. No way would General Jaxx let anyone ruin his immaculate matt-black doors. Also, Enlightened doorways double as airlocks, all of them.

A door, a space deep enough to take six people, then another door. Heavy bolts are fixed above and below each one, ready to lock it down.

'Modular, sir,' says Haze.

'What?' I look at him.

'This whole ship,' he says. 'Each section is a mirror of a bigger section. Boxes inside boxes. The design reflects Uplift theories of the hive.'

I'll take his word for it.

Using a porthole, Neen checks the corridor beyond.

It's empty in one direction. In the other, two guards wait outside General Tournier's cabin. As he watches, two guards become four. A Silver Fist nods, another laughs. And then the first two head towards a bank of elevators.

'Changing shifts,' Neen whispers.

We wait some more.

A few minutes later Rachel blunders through the outer emergency door, and stares around her. She does a good impression of a woman lost. Also drunk, and slightly dishevelled. Shaking out her hair, she turns back and both guards take the bait.

'Wait,' says one.

'No way,' Rachel gives another shake. 'Wrong floor.' She looks at the expensive carpet. 'Very definitely the wrong floor.'

'Where do you want to be?'

'On a water bed,' says Rachel. 'In a hotel overlooking a blue lagoon. With flying fish breaking through the waves and a double sun rising and setting.'

Who knew she could be so poetic?

'You and me both,' says one of the Silver Fist.

To follow Rachel through the door is a misdemeanour in anybody's army; although being on a charge is the least of his worries. Yanking him inside, Franc stabs him through the heart and kicks his twitching body down the stairs. It tumbles as far as a half-landing and jams against a bulkhead.

'What was that?'

Rachel returns to the corridor.

'What?' she asks, walking towards the second guard. 'What was what?' Her knife takes him under his chin and enters his brain. The smile she gives Franc when the rest of us reach her makes me glad she is on my side.

Chapter 49

'ON MY COUNT,' I TELL NEEN. 'FIVE . . . FOUR . . .'

When I hit zero, Neen turns the handle and I kick open the general's door, sliding myself inside, gun combat-ready. Staff officers look up, and the general spins round; over in one corner Vijay's eyes widen.

He's holding a glass. As is almost every other officer in that room.

'Entering emergency shut-down,' announces my gun.

The SIG-37 and I really need to talk about this. It's as irritating as its bloody whirring, and several times more inconvenient. *'Don't you fucking . . .'*

Diodes die before I can finish the sentence.

A dozen Death's Head officers nod, and a handful of them smirk. I'm glad; it lets me know who to kill first. After the Silver Fist, obviously. There are six of these, three on either side of the door. All are armed. And all have guns pointing at my head.

'Sven,' says the general. 'I've been expecting you.' Waving vaguely towards the middle of his cabin, he adds, 'Come in. And bring your friends.'

So in we troop.

Although that is not entirely true, because when I glance back Haze is missing and Rachel is shutting the door carefully behind her.

'Sir,' says the little ADC. 'Perhaps we should disarm them?'

The general considers this.

'Why,' he asks. 'Would it make you feel safer?'

The boy blushes.

Returning my SIG to its holster, I fumble the catch and then unbuckle my belt, dropping it to the deck. At least fumbling is how it's meant to look. One throwing spike now rests in the palm of my hand. At my nod, the Aux put down their guns.

'Search them.'

The boy finds a knife in my boot.

'Anyone else hiding anything?' asks General Tournier. 'If so, you might want to give your weapons up.' There is a drawl to his voice, and a smile on his face that would disgrace a cat. He's obviously hoping we'll ignore his suggestion.

'Lose the lot,' I say.

The Aux do as they're told.

Rachel has a knife inside her shirt, Neen a blade in his boot that the general's ADC missed first time round. Shil just shakes her head. Trooper Emil, our ex-Ninth captain, has a tiny pistol tucked into the back of his belt. Not sure how he expected to get away with that.

'That's it?'

Everyone nods.

'And again,' the general says.

Only this time he is talking to a Silver Fist.

The man starts with me and finds nothing, because the throwing spike is now buried deep under the flesh of my good wrist. Hurts, but then it would. Neen goes next and he's clean. As expected, the man spends more time than necessary on the women.

Stony-faced, Franc waits while he runs his hands over her hips and up the inside of her legs. He misses the blade between her shoulders, but to find that he needs to focus less on her breasts. Rachel just stands there. Shil is less forgiving.

In fact, her slap rocks the Silver Fist on his heels. She is savagely punched for her trouble. As she crawls to her feet, she glances at Neen, who nods. One of the knives on the deck a second before is now missing.

Emil turns out to have a cosh in his boot. When he picks himself up, he sneers at the Silver Fist who hit him and has to pick himself up all over again.

'Just leaves your arm,' General Tournier tells me.

I've been wondering when he would get round to that. When the arm arrived, the screw designed to hold it in place was crusty with rust. Now it's crusted with a mix of new rust and dried blood from the Vals. That makes it damn near impossible to shift without the right tools. When I point this out to the general, he suggests I try using a discarded blade. So polite these Death's Head senior officers.

We might as well be discussing the weather.

'Of course,' he says, 'we'll kill your troops if you try anything stupid. And after that we'll kill you, obviously.' Two Silver Fist point their rifles at me as I bend to pick up a knife.

Don't show any surprise, sir . . .

Haze is inside my head. And yes, I told him to stay out of there, but I'm still glad to hear him. *Listen*, I say. *My fucking gun's dead again.*

Faking, sir.

It can do that?

'Sven,' the general's voice is abrupt.

Looking up, I find the whole room staring at me.

'Anything wrong?'

History is made of questions asked and roads taken . . . So Haze tells me, but he talks shit about stuff like that. What will happen happens, and anything that doesn't happen wasn't meant to happen in the first place. This is our glorious leader's definition of *historical determinism.*

So it is unquestionably right.

All the same, there seems more than one answer to the general's question. And I'm not sure which is right. Presumably, if I say it, then that is what I'm meant to say, and I was never going to say anything else anyway.

'Fuck,' I say.

'What?' General Tournier demands.

'Thinking,' I say. 'Makes my head hurt. Always has done.'

Looking round his room with its carpet and bowls of fruit, and staff officers chatting to each other because this has lasted so long it's become boring, I realize the obvious. 'Should have killed you,' I say. 'Should have just killed the fucking lot of you the first time we met . . .'

He stares at me. 'You're not really a colonel, are you?'

'What the fuck do you think?'

Now I have his officers' attention back. And I am actually beginning to enjoy myself, because facing death does that for me. Then there's our glorious leader's law . . . You know, the one that demands ex-NCOs announce their status, so trouble-makers can be identified early.

'I'm an ex-sergeant,' I say. 'From the Legion.'

'Jaxx sent a sergeant after me?'

'An ex-sergeant,' I remind him. 'A Legion ex-sergeant.'

It is worth saying for the look on General Tournier's face. This man is seriously insulted. As for his staff officers, they're slicking sideways glances at him. This is fine, because it means they're not looking at me.

'Neen,' I say.

Stabbing a guard, Neen flicks the blade to his sister. She kills the one next to her, then goes after a man behind. I'm busy extracting my elbow from the skull of the nearest Silver Fist. And the man who patted down Franc has a new mouth. As I watch, she reaches into the gash and yanks his tongue through the slit.

Serious anger issues, that woman.

We're good, and we're quick. Six dead in less than a second. But guns are being levelled across the room.

'Neen,' I say. 'The SIG.'

Neen wants to say it's dead. Instead, he hooks his foot under the holster and boots it up to me.

Catching the SIG, I rip it free.

'*Haze*,' I say.

The lights go out. Actually, everything goes out. Lights, temperature control, oxygen recycling units, cheesy classical music, the lot.

'Hollow-point . . .'

The SIG-37's loaded up already.

I fire at their muzzle flashes and they fire at mine. Only I'm not where I was because I'm already somewhere else. All of my troopers have hit the deck and rolled towards the nearest bulkhead, which helps. Although I almost trip over Rachel.

She yelps, and then yelps again when I boot her out of the way.

It's dark, and then it's not, because my eyes adjust and I watch the general aim his gun. Seems I'm not the only one with night vision. This isn't looking good. '*Move*,' suggests my gun.

'Too late,' says the general.

'Not really,' says the man standing directly behind him.

Smashing his brandy glass, Colonel Vijay rams it into the general's neck, and twists savagely on the stem to widen the wound. Blood spurts halfway across the room, and then weakens until a final dribble wets the general's boots like piss.

Vijay does this blind. In total darkness. Having memorized his position.

I'm impressed. 'Sir,' I say, 'the command is yours.'

'Carry on, Sven.'

The next job is less pretty.

The general's little ADC has his dagger out and is jabbing it frantically at the darkness around him. He's as likely to stab his own side as ours; but he is frightened beyond caring.

Was I like that? I wonder. When Lieutenant Bonafonte put his gun to my head in the dump. The day the Legion burnt down my village and slaughtered the Junkyard Rats on the road below the edge of Primary One.

No . . . Death would have been welcome. It was probably why Bonafonte spared me. He always was a perverse bastard. Reaching forward to snap the ADC's neck, I find myself hesitating.

Now, I don't hesitate, ever. *I do.*

That is the way this shit works. Stop to think about what you're doing and you're dead. That's what Bonafonte told me, and he was right.

Look what happened to him.

I'm glad it's dark and no one saw. Realizing this makes me angrier still. Since when do I give a fuck what anyone else thinks? But this kid could be me; if I'd grown up rich, of course . . . In a proper house, with schooling and stuff like that.

Grabbing the little ADC's wrist, I twist until he drops his dagger. And then I push my face close to his. 'Hit the deck,' I tell him. 'Crawl towards the door. Get yourself out of here.'

He nods, as if this is obvious. As if he should be listening to orders from an enemy. And while he's still nodding, I jab my own blade hard through the side of his skull and cut his brain stem.

He dies without knowing it has happened.

The others I kill brutally. Gutting some and sweeping the feet from under others, stamping on their necks. I go through that room like the wind, taking down all in my path. Three Silver Fist I simply kill with a single sweep of my blade, opening their throats in a row and welcoming the hot liquid that jets out to spray me. I'm just wiping my mouth when the panic lights come up.

Probably looks like I'm licking my fingers.

Shil turns away and Rachel signs against the evil eye. Even the colonel looks at me strangely. 'All done?' he asks.

'All done, sir.'

'Good,' he says. 'Then let's get out of here. But first . . .' Hacking the general's head from his body, Colonel Vijay lifts his trophy by its braids, and smiles.

'Sir,' I say, 'you want me to rip his implant?'

'Oh no,' he says. 'I'm sure OctoV would prefer the whole head.'

Chapter 50

THE AUX LINE UP. THEY'RE NOT MEETING MY EYES. IN FACT,
they're doing everything but looking directly at me. Must
be the blood on my uniform. So I have Neen bring them to
attention and walk myself down the line. That way they have
no choice. Rachel is crying, but quietly. Franc looks lost inside
herself. And I can't read Shil's expression at all.

'Report,' I order Neen.

'All present, sir,' he says.

And he's right. Because Haze is in the doorway behind us,
looking like sin on a bad day. At a nod from me, Neen tosses
him a spare Silver Fist rifle, and we all watch as he fumbles
the catch.

Colonel Vijay sighs.

'What now, sir?' I ask.

'We find ourselves an escape deck,' he says.

'Sir,' I say. 'What about the missing U/Free observer?'

'He's gone, Sven. Got that from the general himself.'

'Dead, sir?'

The colonel looks at me, glances at the others, and then
walks me across to a corner of the general's suite, his head bent

close to mine. 'Sven,' he says. 'There was no observer. OK? Let it go . . .'

It's my turn to stare.

'We needed cover stories. That was our second. You know, the first one was we're on a cultural mission. And then, for the people who don't believe that . . . we're looking for a missing U/Free.'

'And the U/Free agreed to go along with it, because they think we're here to sign their treaty? But really,' I say, glancing at his trophy, 'we've been here to collect that all along and there was no observer?'

'You've got it,' he says, slapping me on the back.

There are days I fucking hate politics.

Racing up the corridor, a Death's Head trooper from the Ninth Regiment freezes, unsure what's happening. After a second, he salutes. Idiot.

'A false alarm,' I say.

He gapes at me.

'Malfunctioning sirens,' says Colonel Vijay. 'Return to your unit.'

The man nods and turns. Only a Silver Fist captain is turning the corner behind him and he isn't as stupid. He is, however, slow. He's still pulling his pistol when I put a throwing spike in his throat. Colonel Vijay kills the original trooper, who dies still looking puzzled.

Bundling down a corridor, we head for a door. The elevators are locked down. That is good, because it keeps the enemy away. Also bad, because it means we might need to fight on the stairs. Should the Silver Fist work out that having elevators arrive and not leave is a better option still, then we'll really have a battle on our hands.

'Sven,' says my gun as I skid-turn, and rip my fighting arm into the throat of a sergeant rounding a corner towards me.

327

Colonel Vijay shoots the man behind him. The man behind that turns to run and dies with one of Franc's knives in his back.

'*What?*' I demand.

'Remember me?'

You can always tell when the SIG's jealous. It gets snippy. 'This arm's useful,' I say.

'No,' says the gun. 'It's rusty, out-dated, and *ugly.*' The SIG places special emphasis on the last. 'And it's slowing you down.'

'It's not.'

'Weighs more than a combat trike,' it says. 'Bloody thing was meant to handicap you. Only you're so stupid you decided to keep it.'

'You'll get your chance soon enough.'

'So you keep saying.'

Catching up with me at the stair door, Neen opens it and through I go. Takes me ten seconds to reach the first bend and check it is clear, eleven to return. As I step back into the corridor, Neen raises his rifle. 'Sorry, sir,' he says, lowering it again.

'Next time hold your aim,' I tell him.

Colonel Vijay is listening.

'What if someone was coming through behind me?'

He'll remember next time. For an ex-militia grunt with barely six months as an NCO he is turning into a pro. Actually, he's turning into a veteran. Neen goes red when I say this.

'Round here,' says his sister, 'it's adapt or die.'

When Neen shoots Shil a frown, the colonel laughs. 'It's all right,' he says. 'I'm sure Lieutenant Tveskoeg can recognize a compliment when he hears one.'

★   ★   ★

Standing by a Silver Fist launch that looks more like a small space liner, Colonel Vijay says, 'We'll take this one.' The *Wild Wild Wind* has elegant lines, its own escape pods and an array of antennae bristling along the top. It's also easily big enough to take all of us and still have room to spare.

Obviously enough, the SIG disagrees.

The craft the SIG wants sits behind the one Colonel Vijay likes. It's a B79 bomber and a third the size of the launch. A silver skull on its black nose-cone reinforces what we already know. The craft belongs to the Ninth.

'This one,' says the colonel, tapping the little liner.

The SIG is not having it.

As they argue, lights start flickering on the bomber's hatch. At first they're out of sync with those on the SIG. Slowly the sequences begin to match. When they match exactly, the hatch shifts slightly, stops, and then pops open.

'Well, hello,' says the gun.

A second later a ladder folds down.

'B79, new model,' says the SIG. 'Now with sixty-four rockets, instead of forty-eight. Added stealth screening. Uprated quad-barrelled machine gun, fully automatic obviously. Semi AI navigation, fully AI combat brain . . .'

Haze is practically drooling.

He's sold. The others are looking at Colonel Vijay.

'Well?' says the gun.

OK, he's sold as well. Who wouldn't be with that firepower? And we need to move anyway, because the sirens are dying, and that is not good. It means someone is finally taking charge.

'Fighters,' says Haze, glancing at a wall screen. 'They've scrambled fighters.'

'Gets worse,' my gun says.

'How?'

All the overhead strips go out. On cue, the escape deck's

emergency lights fire up. Only to go out just as quickly. A second later, Neen turns on his rifle's torch. It produces enough light for us to see our way to the bomber.

Neen thinks that's the problem solved. He hasn't thought it through.

If the emergency power is dead, then how do we fire the explosive bolts holding the outer wall in place? Without these, the wall remains and the escape deck keeps us trapped. Until their CO works out a way to hook us out of here. Personally, I would flood the place with nerve gas.

Colonel Vijay agrees. 'Has that bomber got an air system?'

'Of course,' says the gun. 'It's got an Alexo3 ferric—'

'Everyone inside,' he says.

The SIG's still running its sales pitch for the purifier, though it stops when it realizes no one is listening. The steps flip up, and the door hisses down, and we are airtight inside fifteen seconds. I'm beginning to like this machine.

'Permission to . . .'

Colonel Vijay nods. 'Go ahead, Sven,' he says.

Slapping my hand on a plate next to the pilot's seat, I let the B79 scan my palm and then give it my name, rank and service number. I give it the real ones. If it is as clever as the gun says, then it can match the hand scan to my service records anyway.

A line of words scrolls across the glass plate.

Information already entered.

'Genotype human equivalent. Status DH class 2, override . . .'

It's reading a bloody identity chip fitted when I was on the general's mother ship. Knew I had one in that arm Colonel Madeleine made me. Obviously got one under my skin somewhere as well.

There are three combat seats in the B79.

The colonel gets one, because he's ranking officer. I get

one, because I'll be handling the cannon. Also, Vijay might be younger than Neen, but he is not stupid, he knows who's winning this war for him.

Haze gets the last seat, because he's a braid.

I run that thought back, decide I agree with it, and realize just how bloody odd that sounds. 'Sit there,' I tell Haze. 'Before I change my mind.'

Emil is not happy. He outranks Haze in theory. As do Neen and Franc. But they're not braids, and they don't chat up machinery the way the rest of us joke with whores. That leaves five people without proper seats.

A low ledge runs round the back of the crewpit. Five people sitting together on the ledge should help cushion each other from the worst of the acceleration shock. All we have to do is what we did in that tug.

'Tie yourselves into place.'

'Sven,' says Emil, sounding horrified. Turns out, he's flown in a B79 before.

'So you'll know what to expect,' I tell him. 'And it's *sir.* You're a trooper in the Aux and you'll remain one until I tell you otherwise.'

Chapter 51

LIGHTS FLASH IN FRONT OF US. FLASH, FLASH FASTER, AND THEN stutter to a halt. A second run ends the same way. And then a third. I know what the ship's AI is glitching against, but we have enough time to let it reach its own conclusions.

'Give me three sixty.'

Screens come to life around the crewpit.

At my nod, Haze revolves the entire pit, letting me check the new arrivals. The lenz in the hangars might be blind, but we have our own on this ship and they're showing us a major and fifty Death's Head troopers bundling through an emergency door, and stopping in the darkness, backlit from the stairs.

'Idiot,' says Neen.

Also lazy and arrogant. Any half-decent NCO would kill those lights before coming through. If we were out there, we'd have cut them down by now. But luckily for the major, we are in here and keeping the surprise.

At an order from a corporal, the lights go out.

Lasers play across the emptiness of the hangar. A couple of NCOs turn on the torches on their rifles. And then, the panels on the ceiling above us all flare into life again.

'Sven,' says Colonel Vijay. 'Perhaps . . .'

'We should think about leaving?'

He nods.

'And maybe not,' the SIG says.

Lights or not, the wall bolts are still powered down.

As Haze checks that the SIG is right, a dozen Silver Fist hurl themselves through the opening doors of an elevator, guns drawn. They stand down the moment they realize there is no enemy in sight. Another three elevators open a second later. We're drawing ourselves a big crowd, and soon someone is going to begin scanning the pods and work out where we are.

'Sir,' says Neen. 'Do you want me to take the attack outside?'

'No,' I tell him. 'It's all going to plan.'

That earns me a stare from Colonel Vijay.

So I grin, letting adrenalin flood my body. This is the bit I like. Only we're not there yet. More troopers must be on their way, and I would hate to deny anyone their share of the fun.

It takes five minutes before a braid appears.

The first thing he does is send a dozen Silver Fist to check the fancy-looking launch next to us. Maybe he reckons we can't all get into the B79 bomber. He's wrong, but looking at Shil, Rachel, Franc, Neen and Emil tied under a cargo net behind me, I can see how they might feel he's right.

When the Fist start coming towards us, I decide it's time to move. 'OK,' I say. 'Let's go.'

'Sven,' says Colonel Vijay. 'The bolts are still dead.'

I know that. Why does he think the B79 won't start? My gun is going to override the safety routine that prevents ignition. 'Fuck the bolts, sir,' I tell him. 'I'm going to put a rocket through the wall.'

'You can't,' he says. 'There'll be an *equal and opposite.*'

'A what, sir?'

'Newton's Third Law,' he says. 'You must remember.'

God . . . Do I look like someone who knows Newton's Third Law?

Turns out it's not a problem. If firing a rocket will make us slam into the escape craft directly behind us, then surely all we have to do is fire our engines at the same time? One can cancel out the other.

Seems I have reduced Colonel Vijay to silence. But that's OK, because the SIG is back up and chattering probabilities.

Our best choice is three rockets, apparently. That gives us a seventy-eight per cent chance of removing the wall, with only a thirty-eight per cent chance of killing ourselves. Four rockets would guarantee the wall but total our odds of surviving in one piece.

Two rockets, barely worth discussing.

'Three,' I say. 'Fire the engines at the same time. And then hold us steady.'

The gun wants to tell me this can't be done and then decides it can. Obviously, such a feat will take brilliance and inhuman levels of skill.

It's disgustingly smug as it says this.

As I wait for the SIG, a helmet drops from the crewpit roof, so I slot it over my head. Flipping down the visor reduces the pit to a ghostly haze. I have schematics where the bulkheads are. And I'm looking at the hangar outside as if there's no hull in the way.

'Not meant to work like that,' says Emil.

Flipping the visor up, I discover my helmet schematics are also on screen, and the ex-Ninth officer is looking around at the walls of the crewpit in shock.

'Get used to it,' says Neen.

★　　★　　★

334

Every fucking thing in the hangar not nailed down begins moving as the wall blows out and vacuum sucks away what it can. Firing retros, the B79 lurches forward and then reclaims its position.

The troopers closest to the blast are lucky. They die quickly. As do the ones standing behind our engines. It's the rest who suffer. A roiling wall of flame swallows them for a second, before they're sucked into space, their lungs rupturing as air is dragged from their bodies.

It is a bad way to go. We know it without needing to see it on screen.

'Behind us,' shouts Haze.

Slipping to the left, the B79 shudders as something glances off its side. Retros fire, and we stabilize again. 'Neat,' says the SIG. 'Though I say so myself.'

The vessel it dodged tumbles once, slides sideways and blocks our exit. It's bigger than we are, a lot bigger. We're staring at the general's launch.

Emergency routines are running in the hangar. If a whole hangar has to be sacrificed that's what will happen. The troopers nearest the exits aren't stupid, they know that. That is why they're gripping on for dear life, while scrabbling over one another to get out.

A sergeant fails to make it through a door.

We get one half, from shoulder to knee, which is sucked towards the broken wall. The rest of him disappears inside the elevator. It's not going anywhere because the lift shafts have already sealed themselves. 'Clear our way,' I tell the gun.

'My pleasure.'

Launching a fourth missile, it fires a fifth just for the hell of it.

As the general's little liner shatters, a lieutenant is sucked off his feet, his hands scrabbling for anything to grip. As we watch, he's dragged across the deck and disappears. Just one of a hundred.

'You know how to fly this?' demands Colonel Vijay.

'Of course.'

Haze looks surprised.

'Flew a skimmer round the landing fields,' I tell him. 'At Bosworth. How different can it be?'

Opening his mouth to answer, Colonel Vijay realizes it's a joke and shuts it again. Leaning across, he offers me his hand to shake. That is how I know he expects to die.

Chapter 52

ACCELERATION WELDS MY COMBAT ARM TO THE CHAIR AND squeezes air from my lungs. As we roll, my ribs creak and my shoulders try to dislocate. Everything around me is turning black and white. Only there is no *around me*, because all I can see is directly ahead.

A shrinking circle going fuzzy at the edges.

'Seven g,' says the gun. 'Twenty-five seconds.'

Colonel Vijay is unconscious. Other than me, only Haze is awake, and he looks terrified. Turning to forward again almost breaks my neck.

'Nine g,' the gun tells me. 'Thirty-two seconds.'

It hesitates.

'Say it . . .'

'Going to kill them,' the SIG says.

'No, they'll pull through.'

'Not those two,' the gun says. 'That lot.'

A screen flickers to show me Rachel, Shil, Emil, Neen and Franc . . . They are twisted into the bulkhead. Far from helping, the curve of the crewpit seems to be forcing them into a single mass. One of the straps holding their net has snapped, another cuts so deep into Rachel's arm it is bruising already.

'Thirteen g,' says the gun. 'Thirty-seven seconds.'

'What's the tolerance . . . ?'

'For them?'

'No,' I say. 'For this ship.'

The SIG feeds me a figure so high we will be slop in a bucket long before I can shake the engines off this thing. As always, the limits are our own.

'They're human,' says the SIG.

'So am I.'

It laughs, darkly. 'You really believe that?'

I'd nod, but g-force glues my skull to the seat. So I grunt, ease back a little and roll a turn. We just miss a Z7x fighter, which explodes as our rocket hits.

'Five,' says the SIG.

My gun is firing, the combat AI target-spots, and I fly. Should be Haze, but he's away with who knows what. So far the combination works. Hekati is behind us. A bloody great ring hanging off the edge of a mined-out—

'Concentrate,' says my gun.

Another fighter explodes in front of us.

Out here, you don't get sound; you don't even get shock waves. You just get a burst of light and endless high-speed shrapnel. The trick is to outrun the shrapnel, or slide it off your force field like flat stones off water. Easier to describe than do.

My screen shows a fighter coming up behind. No way is it going to miss from this distance. As I roll the B79, the Silver Fist fighter fires, and the SIG burns each of its rockets in turn with a short pulse of cannon.

Rolling again, I loop my own path to take the Z7x from the rear. It goes up in a ball of flame, and enough shrapnel to make me twist viciously.

'Sven,' says the gun.

'What?'

'You're killing the Aux.'

'If I don't do this,' I say, 'they're going to be dead anyhow.'

'Well,' it says. 'Perhaps they'd rather be killed by the enemy.'

'How are they going to know?' I ask, checking a screen. 'They're all unconscious anyway.'

The gun says nothing. Probably not a good sign.

Taking a slow curve, I see the edge of the asteroid belt.

It is that jumble of rocks, slashed like a broken line inside my screen. Should have thought of it before. 1500 klicks. *We can do that.*

'Behind you,' warns the SIG.

There are two of them, fighters in tight formation. And then, when I check again, I see it is three. One waits higher than the others, further back. That one intends to kill me. The others are just along for the hunt.

To unsettle me.

'Incoming,' the SIG says.

Yeah, I've seen them. The outriders sweep in behind me.

They intend to cross, which means they're flying staggered. Although both open fire at the same time. Give me a knife, and I'll take down anything. But this, slamming around inside some bloody machine, it's not natural.

If I'm going to kill someone, I want to see their eyes.

Firing the retros makes Haze double over and lose the contents of his gut direct into his lap. Proves he's still alive, at least. The SIG swears, but that's only because it is flipping across the crewpit to hit a screen.

Somewhere in the middle of that, the SIG thinks *cannon*, and reduces both fighters to shards of metals, exploding gas and a flash of blinding light. 'Ungrateful bastard,' it snaps, when I remain silent.

But I'm too focused to answer.

Anyway, the third Z7x is beginning its run. The pilot is spooked, which makes him careless. This isn't what he expects. Coming out like that in a group of three, only to be alone. Now, me . . .

I was alone to start with.

And here he is, chasing an enemy towards the edge of the asteroid belt. An enemy who's just killed both his companions. It is not a big jump to deciding he's next.

The fighter comes in fast, and I loop, with darkness eating at the edges of my vision until the world becomes a tiny circle of *straight ahead*. What I need is to get behind the enemy pilot and let the SIG do its thing.

How hard can that be?

As the Silver Fist opens fire, I pull up and it flicks below me. Looping takes all of my concentration, and as we level out again the SIG starts firing. You can see pulse cannon in space. It burns green. Don't ask me why.

This guy is good. He twists away, and I follow. As he jerks up, I begin to follow him into a loop and suddenly he isn't there, because he's out of the loop and back on his original heading. Any moment now, he'll do a second twist and roll himself behind me.

'Wait,' I tell the SIG.

Slipping sideways, I flip the B79 and fire boosters. The kick nails me to the chair and turns my vision to a tiny island of light surrounded by waves of blackness. As we level out, the SIG sights.

Looks like a clear shot to me.

'Targeted,' the SIG says.

'Take it.'

Warnings obviously fire inside the fighter, because the pilot weaves from side to side and then rolls into a dive. There is no gravity out here, but that dive instinct still kicks in.

As we go for a kill, the pilot kicks in extra boosters.

Heat flares from his afterburner. And the fighter explodes into a weirdly flattened ball of flame and razor-sharp fragments. Only the shrapnel's all heading in our direction. On the far side of where the fighter was, lights spark in their millions.

'*Pull up*,' shouts the gun.

At this level of g-force, that is easier to say than do. Executing a tight turn, I roll the B79 into the early stages of a loop and begin to climb.

'*Tighter.*'

Bastard SIG.

Somewhere down the line, I black out.

Doesn't matter, the combat AI keeps me on track, and I'm awake before it can turn one loop into two, or do something stupid like go take a closer look at all those little explosions.

'What the fuck happened?'

An area of blank space hangs between us and *Victory First*, with Hekati looking vast behind that. There isn't a Z7x to be seen.

'All gone,' says the SIG.

'Fuck, how many?'

'Twenty-three.'

We killed twenty-three fighters . . . ?

'Fish in a barrel,' says the SIG, sounding disgusted.

'Them?'

The gun snorts. 'Us,' it says, and tells me why.

We didn't kill that fighter. It crashed into the inside edge of a force field *Victory First* threw up the moment this battle began. If the field can destroy their fighter, it can destroy us.

And I have problems that are more pressing. We are almost out of fuel, our oxygen's nearly gone, and we're using what is left faster than the converters can replace. Eight people in a B79 bomber designed for three is a shit idea. Even if it was mine.

Also, we're suffering.

My sight is blurred and my throat sour from the kyp. Haze is sticky with his own vomit, and what didn't glue itself to the walls or the rest of us now hangs in the air, tiny spit balls of half-digested supper.

As for the others . . .

Colonel Vijay is unconscious. But at least he's upright and safe in a chair. Looking at him reminds me of a very young General Jaxx, which is weird enough to make me decide to think about something else.

It is the rest who need help.

Shil's chest rises and falls as she struggles for breath. A shoulder tab on her uniform reads orange. She has taken damage, but it's not yet fatal. At least, not if we can get help and that's one hell of a—

'Sven,' snaps the gun.

'*What?*'

'You might want to pay attention.'

Chapter 53

ONE WHOLE SIDE IS RISING FROM *VICTORY FIRST*. IF THE Enlightened ship is a city, then an entire neighbourhood is detaching itself to lift slowly away. It reveals a hole in the mother ship that begins to close as walls shift and hangar doors move.

Soon the *Victory First* will look as it used to look. Just a bit smaller. 'What the fuck is that?' I demand, pointing to the detached bit.

'Epsilon-class cruiser,' says the gun.

We can play question and answer or I can use the kyp. The thought doesn't make me happy. 'Using it already, sir,' mutters Haze.

Blood beads his lip. It wells into little blue spheres and flips free like floating pearls to join the vomit, spittle and all the things we forgot to lock down.

Blue? I think. And then I have my answer.

Oxygen loss starves haemoglobin. In a flash flood, I understand more than I want about human biology. And Haze is human; well, as human as I am. Just as quickly, I dismiss the fact.

Who needs memory when this stuff can be pulled from the air?

The cruiser is epsilon-class, a kilometre long and 330 metres wide. It's vast, armed with fifty cannons and has flight decks for three combat wings . . . That's a hundred and fifty Z7x fighters.

A list comes up before my eyes. Battles won by a single epsilon-class.

Victory First is made of nineteen epsilons slotted together. That is the beauty of Enlightened technology. It's cumulative. The Z7xs fit into the sides of the cruiser, the cruiser slots alongside other cruisers to make the mother ship. If needed, the mother ship can be slotted with others to make . . .

Something the size of a small moon.

A ray-traced sphere flickers into my vision and then goes, along with coordinates that put it half a spiral arm away from us.

Speed?

Faster than we are. Well, the cruiser is. Although it takes time to get ramped up enough to use its ion jets.

And distance?

It could cross the galaxy, if the U/Free ever let it get that far.

All this makes me wonder how we outfight the Enlightened, because we do. Every planet they take, we retake, or take one in its place. The figures are vast, tens of thousands of suns and hundreds of thousands of planets. It seems impossible, beyond counting; until that thought brings the number of stars in our galaxy.

A million million.

Our glorious leader, OctoV . . . And the Uplift's hundred-braid, Gareisis, the Uplifted and Enlightened. They mean so little to Letogratz that the United Free will accept any solution that stops us fighting. Doesn't have to be fair. Why would it be? Not much else in life is.

Makes me wish I were still at Fort Libidad, scanning the dunes for ferox and desert tribes. And that makes me wonder what an ex-sergeant, who couldn't count above twenty until a few months back, is doing counting stars.

'So,' says SIG. 'You're back.'

It shows me the cruiser on screen. 'You plan on fighting that?'

'Got a better idea?'

'Well,' it says. 'We're out of rockets, our shields are screwed and the power bank for the pulse cannon is critical.' It pisses me off when the SIG gets snotty.

'You forgot oxygen.'

The SIG begins to tell me it doesn't need—

So I point out that unless it's happy to drift in space with rotting bodies for company, it will factor oxygen in too. It's still sulking when I use most of our remaining fuel to take us over the top of the cruiser, round the outside of the mother ship and over the edge of Hekati itself.

Red lights start flashing. A buzzer joins in. And, just in case we need more distraction, the crewpit screens override with a critical fuel warning.

'Sven . . .'

'Look,' I tell the gun. 'I know what I'm doing.'

'There's always a first time.'

The mirror hub is ahead. A small silver castle where the struts meet in the centre of Hekati's ring. Brightness flares our screens as we get between a mirror and the sunlight it's reflecting at the glass that gives this habitat its sky. What fuel is left, I burn entering the hub itself and slotting ourselves into a dock.

Obviously enough, it's fuel we can't afford.

★   ★   ★

On the far side of the airlock, Ajac takes one look at my vomit-splashed uniform and steps back. Could be the stink, could be the bloodstained blades on my combat arm, or it could be the foulness of the air belching out behind me.

Iona stands beside him. She's carrying Colonel Madeleine's handiwork.

Yanking my combat arm free, I see her glance away. She waits until my old arm is in place before glancing back. 'Knew you'd return.'

More than I did. Needles pierce flesh. After a second, I flex my fingers. Good enough for what I need to do now.

It takes me a minute to cut the net, remove the straps and begin carrying my crew into the corridor outside the airlock. Shil is first, and she weighs less than I expect. Her right shoulder is dislocated. As I settle her on the deck, she whimpers.

'Shil,' I ask. 'Can you hear me?'

She nods.

'This is going to hurt.'

A thump of my hand against her shoulder puts the joint back into place.

Spittle dribbles from her mouth; she has bitten her lip and wet herself, although Ajac pretends not to notice. His manners are better than mine are. 'Can't see,' she says.

'It's the g-force,' I say. 'Makes your vision blurred.'

'Can't see,' she repeats.

'Shil,' I say. 'You'll be fine.'

Ajac gets Franc out. If anything, she is even worse. When I look round from unbuckling Colonel Vijay, I see Ajac still kneeling next to her. Franc's eyes are open and she's staring at nothing. She's staring at it intently.

Climbing unsteadily from his seat, Colonel Vijay says, 'You want me to look at her?'

'You can help, sir?'

'Probably . . .' He hesitates, reassesses. 'Well, I can try. And there has to be a medical bay round here somewhere.'

We need a way out of here. We need a way to kill the cruiser. We need a way to get home. Three big needs, for a group relying on a B79 bomber down to five per cent of its power. There are ten of us now. And the bomber is still only built to take three. Answer is obvious, really . . . We need a bigger ship. More weapons. A better plan.

'Haze,' I say. 'Don't care how you do it. But check the power status of every ship docked in the hub.'

A roll of his eyes and he's gone.

'Doesn't it freak you out?' says Neen, then remembers to add *sir*. 'I mean, when he does that?'

'Freak you out when I do it?'

Neen wants to say that is different, but it isn't. So I clap him on the shoulder. 'Be glad I've got Haze to do it for me.'

There are seven vessels, including our B79 bomber. Three of the oldest are near dead, reduced to whimpering their names and begging for fuel. If Haze is right, one has been doing just that for over five hundred years.

Of the other four, the B79 is down to local boosters and an ion drive that might work if we had enough dry thrust to get it up to speed. That leaves three vessels. One is ours. Well, the U/Free hopper we arrived in. Another is so old the only reason it's not dying is it's dead already.

The final ship is chosen by default.

A Z-class tug ancient enough to have fins and dumb enough to be proud of a ten-foot nude painted on its nose. It's old, it's rusting inside, it's filthy. I don't care, really don't care. Not after I crawl around inside a bit, and then go tell Colonel Vijay about its cargo.

Kyble was right. Luck is a whore.

But Luck likes fighters, and I think of her as a Val: magnificent tits and a dangerous smile. Always ready to step up beside you when it comes to making a stand.

Chapter 54

'IT'S GOT ENOUGH SEATS, YOU SAY?'

Yes, I thought that would appeal to Colonel Vijay. Looking around, the colonel spots the telltale signs of gravity flooring and that appeals to him even more. There is only so much floating vomit a well-brought-up young officer can stand.

'What?' he demands.

'Glad you like it, sir.'

'And this is what you wanted to show me?'

'No, sir. That's down here.' He stares into a filthy hold revealed by the trap door I open.

'Yes,' he says. 'Of course it is.'

A ladder leads to a crawl space below. Carrying a light from one of the rifles at my suggestion, the colonel flicks its beam across boxes, and then more boxes, piled into an area maybe ten paces by ten paces, but only half our height.

'What's in them?' he demands. And then answers his own question by running his light across a long box stencilled with a skull in flames.

Danger.

Keep safe.

Do not expose to heat.

There are other warnings, but he has the message.

He's crawling round the hold of a Z-class cargo tug packed with out-of-date and probably unstable explosives, *asteroid miners, for the use of . . .*

Each case is sealed in clear wrapping against damp and secured with double bands of cheap steel. Cheap enough to cut with my knife. Slicing the side from a case reveals blocks of something that looks like clay and smells like stale cake. 'That what I assume it is?' the colonel asks.

I nod.

'Sven,' he says, 'I think it's time you told me your plan.'

For something I make up as I go along, it's quite convincing. That is the thing about senior officers. They'll believe anything, provided you sound like you really, really mean it.

'You know,' says Colonel Vijay, 'it might work.'

So, we have explosives, and a tug with enough power to get us to the asteroid belt. But we also have a Silver Fist mother ship, an epsilon-class cruiser hunting us down, and a force field locking us into the area around Hekati. What we don't have are detonators.

'Bound to be here somewhere,' the colonel says.

Dragging cases aside, he finds a smaller box pushed against a bulkhead. The fuses are simple enough. Much like the ones the Legion use when cutting roads through mountains: one pulse to prime and another to fire.

'OK,' I say. 'Here's what we do.'

My troopers are patched as best we can manage.

Mostly this involves painkillers, amphetamines and re-hydrating salts from the medical bay Colonel Vijay tracked down. Shil still stumbles occasionally and Rachel rubs at her hip. But neither one complains and that is good enough.

Emil pre-primes the detonators I give him. Colonel Vijay, Shil, Ajac, Haze, and Rachel begin carrying boxes of plastique from the tug to the B79 bomber. Franc's off somewhere, licking her wounds in private. I only know that's what she is doing because it's what I would do myself. And Iona? Hanging round Neen as if they are joined by invisible wire.

But I have more pressing problems.

So far, the Silver Fist cruiser has taken itself out to the edge of the force field, to run a scan of the whole area. After this proves fruitless, it begins a more careful sweep; one that will take it over Hekati's mirror hub in about five minutes. That is how long we have to make this plan work.

'Four minutes, fifty-eight seconds.'

The SIG keeps with the updates until I tell it to stop.

We now have three minutes left before the cruiser passes overhead. Enough time for Neen to pack the nose of the B79 bomber with explosives. When he's done, there is still room for more. So Shil, Haze and Rachel race back for extra boxes, and Neen stacks these inside the nose-cone as well.

The detonators go everywhere.

He could use only one, but why bother? We have a hundred, and they're all set to the same frequency.

'Two minutes ten,' says the gun.

Colonel Vijay is watching. Well, half of him is. The other half focuses on Neen, who is bundling out of the B79's hatch, looking pleased with himself.

'Two exactly,' the gun says.

Above us, a shadow can be seen. Our own little eclipse.

The cruiser already hangs between the sun and the mirrors. And now its shadow begins to creep down the inside wall of the mirror hub. Soon we'll be able to look up and see the cruiser itself.

'One fifty.'

'Sir,' says Neen. 'We need to get it launched.'

'How long do we have?'

'Now is optimum,' says the gun. It likes fancy words. 'But we've got a four-minute window.'

The colonel is staring at the B79. He's obviously making his mind up about something, and his decision is to stay silent. When someone like Vijay Jaxx remains silent it's because he believes events have moved beyond what his words can change.

Marching up to him, I salute.

'Sven?' he says.

'What am I missing, sir?'

Glancing at the Aux, he shakes his head. His look says, *let this go* . . . Only I'm not good at that.

'Sir?' I say.

'Found a glitch,' he says. 'You're not going to like it.'

'No, sir. Probably not.'

The Silver Fist are going to scan our bomber for signs of life, and they won't find any. That's what he tells me, keeping his voice low. The moment their braid realizes there's nothing alive on board he will either jam every channel we might use to trigger a bomb. Or he'll spam a fire command, and blow the B79 to bits before it can get close enough to do damage.

To make it work, we need a voice link between us and the bomber to make it sound as if we are on board. And we need to find a way to stop the bomber from showing up as empty when scanned for signs of life.

'Half a dozen goats would do,' says Colonel Vijay. That's a joke, apparently.

'Cruiser coming into sight,' says the SIG.

And my gun's right. The Silver Fist cruiser is that bloody great shadow above us blocking out the sun. As we watch, its nose creeps over the edge of the hub.

'No time,' I say. 'We launch now.'

'And then?' asks Colonel Vijay.

'We take the tug and head in the other direction—'

'As fast as we can,' he finishes for me.

It is not much of a plan, but it's what we've got. And would remain so, except for Franc, who has suddenly reappeared on the edge of our discussion. 'Permission to speak, sir?'

I nod.

'To Haze, sir.'

'Make it quick.'

Franc's lip twitches. 'Yes, sir,' she says.

When she speaks to Haze her voice is a whisper, her words swift, and I can almost feel the tension burning off her. Just once, he tries to interrupt her, and she shakes her head. 'My life,' she says, loudly enough for the rest of us to hear.

'Franc . . .'

'You said so.'

Reaching for his hand, she opens his fingers and touches his palm to her lips. Then he puts his hand on her head and says something so softly that I doubt even Franc can hear.

'Sven,' says my gun. 'We're running out of—'

I slap it into silence.

Keeping her shoulders back and her chin up, she marches briskly towards me and stamps to attention. Should be Colonel Vijay she asks, but he is too busy looking appalled. As I return her salute, I already know what she intends to say.

'Please, sir,' she says.

And proves me wrong.

'Take this,' I say, ripping off my arm again. 'It's chipped,' I add, when she looks puzzled. *Genotype human equivalent. Status DH class 2 . . .*

Reaching up, she kisses my cheek.

'Thank you.'

For letting you kill yourself? I think. She must see that thought in my eyes, because she smiles. 'For trying to give me back my scars.'

'Trying?'

'Already fading,' she says. 'The U/Free really fucked me over.'

Sweeping her gaze across the Aux, she goes for a smile. Most of them are playing catch-up, and Iona and Ajac don't realize what is happening until Franc is inside the B79 and its hatch is hissing shut. And even then, they're not sure they believe it.

Bolts blow, grapples release. The B79 shivers, and drops away.

A few seconds later, it lurches through the mirror hub to stop a mile or so above us, and away to one side.

'Piggyback her calls,' I tell the SIG.

Only it's doing that already, and we hear Franc's first contact. Most people would try for a hailing frequency. Franc punches the emergency button and relies on it to override everything else.

'Three-braid Carson,' says a man. 'Who is this?'

'Trooper Franc,' she says. 'I'm flying the bomber . . .' Franc hesitates. 'Well, it's flying itself . . . No,' she says. 'It's not flying at all. But when it does, it flies itself. Mostly . . .'

Never underestimate metalhead contempt for the un-Enlightened.

And don't forget, she is female and militia, talking to a Silver Fist officer. He's probably surprised she can talk at all. We wait, as he says something off screen, and then he is back.

'Let me talk to your senior officer.'

'You can't,' says Franc.

'Why not?'

'He's unconscious.'

Anyone running software will know she is frightened. Assuming they're too stupid to pick that up just by listening.

'Everyone's unconscious.' She sobs, stops herself. 'No,' says Franc. 'Not true. Mostly they're dead, I think.'

'*You think?* Can't you run scans?'

'No,' says Franc, sounding young. 'Don't know how.'

The three-braid sighs.

'I want to surrender,' she says.

'And your officer is alive?'

'Yes. Only his mouth's turning blue.'

'*Oxygen starvation,*' someone mutters almost out of range.

The three-braid hisses him into silence. The Enlightened is thinking. Unless he is scanning her. So we wait where we stand in the corridor, and Franc waits inside her bomber. Anything said between us will be overheard, so we say nothing. Three-braid Carson finally comes back on air.

'Your weapons are active,' he says. 'Shut them down.'

Franc says nothing.

'Did you hear me?'

'Yes,' she says. 'Only I don't know how.'

Overdoing it, I think. And then I realize she's not overdoing it at all. Franc means it. She's not sure how to shut the cannon down. We leave her being talked through the control panel by a pilot from their end.

He's good, and we've just got to, *See the third touch-pad on the right, the orange one, well tap the bottom right corner twice* . . . when I decide it is time for us to get out of there.

Chapter 55

SETTING OUR BOOSTERS TO SLOW BURN, HAZE KEEPS IN THE B79's comms shadow as our tug drops away from the hub and leaves Hekati's mirror ring high overhead. We're going to be a small blip below a bigger blip.

Also, that hub contains Hekati's AI, which should throw up enough electronic chatter to mask us from the braid in the cruiser above. At least, that is the theory.

'Don't need to know the detail,' Colonel Vijay tells Haze. 'Just need to know it's going to work. It is going to work, isn't it . . . ?'

Seeing me listen, the colonel blushes.

Yes, I've heard his father say that too.

'Suit check,' I say.

Everyone scans their read-outs.

We've all got suits this time. Old mining issue, with outdated radiation patches on the breastplates, clumsy clasps, and out-of-date fasteners. But they're water-lined against g-force, and all have full oxygen tanks.

The SIG's meant to keep checking our safety status. Only it is far more interested in what's going on above.

'Oh for fuck's sake,' I say. 'Put her on the speakers.'

My gun does as it's told.

'Trooper Franc,' says the three-braid.

'Sir,' she says.

Nice touch, I think.

'Bring it up slowly . . .'

'I'm trying.'

Another voice comes on, telling her how to feather the boosters. I've no idea what he means and nor does Franc, but she concentrates as he talks her through which buttons to tap.

'So,' says Franc. 'Tapping up makes me go faster?'

'Yes,' the pilot says.

'So I want to tap down?'

He agrees this would be good.

The B79 obviously slows, because the pilot's next comment is to congratulate Franc and suggest she steer towards the middle of the cruiser. 'You're too close to the engines,' he says.

'Put it on screen,' I tell Haze.

'Sir, that might—'

'Do it,' says the colonel.

Haze shrugs, which is close to outright insolence for him. Our braid's turning into someone else. I'll deal with that later. For now, my attention is on the B79 that suddenly appears on our screen. We're locked into one of Hekati's own cameras.

The B79 hangs below the cruiser like a tiny fish nosing towards a floating alligator. Although it's hard to see much more from this distance.

'Bring the picture close.'

Haze wants to object, but he tightens the focus anyway.

The mirror hub is above us, and Hekati's habitat is a vast circle around that. The struts that hold the habitat to its hub revolve slowly overhead. I want to be up there with Franc, but that's absurd. This only has meaning if she does it by herself.

The sacrifice of one for the many. I can't think of anything that Franc could do that would make me prouder to have known her.

'Sven,' says my gun.

'What?'

'She's priming detonators.' The SIG's voice is flat, emotionless. Didn't know it could run in that mode. 'You want me to piggyback their lenz?'

'It'll—'

'Sir,' says Haze. 'They know already.'

A jumble of shouts blares from our speakers. The pilot's voice is replaced by that of the three-braid who sounds furious. And then he's shouting orders at Franc, and when that fails, he starts shouting them at someone else.

Panic, you bastard.

'Piggyback,' I tell the SIG.

Our screens flip to their point of view.

And suddenly we're the Silver Fist watching us. Well, watching Franc; and the B79 is closing that gap fast. We're seeing her through a lenz hung directly under the cruiser itself. A pulse cannon fires out of shot, but Franc is too close to the cruiser for the barrels to lower far enough. The weapon is limited by its own safety routines.

A panel slides back above her.

'Fighters,' says Haze.

I've worked that out for myself. Lurching forward, the B79 disappears through the opening hatch before the first Z7x can emerge.

And then there is light.

'*Fuck,*' says Neen.

No one will be putting Franc back together again, not this time.

Shil's crying, Rachel also, from the noise behind me. 'Sven,' says the SIG. 'You might want to watch.'

The explosions begin slowly, with a ball of flame. Oxygen burns, and that is what catches fire. A high-oxygen/low-pressure atmospheric mix that we use in our ships as well.

As we watch, a side panel blows out, flame blossoming behind it. The explosions spread, fire obviously running down corridors and rising up elevator shafts to blow out panels elsewhere.

It has, as Colonel Vijay points out, a terrible beauty.

A hatch irises open, to release a fighter that is eaten by an explosion that rips out of the flight deck behind it. There are a hundred and fifty troopers on board that cruiser, three flight wings, one three-braid and eighty crew.

The figures fill my head.

'Sven,' says Colonel Vijay. 'Are you all right?'

My throat tastes sour.

'Fine, sir.'

As I watch, the cruiser cracks at the stern and lights go out behind the break. Hekati's gravity twists the dying vessel on its axis, and then an explosion rocks the engines and snaps the cruiser in two.

A fuel store? An arms depot? The engine itself?

Don't know and don't care, because I'm watching shrapnel. If that is the right word for spinning thousand-ton fragments of cruiser. As another explosion rips the segment, and the bridge goes up in a fountain of flame, an antenna scythes away into space like a thrown blade.

'Shit,' says Shil.

Vacuum is sucking at the segment's guts to swallow dying troopers and broken fighters.

'Wait for it,' says my gun.

All our screens blank as the electromagnetic wave rolls over us. A Casimir coil exploding. Or perhaps it's an ion drive.

Machinery isn't my thing. All I know is that one third of a burning Silver Fist cruiser has ceased to exist, and the other two thirds is racing into the distance.

'Equal and opposite,' says Colonel Vijay.

'Sir,' I say. 'Permission to give chase?'

His lips twist. 'Feel free,' he says.

Imagine one point nine million tons (roughly what two thirds of an epsilon-class cruiser weighs), punching into a force field generated by a mother ship and then trying to keep going. It is like watching a steel post being fed to a chipper. The field blazes with cold flame that struggles to eat section after section of the cruiser. And still kinetic energy keeps the cruiser coming.

Our screens go lunatic. Waves of energy ripple like storms.

Colours clash and lightning flickers. Only that is impossible in space. What's not impossible is the sheer power being consumed by the field, as it tries to swallow everything the cruiser feeds it.

Force fields exist to stop incoming missiles.

And then somewhere back down the line a weapon's geek realizes if it works on incoming missiles, then it works on incoming fighters. And what works for incoming fighters can be applied to outgoing fighters as well.

Must be impressive, the first time that trap is sprung, and an enemy discovers they're locked into a free-fire zone. But it doesn't work for vessels much larger than a frigate. So it's definitely not meant to deal with a cruiser. Not even a burnt-out, ripped-open two thirds of one.

'Count me down,' I tell the SIG.

Something whirrs behind its pistol grip. 'Fifteen seconds,' it says. 'Fourteen seconds . . .' My gun keeps counting. And we're all counting along inside our heads. So it is my own voice I hear as the tally hits zero.

'Do it,' I tell Haze.

And we crash our Z–class through the crumbling force field into the emptiness of space beyond.

'Damage report,' I demand.

'Significantly less than you deserve,' the SIG replies tartly.

'Well,' says Colonel Vijay. 'That was interesting.'

'As in, *insanely suicidal?*' the SIG asks.

He laughs.

Iona claps, and after a second Neen does too. Haze blushes, but that's Haze for you. A moment later, the others join in the clapping, even Shil, who stops the moment she sees I've noticed. So I grin at her, and that makes her scowl even more.

Chapter 56

WHEN OUR EXCITEMENT AT BREAKING THROUGH THE FORCE field fades, Colonel Vijay suggests I say a few words. And I agree that words need saying for Franc, but I am sick of the soldier's prayer. Sick of reciting, *Sleep well and a better life next time.*

Done it once for Franc already. I owe her more than that. We all do.

'Listen,' I say. 'Met Franc on a battlefield. Didn't expect her to live out the day. Didn't expect her to keep the rank of corporal. Never met a better cook. Never met anyone better with—'

A knife, I want to say.

Only the kyp's begun shitting in my throat.

And the tug's crewpit loses focus as a vicious wave of emotion washes over me. Not my emotion, I know that. I'll do sorrow for Franc. I'll do respect, because she deserves it. But I won't do panic.

'Sir,' says Haze.

'*What?*' Got my voice back.

'You might want to look at this.'

Tapping a screen, he cuts the focus to bring Hekati closer. The engines on *Victory First Last and Always* glow with heat. I don't mean its boosters, because this isn't about shifting position or running a routine to check the coils still work. The fucker's coming after us.

Eight nozzles, each the size of a cathedral dome, begin to shimmer with flame. The web of tubes lashing the Silver Fist mother ship to Hekati's ring is still in place. As we watch, they begin snapping. And the sheer force of those engines tips the habitat out of true.

A torus is strong, but no engineer has allowed for this.

The panic I can feel comes from Hekati herself, and Iona can feel it too. That's when I realize she's precog. 'Stop them,' she begs. 'Please. Do something.'

'He won't,' says Ajac. 'He caused this.'

Neen dumps the unconscious boy into a chair and abandons him without a glance. And, rubbing my fist, I decide Ajac will learn. He's Aux now. It's not as if he has anywhere else to go.

Looking at Neen, Iona says, 'Hekati wants our help.'

'You can talk to her?'

The girl shakes her head. 'No,' she says. 'I feel it here.' She touches a fist to her heart, which tightens her tunic, and makes her breasts look bigger still.

Neen has trouble meeting her gaze.

And Shil's shooting daggers at me, as if this is somehow my fault. But I'm busy thinking about what Iona said. *Hekati wants our help.*

We're a Z-class mining tug. Slow, if good at manoeuvring. We have harpoons and a drilling laser. All our explosives went with Franc. Even if we manoeuvre over there before the *Victory First* finishes ripping itself free . . .

What do we fight it with?

Handguns?

'Incoming message,' says Haze.

In place of Hekati, we get a nine-braid.

A brigadier stands beside him. He was Death's Head once. Ninth Regiment, the emperor's own. Although it's been a while since he was anything I would consider Death's Head.

Colonel Vijay steps forward. But I'm already there.

'A snakehead and a traitor,' I say. 'What a pair . . . You know,' I add, looking at the brigadier, 'you're a fucking disgrace to that uniform.'

Opening his mouth, he shuts it at a glare from the nine-braid. Seems I should have insulted him first. The slight wasn't intentional, but I am delighted all the same.

'Surrender,' says the braid.

He has a hundred and fifty dead, thirty-five missing Z7x fighters and an epsilon-class hole in his mother ship. We tricked his three-braid with a false surrender, and we fucked his systems destroying that force field.

And still he claims we can surrender.

Just how stupid does he think we are? Turning to Colonel Vijay, I say, 'You want to do this bit, sir?'

He smiles at me. 'Sven,' he says, 'you're doing fine.'

Turning back, I look at their commander. He's smaller than most Enlightened I've seen. A shock of metal braids sweeps back from his forehead and falls onto his shoulders. I can see shining bits of skull where the virus has turned his scalp to shell. He's bare-chested, because braids are always bare-chested. No one has come up with a jacket that fits someone already wearing a bathroom's worth of piping. His weathered face watches me examine him. And when I'm finished, his gaze holds mine so tightly it takes an effort not to look away.

'Your name?' I say.

The nine-braid stares at me.

'It's just,' I tell him, 'I like to know who I'm going to kill.'

He sneers. An Enlightened's contempt for the rest of us.

'We will crush you,' he says, and I'm glad. It means we have all that shit about surrendering out of the way.

'Sven,' says Colonel Vijay, keeping his voice low. 'Is this going anywhere?'

'Want his name, sir.'

'For when you kill him?'

I nod.

The colonel sighs. Seems the braid isn't amused either. Glaring at me, he says, 'Your deaths will be painful.'

'Is that a threat?'

'No,' he says. 'It's a promise.'

There has to be a class somewhere to teach these people. Or perhaps they come out of the egg like that. He scowls and I grin, because this is more fun than I thought it would be. And then I remember Hekati, and it stops being funny.

'Let me see the habitat,' I demand.

Haze and the SIG scramble to put it on screen.

Between them, they clear our screens of the nine-braid's face, and throw up pictures of Hekati instead. Some are taken from a comm sat, a few from inside the habitat, and one from *Victory First* itself.

They all show variations on the same thing.

The lines lashing the Silver Fist mother ship to Hekati are gone. The fat tube stealing Hekati's air now bleeds into empty space. Water roars from the end of a broken pipe to split into a million droplets that separate, join, and separate again. Inside the habitat itself, high winds have risen to rip trees from the valley floor and scour grit from the mountainsides.

Only there is worse. Far worse.

A slab of Hekati's outer shell the size of Zabo Square is missing where the *Victory First* ripped her anchor free. Multi-legged bots crowd the wound, but there is little they can do except kill themselves trying to mend a hole that cannot be mended.

'Oh shit,' says Haze.

Lining the hole is rubble and steel mesh as thick as trees. The mesh is broken, and rocks the size of Farlight cathedral tumble into space as the habitat revolves. Vast asteroids returning to the belt. Hekati is losing more than her air and water. She's losing bits of her ballast. 'Too late to surrender,' says the colonel.

He sees my look.

'Can't save Hekati now.'

It hadn't occurred to me we could.

Chapter 57

IT MOVES SLOWLY, THE ENLIGHTENED MOTHER SHIP, THE GAP between Hekati and our enemy seeming to remain the same, although our sensors say it is widening. A Z7x fighter is fast, but with shit range. *Victory First* can follow to the other edge of the galaxy and beyond. We can't outrun it once its engines hit full power, and we can't outshoot it. All we have going for us is a head start. And that is not going to last us long.

'Asteroid belt,' says Colonel Vijay. 'We'll hide there.'

'Sir,' I say, 'they've got enough firepower to turn the belt to dust.'

'And us with it,' adds the SIG.

The colonel grins sourly. 'So much for that idea.'

'We could try U/Free space.' Haze is right, we could . . .

Only Paper Osamu won't be happy if we come trailing an Enlightened ship behind us, and General Jaxx will be furious. Any sentence passed by court martial on one of us is passed on the others. Little point getting home, only to be executed for treason. We need a better plan.

'Hekati's dying,' says Haze.

'Sven?' Colonel Vijay says.

'Thinking, sir.'

My gun snorts.

I've seen battle, I've killed. This is different. It's *genocide*, which is a term I've only heard the U/Free use. But it sounds right for destroying a habitat and killing those inside. *Hekati wants our help.* I run Iona's words again.

And we want Hekati's . . .

'Back through the ring,' I order. 'And take us out to the belt.' To his credit, Colonel Vijay says nothing when I steal his plan.

'Make it fast,' I tell Haze. To Shil, I say, 'Arm the harpoons.'

She scowls at me.

'It's what we've got,' I say. 'Only take the bloody tethers off first.' The last thing we need is to drag some wounded Z7x in our wake. Assuming we're still around to hit one.

'And the drilling laser,' I tell Neen. 'Put that on standby.'

Hekati's hub is so badly out of true we scrape an inside edge, shattering a sheet of glass higher than the tallest building in Farlight, because the hub is only small compared to the habitat itself. We shudder as we hit, my SIG feathers the retros and we are through.

The asteroid belt waits ahead.

Also behind us is the vast bulk of the mother ship, turning as fast as its boosters will allow. We've long since lost the braid. He broke audio as soon as he realized we'd stopped listening to him. Braids hate that.

I mean, most people hate being ignored, except me. I'm happiest in my own company. But braids take it personally. It pisses them off when lower species don't know their place. And ours is out here in the belt.

'Fighters,' Neen says.

Three of them, coming in tight. Not the cleverest of formations.

'Take them all,' I say.

Our mining laser is meant to crack rock. So it's not subtle. That makes it hard to aim and crude, but it's still a laser and one of the Z7xs comes apart with a satisfying flash. It's good luck that makes it wipe out the other two as it explodes.

'Those harpoons ready?'

'Yes, sir,' says Shil, her voice clipped. If she's afraid, it is well under control.

'Well, use them.'

Another three fighters are moving to intercept us.

They come in hard and fast, and they're being careful this time. Two fly ahead, the other waits behind, high enough to avoid any explosion that kills its outriders.

'Missile about to launch,' says the SIG.

'Change its mind.'

'Haven't got time,' it says. 'I'm busy.'

'You can be replaced.'

'Sven,' says my gun. 'You don't mean that.'

'Try me.'

The SIG stops what it is doing, which turns out to be keeping us steady. As everything lurches, my head hits the side of my chair and we start to spin. 'I'm sorry,' says the gun.

The rear Z7x launches a missile that flicks past us, and turns in a tight curve to head straight back for a second go. 'Really,' we hear the gun saying. 'You've got this completely wrong.'

The missile disagrees.

So the gun copies the ID patch from the fighter, pastes it onto our tug and deletes the original. 'See,' it says. 'I told you.'

Avoiding us in a blur of white heat, the missile takes out its original owner. A split second later we have a blizzard of steel fragments, ceramic shards, traces of organic matter and some water vapour. I only know because the SIG tells everyone.

'Thank you,' I say. My gun pretends not to hear.

At the last second, the next attacker loses his nerve and stands down his missile.

'Get him,' I tell Shil.

She fires, and a harpoon streaks away. She's left the tether attached. I am about to bawl her out for being stupid when I realize the wire is free at our end. When I said untie the tether I meant at the harpoon end.

Obviously.

Well, it's obvious to me.

As we watch, her harpoon flips ahead of the fighter; which hits the quarter-mile length of industrial hawser dragging behind it. A Z-class mining tug, and we're a Z-class mining tug, can drag a ten-thousand-ton asteroid out of orbit. Dragging is the easy bit. It's getting the asteroid moving first that is tricky. That's where the wire comes in.

Thin it might be, but God it's tough.

The Z7x spins away. One wing is sheered off close to its fuselage. The fighter has lost the wrong retro to halt its spin. The next thing we see is an explosion as the Z7x hits the outer edges of the belt.

'Good shot,' I say.

'Thank you, sir.'

'My pleasure. Now do it again.'

'Kinetic energy/hit-to-kill,' my gun announces suddenly.

We won't be talking this missile out of anything. It's dumb as a stone. No targeting AI and no warhead, just a length of titanium-tipped steel. The speed of the incoming fighter gives the steel bolt its power. And because the hit-to-kill launches head on, our speed is added too. We're talking closing velocities of three point five miles a second.

370

'Haze,' I say.

'Sir,' he says. 'I'm on it.'

'No . . . Hand navigation back to the SIG.'

'Sven,' says Colonel Vijay.

'Know what I'm doing, sir . . . And, I need Haze.'

'Switching roles now,' says our pet Enlightened. His face blanks, and then we're spiralling away as the SIG twists us out of the way of the first hit-to-kill. Another fighter flicks past and the SIG twists again, but that's unnecessary.

This fighter still has its bolt slung underneath its fuselage.

Now the Z7x has to go round again. That's going to be a long loop, because it will need to ramp up its speed for the next hit-to-kill.

Except that fighters are shaking free from *Victory First* like bees from a hive. As for the mother ship, that's turning for the asteroid belt. Read-outs on the heat signature say it is about to gather speed.

Desperate times, my old lieutenant used to say, *desperate measures.*

You take ground and then you keep taking ground until casualties make further advance impossible. Life used to be so much simpler in the Legion. Reminding myself of that doesn't make me happier. But what does happiness have to do with it? If I have to embrace the kyp then that is what I have to do . . .

'Haze,' I say, my voice harsh. 'On my count.'

'Sir?' he says.

'Lock me down.'

A wall rises around me as my count hits zero.

I'm somewhere else. Although my body is back in a Z-class mining tug. Has to be, because it's not here. The wall smells like ice and tastes like . . . Who the fuck knows? How do you put words to something like this?

'*Hekati*,' I call.

The air inside her shell is thin, getting thinner. The sea is gone. All the mirrors in the hub are broken or ripped out of true and those towns not crumbling are burning up. The oxygen mix is so thin the grass no longer burns, it chars direct to ash.

A young woman grabs her child and runs. She dies under the feet of men running in the other direction. Whole villages flee for safety they don't find. Because safety no longer exists in Hekati and will never exist here again.

Everybody has stuff that shames them. Troopers more than most, but we do our job so other people don't have to. At least that is what I believe.

This, I tell myself, *this is different.*

Hekati agrees.

She's dying in front of my—

Fighting free of the horror, I find myself on my knees in the crewpit. The kyp in my throat is so excited it is trying to crawl its way out of my mouth. It can't, of course. Those hooks go too deep into my gullet.

It'll kill you, Paper told me. Right around now, I believe her.

Colonel Vijay tries to lift me into a seat but I shake him off. 'Shouldn't be here,' I tell him. 'Should be back there. Haze . . .'

Haze nods.

Hekati's waiting for me this time. A firestorm of emotions and a thousand clashing voices all joined into one scream. She's scared, and she's furious, and she's so tired of life that it hurts. Not sure I want to know this stuff.

'*Sir*,' says a voice. '*Sir.*'

'Leave,' I tell Haze. 'Get out while you can.'

Who are you? Hekati says.

Sven.

Human? Had this conversation once before. A few months

back. But that was with a ferox. And everyone knows that ferox can't talk.

Mostly, I say.

But not now?

No, I say. *Not now . . .* Rummaging among the million images she's receiving, I find one of the *Victory First.* It is seen from Hekati's view, little more than a heat signature laid over six exhaust cones. Only now, the exhausts look tiny.

This is what hurt you, I say.

Hekati probes the edges of that thought.

It stole your air and water; it ripped a hole in your shell; it broke the mirrors and took away your sun; your hills are crumbling, wind's stripping dirt from the fields; the people now dying inside you are dying because of what this thing did.

The people now dying inside you . . .

Pavel's in there and I don't care what happens to him. But so is his daughter Adelpha, and her new husband. So is Kyble, and the boy with the dog, who found enough courage to challenge our shadows in the night, and the girl who pissed on her own doorstep, not knowing she was watched. For all I know, the miners we met on the river bed are still in there. If they lived this long. A world is dying, and those dying don't even know why.

That machine will kill another like you, I say. *It will kill again. If you don't halt it now . . .*

Doubt fills her.

As what I have said isn't true, I don't blame her. Only I realize it's not doubt about the Silver Fist ship killing another habitat that troubles Hekati. It is the thought of having to kill her own people.

She's quick.

Already aware of what I am asking.

You're dying, I tell her. *Your shell is ripped and your mirrors are broken. You cannot stop what is happening. When you die, those you protect will die.*

The fact Hekati doesn't disagree tells me she knows it.

Why let them suffer in darkness? I say. *There is a kinder way . . .* I feed her the memory of my blade sliding beneath Franc's ribs.

Chapter 58

'DEATH OR GLORY,' I TELL THE COLONEL.

He smiles, realizes I mean it and loses the smile. You don't need to be Haze to work out which of these is more likely.

'Endgame?' he asks me.

'Yes, sir,' I say.

'Carry on.'

Firing up the drive, the SIG charts our quickest route into the asteroid belt. We have a hundred fighters looping in a circle towards us but we can reach the belt before they reach us if we burn everything we have.

'Neen,' I say. 'Kill anything that gets in our way. Use the lasers.'

He salutes.

'Shil . . .'

She looks at me. 'Yes, sir?'

'I'm sorry.'

'About what, sir?'

The fact you were captured. The sheer bloody mess in which we find ourselves. The fact people don't always like chaos, and I forget that.

'Ilseville,' I say.

Shouldn't have said some of the things I said to her there. Shil almost shrugs, and then catches herself. 'I'm sorry too, sir.' Sounds like she means it.

'Refasten the harpoon ropes.'

Saluting, she turns on her heel and leaves the crewpit. I send Rachel and Emil after her with orders to calibrate the harpoon guns. I have no idea what it means, but the SIG assures me it's necessary.

'Haze . . .'

He turns, face slick with sweat.

'You all right?'

He takes a deep breath, steadies himself. 'Yes, sir,' he says. 'The braid knows you talked to Hekati. He doesn't know what you said.' There's something envious in his gaze. I've talked direct to a habitat.

The timing on this is going to be tight.

An asteroid field waits. A few minutes for us, and fifteen seconds for a Z7x, running at half speed. But fighters are short-burst machines, and we are luring them away from their mother ship. Plus the visible edge of the field might be ahead, but we're already passing into its margins. An area that contains dust and grit. Even tiny slivers of rock will kill you if they hit you fast enough.

Hekati . . .

No answer.

Just rage and sadness.

And a slow burn in a power core that once kept mirrors angled to the ring and air scrubbers working, and tides running around a ring world, when physics says this was impossible.

When that core blows, it is going to destroy everything in its path including us; unless we can hide ourselves behind something big enough to protect us from its blast. And the only thing big enough out here is an asteroid. Of course, to be protected, we're going to have to tie ourselves to the asteroid first.

'Sir—' says Haze.

'I know.'

Leaving him standing there, I go to find Rachel and Shil. They're in an observation bubble slung below the tug's nose. That's how old this craft is. The glass is thick, though its radiation shielding is worn and dust has frosted the bubble enough to make the emptiness beyond look grey not black.

Our ship twists once.

'A fighter,' says Neen, his voice echoing from a wall speaker.

'Status?' I demand.

'All clear,' he says.

What we felt was the SIG taking evasive action. The fighter doesn't have time to loop round again. It doesn't have room either. We're closing that gap on the asteroid field fast.

All we need now is for this to work.

A fold-down sight hangs open in front of Rachel. She is making cross-hairs line up with each other. 'You almost done?' I ask.

'Yes, sir.'

'Sir . . .' Haze has panic in his voice. 'Hekati's core is going critical.'

Looking up, Shil glances at Rachel, and then catches my gaze. 'That's good,' I tell her.

She looks like she wants to disagree.

'Shil,' I say. 'Trust me.'

Strange how women always twist their mouths when I say that. After choosing a vast asteroid, I have my gun position us behind it. And then I tell the SIG-37 to take us as close as it can without crashing into the thing.

'OK,' I say to Rachel. 'Now fix me a line.'

Should be easy. We're a Z-class mining tug for Godsake.

377

And I'm sat in an observation pod – with five harpoons slung below me, a joystick for aiming – next to one of the best shots I have ever met. 'Do it,' I tell her.

Rachel's first harpoon skids across the asteroid's surface, disappears into space and drags the line behind it. Shil has re-fixed the wires. I know that, because the whole tug twitches slightly when the harpoon reaches the end of its run.

'Concentrate.'

She aims carefully.

This time a small section of asteroid cracks free.

'*Sir,*' says Haze. '*We should—*'

Only I'm not listening, because I am staring at the shiny scar revealed by the last harpoon. Rachel's third attempt snags on a small outcrop, but begins to come free the moment we start the winch. So we stop winching and leave the harpoon snagged where it is. Whatever is under that asteroid's skin, there's no way we are going to fix a harpoon into it. We might as well try to hang a picture by nailing glass.

'Haze,' I say. 'How long?'

He knows what I'm asking. *How long before Hekati explodes? How long before the mother ship gets us in range? How long before a Silver Fist fighter noses its way through the boulders out there and takes another shot?*

'A minute,' he says. 'Maybe a minute thirty.'

It takes me ten seconds to scramble out of the harpoon pod, another fifteen to grab a helmet from the wall and fix it over my suit.

'Running safety routines,' the helmet says.

It shuts down in a squawk of protest as I override its routines. 'Open,' I tell an airlock.

The bloody door stays shut.

'SIG,' I say.

Lights glitch on a control panel, and now I have two emergency systems screaming at me. They're wasting seconds

I don't have. They're wasting seconds none of us have. Inner door opens, inner door shuts.

The outer door blows at the SIG's command. And I exit the tug like a cork from a bottle, straight into the side of the asteroid. I might as well try shoulder-barging a cliff.

'Take care,' says a voice.

How sweet of Colonel Vijay to remember me at a time like this.

A rib broken, I think, *perhaps two*. Blood fills my mouth, but that's me biting my tongue when I hit. I barely notice, because I'm too busy clinging to the asteroid surface.

'Please, God,' someone says.

Sounds like Shil. We can't end like this. I won't let it end like this.

As my fingers hunt for a fresh grip, my boot finds a crack and I scrabble hand over hand towards the harpoon above me. It straddles a gap between the floor of the asteroid and a rocky outcrop. The line is kinked round the harpoon's middle and that helps keep it in place. A simple yank will set it free.

But I don't want to set it free. I want that line tied tight enough to tether us to this bloody great rock.

'He's not going to make it . . .' They have the comms channel open, and I can hear resignation in Colonel Vijay's voice.

'Yes, he is,' Shil says firmly.

I grin.

'Sir,' says Haze, 'Hekati's about—'

'Closer,' I order. As the tug shifts, I grab the line and wrap the slack once round the outcrop. I'm about to wrap it a second time when Haze's scream tells me to let go the line. He's right. As the world ends, it snaps the line tight and ties us to the outcrop. At least it feels like a world ending.

Hitting a glancing blow, the Z-class slides off the asteroid and yanks at its new tether. Sound doesn't travel in space. But I can feel that wire hum in my head.

Cut me in half if it snaps, I think.

The wire holds, and the tug swings back to glance off the asteroid again, only less violently this time.

Imagine a storm. Then make it a thousand times worse.

Instead of wind, imagine flames from an exploding nuclear core.

Replace torn scraps of paper, dead leaves and broken bottles with chevron glass ripped from the roof of a world and rubble collected to act as shielding. Mix in armour plating from a splintering mother ship, ion drives the size of a small town, disintegrating Z7x fighters and body parts from four thousand troopers. Then add the scream of a dying AI. A scream that echoes so loudly it adds new colours to the inside of your head.

That doesn't even come close.

Hekati explodes in all directions.

But the mother ship is between Hekati and us. So pieces of both come our way. Instead of water, it rains rubble and molten metal. And the bulk of the asteroid we hide behind is the only thing that protects us from a firestorm of slowly cooling plasma where Hekati used to be.

Shutting my eyes makes no difference.

Anyway, why would I want to shut my eyes? How often does anyone get to watch shit like this? It is the biggest bang we will ever see.

'Boss,' says Neen.

'That's *sir*,' I say.

Rachel laughs. And though there is hysteria in her voice, it's under control when she speaks, which is only a second later. 'Should have known you'd be all right.'

'Yeah,' says Shil. 'Impossible to fucking kill.'

'I heard that.'

'You were meant to.'

We have lived through the destruction of a world. We've

taken down a mother ship, or, if that's too big a stretch, we took down an epsilon-class cruiser and we'll give the mother ship to Hekati. May she sleep well and have a better life next time.

As I cling to the rock and listen to their chatter, I know they're writing their own legend. We have no right to be alive. Mind you, no one does. That's line one, paragraph one of the Octovian constitution.

Chapter 59

HAVING HELPED ME INSIDE, COLONEL VIJAY OFFERS ME HIS hand. That's officers for you. Real ones, I mean. 'Officer on deck,' shouts Neen.

The Aux come to attention.

Undoing my helmet, the colonel grips it by its lower edge and twists, freeing it from its safety locks. As I drag air into my lungs, he says, 'You left that a bit tight.'

'I'll try to do better next time.'

The colonel looks at me and shakes his head.

Rachel has vomit down her front; Haze has a nosebleed, as always. Neen is watching his sister, something unreadable in his eyes. Emil is smiling. But we have a couple of people missing. 'Where's Iona?' I demand. 'And Ajac?'

Neen leads me to the crewpit.

Ajac is on his knees, cradling Iona. Her mouth is open in a scream so loud and long that only its echo is left in the misery of her face. She's precog, God knows what she felt when the habitat died.

'Stand her up.'

My slap flips her head to one side. I don't get to land a

second, because the gravity carpet on this ship is so old she hits a bulkhead and lands in a heap beneath a safety notice.

'Iona,' I say. Only then does something human return to her eyes.

Don't get me wrong, I'm not impressed with being human either. But it's what she is and what she's going to stay. Well, if I have anything to do with it.

'*It was Hekati's choice.*'

She stares at me; they all do.

That's when I realize not even Haze knows exactly what happened. 'You saw the size of the piece that the Enlightened ripped from her shell,' I tell them. 'Hekati was dying. She chose to take the Silver Fist ship with her.'

'Hekati's gone?' Ajac says.

'Everything's gone. It's just us now, and half a million new rocks.'

When Iona starts crying, Neen puts his arm round her shoulders and tries to wipe away her tears. I can think of half a dozen more useful things he could do.

'Check our food supplies,' I tell him. 'And look at the oxygen levels.'

He salutes.

'Take her with you.'

Iona might as well learn how life works around here.

It's a while before they come back and Iona is still adjusting the buckles on her spacesuit when she does. Grief does that to people. After the slaughter at Fort Libidad, I fucked myself stupid for a week.

'We've got food for eight days,' says Neen. 'And the oxygen scrubbers are working at near ninety-nine point ninety-nine.' He means we'll starve before we choke.

This is a Z-class tug, mining issue. It's not built for speed. It's not built for system-hopping. The damn thing is designed to drag rocks from here to Hekati.

But that is OK.

Because I'm Sven Tveskoeg, Death's Head lieutenant, Obsidian Cross second class, and I have a better plan up my sleeve. 'Haze,' I say. 'Fix me a call.'

We've been here before.

'You want me to spam the whole galaxy?'

My grin is wide enough to scare Colonel Vijay. 'Hell, no,' I say. 'I want a one-to-one with General Jaxx.' And that scares the colonel even more. All the same, he asks only one question.

'Sure you know what you're doing?'

'No, sir.'

'He makes a bad enemy.'

'Sir,' I say, 'we can die here or take our chances with your father.'

'All right,' he says a minute later. 'Make your call.' I'm not sure it should have taken Colonel Vijay that long to make his decision.

Haze sets up the link.

I don't know how he does it. That's fine, I don't want to know. I just check it can't be traced and that it can't be broken. When Haze begins to talk about piggybacking comm sats, I wave him into silence and stand to attention in front of the lenz, only to stand myself down.

I'd send the Aux out of here. But *out of here* is free-floating in space, and even I am not that hardcore. Although I open my mouth to issue the order.

'Go wait in the airlock.'

They look at me.

'You can helmet up if you want.'

The Aux go as they are. It shows touching faith.

'Sir,' I say, when Colonel Vijay turns to follow.

'I'll be with the others,' he says.

Having heard the inner door lock, and watched the light

flicker on that tells me I can open the outer door if I want, and dump them all into space, I leave the Aux and Colonel Vijay to their thoughts. Who knows? If I were to dump them, maybe I'd have enough oxygen to take me somewhere useful.

And maybe I won't.

'General . . .'

'Who is this?'

Haze has done what I ask to the letter. I am through on the general's private line, minus a picture. And it doesn't sound as if General Jaxx is too happy about being interrupted.

'It's me,' I say, fumbling with screen controls.

Not the greatest opening line in the world, but it's too late to worry about that. As I punch buttons in irritation, something shifts and a lenz starts working.

'*Tveskoeg . . . ?* Now this is a surprise.'

I can almost hear his thoughts turn over. As a woman behind him is busy forcing her full breasts into a skimpy bra, I have obviously caught him at a bad time. It's Caliente, from the brothel on board the general's own mother ship. The fact she smiles when she sees me doesn't help either.

'Go,' he says. For a second I think he is talking to me. And then I realize he isn't. 'I'll call for you later.'

Her smile tightens. Turning her back on both of us, she climbs into her skirt, slips on a blouse and vanishes off screen. A second later, I hear a cabin door slamming. It sounds so close it makes me wonder what I'm doing here.

Only I know what I'm doing.

I'm obeying orders, more or less. And using my initiative. Even a general like Jaxx can hardly ask for more. Although he will. Generals always do.

'Tveskoeg,' he says. 'I thought you were dead . . .'

'Not here,' I tell him. 'And not yet.' I end explaining that's an Aux saying, and we're sticking with it.

385

'Aux,' he says thoughtfully. 'That's your little group, isn't it?'

'Yes, sir.'

'How long have you been together?'

I admit it's only a matter of months. And he laughs at the idea of us having traditions, then decides it is not a laughing matter after all. Seems he's recently taken a call from Paper Osamu. She regretted to announce I had been killed in a tragic accident. When I ask where, the general names a planet three systems away from here. I was on safari, a guest of a well-known anthropologist.

After telling me what *anthropologist* means, General Jaxx admits he did find it unlikely. 'So where are you?' he says. 'And what's with that absurd arm?'

'Combat issue,' I tell him. 'Killed a couple of Vals with it.'

'Did you now?' he says.

'Yes, sir. Got their implants in a jar. Intend to ship them back to Val Central if I get the chance. Feel we owe them that.'

'And you're where now?'

On a mining tug, floating in space, off the edge of a dead habitat. Where the fuck do you think we are? I don't say it, obviously. But something about his question worries me.

Of course, the fact I'm talking to General Jaxx at all should worry me. Any general is dangerous. A Death's Head general takes danger to new heights. And Jaxx commands the other generals. If half the things said about him are true, you could float entire planets in the blood he has spilt.

Life was simpler in the Legion. Only I'm not in the Legion any more.

'Sir,' I say. 'Did Paper Osamu say why she wanted us? I mean originally, when the U/Free first borrowed the Aux?' This is big-picture stuff, not something a lieutenant should ask a general. I know that, even before General Jaxx scowls.

He's about to break the connection.

'All I'm asking,' I say, 'is, was the job legit?'

The general looks puzzled.

'It was one job, right?'

'Right, *sir.*'

I ignore him. *What's he going to do?*

'One job, that's right?'

His nod is slight. He seems to be watching, and I can see his eyes focus on something behind me. It's probably one of the safety signs. Our tub is littered with them: although I can't see the point. Anyone who doesn't understand that explosives go bang or stepping into space without a suit kills is too stupid to be alive in the first place.

'Sven,' he says, 'where are you?'

'In a Z-class mining tug.'

He sighs. 'I don't want to know, do I?'

'Sir,' I say, surprising myself. 'What was the job?'

The general glances out of screen, stands up and disappears. When he gets back, he's clutching a floating lenz. This says some interesting things about his sex life. Although who am I kidding? I'd probably record my own, if I could afford the kit.

'Capture or kill,' he says. 'You already know the target.'

Except I don't, or maybe I do . . . One of us is in for a shock, and it is probably him. And since generals don't like shocks, and I don't like floating around in space miles from home, I am going to have to be careful how I word this.

'Did you know about the party?'

'On arrival?' He nods, his smile mocking. 'Oh yes,' he says. 'We heard all about your party. Quite the social animal.'

'And did you hear about the person I killed?'

He goes still.

'Sven,' he says. 'No one died at that party.'

'They didn't?'

387

'No,' he says firmly. 'They didn't. There was, however, a tragic accident later that evening. As you know—' He catches himself. 'Well, maybe you don't.'

General Jaxx shakes his head.

'Oregon Marx, the U/Free president,' he says. 'Died in a fall. You had nothing to do with that . . .'

'I didn't?'

Turns out the general isn't telling me. It's a question. 'Sven,' he says. 'Tell me you didn't have anything to do with that.'

'*I didn't have anything to do with that.*'

He sucks his teeth. Now generals don't suck their teeth. Militia troopers suck their teeth. And then he looks at the lenz, checking it really is turned off. And he flips open a pad to pass his fingers across the top.

'This line,' he says.

'Is secure . . . Haze set it up,' I add, when the general looks doubtful.

'Your pet Enlightened?'

'Yes.' I had forgotten he knew about that.

'That party,' he says. 'Nothing happened.'

'No, sir.'

'You understand?'

'Completely, sir,' I say. 'At that party Paper Osamu's grand-father didn't ask me to kill the president . . .'

The general shuts his eyes.

'What about Hekati, sir . . . ? Also the general and the mother ship. What's our position on those?'

He looks up from under half-open eyelids. And I've seen cats torturing half-dead mice look cuddlier. '*Hekati,*' he says. '*The general . . . Mother ship.*' A space is left between each item.

'Yes, sir,' I say. 'What's our position on those?'

'Sven,' he says. 'There is no *our* . . . I'm here; you're floating in a tin can somewhere. And this conversation is over.'

'I know about the Ninth.'

General Jaxx halts, his hand an inch away from a switch that will shut me off and leave me floating out here. Because I have just realized something. The U/Free think we're dead. So they're not going to come racing out here to collect us either. But someone might find us, and he is not sure he can take that risk.

'Where are the others?' he asks me.

'In the airlock, sir.'

The general looks at me, very strangely.

'What are they doing in the airlock?'

'Waiting, sir. I locked them all in there. Didn't want them overhearing this conversation.'

General Jaxx sweeps his hand back across his skull, and then discreetly wipes his hand on his uniform trousers. Buttoning his shirt, he tucks it in and stands up to put on his jacket.

'If I tell you to dump them all into space?'

'Then I pull the lever, sir.'

'I believe you would.'

'Yes, sir.'

He sighs. 'You have no notion,' he says, 'how tempting I find that idea.' Sitting down again, he leans forward. 'This was a simple mission, Sven. A basic infiltrate and terminate. Sounds to me like you messed up.'

Thinking back over the past three weeks, I can see how he might think that.

'What are your casualties?'

'Franc, sir.'

'That's it?'

'Yes, sir.'

'What about enemy losses?'

'Don't know, sir.'

He must hear something in my voice, because he leans closer to the lenz. 'Sven,' he says, 'give me a figure.'

I shake my head, but it is not insolence. I really don't know. 'How many people are there on a mother ship, sir?'

He sits back. 'You destroyed a mother ship?'

'Yes, sir. It killed Hekati—' I hesitate. 'Well, it wounded Hekati.' My mouth tastes sour with the recollection. It will be a while before I scrub the habitat's dying scream from my memory. 'The mother ship split,' I tell him. 'Birthed a cruiser.'

'We're talking about *Victory First Last and Always*?'

What does he think we're talking about? That's the problem with senior officers. They're too busy thinking about half a dozen other things to listen to what is being said.

'Yes, sir.'

'So we're talking about an Uplift general?'

'No, sir. I'm talking about General Tournier.' This is getting more complicated than I like. And something in the general's gaze tells me I know too much for his comfort or my safety.

'General Tournier died in battle, gloriously.'

'I'm sure he did, sir.'

'OctoV announced it. General Tournier died in battle. As did the entire Ninth Regiment. They fought heroically, to the last man.'

'Ah,' I say. 'That explains it . . .'

He asks the obvious question, *Explains what?*

And I'm doing my best to come up with an answer when I think of Franc, whose self-inflicted scars were the only things tying her to reality. And before that, something a colonel once said after Haze referred to a dead Uplifted as a machine.

I have my answer.

'General Tournier had braids . . .'

'*Sven.*'

'Braids, sir. All the senior officers did. And there were . . .' I try to remember. 'At least a hundred of them, maybe more. Many more.'

'A thousand died at Jade3.'

'Yes, sir. I'm sure they did. Died gloriously.'

'You're saying that's a lie?' The general's voice is hard. He's lost his silky smoothness, skipped the bit where his words are meant to go icy.

'No, sir. I'm saying the Uplifted brought them back to life.'

'Fuck,' he says. 'You're good at this.'

It's the first time I've ever heard Jaxx swear. I'm negotiating for my life here; we're both aware of that. I'm negotiating for the lives of my troopers. And then there is Aptitude. I swore to her mother that I would stick around to protect her. I intend to keep that promise.

'Sir,' I say, my voice firm. 'The Enlightened obviously resurrected an entire regiment.' Sounds like the truth to me. And it will be the truth by the time I've finished with it.

'Go on,' he says.

'I don't imagine the U/Free knew about that. But, honestly, how could we be expected to sign a treaty with our own dead?'

'Sven,' the general says. 'Talk me through this.'

We get to the bit where the Silver Fist cruiser sends fighters after us and we kill them. And then hide in the mirror dock of a habitat. 'Where you found the tug?'

I nod. 'Yes, sir. We were almost out of oxygen.'

'And then?'

'Franc flew a suicide mission.'

The general looks interested. 'How did you choose?'

'She volunteered.'

He smiles, because that pleases him. He's impressed by stuff like that. And his smile gets wider as I run him through the rest, how we destroyed a B79 bomber and crashed an epsilon-class cruiser into a force field and used the power drain to make our escape in a mining tug. Although his smile falters when I tell him about persuading Hekati to explode.

'She was dying?'

'Almost dead,' I say. 'Beyond saving.'

'Good,' he says. 'The U/Free will want to know that.'

It is the first thing he's said that suggests I won't be spending the rest of eternity floating on the edge of an asteroid field. His next sentence confirms it.

'I'll put in a call,' he says. 'Talk to Paper Osamu myself. I'm sure she'll be with you soon enough.'

'Sir . . .'

He looks at me.

'Thought you might want to collect us yourself.'

Set the hook, my old lieutenant used to say. Set the hook and reel them in. Only, this time, it's not just a saying. Well, the reeling in bit isn't – we will get to that.

'And why would I want to collect you?' General Jaxx is too interested to be outraged.

'Three reasons, sir.' Opening my shirt, I hold up the planet buster.

'Is that what I think it is?'

'Yes, sir.'

'It's a good start,' he says. 'What are the others?'

So I tell him the tug is tied to the biggest chunk of crystalline carbon I've ever seen. And he knows what our glorious leader is like about diamonds.

'And the third?'

'Vijay,' I say.

The general closes his eyes. It's brief, and he catches it fast. General Jaxx doesn't show weakness or forgive those who see it in him. With his son's name, I undo all the good I have done myself in the previous ten minutes.

'He died well?' There's more hope than belief in the question.

'He did as ordered,' I say. 'Killed General Tournier. Cut his throat and hacked off his traitorous head. I have the head with me.'

'That makes four things,' says the general.

'Yes, sir,' I say. 'Never was good at counting.'

'And my son? He died bravely?'

'Colonel Vijay's here, sir.'

'Sven,' says General Jaxx. 'Are you saying my son is in the airlock with your troopers?'

'Yes, sir,' I say. 'That's exactly what I'm saying.'

'The airlock you're planning to blow if I give the order?'

'Yes, sir.'

General Jaxx looks impressed.

Chapter 60

GLANCING AT A FORK, I CHECK THE OTHER FIVE FORKS NEXT TO it and wonder what is so special about this one anyway. Six forks, seven knives, four spoons and three glasses. All made from silver.

Apart from the glasses, obviously.

They're milled from blocks of natural crystal.

In front of me sits a *roundel* of beef. At least that is how it's described on the menu. The beef is thin as tissue and wind-dried on the shores of a small sea two systems away. Wind-drying the beef seasons it with rare salts. And yes, it says that on the menu too.

'Begin at the outside,' says Paper. 'Work your way in.' She is talking about the forks. When I reach forward to pick up the beef with my fingers, she rests her hand on my wrist. 'Don't,' she says.

And when I scowl, she adds, 'Please.'

Imperia is the oldest restaurant in Farlight. It sits in a narrow street five back from Zabo Square and looks like someone's house. Obviously, everyone in Farlight has heard about it except me. Even Angelique is impressed. Although she is less impressed when she discovers who's asked me to supper.

As for Shil, she just slams a door on her way out.

A limousine hover picks me up from Golden Memories.

Actually, it doesn't. Paper thinks it does, but the driver she hires knows he'll be robbed blind before he gets halfway there. So he puts in a call and I agree to meet him halfway.

Don't think I am what he's expecting. Might be the uniform, might be the dagger at my hip. Might be the fact my SIG-37 takes one look at the smoked-glass windows and chrome grille on his hover and laughs.

'So,' says Paper. 'What do you think?'

Looking at my plate, I realize I have eaten the lot.

'It was all right,' I say.

She sighs.

Our only conversation so far was brief. And Paper's been frowning ever since. All I asked was whether she had visited an area north of Karbonne where the ancient dumps are. She asked me which planet. When I told her, she said no, she didn't think so.

A waiter delivers a plate of Sabine ice fish. It's caught by hand, gutted immediately and packed in freshly fallen snow. Imperia guarantees that any ice fish served in the restaurant has been caught within the last twenty-four hours. Given the distance between Sabine and Farlight, I'm impressed. I didn't know cargo ships could travel that fast.

Mind you, we only have the menu's word that this is ice fish. It could be anything. Personally, I like food I can recognize.

When the waiter has gone, Paper leans forward. *Here it comes*, I think.

'Must have been tough.'

'What, Hekati?' Seems like a reasonable guess to me.

Paper Osamu shakes her head. 'Growing up in the desert. Living with the soldiers who killed your family.'

'Troopers,' I tell her. 'We call them troopers.'

She looks at me.

'Paper,' I say, 'I don't think about it.'

The U/Free ambassador nods sympathetically. 'Yes,' she says. 'I can understand that.'

I could say, *No . . . I simply don't think about it.*

But what's the point? So I clear my plate and wipe it clean of melted snow with a chunk of bread. There's something nagging me. So I decide to get it out of the way. 'Why are we here?' I ask.

Raising her wine glass, Paper says, 'To celebrate your safe return.'

'But the mission was a failure.'

'*Sven,*' she says.

'For the U/Free.'

Paper Osamu looks puzzled. 'For us?'

'The treaty,' I say. 'The one that would have folded OctoV back into the mind of the Enlightened and Uplifted, ended the war and bound us by treaty to the United Free . . . You must be upset.'

She puts down her glass.

'Unless, of course, you didn't really want it signed at all . . .'

'You know,' she says, 'I'm not sure what you heard when you were staying with us in Letogratz. But I think you might have misunderstood what was said.'

'I might?'

Nodding, she touches my hand. 'Diplomacy can be complicated,' she says. 'Particularly for . . .'

'Savages?'

Her mouth sets in a tight line.

This isn't the way our dinner is meant to go. We both know Paper has taken a suite at a hotel near the cathedral, while her embassy is redecorated. Imperia is less than a minute from the hotel. We have the whole night ahead of us and she's wearing a dress cut so low I can see her nipples every time she leans forward.

So can the waiter who delivers our food.

Another three courses of fancy food and we can stumble our way to bed, via a fuck against an alley wall if that excites me. I'm ruining the atmosphere. But that is fine, because I'm going home when this is over. Although I'm not sure Paper realizes that yet.

'Sven,' she says. 'Have I upset you?'

Behave, General Jaxx told me. So I do. Sitting back, I say *Of course not.*

After all, it could be someone else at the dump. Another U/Free with Paper's face watching while a squad from the Legion slaughter the Junkyard Rats, kill my sister and burn my village. And what's a dead auxiliary between friends? Even if Franc was better with a knife than anyone I know, except me.

The sky's dark and Zabo Square deserted as I cut around the cathedral, make my way under an arch and through a public garden where a Death's Head major once tried to put a flechette through my head.

He's dead and I'm alive, for now.

It is late and Farlight's boulevards are quiet. A man smokes a cigar in the upstairs window of an ornate mansion. I can smell the richness of burning tobacco. Although maybe that's just my imagination.

In a doorway a girl freezes, watching me over a boy's shoulder as I pass.

A security guard moves forward to challenge me a few minutes later, sees my uniform and turns his challenge into a salute. The Death's Head colours do that to people. If he wonders what a lieutenant is doing heading for a barrio on the upper edges of Calinda Gap, he has the sense to keep that question to himself.

'Night, sir,' he says.

'Which regiment?'

He served with the XI Légion Etrangère. His name's Paulo, he wants to know how I knew about the Legion. I tell him it leaves its mark on people.

Taking the coin I offer, he sees it's gold.

'Knew someone in the Legion,' I tell him. 'A good man.'

'What happened, sir?'

'He died.'

The security guard nods, as if that's the obvious answer. And it is. We both know that.

Returning his salute, I head uphill until I reach a street I recognize. A cable car runs through here day and night. Aptitude told me about it. But I prefer walking anyway.

At a café below the landing fields, I stop for a coffee and a brandy. The café is small, used by people unloading cargo or working the repair yards. A man looks up briefly, looks up again and mutters something. A woman opposite slides me a glance, and then quickly looks away.

'Brandy,' I say.

So nervous is the young woman behind the counter that the entire room hears her rattle the bottle against my glass. She slops my coffee delivering it. And spends a full minute apologizing.

Time was, I'd ask her name. Ask what time she got off. Maybe ask if she has a sister who would like to join us for a meal. Either I'd get my face slapped or we would all end up in bed. The uniform works against this.

Finishing the brandy, I leave my coffee undrunk.

Golden Memories is in darkness as I work my way round the side of the landing field at Bosworth. *Must be late*, I think. Then check the sky and realize it is almost morning.

The front door is locked and bolted from the inside.

A metal grille closes off the rear entrance and all the windows are shut. Nothing for it: slamming my elbow through a pane of glass, I reach inside and have my wrist grabbed. Neen discovers you can't nail a burglar to a wall with a knife if his hand is metal. 'Fuck,' he says. 'Boss?'

'Yeah. Me.'

Opening the door, Neen waves me inside. 'Thought you'd be—'

'Yeah,' I say. 'Well, I'm not.'

Chapter 61

THE CATHEDRAL IN THE CENTRE OF FARLIGHT IS SO VIRUS–RIDDEN it has sunk into the caldera floor on which OctoV's capital is built. It sits, faded and half melted facing Zabo Square. Cafés line the square around it, and a statue of a young woman sits under a colonnade a hundred paces away from where I am standing. She is made of bronze, and naked, obviously. Statues in Farlight always are.

The statue bears a striking resemblance to the girl next to me. At least, the face does. I can't swear to the rest of it.

'My great-grandmother,' says Aptitude.

I look at her.

'She was sixteen.'

There are things about Farlight I don't understand. How the rules work for the high clans is one of them. What kind of family puts statues of themselves naked in public for the entire world to see?

But knowing I don't know is a start.

Ask me six months ago and I would have said the rich and powerful don't work to any rules at all, because they don't have to . . .

It's not true. They have rules. Just weird ones.

Where I come from if someone injures you, then you kill them. Provided it's serious enough. Round here, you invite them to a party and then patronize them to death. Aptitude has to tell me what *patronize* means.

I look at her to check if she's joking; she's not.

Aptitude is good with words. She's good at cooking too. She has taken over the kitchens at Golden Memories; and now people actually come to eat, instead of regarding eating as an inconvenient fuel break between drinking and fucking.

Only we're not in Golden Memories.

As I said, we're standing outside a café on Zabo Square, in the shade of an umbrella, looking at a bronze girl with perfect breasts and a smile that is missing from the face of the young woman beside me. Aptitude is shaking. It's not from the cold, because the sun is so hot that sweat drips down the inside of my jacket.

The last time either of us was here, she had just got married. And shooting her husband was my first job for the general. As far as we know Jaxx thinks she is dead. Her ex-husband certainly is. But in that case . . .

'*I don't know,*' I tell Aptitude.

She looks at me, eyes made large by fear.

Neen is outside the cathedral waiting for me. He is in full uniform, as are the rest of my troopers, minus their rifles. It's not just us; everyone invited to this afternoon's service is minus their weapons.

Paper Osamu has been strict about this.

As U/Free ambassador to this section of the spiral she will not attend any function at which weapons are displayed. Although my gun is the exception. It has full citizen status under U/Free rules.

When it's pointed out that Paper's demand means no one can wear swords, she says the rule doesn't apply to ceremonial weapons. Apparently, swords aren't dangerous, they're decoration. Shows what she knows.

Although who knows what Paper Osamu knows? Not me.

I don't want to know, either. Sure, she is beautiful, intelligent and ambitious. She has the body of a teenage hooker, matched to the morals of an alley cat. This usually works for me. But she also has the mind of a snake.

And her grandfather is the new U/Free president.

It's a titular role, obviously. That means he has no real power. But then nor do the U/Free if you listen to Paper Osamu. They're just sweet lovely people who want to help the rest of the galaxy find peace and harmony, learn to love art and live for ever.

'What are you thinking?' asks Aptitude.

'About Paper Osamu.'

'You—' She blushes. 'Didn't you?'

I nod.

'Why?' Aptitude has grown in the last few months. Either that, or she's been storing up questions. She asks them with a new confidence. It comes, I guess, from having to cope on her own while I was away.

'It was expected.'

She stares at me.

'Also,' I tell her, 'I needed information.'

'And *that's* how you get information?'

'One of the ways,' I say. 'You can learn a lot in bed. Who pays protection? Who demands it? Places not to go . . . Seems the rules that apply at my end of the scale apply at the other.'

Aptitude sighs when I say this.

'Officer on deck,' shouts Neen, as I approach.

As one, the Aux snap to attention.

A militia major glances across and begins to scowl. Then he sees my arm, which is piston-driven, but minus the spikes, and recognizes my face. He lets me go into the cathedral first.

The Aux have places at the back.

Aptitude has a seat. It might be behind a pillar and on the outer edge of a nave, but it is a seat . . . And that's more than half the crowd have in this place. As for me, I stamp my way to the altar step and take up my position beside General Jaxx.

'Sven,' he says. 'How good of you to join us.'

We've kept him waiting, I realize. We've kept them all waiting. From the look on the general's face, he regards this as a huge joke. I'm glad; he could equally regard it as a shooting matter.

'Your niece is here?'

I nod, my expression flat.

He smiles. 'You,' he says. 'A family man. I can't tell you how surprised I was. And to fly her halfway across the spiral like that . . . Our glorious leader told me,' he adds, seeing my surprise.

'OctoV?'

'We are but falling sparrows in his eyes,' says the general.

I'm still trying to work out what the fuck that means, when a wind blows through the cathedral and the lights flicker. In my throat, the kyp goes berserk, as the air begins to taste of electricity.

OctoV could enter quietly if he wanted to. But why would he bother? When he can appear in the centre of a storm, and have even the U/Free blinking and wondering what the little psychopath is up to this time?

Sven, says a voice in my head.

I snap to attention.

That isn't kind. After I lied about Aptitude for you.

Everyone looks at me. Well, the general, the archbishop and all those choirboys who have been shooting glances at the bishop up to this point. There are days when I want to burn this bloody city down.

Believe me, says the voice in my head. *There are days I want to burn it down too. But it's the only one I have.*

This isn't true. OctoV rules ten thousand systems. He has more cities than I've had whores.

Maybe, the voice says petulantly. *But this is the only one I like.*

I wait for the punchline and inside my head OctoV laughs. It's a terrifying feeling.

You're right, he says. *I don't even like this one that much.*

I want to wipe sweat from my skull, but I'm damned if I'll give OctoV the pleasure. This time when he laughs everyone hears it. He looks about twelve and sounds younger. From what Colonel Vijay says, this is his first public appearance in more than a hundred years.

'Well,' says OctoV. 'I suppose we'd better get on.'

Stepping up to General Jaxx, our glorious leader extends his hand and waits for the general to sink to his knees. I sink to my knees behind him. Although I'm not important enough to kiss the emperor's hand.

At OctoV's suggestion, I'm replacing the general's ADC for the day. Reward for my part in overthrowing an evil Uplift plot. My rank of lieutenant is confirmed and the Aux now have official status. We're going to be paid. Although I'll believe that when it happens. I'm also officially part of the general's staff, which allows me a second twist of silver braid.

The general's rewards are more impressive.

General Jaxx is now Duke of Farlight. As of last night, fifteen families have gone into exile at this sign of imperial favour. His political enemies are crawling over one another in their desperation to become his friends.

If I were OctoV, I'd be afraid of putting this much power in the hands of one man. Particularly a man like General Jaxx.

But I'm not OctoV.

The choir does what choirs do, loudly and endlessly.

Although I can see from the faces of those around me that they find it delightful. OctoV makes a speech in which he thanks Paper Osamu for her understanding.

He means for overlooking the fact an Octovian mother ship suddenly uncloaked in Uplift space. And then he does something strange. Our glorious leader stares out over a congregation made up of empire ministers, courtiers, generals and heads of the trading families, and calls my intelligence officer to the front.

Being Haze, he trips on the steps to the altar rail.

OctoV smiles indulgently.

'Fuck,' says my gun. 'Now what?'

Everyone around us is far too polite to notice.

At a sign from the emperor, Haze removes his helmet and shakes free two braids, which drop around his shoulders. This part of OctoV's speech is short, to the point and brilliant. The Enlightened might discriminate against Octovians, but Octovians do not discriminate against the Enlightened. Haze-ben-Col chose to serve OctoV in an elite sub-group of the Death's Head.

That's one way of putting it. And the general, at least, isn't happy with that description. Although he swallows his expression quickly enough.

But OctoV has a new job for Haze. He's to be our ambassador to the U/Free. When OctoV says this, Paper Osamu blinks. And then she smiles, twisting her lips into something close to amusement and nods approvingly. She's impressed, and the whole galaxy can see she is impressed because we are all on lenz.

Kneeling, Haze takes a letter of introduction.

As he stands again, he catches my eye and for a moment looks apologetic. But I know how these things go. So I step back, to give myself space, and come to attention, saluting smartly.

It's worth it for the appalled expression on his face.

'Swings and roundabouts,' says OctoV. 'Swings and round-abouts.'

A wind is rising around him. The lights in the cathedral have gone back to flickering. We know our beloved leader is about to disappear before our eyes. Well, I do, and the others do if they have any sense.

Stepping back, the new Duke of Farlight joins me in a salute. We wait at attention until the wind drops and the lights come back up and we realize we're saluting an emperor who is no longer there.

The crowds clap. An organ breaks into a tune I vaguely recognize. And the general's real ADC rushes forward to escort General Jaxx out of the cathedral. The glare Leo Thomassi shoots me is poisonous.

'It's all right,' says my gun. 'He doesn't want your bloody job.'

'Don't you?' asks the general, turning back.

The ADC looks worried. Whether at being the centre of attention or from fear he's about to lose his position is hard to say.

'No, sir.'

'Why not?'

'All that standing around being smart, sir.'

'Are you for real?'

What kind of question is that? 'Yes, sir,' I say. 'Damn near humanoid original, apparently. Apart from my arm. That's metal . . .'

The general barks with laughter. He's still furious that OctoV talked to me direct. Perhaps he's even worried about what our glorious leader might have said. But he no longer looks like he wants to put me up against the nearest wall.

That's a start.

'You,' the general tells his ADC. 'Wait outside.'

406

The whole crowd watches the major march for the door. Because the whole crowd freezes where they stand. No one can move until the new Duke of Farlight leaves the cathedral. Not even Paper Osamu.

'His job is yours,' says General Jaxx. 'If you want it.'

Keep your friends close. And your enemies closer. 'Thank you, sir, but no . . .'

'And if I order you?'

'Then I'll do it, sir.'

'To the best of your ability?'

'I do everything to the best of my ability, sir.'

He looks at me and smiles. 'You're a fool,' he says. 'There are senators willing to pay thousands in gold to get their sons on my staff.' The general jerks his chin towards the door through which his ADC has just vanished. 'I took both his sisters in payment, plus a country estate.'

'I don't have an estate,' I tell him. 'And my sister is dead.'

General Jaxx sighs.

'Go home,' he says. 'Get drunk, get laid . . .' We could be alone for all the attention he pays those around us. 'You'll be called when I need you.' He turns to go, and then turns back one final time.

'Sven,' he says. 'There's been talk of a new crime syndicate, based out in a brothel on the edge of the landing fields. Ruthless, efficient, unforgiving. You wouldn't know anything about that?'

'No, sir.'

He nods. 'Thought not.'

Chapter 62

DRINKS ARE FREE TONIGHT. WE'LL MORE THAN MAKE THE COST back on the sale of Aptitude's cooking. The girls upstairs are working overtime. Everyone is having a good time. When we finally hit midnight, the bar is so crowded our customers are spilling into the street outside.

A man from the landing fields called Per Olson wraps one arm around Lisa's shoulders to cup her breast. From the way his kid grins as she slaps his hand away it's not the first time that has happened.

I'm not sure what we're all celebrating.

Being alive, probably. That's what most parties are about.

The fireworks outside celebrate General Jaxx's promotion to Duke of Farlight. He's no fool. Down in Zabo Square whole cows turn on spits over fire pits dug into the flagstones. Up here, in the barrio, where the air is cleaner but water rare, we're making do with goats.

The smoke from our fire is so greasy it sticks to my skin.

Aptitude barely notices.

She's too busy being chilled about Vijay. He's been up to

Golden Memories three times since we landed and should be down in the square with his father. The first time was to see where we lived. No one has any doubts about why he came back a second and a third time. He's glued to Aptitude's side tighter than her shadow. Not quite touching, as she moves from spit to spit, pouring oil onto crisping meat and slashing great cuts in each goat.

I seem to be the only one aware how skilfully Aptitude handles her knife.

'Lisa,' I say.

Unwrapping herself from Olson, she winds her arms round my neck and tries to kiss me. 'You're no fun,' she says, when my glance flicks to Aptitude, who's watching from the corner of one eye.

'Who taught her to use a blade?'

Lisa decides to tell the truth. That's one reason I like her. Attention span of a goldfish and way too lazy to lie. 'Me,' she says. 'Gave her the knife too. I mean, it's not our fault if you fuck off for three months at a time and leave us to fend for ourselves.'

I scowl at Lisa.

She scowls straight back. 'You should be pleased,' she says. 'A girl can't be too careful these days.'

Leaving Aptitude and Lisa to their admirers, I go looking for Shil, and find Haze instead. He's under a tree, playing with Aptitude's cat, which is now nearly full grown and three times fatter than when I last saw it.

Haze scrambles to his feet.

Then looks embarrassed as he realizes he doesn't have to do that any more. I should probably salute, but that would be too odd for both of us. So we shake hands instead.

I am surprised he's here at all.

That doesn't mean I don't want him here.

He's Aux; he will always be Aux, even when he is something

else. All the same, I thought he'd have more important things to do. After all, Paper Osamu is giving a party to celebrate the general's promotion.

'Needed to say goodbye properly,' he says.

It's not hard to work out who he's been saying goodbye to . . .

Rachel is drunk.

Given how she feels about Haze, that's not surprising. Dropping to a crouch in front of her in the yard, I grip her shoulders. She shakes me off.

'Haze asked me to go with him.'

'What did you say?'

She glares at me, glares at the 8.59mm Z93z long-range rifle, with adjustable cheek piece, ×3–×12–×50 spotting scope and floating barrel, that rests on an oilcloth on the ground in front of her, and strips it into fifteen pieces with quiet fury.

'This is my rifle,' she says flatly. 'There are many like it, but this one is mine. Without it I am nothing.'

Fifty-five seconds later, it is back in one piece.

Serves me right for asking.

I find Neen in the stockroom, killing a bottle of cane spirit as efficiently as he kills most things. A girl sits facing him on his lap, her legs wrapped around his waist and her dress tumbling either side of his knees. From the unfocused look on Iona's face there is more going on under the surface than I want to know.

That's also what Shil thinks.

'Come on,' I tell her. 'He's young.'

She nods, lips tight. So I take her outside and cut down a track to a ruined shack on the edge of a slope overlooking Farlight's centre. It was a bar once, before a storm washed away its foundations and dumped most of its customers over the side.

'Sit,' I say.

Leaning against a dirt bank, we stare at the stars. I've forgotten how many there are. Pretty soon I'll forget I ever knew. Until the next time the kyp ties me into the information storm slopping round this edge of the galaxy.

I'm drunk, but that's fine. Shil's drunk too. Pulling a bottle from my pocket, I fill two shot glasses and toast the new Duke of Farlight's health. In the circumstances I'd be better off toasting my own.

'What aren't you telling me?' she says.

'That's—'

'Yeah, I know. What aren't you telling me, *sir*?'

'Things are going to change . . .'

There, I've said too much or not enough. Silence tells me she's waiting to find out which. That's one of the things about Shil. She knows how to keep quiet. 'Our glorious leader, beloved and victorious, whose very sweat is perfume to his subjects . . .'

Shil thinks it's a toast. She must do. She raises her glass.

We drink. I refill.

OK, where was I? 'He offered me a reward for destroying the Uplift mother ship.'

'What?'

I look at her. Well, it's more of a drunken squint.

'Sven,' says Shil. '*What* did he offer you?'

'Anything I wanted.'

Somehow I end up telling her about Paradise and how I met Aptitude's parents. Senator Debro Wildeside and Anton, ex-captain of the palace guard. We touch on my taking over the prison. Although I drop the body count a little.

'This has to do with what you chose?'

It has.

What do you do when offered whatever you want? I don't know. It's never happened before. Probably not going to happen

411

again; and maybe I made the wrong choice, but that wouldn't be the first time – and I'm still here.

'Sven,' says Shil. 'You OK?'

'Sure,' I say. 'I asked him for Anton and Debro's freedom.'

'Shit,' she says. 'Does Aptitude know?'

'Not yet. It's a surprise.'

'So why aren't you happy?'

I want to say happiness is overrated. My sister told me that. Sounds like something Debro would say as well. Only Shil is right. 'Because Jaxx doesn't know yet.'

And then I have to tell her about killing Aptitude's husband, Senator Thomassi, and how I was meant to kill Aptitude and who gave the order . . . Shil's looking at me as if I'm mad, and there are days I am, but this isn't one of them.

'The general's going to be furious,' she says.

That's the least of it.

Jaxx will want me dead.

I don't say that. I don't need to. Shil's smart. She'll work it out. And there's something else, to do with Farlight itself. Something that's been nagging me from the moment I walked out of the cathedral after Jaxx was made duke.

'Can't you smell it?' I say.

'Smoke from barbecues,' says Shil. 'That's what I can smell.'

Also dog shit, pollution, stale drains and static from the landing field. Yes, I've got those as well. A rocket breaks for the sky from the square below. We get coloured stars to hide the real ones. All of the scents we mention are out there. Plus smoke from the fireworks. But there's something else. Something deeper.

'Well?' she demands.

What can I smell that she can't? What I can always smell, just before things get really nasty.

'Trouble.'

412